HEALING STONES

HEALING STONES

Nancy Rue and
Stephen Arterburn

THOMAS NELSON
Since 1798

NASHVILLE DALLAS MEXICO CITY RIO DE JANEIRO BEIJING

Published in Nashville, Tennessee, by Thomas Nelson. Thomas Nelson is a registered trademark of Thomas Nelson, Inc.

Thomas Nelson, Inc., titles may be purchased in bulk for educational, business, fund-raising, or sales promotional use. For information, please e-mail SpecialMarkets@ThomasNelson.com.

Publisher's Note: This novel is a work of fiction. Names, characters, places, and incidents are either products of the author's imagination or used fictitiously. All characters are fictional, and any similarity to people living or dead is purely coincidental.

Library of Congress Cataloging-in-Publication Data

Arterburn, Stephen, 1953–
Healing stones / Stephen Arterburn and Nancy Rue.
p. cm.
ISBN 978-0-8499-1890-2
I. Rue, Nancy N. II. Title.
PS3601.R76H43 2007
813'.6—dc22

2007033922

Printed in the United States of America
09 10 11 12 13 RRD 17 16 15 14 13

For Joey Paul, who understands healing
and trusted us to tell its story.

CHAPTER ONE

I sneaked down to the boat that night to say this couldn't happen anymore.

Mind you, I didn't want to. Ripping a man's heart out wasn't up there with things I relished. I don't know what I thought would come of things in the end, but I never envisioned this. "This" fell into the "have to" column. When you've made a mess so major you can't hope anymore that somehow things will turn out all right on their own, you have to fix them.

I made my usual way through the shadows, glancing back out of habit to be sure no one saw me. No one frequented the Port Orchard Yacht Club on late February evenings, and even I wouldn't have to anymore after tonight.

I sucked in damp Washington air and breathed out my urge to run from the pain. Then I slid my hand into the pocket of my P-coat, felt the key card waiting in its satin hiding place, and curled in on myself, plastic card digging into my palm.

Would everything that reminded me of Zach torture me from now on? This was just the key to the ramp. What was going to happen when I saw his face?

I managed to get the gate unlocked and then closed it behind me, clanging like a prison door. Yes, I waxed dramatic, but everything inside seemed to hold a piece of him. Zach always had a field day with the curled-up ad on the bulletin board asking for a stud for a Yorkshire terrier. Every time I picked my way in the dark down the puzzle grating on the gangplank, I anticipated his arms around me.

I started down narrow Dock C, the open-ceilinged hallway lined with cheerful doors that led to covered, inside boat slips, and

I could hear Zach chuckling over the limp Valentine's Day wreath that hung over a faux porthole, reds and pinks oozing damply into each other. I belonged on this slender path to Zach's door. It always seemed to close behind me—holding me in that one safe place.

How, then, would I get out after I'd said what I came to say? My, my, Demitria. You sure know how to arrange things.

My hand was barely on the knob when the door to his slip came open and Zach filled the doorway, and me.

"Hey, Prof," he said.

Standing there with him so close I ached, I fought to remember how I'd steeled myself for this. I was doing it for Rich and our kids—because it was the right thing—because I couldn't do the wrong thing anymore.

Zach stood silhouetted with the boat rocking behind him until he pulled me through the doorway onto the enclosed dock—and into the intoxicating musky smell of his neck. Then he was too real.

"Okay, what's wrong?"

I couldn't answer, not with my face pushed into the black wool of the sweater stretching across his chest.

"You sounded stressed on the phone. I can feel it in you." He held me tighter and pressed his chin on top of my head. I didn't have to look at him yet, but I could see him all the same.

His dark thicket of brows drawn together. Blue eyes closed, I knew, squeezing the worry lines into fans at their corners. I tried to push myself away, but he cupped my face in his hands and soaked me in. I'd been right about his expression. The only thing I'd missed was the rumple in his wiry, almost-gray hair, where he'd apparently raked his fingers.

"You're scaring me, Prof." He tilted his head to kiss me, but I peeled his hands away and stepped back.

"Can we get on the boat?" I said.

I didn't wait for an answer but maneuvered around him and hurried down the dock to *The Testament*'s stern. Every squishy step of my rubber soles echoed like a taunt. *This is the last time. This is the last time.*

I stepped aboard and stopped to stare into the cabin. Candles dotted every horizontal plane, flames casting halos on the polished teak. I was walking into a sanctuary.

"You sounded like you could use a little candlelight." Zach eased the cabin door shut behind us. "What else do you need?"

What I needed was for him not to use that voice right now—the clear, bottomless voice that asked the right questions and gave me my nickname and always said if I wanted him to stop I should tell him before he wouldn't be able to.

"I need to talk," I said. "And I need you to listen."

"Always." Zach pulled me toward the pillow-piled seat that banked the corner, but I wriggled my hand free.

"I can't sit next to you for this."

"Okay, Prof." He ran a finger under my chin. "This is your meeting."

He swiveled the captain's chair to face me and perched on its edge. His long legs, clad in jeans that followed the commands of his thighs and calves, draped to either side.

"Rich?" he said. "Does he know?"

"Zach, let me—"

"If he does, so be it. You know I've got your back." He shrugged his squared-off shoulders. "I've been saying you should tell him."

I couldn't help smiling. I could never help smiling at him. "Am I going to have to duct-tape your lips?"

The lips in question eased into a grin. "I'm listening. Talk to me."

Of course I could talk to Zach. He would even understand this, which, ironically, had put me in this impossible situation in the first place: because I could talk to him like I could talk to no one else. There was never a need for caveats—and the undivided attention was as addictive as everything else about us.

Yet I had to say it.

"We have to end this. I mean us—we have to stop being us."

He didn't move.

"I love you—you know that. You're the rest of me that I could never find until you, and this place." I swept my gaze over the walls.

The candle flames flickered frantically as if they registered what Zach didn't seem to. "I want to be with you. I want the life I know we could have, only I can't have it all tangled in secrets and lies. I don't want anything about us to be wrong, and this is, and I can't anymore . . . Zach—say something."

"You told me not to."

"Do you always have to do what I ask you to?"

His face went soft. "One of the things I love about you is that you're the kind of woman who'll go back to her husband. I can't argue with your integrity, Demi."

I actually laughed. "What integrity, Zach? I'm a married woman and I've been having an affair with you for five months."

"Five months, three weeks, four days."

"That's not integrity—that's adultery."

"So you've said—at least one thousand and three times." He cocked his head at me. "But if you could see yourself. This is tearing you apart and has all along. A woman without integrity wouldn't care about right or wrong, especially after the way Rich has treated you—"

"He's still my husband."

"Exactly my point."

I pushed my hands through my hair. "I wish you would stop turning me into a saint. I'm trying to do the right thing here."

"I know. And I hate it and I love it at the same time." He leaned toward me, touching me without touching me. "It makes you even more beautiful."

I pulled my knees into my chest, the soles of my boots divoting the corduroy. *This must be what withdrawal feels like.*

"Prof, I can see into your soul. It's hurting."

"I don't care if I'm wonderful or scum—I still have to end this." I unfolded my legs. "I'm going to walk out of here, okay? And I'm not coming back."

He watched me. The liquid-blue eyes, the color of Puget Sound, swam, until I realized I was the one on the verge of tears. He made a move to come toward me, but I put my hand up.

"This is breaking your heart," he said. "I don't know if I can stand that—I want to help."

"We'll have to stay away from each other."

"How do you see us doing that? We'll be tripping over each other in the hall." He pulled his brows together. "No matter. I can't go anywhere on that campus without seeing you, even if you aren't there."

I watched him swallow.

"Our lives are too enmeshed for us to walk away from this," he said. "What about the Faith and Doubt project? That's a baby you and I brought into this world." His face worked. "We have students who would have completely turned their backs on Christianity if we weren't working with them. We have a responsibility—"

"We won't let that go," I said. "We're grown-ups, Zach—we can hold it together for the kids."

"I don't know if I can. A man in love isn't a grown-up." Zach leaned back. "At least not this man. He's a spoiled-rotten little boy who knows what he wants, and he won't be without it."

"You have to be without me."

"Forever?"

"I have to know if my marriage to Rich can work—"

"Haven't you tried hard enough?"

"Not enough to walk away from twenty-one years."

Zach pressed his palms on his thighs and wiped at his jeans. Zach Archer didn't do desperate, and I could hardly bear it. "A relationship needs two people to work," he said. "Do you think Rich is going to—"

"Zach, stop."

He did, just short of the line he'd promised never to cross.

"I'm sorry. I've never put him down."

"No, you haven't, Doc, and please don't start now."

Pain shot across his face, and I wanted to bite my tongue. I'd told myself I wouldn't use his nickname.

"You love me," he said. "I know you do."

"That isn't—"

"Then do what you have to do. I have to set you free for that."

I closed my eyes.

"But I have to say this one thing, and I want you to hear me." He hesitated as if he were waiting for my permission. "This—what we have—this is true love, which will win out if we let it."

"But we can't let it *this* way." I opened my eyes. "If we put us before God, then that can't be true."

We both stared at the space between us, as if a third party had entered the cabin and spoken. The thought had curled in my brain like a wisp of smoke for—five months, three weeks, and four days. Longer than that if I counted the weeks watching him at faculty meetings, the days dreaming up reasons to drop by his office, the stolen moments I collected like seashells to hold later. Now that the thought was between us, it cut a chasm I couldn't walk around.

Zach leaped across and came to me. I straight-armed him before he could touch me and make God disappear.

"Please don't make it any harder," I said.

"Can't happen. I'm already in shreds."

"Then let me go—please—and we can both start to heal."

He brushed the hair off my forehead with one finger. "I'll never get over this, Prof."

And then he gave me the look. Our look. The look that destroyed me and threw me right into his arms—to the place where I didn't care what I was doing, as long as it felt like this.

Our clothes were halfway off within seconds. We had that part down to a passionate science. I was once more ripped from in-control to out-of-my-mind, lost again on the wave I wanted to ride all the way, no matter where it took me. I'd thought in every guilty-afterwards that this must be what a drug addict felt like.

I clung to his chest and let his mouth search for mine. He found it just as the cabin erupted with light. Over my heartbeat, I heard the unmistakable click and whir of a camera.

CHAPTER TWO

What? Zach—what?"

That was all I could say—in a voice whose panicked pitch couldn't possibly be mine. Another flash jolted my vision into misshapen rings of light—then another and another—while I found my jacket and tried to pull it over my face. The satin lining was cold against the bare skin on my chest but I couldn't get it turned around. I felt a flailing sleeve hit something. A flame zipped along the floor and grabbed at a pillow that had tumbled there, startling it to light.

"Go, Demi!" Zach called from somewhere.

The camera's auto-winder chattered like a squirrel as I snatched up articles of clothing and tried to hold them against me with one hand while I grabbed for more with the other. Parts of Zach jerked surreally as if he were moving through strobe lights, slapping at the fire. But it was Rich's voice that shouted in my head.

In a fire, you gotta move quickly, but don't panic. Stay low—don't run.

I lunged for the door and flung it open, my clothes in a bundle across my nakedness.

"That's enough," I heard Zach say.

I stumbled across the stern deck and hoisted myself onto the dock. Something slithered out of my arms, but I didn't stop to get it. I didn't stop at all until I was at the gate, tearing crazily at the handle. My hands were already so drenched in sweat they slipped off, and I fell backwards onto the ramp.

For an insane moment I considered throwing myself into the inlet and swimming for shore. It was only slightly less psychotic that I kicked my bra and camisole over the side of the gangplank, shoved my arms into the sleeves of my P-coat, and climbed the gate like an escaping ape. I managed to get myself into the Jeep and down Bay Street.

I'd passed city hall before the first rational thought shot into my mind. Two rational thoughts.

One—what was I running from? No one was chasing me. The clock on the hall read a quarter to nine. Drivers passed by on their leisurely way home from eating calamari at Tweeten's or picking up kids from basketball practice, but no paparazzi tailed me with their 35-millimeters hanging out the windows.

I slowed down.

Two—I'd left Zach alone, smothering a fire and dealing with—who? Who hid on his boat, waiting to take pictures of us—*half naked*?

I pulled to the curb and pressed my forehead against the steering wheel. I'd imagined our affair being discovered a hundred different ways—from Rich following me to *The Testament* and dragging me up the gangplank to my eighteen-year-old son hacking into my secret e-mail account. None of them had involved a photographer crawling out of the galley of the cabin cruiser and shooting us groping each other by candlelight.

Now whoever it was had pictures—of our last time together. I pummeled the steering wheel with my fists, and then I sat up. With chicken-claw fingers I buttoned my jacket. Zach wouldn't let anybody get out of there with that film. He'd sounded so calm when he said, "That's enough," as if it were going to be no trouble at all to disarm whoever it was. By now he'd probably already called the police, or brought the full power of the Dr. Zachary Archer charm and intensity to bear on the situation.

Zach wouldn't have hit the jerk. That was more Rich's MO. Back when he'd cared enough about anything to throw a punch at it.

I pulled my cell phone out of my purse, which I'd left in the car, and turned it on. Pulling my lapels together with one hand, I was reaching down to turn up the heat when the tiny screen signaled one new voice message. Already dissolving into relief, I poked in my password.

"Hey, Mom?" It was the indignant tone only a thirteen-year-old girl can achieve. "Could you come get me?"

I could see Jayne's eyes rolling. But I could also hear the whine of uncertainty, even over the siren now screaming in the distance.

"Rachel was supposed to take me home from rehearsal, but I guess she forgot me. Could you call me when you get this?" The whine reached a peak and fell into a teeth-clenched finish. "Never mind. I guess I'll have to call Christopher."

I searched the screen. She'd left the message at eight—forty-five minutes ago. Fighting back visions of child abductors in black vans stalking Cedar Heights Junior High, I shoved the Jeep into gear, then shoved it out again. I dialed my home phone.

"You *so* owe me," Christopher said, in lieu of "hello."

"Did you pick Jayne up?"

"Like I said, you owe me."

"Is she okay?"

"She's in her room with the lights out and that music on that sounds like some chick needs Prozac." Christopher gave the hard laugh he'd recently adopted. "Which is what she always does, so, yeah, she's okay. Where were you?"

I was suddenly aware of the nakedness under my jacket.

"I had a meeting," I said. "Has your dad called?"

"I called *him* to see if he was okay."

"Why?" I said. My chest tightened automatically—the Pavlovian reaction of the firefighter's wife.

"Fire at that 76 station on Mile Hill Road. Heard on the radio on my way home from the library. They said it was contained, so I called him."

I told myself I was imagining the innuendo of accusation in his voice, the *Why didn't* you *call him?* I chalked it up to the overall attitude of superiority my son had taken on now that he was a college freshman and knew far more than his father and I could ever hope to. I was forty-two with a doctorate in theological studies, but Christopher Costanas could reduce me to the proverbial clueless blonde.

"He said they got another call and he's going out on it," Christopher said. "Even though his shift's over—you know Dad."

Thank you, God, I thought as I hung up. Although God helping me keep Rich out of the way until I could find out what had just happened wasn't something even I could fathom. Funny. All through my affair with Zach, I'd continued to talk to my God, asking His forgiveness over and over, every time I left the yacht club, knowing I'd be back. Now that I'd ended it, I couldn't face Him. In His place was a rising sense of unease.

Rich's Harley wasn't in the garage when I got home. Christopher answered with a grunt when I said good night outside his door. I tiptoed into Jayne's dark bedroom, but all I saw was a trail of strawberry-blonde hair on top of the covers and a rail-like lump underneath them. I kissed the cheek that was no longer plump and rosy, now that my daughter had abruptly turned into a teenager. She didn't stir, even when I whispered, "I'm sorry about tonight. We'll talk tomorrow."

Whatever "tomorrow" was going to look like. The uneasiness rose into full-blown nausea as I pulled on an oversized Covenant Christian College nightshirt and crawled into our empty bed. Tomorrow would be the first day of a new existence—without Zach to make me okay. When I woke up, I would be completely Rich Costanas's wife again, and nothing would be any different from the first moment when I'd admitted to myself that I'd fallen in love with someone else.

Tomorrow I would still try to be cheerful as Rich silently, sullenly sat like he was walled into a dark room he wouldn't let any of us into. I would kiss him on the cheek before I left for work, and he would mumble "have a good day." He would go to the station for the evening shift before I came home, leaving no note, making no phone call, giving me vague, monosyllabic answers when I called him. I'd stopped calling three months ago.

Tomorrow I would do the right thing: give up a relationship that made me feel alive and loved and necessary, and attempt to revive what Rich and I once had, before September 11, 2001, drained the life out of us. I'd found a reason to keep breathing. I wasn't sure Rich ever would.

And yet, tomorrow I would try. Only it would be a different person doing the trying. I was now a person who'd manufactured lies so she could meet her lover. A person who'd stripped herself down to betrayal, just to feel connected again. A person who'd been caught in the flash of a camera with her clothes on the floor around her.

I churned in the bed, tangling my ankles in a knot of sheets. I had to see Zach and find out what had gone down. And I had to make sure that he knew we were over—and I was really gone.

Though I pretended not to be, I was still awake when Rich fell into bed beside me, smelling of smoke and the Irish Spring attempt to wash it away.

"Hi, hon," he said.

I stiffened. Why did he choose this night to sound like the old Rich? His voice hadn't held that smushy quality for—what—two years? It sounded the way it used to when he wanted me to rub his head or make him a fried egg sandwich.

"How was your shift?" I said.

"I've got bad news for you."

My eyes came open. The answers I'd heard for months had tended toward *It was all right* or *The same as always.* They always implied that I'd asked a stupid question that was more than annoying. I propped up on one elbow and tried to sound sleepy. "What happened?"

"We hadda fight a boat fire—down at Port Orchard Yacht Club."

I curled my fingers around the pillowcase.

"Does your friend—that guy who took us out that one day—does he still own that Chris-Craft?"

He didn't know. He didn't know.

"Uh, yeah," I said—and then my heart clutched at itself. "*His* boat?"

"Had to be—total loss too." Rich punched at his pillow and wrapped it around his neck in his usual preparation for going into a post-fire coma.

But I had to ask.

"Is Zach—was he hurt?"

"Dunno. He wasn't around. I don't think he was there when it started." He gave a long, raspy sigh. "It was a mistake to ever leave New York."

I struggled to keep up. "Tell me some more," I said.

"I don't belong here, Demitria. I'm a fish outta water."

How many times had I turned myself inside out to get him to open up? Six months ago, I'd have had our bags half-packed already, willing to do anything to bring him out of his cave. Now I said nothing, because I felt nothing—except terror at the vision of Zach as a charred version of his former self, buried in the rubble of *The Testament*.

Rich sighed heavily and flopped over, leaving me on the other side of his wall of a back, the one I'd stopped trying to hoist myself over. "There's nothing we can do about it now," he said.

I sank back stiffly onto my own pillow. "Not tonight," I said.

"I didn't mean tonight."

There was the edge that implied I was of no help to him whatsoever, and why did I even think I could be?

I turned my back and moved to the far edge of the bed.

The next day couldn't dawn soon enough. Most of the night I watched the digits on the clock change with maddening slowness, and planned how to get to Zach before I lost my mind.

I was up, dressed, and making coffee by six thirty. Fortunately—and not surprisingly—I didn't hear a sound out of Christopher, but Jayne slipped into the kitchen in ghostly fashion at six thirty-five. Guilt scratched at me like an impatient dog.

"Hey, girlfriend," I said. "You're up early."

"Mom, I'm always up at this time. I have to catch the bus at seven."

I didn't see whether she rolled her eyes. Her face was already in the pantry, where she pawed at the cereal boxes. From the back, she was still a waif of a child, with little-girl-fine golden tresses and a penchant for long flowy skirts, an echo of the tiny days when she fancied herself a fairy princess. Her front was a different story, where late-blooming breasts and a well-rehearsed disdain proclaimed her as *teenager*.

"Silly me," I said.

"Unless you want to take me to school," she said into the cabinet.

Her wistfulness slapped me in the face.

"I can't today, Jay," I said. "I have an early meeting."

I'd made up half-truths so easily until now, but this lie stuck to my tongue like a frozen pole.

"What happened to Rachel last night?" I said.

"I don't know. She ditched me, I guess."

"I'm sorry I didn't get your message right away. I had—a meeting."

Jayne turned and looked at me over the top of the Rice Krispies. "Is that all you do—go to meetings?"

"Sounds like it, doesn't it?"

"Whatever." She shook her hair back and turned the box upside down over a bowl. Two pieces of cereal bounced into it. She curled her lip.

"So—how was rehearsal?" I asked.

I tried to listen as I filled my coffee cup and twisted the lid on. If I didn't get out of there, I wouldn't get to talk to Zach before his eight o'clock.

"I got a different part," Jayne said.

I fumbled for the appropriate reply. "I thought you were playing Mary Warren."

"Mercy Lewis." She gave a disgusted grunt.

"Oh, so—who are you now?"

"Abigail Williams."

The sudden light in her always-serious brown eyes made me hunt through my faded memory of *The Crucible.*

"Isn't she a main character?"

Jayne nodded. The shyness that had disappeared with her twelfth year glowed on her face. I felt my throat thicken.

"Jay, that's amazing!" I said. "Congratulations!"

"Rachel didn't learn her lines and she kept messing around during rehearsal, so Mrs. Dirks bumped her and gave the part to me." She tilted her head like a small bird, spilling a panel of wavy hair across her thin cheek. "Maybe that's why she left me last night."

"Ya think?" I willed myself not to look at my watch. "Well, from now on, I'll pick you up from rehearsals."

"What if you have a meeting?" she said, adolescence slipping cleanly back into place.

"I'm not going to be having so many meetings from now on." The thickness hardened in my throat. I couldn't even say good-bye.

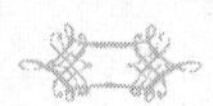

I'd just turned off Raintree Place when my cell phone belted out its disco version of the "Hallelujah Chorus," the ring tone one of my students chose for me. My heart sagged when the number on the screen wasn't Zach's. It was a college number though.

"Dr. Costanas, this is Gina Livorsi," said the California-crisp voice on the line.

Dr. Ethan Kaye's assistant. As in president of Covenant Christian College. My boss and my friend. So was Gina. My stomach tightened. Since when was I "Dr. Costanas" to her?

"Why so formal?" I said.

"Formal occasion." She sounded guarded. "Dr. Kaye wants to see you in his office. Soon as you can make it."

It was already after seven. Zach liked to be in his classroom by seven forty-five—

"I have a class at nine," I said. "I can be there after that."

Gina paused—uncomfortably, I thought.

"He says to cancel your class and be here at eight if you can."

"Do I have a choice?"

"Unh-uh."

"What's this about, Gina?"

"He didn't say."

"He didn't have to," I said. "You always know."

"Can you be here by eight?" she said.

My fingers tightened around the phone. "Yeah," I said. "Sure."

Why this summons? Something so secretive I couldn't even get it out of the secretary Zach and I had affectionately dubbed Loose Lips Livorsi?

I went cold.

CHAPTER THREE

Zach wasn't in his office when I arrived. Normally by seven-thirty there were several students hanging out with him, drinking Starbucks and discussing Habbukuk.

"Where's Dr. Archer?"

I jumped.

A lanky redhead in a hooded sweatshirt loped toward me—Brandon Stires, a junior who thought Zach hung the moon.

"You seen him, Dr. C.?" he said.

"It's not my day to watch him, Bran."

"He's not in his classroom either." Brandon peered into the narrow window in the door. "He's always here by now."

"Is he?" I said. I felt more transparent by the second.

While Brandon continued to muse on the weirdness of Zach's absence, I headed for the only other place Zach would be this close to the start of class.

Freedom Chapel stood at the bottom of the gentle slope that led down from the back of Huntington Hall, the administration building. The chapel's position always bothered me, behind and below the ostentatious structure named after one of the college's original donors. Law overshadowed creativity as the stalwart stone and timber blocked Freedom's silvery-white, winged roof. On paste gray days like so many in the Pacific Northwest—like this one—I wanted wings, not tradition.

The glass doors sighed shut behind me as I stepped into the dim narthex. I saw no heads silhouetted in the weak sunlight seeping into the sanctuary. I ventured in further, knowing the minutes were ticking relentlessly toward eight o'clock. Sometimes, Zach told me, he would come here before a class and imagine Ethan Kaye preaching from the center of the aisle.

Ethan's sermons were an undercurrent in my thoughts as well. He urged us all, students and faculty alike, to eschew the God-talk that depersonalized God into an abstraction. "Go to the Gospel," he'd tell us, "and listen to our Lord's speaking voice. He awakens our imagination so we can experience how His words work."

A chill settled over the sanctuary, and I put my hands in my coat pockets and squeezed myself in. Didn't help. This cold signified the absence of something. Perhaps of Zach. More likely the gaping space where Jesus' voice should be. I didn't want to hear what He would have to say to me right now.

As I hurried up the hill toward Huntington Hall on the path lined with still-bare trees and the first pokings of daffodils, I wasn't particularly anxious to hear what Ethan Kaye had to say either. Ethan and I—and Zach—were friends, drawn together by our common ideas. One of the reasons I'd accepted the teaching position here four years ago was that he sat at the helm.

Ethan had a reputation for wanting his college to be a place where students could face their doubts and ask their questions in an attempt to make their beliefs and convictions theirs and not the dictates of parents or professors. "Doubt isn't the opposite of faith," he said to some student at least once a week. "Doubt is an element of faith." He refused to let the fear of the more legalistic faculty members turn CCC into a dogmatic prison of peer pleasing and rule keeping. That, he said, denied everything personal and free in a relationship with God.

Which accounted for the positive reception he gave Zach and me when we proposed the Faith and Doubt project. I buried my hands in my pockets and took the hill at a slant, only tangentially aware of the infant forsythia that promised spring. I remembered sitting in Zach's office one afternoon, early on in our friendship, studying the wet-gold leaves plastered to his window. We'd been listening to yet another student tell us over lattes that his early experiences in the church left him feeling less than Christian.

"Everybody talked about the joy you were supposed to feel in the

Lord," Brandon Stires told us. "I'd walk out of the church feeling like roadkill."

"They're stuck, Doc," I'd said to Zach. "These kids that were raised in strict homes think God gets mad at them because they even *have* doubts." I'd looked at him—not expecting the liquid blue look I got back.

"Then let's get them unstuck," he'd said. "Because if anybody can get them free, it's you."

I stopped now, my hand on the knob of the back door into Huntington, the small door Zach and I always slipped through to get up to Ethan at the end of the day, when he could take off his ever-present tweed jacket and his battle-weary face and hear us wax on about plans, process, results. This method was working—students were going out into the community and interviewing seekers, people who wanted God and were in various places on the path to finding Him.

Ethan stood behind the project even when faculty members like Kevin St. Clair saw it as creeping liberalism. Zach called him "Kevin St. Pompous" during our after-hours discussions over Chinese food in the president's office. Ethan always grinned.

I started up the back steps, planting my feet in the worn places in the wood where three generations of students had climbed. Each step grew harder to take, because I knew that as steeped in compassion as Ethan was, he took a hard line when people behaved stupidly. I tried to convince myself this urgent meeting had nothing to do with my recent stupidity, or with the possibility of Zach's horrible demise in the boat fire, but my insides were a large, gelatinous mass by the time I walked into the outer office. When I heard voices in obvious conflict on the other side of his door, I clung to the hope that Zach had been called to the president's office too.

I grabbed onto the corner of Gina's desk to steady myself. She didn't turn from her computer monitor.

"Who else is coming to this meeting?" I said.

"Don't ask," she said. "Dr. Kaye said to go on in."

"Gina—"

She twisted to look at me, face as white and expressionless as porridge. "This is one time I can't tell you, because I honestly don't know." She glanced warily at the double oak doors. "All I can say is that I have never seen him lipid before."

I blinked. "You mean livid?"

"Whatever. He's ticked."

I swallowed hard to keep from throwing up.

Four faces swiveled toward me when I entered Ethan's office. None of them belonged to Zach.

Oddly, the one I noticed first belonged to the man sitting apart from the others. Andy Callahan. Attorney to the college. Thin man with the kind of unflappable manner you want in your legal advisor, though at the moment his presence fanned the flames of my anxiety. Why did this meeting require a lawyer?

Ethan himself sat on the edge of his wide desk, just shy of the stacks of files that were perpetually there. He looked the same as always—prematurely white hair brushed close to his round head, eyes direct over the Roman nose that gave his profile power, a permanent vertical line etched into the ruddy skin between his eyebrows. He wore the usual tweed slacks and hung clasped hands on the leg that didn't touch the floor.

I'd only seen Ethan Kaye angry a few times. I could add this to the list.

At least the fury didn't seem to be directed my way. In the instant before his eyes found me, they were drilled into the man in the padded Windsor chair to his left. I stifled a groan.

Kevin St. Clair was head of the religion department, so I saw him daily. But even if I hadn't, he bore too close a resemblance to a blowfish for me to ever mistake him for anyone else. His thick lips consumed the lower half of his face, and his eyelids nearly met the bags beneath them when he scowled, which was often.

"Dr. Costanas," he said. His voice was the worst thing about him. He hailed from Ohio, but he always spoke like a Georgia preacher, as if he'd learned to speak Church in divinity school. "We've been waiting for you."

Ethan shot him a look. "You're right on time, Demi. Why don't you have a seat?"

His voice I loved. Ethan actually was southern, born and bred in Tennessee, schooled at Vanderbilt. He possessed a gentle firmness only true gentlemen from below the Mason-Dixon Line seemed able to master. Even with the tension in the room as thick as dough, I felt better as I took the chair opposite Kevin, next to the other man.

I didn't know Wyatt Estes very well. He was a sixtyish businessman with a large head of iron-colored hair that looked as if it had been commanded to shoot back in large waves. One of CCC's major financial donors with, according to Gina, money in his genes. Huntington Hall was named after his grandfather, Howard. Mr. Estes wasn't on the same side of the theological fence as Ethan, though he never pretended gentility the way St. Clair did. He was a straightforward Washingtonian to the core, the kind of man I'd grown up around.

He barely acknowledged my presence. He seemed far more interested in a manila folder on the low table between himself and Kevin. He ran his thick fingers along the edges as if he were trying to straighten them.

St. Clair cleared his throat. "To get back to what I was saying—"

"I think we've wrung all the juice out of that topic," Ethan said. "Let's get this over with."

Kevin slanted against the back of his chair, arms folded like a belligerent child. Ethan looked at me, reluctance in his eyes.

"I still say Archer should be here," Kevin said.

"This doesn't hinge on his presence." Wyatt Estes's voice was surprisingly high-pitched, like the bark of a terrier.

"You did try to get in touch with him?" Kevin said to Ethan.

Ethan turned to me. "Do you know where Zach is?"

The question wasn't accusatory, but the tone was grim. He knew. I sucked dry air.

"I haven't seen him today," I said.

Wyatt Estes flipped open the folder. "Was this the last time you saw him?"

I stared at the contents he thumped with his index finger, and I gasped. It was a picture of me. It could only be me, though I'd never seen myself in a moment of passion before—eyes half closed, mouth half open in the expectation of ecstasy as Zach's hands gripped my bare shoulders and his lips hovered over mine.

Estes pushed that one aside to reveal another—my eyes startled like a doe's, hands holding Zach's head against my collarbone. Then another, showing more of me than a camera had ever captured before.

"All right." Ethan slid the folder off the table and tossed it behind him onto his desk. "You've made your point."

"No." Kevin pursed the blowfish lips at me. "I think Dr. Costanas has made it for us."

Only the fact that Kevin St. Clair had seen a picture of me bare-chested kept me momentarily speechless.

St. Clair leaned toward Ethan. "I have to wonder—has Dr. Costanas somehow gotten the message that this kind of behavior is acceptable on our campus now?" He pulled his lips into an upside-down *U.* "And that of course begs the question of whether or not our students have been similarly impacted. Of course, we can't know that. We don't have pictures of *them*—"

"Here's the bottom line, Kaye," Wyatt Estes said. His jowls jittered like nervous hands. "I'm not the only donor who will pull his support if something isn't done. Fowler—Gentry—Collins—if any of them knew that this kind of thing is allowed to go on—"

"'Allowed to go on'?" I said.

St. Clair and Estes looked at me as if they were surprised I remained vertical, rather than cowering under the table. I pressed my hands to my thighs to conceal their shaking.

"Do you think Ethan knew about this and said, 'Oh, sure—you two kids go ahead'?"

St. Clair grunted. "Possibly you could have inferred it from one of Dr. Kaye's sermons—"

"What am I, twelve?" I said. "*I* committed the sin, Kevin—on my own. It was my decision, and I never thought for a minute that Ethan would approve, or even look the other way."

The blowfish lips drew into a sanctimonious purse.

"I fail to see what this has to do with Ethan," I said to Estes.

The man's nostrils flared like apocalyptic horns. "This happened under Dr. Kaye's watch. He is the one ultimately accountable for the morality—or lack thereof—on this campus."

"Look, what do you want?" Ethan's voice veered close to an edge I didn't want him to cross.

"We want your resignation, Dr. Kaye," Wyatt Estes said. "Tender it, and this mess goes away."

"What?"

Once again they looked at me, this time in apparent annoyance that I was still there, still daring to speak.

"That is the most—inane thing I have ever heard," I said. "If anyone should resign, it should be me."

The words came of their own accord—and yet they were the only ones I could say.

"Demi—" Ethan said.

"For you to step down over something *I* did makes no sense, Ethan. I would expect you to fire me anyway, now that you know." I looked at Wyatt Estes, who watched me through narrowed eyes.

"Not that it's any of your business," I said, "but I went there last night to end the relationship *because* I could no longer teach here in good conscience and continue the affair."

"That was good-bye?" Kevin said.

"Shut up," I shot back.

Ethan put up both hands, eyes closed like a weary father. "I can't let you do this, Demi."

"You have no choice. It's done." I looked at Wyatt Estes again. "Your 'mess' has gone away."

He arched an eyebrow at Ethan. "And Dr. Archer?"

"What about him?" Ethan said.

"You'll ask for his resignation as well?"

St. Clair's eyes bulged from their pouches. "What are you saying, Wyatt? You're going to take their resignations over his?"

"I see no reason to do otherwise." Wyatt Estes swiveled his big head toward Ethan again. "But I give you fair warning. If there is one more incident of misconduct, you will either resign, or I will withdraw my financial support."

"What about last time?" St. Clair said.

Wyatt Estes merely got to his feet. "I think we're through here."

"Not quite." Dr. Kaye reached behind him and picked up the folder. "I want the negatives. There is to be no publicity about this—absolutely none. Dr. Costanas has already punished herself—"

"You see?" St. Clair waved a finger at Estes.

"—and I see no reason to put her family through any unnecessary pain."

"You have children?" Estes said to me.

"Yes."

His lip curled, but he nodded. "Agreed. Kaye, I'd like copies of both letters of resignation."

"As soon as you turn over the negatives," Ethan said.

Wyatt Estes nodded again and exited. Kevin stared after him, lips parted, and then seemed to collect himself. He elongated his neck, looking for all the world like E.T., and departed through the slit of an opening Estes left him.

Ethan crossed the room and pushed the door shut. The click of the latch snapped in my head. Except for Andy Callahan, who made himself invisible at the window, I was alone in the room with the man I looked up to most in the world and a file full of pornographic pictures of myself.

"I'm so sorry, Ethan," I said.

He stopped me with a look that reached into my chest and pulled my heart out. "What were you thinking, Demi? What in the world were you thinking?"

I stared down at my hands. "I wasn't thinking at all. I was caught up in a feeling—like I was obsessed—and I couldn't get free."

It sounded so pathetic. I could have been any angst-ridden adolescent, begging to be understood.

"You've put me in a very bad position."

"I know that," I said.

"Do you?" Ethan leaned against the front of his desk. "You've let me down—the students—the whole college."

I didn't answer. What, actually, was there to say? He was laying out everything I'd already butchered myself with.

"Did you think about your Faith and Doubt project?"

"I can't stand that I've jeopardized that."

"That's what I don't understand." Ethan's voice sank. "Something is very wrong for you to risk all of that."

"I've never done anything like this before—I didn't even think I could—"

The pause was so long I thought I would die in it.

"I can't quite wrap my mind around all this yet," he said finally. He started toward the window, hand running down the back of his head, and stopped as if he'd just realized Andy Callahan was still in the room. He sat stiffly in the chair Wyatt Estes had vacated, looking hard at me.

"I trusted you—both of you. You were the only people I thought I could share my concerns with about the direction things are taking."

"I haven't betrayed that, Ethan."

"Did you miss the little scene that just took place here? This was exactly what they needed to put me in the place I'm in right now. If I step down from this presidency, you know they'll bring in somebody Estes could work like a puppet. I want to continue to guide this college in the direction I think God wants."

I bit down on my lip.

"If I stay and this gets out—and I don't take any action—I'll be misrepresented as some radical and suffer the withdrawal of funds."

"That's why I resigned," I said. "I wasn't trying to be a martyr."

Ethan shook his head. "I know that. I also know that if it weren't this, they'd have found something else eventually. It isn't over." He grunted softly. "I allowed you to get the best of him in front of Wyatt Estes, and he's not going to forget that."

"But now you won't have Zach and me to run interference for you."

He seared me with a look.

"In the end," I said to my lap, "we almost took you down, didn't we?"

"*We* being the operative word."

"I don't understand."

"You didn't do this alone."

My head came up.

"You don't have any idea where Zach is?"

"I checked his office and the chapel," I said. "One of his students said he wasn't in his classroom."

"Gina hasn't buzzed me. He hasn't shown up."

I could hear my pulse in my ears. "I don't know what happened after I left the boat last night. There was a fire—"

"I saw that in the paper—"

"But I still thought he'd take care of the film—unless he couldn't because he was injured." My gaze locked with Ethan's. "How did Estes get the pictures?"

"I don't know. He wouldn't say, except that they were brought to him last night. He called St. Clair . . ." He let the rest fade into our silence.

Too much had slammed into me at once. The things that held me together were shattering one by one.

"I have to ask you a few questions."

I sat up straight and dried my palms on each other. "Ask me anything you want."

"Who else knows about this—thing with you and Zach?"

"Nobody."

"You didn't tell Gina?"

I felt my eyes bulge. "Are you kidding? I'm not exactly proud of it. I haven't told a soul."

"I'd appreciate your keeping it that way—with one exception." The wise eyes I so respected searched my face. "Look, Demi, this whole thing is so un-you. You are a good, moral woman, and I know something has gone wrong for you to make a choice like this. Please get help."

"Help? You mean like—"

"I mean a good pastoral counselor or a therapist. I know a—"

"Thank you." I stood up. "I appreciate your concern, Ethan—I do. But I know what happened, and I'll make sure it never happens again."

I fumbled for my purse and found the door.

"If you need anything at all—"

"I'm fine," I said to the doorknob.

"You'll be missed, Demi," he said.

As I hurried down the front steps of Huntington Hall in the midmorning drizzle, I knew I would miss me too. Because I was leaving a chunk of myself behind, and I had only myself to blame.

CHAPTER FOUR

I canceled my classes and stayed cocooned in my office all day, ostensibly to write my letter of resignation. In truth, I clung to mugs of coffee I never drank and watched my e-mail like an obsessed hawk.

Every footfall in the hallway sent me running to the door. I called Zach's cell phone on the half hour. I even pressed my ear to the shared wall between our offices, until I told myself I'd need quaaludes if I didn't get a grip.

Zach always promised he would sweep the stars aside to be there for me. He would show up. And I had to see him. Surely he didn't know we were "resigning."

But the sense that he hadn't believed I was leaving him gnawed at me most. It was now a matter of photographic record that I hadn't done much to convince him. If I could talk to him—that's all—one more time . . .

And make sure that he was still alive. As hard as I'd worked for twenty-one years to deal with the possibility that my husband could die in a fire, the idea of my lover dying in one was painfully ironic.

He didn't appear, and I finally put a Do Not Disturb sign on my door so Brandon and Marcy and a myriad of other students would stop coming in to ask me if I knew his whereabouts. One thing was clear: the fact that I almost always knew where Dr. Archer was hadn't escaped them. Who did I think I'd been kidding?

Actually, I was waiting for Rich to leave for work at two-thirty before I went home. Even after I gave up on the resignation letter and tried to formulate a reason to give my husband for my sudden exit from Covenant Christian, I wasn't even close.

After all the lies I'd told him in the last six months, you'd think I could come up with one more. But there was too much piled on me, like the rubble of an earthquake. Too much pain and anger and guilt and shame and fear. I couldn't dig my way out enough to even look at Rich, much less tell him our income had just been slashed by three-quarters and that I probably wouldn't be able to get another job in Christian academia.

I tried distracting myself by writing out a financial review. Rich didn't make enough as a firefighter to support our lifestyle, especially with Christopher in college. We had some savings, a few investments. And the nest egg we'd gotten for Eddie after 9/11. I actually snapped the pencil in half at that thought. No way we were touching the "compensation" money from Rich's brother's heroism to make up for what I'd done. And that went for the inheritance from Rich's parents' house too. Those precious people were not going to pay for my mistakes.

I abandoned the money issue and went back to scribbling reasons to give Rich. Although I'd chattered to him about everything I did at CCC—until I found an actual listener in Zach—he probably hadn't heard half of it from his cave. He might accept anything I told him.

But teaching religion had been my passion ever since he'd known me. He used to say it was the thing that made him passionate about *me,* the way I lit up when I went on ad nauseam about my students learning to embrace the parables . . .

I scratched everything out until I scraped a hole in the paper. Rich would never buy the idea that I just quit. The only thing close to the truth was that the constant conflict between Kaye's vision for the college and St. Clair's had finally gotten to me and I couldn't be part of it anymore. Finally, I put all my attempts through the shredder and drove home to the hammer of rain on the Jeep's soft top. The sound used to soothe me when I left Zach to go home to Rich. Now it accused me.

I had until the next morning to think of something, maybe even days before he noticed I wasn't going to campus . . .

That hope faded the moment I pulled into the driveway and opened the garage door. Both Rich's Harley and our green Range Rover were tucked inside. I glanced at my watch. After three. Rich should have left for the station forty-five minutes ago. A dread so heavy settled over me, I could barely climb out of the car.

I pulled off my boots in the mudroom, chest seizing. There was no Zach to run to now, to tell me I was right. I padded into the kitchen and set my briefcase soundlessly on the counter. The house was so eerily quiet even my socks on the plank floor announced every footfall, as if something had come in and sucked out all the sound waves.

The ground floor of our log home was one large open space, sectioned off by American Indian rugs we'd bought on our attempts at family outings and by cozy groupings of big-stuffed furniture that my two teenagers often rearranged to suit the need of the moment. Right now, the pair of russet recliners in the TV area were pushed to within a foot of the screen.

At the other end of the room, the pellet stove sat cold and silent, giving the place an unusual dreariness. As soon as I changed into something sloppy and comforting, I'd get it going. Some cheer might help me think. I headed for the staircase.

"Demitria."

Rich's voice boomed from somewhere in the cavernous room.

I stopped, hand on the banister. "Where are you?" I said.

His head rose from one of the recliners, and he stood, his back to me, broad shoulders so stiff they tortured the stretch of the navy blue South Kitsap Fire and Rescue T-shirt. Circles of sweat had formed under the sleeves. With a straight steel band of an arm, he lifted a brown envelope and held it above him.

"What's that?" I said.

Instead of answering, he came out from behind the chair and opened the mailer as he crossed to me. By the time he reached the bottom of the stairs, he'd pulled out the contents. The room tilted, and I sank to the steps.

"Oh, Rich, no," I said.

He still didn't speak as he dropped the photographs one by one, face up, on the floor below me. For the second time that day, my body and Zach Archer's were exposed to eyes that were never meant to see them that way.

"Where did you get these?" I said, in someone else's stricken voice.

"They were in my box at the station today," Rich said. He sounded dead. "I don't know who put them there. I don't care. I just want to know—"

He stopped, and in the space I could almost hear his blood pounding.

"I want to know—why, Demitria?"

I'd given myself a hundred reasons that had until this moment made sense to me. Right now I couldn't think of one. All I knew was the twist of my husband's face as he looked at the images of what I'd done to us.

"I was wrong, Rich," I said.

A hiss escaped between his teeth. A New Yorker can imply a paragraph of swearing in one long Brooklyn *S*. I cringed as if he'd slapped me.

"Where did this happen?" he said, his gaze still riveted to the pictures, voice low. "Here, in my house? In my bed?"

"Of course not. We were on his boat—"

Rich snatched up a picture. BBs of sweat glittered on the dark stubble of his upper lip. "Who is this?"

It hadn't occurred to me that Zach's face never showed in the photos.

His voice rose for the first time. "Who is it?"

"Zach Archer."

Rich pulled the picture closer to his face, his heavy brows wrenched together. I felt a stab. All he'd seen in those photographs until now was me.

He flung the photo from him and stared at me. Stared as if I were a stranger who'd appeared to tear his life apart.

"I've been on that boat—he took us all fishing."

"I know."

"Was that before or after he got you in bed?"

I clapped my hand over my mouth.

He put up his hand, its glistening palm facing me and shaking. The 9/11 hero was trembling.

"This wasn't no one-time thing," he said. He shoved the first photo with the toe of his boot. "How long?"

"Five months," I said. "But last night—when these were taken—I went there to break it off, because it was wrong."

Rich looked at me. "Took you five months to figure that out? Took me five seconds."

From stone stillness he thrust out his leg and kicked, so hard I felt the vicious air at my face. Images of my infidelity scattered to the corners of our home. Rich caught his balance and turned his back to me, his shoulders heaving, hands clenched on his hips.

"It's over," I said.

"How many people know?"

"Ethan Kaye. Kevin St. Clair. A man named Wyatt Estes—he's a donor. That's all."

"Oh, that's all?" Rich scraped his hand down the back of his head, making a salt-and-pepper path that ended with his nails digging at his neck skin. "That's half your college."

I drew in what air I could find. "It's not 'my' college anymore. I had to resign. It was either me or Ethan," I said. "I couldn't let him take the fall for me."

"You have a conscience for Ethan, but not for me."

I didn't say anything. The gutsy belligerence I'd mustered so easily for Kevin St. Clair no longer existed.

"So," Rich said. "You're fired. These bigwigs know. How long before this makes the news?"

"It won't." I sounded like a ten-year-old. "Ethan made them promise there would be no publicity. They're giving him the negatives."

He did swear then. "Other men have seen you half naked?" Rich poked up fingers. "One—two—three—oh, and—him."

He pulled in his breath and his hands and the gaze he pierced me with.

"Don't, Rich," I said. "We have to talk about this."

"There's nothing I want to say and nothing I want to hear." He took a step backward, but then he drew his hands to his hips again. "No, I do want to know one thing."

"Anything."

"I want to know how you could get up every morning of your life and read the Bible and go over there to that school and teach kids how to live, and do—*this*—at the same time. Tell me how you could do that."

I steepled my fingers to my forehead and closed my eyes. It was the one question I didn't know the answer to.

He went so quiet, so still, I was sure he'd simply dissolved from my life. Until he said, "I don't even know who you are."

The front door slammed—and I wanted to die.

I'm not sure, during the time I sat there paralyzed on the steps, when the questions began to batter me. Would it have been different if I'd called him and told him right after the meeting in Kaye's office—if he hadn't seen the pictures?

And who on *earth* had delivered them to Rich? Estes had promised no publicity, and he didn't seem to want my family hurt. My focus narrowed on Kevin St. Clair. The slimy blowfish was capable, but his wasn't a vendetta against me—it was about Ethan.

Finally, in the midst of that tangle, I sagged against the steps. Why did it matter? Rich knew now, and in the worst possible way. We were scraped down to the bone—naked and raw. He'd summed it all up, as he always could. Time and time again in our marriage, I waxed eloquent on an issue for thirty minutes, only to have him pack the essence into one neat irrefutable sentence.

I don't even know who you are.

That made two of us.

I probably would have sat there, frozen, through the night, if I hadn't heard the school bus lumber to the curb.

Jayne was home.

Nerves sizzled to life as I half-crawled, half-ran around the room, gathering up the photos, dropping them, seizing them again. Frantically I looked for a place to stash them, suddenly unfamiliar with my own house. I'd never needed a place to hide shame before. As the mudroom door opened, I flung open the stove and thrust the pictures inside. I was shoveling in pellets when Jayne passed through.

"Why is it so cold in here, Mom?"

I didn't even know where to start.

That night I didn't say anything to either of the kids. I managed to conjure up an image of Rich coming home from work at midnight, ready to talk things out, and I hung onto that while Christopher and Jayne and I ate pizza in front of the TV, and I took Jayne to play rehearsal and picked her up.

Christopher, mercifully, spent the rest of the evening at the library at Olympia U. He gave no indication that he saw me curled up on the couch in front of the stove when he came home at eleven-thirty and went up to his room. I watched him disappear up the steps, his thin frame so unlike Rich's shorter, solid powerhouse self in every way. Except his temperament. Like his father, the boy could hold a grudge longer than most people lived.

That thought shattered my fragile hope of Rich being open to a reconciliation so soon. Still, I ran to the kitchen to meet him when I heard the Harley pull into the garage. His swarthy skin was chapped and his dark eyes swam in a stinging mist. He didn't even look at me.

"Rich, we have to talk about this," I said.

"Nothing to say."

He started through the kitchen. When I dove to grab his arm, he yanked it away as if I'd come after him with a branding iron.

"Don't, Demitria," he said. "Let me be."

"Let you be what? Miserable?"

"What do you expect me to be?"

I opened my mouth, but he swore.

"We'll talk tomorrow then," I said.

I stayed put while he pounded up the steps, prayed the noise wouldn't wake Jayne up. *Prayed* is actually the wrong word. I had yet to crawl to my God with any of it.

Working deliberately, trying to stay focused on every step, I made coffee for the next morning. Not that I expected to need anything to wake me up, since sleep was out of the question. I loaded the dishwasher. Emptied the trash. Crossed the notation about a faculty meeting off the calendar. Tried not to wonder if Zach was in a burn unit in Seattle.

When I was sure Rich would be in bed, I went upstairs, planning out the first sentence I would try when I climbed in beside him. I stopped at the top.

He was leaned over outside the bedroom door, stacking items on the floor in the hall.

"What are you doing?" I said. "What's wrong with my shampoo?"

He set the bottle on top of what I now realized was my makeup bag and my blow-dryer.

"It was in my bathroom," Rich said.

"Your bathroom?"

"Find another place for it. And another place to sleep. I'll get your pajamas."

"Rich, stop! This is absurd—"

Across from our room, light slipped out from under Jayne's door. I went to it and pressed my face to the doorjamb.

"It's okay, honey," I said. "Go back to sleep."

"Whatever," came the sleepy reply.

I turned back to Rich, who was in our doorway with a pair of my sweats and a bathrobe.

"You can get the rest tomorrow."

I went close to him and whispered, "You're kicking me out of our bedroom?"

"I can't sleep with you." He nodded at the pile on the floor. "You need anything else?"

"I need you to listen to me!"

"Good night," Rich said. And he shut the door in my face. I heard the lock click into place.

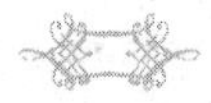

The next day was the first of March, a Saturday, without a hectic morning schedule to hide the fact that my toiletries were living in the downstairs bathroom, or that Rich and I weren't speaking to each other. The kids were used to that part, in a sense.

They were accustomed to his sleeping past noon, even on his

days off, and giving one-syllable answers to their questions, and watching re-runs on television until even their eyes glazed over. It had happened so gradually since we'd moved from New York, neither of them ever asked me, "What's wrong with Dad?" Maybe they were so wrapped up in adjusting to the culture shock, they didn't see it happening.

But I wondered at times if from ages ten and fifteen to their current thirteen and eighteen they'd forgotten what their father was like before 9/11. "He's depressed" seemed so obvious; surely they'd figured that out. Who wouldn't be after what he'd been through?

But who wouldn't have gone for the counseling offered to him in New York in the aftermath of the attacks? All his buddies did.

Who wouldn't have at least tried to accept help when he was ordered to take a leave of absence? His refusal cost him his job.

Who wouldn't have appreciated the welcome he received here from Orchard Heights, Station 8, the arms open in near-worship to a World Trade Center hero?

I was the one who had suggested the move to my home state, yes, yet he'd shown a glimmer of hope that it would distance him from bitter memories and give him a new start.

But who else would have pushed away the one person who ached in every fiber of her being to help him?

After surprising him with a boat and a motorcycle, bringing on the candles and the massage oil to try to please him in bed, and begging him in tears to open up to me, I would have had no answers for my children if they had asked me why their father was disappearing into himself.

Maybe that's why they never asked.

But Rich's customary distance had an edge to it that morning that even a thirteen-year-old in her own world couldn't miss.

"Turn that thing off," he barked at Jayne when she settled in front of the TV with a piece of toast.

"We always watch—"

"I said turn it off! I can't stand that noise."

Jayne retreated to the kitchen where I was cleaning out the refrigerator and parked herself at the snack bar. Her hair dipped over her plate.

"It's not you, Jay," I said. "He's dealing with some things."

"Does it have anything to do with you sleeping on the couch?"

I looked up at my son, who had materialized next to the coffeepot. He was still in the boxers and Olympia University T-shirt he used as default sleepwear, and his sandy blonde case of bed head matched the puffy eyes. But from the way his gaze poked at me, I knew his mind was wide awake.

"I was restless," I said. "I didn't want to disturb him."

"Looks like you disturbed him anyway," Christopher said. "I heard him cussing in the garage."

Jayne's head came up. She looked at me briefly and went back to tearing her toast into confetti.

"We're having issues," I said. "You two don't need to worry about it."

Christopher arched an eyebrow and picked up the coffee carafe. "'Issues' is he doesn't take out the trash and you leave your pantyhose soaking in the sink."

I dumped a lump of pink mashed potatoes into the garbage disposal and concentrated on scrubbing out the Tupperware it had been growing in.

"I also know Dad throwing tools isn't about 'issues.'"

I stopped scrubbing. "He threw something?"

"Have you looked in the garage this morning? Looks like Mr. Goodwrench went ballistic in there."

I nearly scoured the logo off the bottom of the container. Rich didn't hurl screwdrivers and yell at his kids. He'd never even spanked one of them.

"So, yeah, Mom," Christopher said. "What's going on?"

"Maybe it's none of our business," Jayne said.

Christopher held his coffee mug halfway to his lips and looked at her through the steam. "Is it my business if they sleep together?"

"No," she and I said in unison.

"Does it become my business when my father turns into Attila the Hun? Yes. Do I have a right to know what's going on when I'm afraid to walk around in my own house? No doubt." He took a noisy sip from the mug and surveyed me. "So what gives, Mom?"

Jayne pushed her plate across the counter and slid off the stool.

"Don't go anywhere, Sissy," Christopher said. "We need to hear this."

Only Christopher's use of his childhood name for his sister pushed me toward telling them something to ease their minds. "Okay, listen," I said.

Jayne slid one bun-cheek back onto the stool and examined her split ends. Christopher took another drag from his coffee.

"I did something that upset your dad," I said. "So he asked me to sleep downstairs until we can sort it out."

"Geez, Mom, what did you do?" Christopher said. "Cheat on him?"

The flicker of shock I registered lasted only until I saw in his crooked smile that he was kidding. But it was long enough. Christopher set his mug on the stove and stared at me.

"Dude, that's it, isn't it?" he said. "You slept with some other guy."

"You told them?"

Rich was there, out of nowhere, the way everything suddenly seemed to be. His eyes bit into me.

"No," I said lamely. "He guessed."

Rich hissed. "He grabbed it out of thin air—"

"So that's why you're never here," Christopher said. "That's why Jayne has to call me to pick her up—"

"It's over, Christopher," I said.

That didn't seem to make any more difference to him than it had to anyone else I'd said it to. He drew his mouth up to his nose. "How could you do that to Dad? You're a hypocrite."

"I know," I said. "I've hurt your father—now I've hurt you kids—and I'm so sorry."

"Like that's supposed to change anything." For a horrified moment I thought Christopher was going to spit at me. Instead, he turned to his father, but Rich was honed in on me, wearing an expression identical to his son's.

"Come on, Sissy," Christopher said. "Let's go for a ride."

Jayne looked at me. There wasn't an eye roll within a hundred miles. Only heartbreaking confusion splashed across her face.

"Go with your brother," I said. "We'll talk later."

Christopher nodded Jayne toward the mudroom door. His last look before his exit was for Rich. "Anything you need, Dad," he said. "I'm here for you."

Both Rich and I stood there, not moving, not speaking, until Christopher's pickup roared out of the driveway.

"Why did you have to let them find out?"

"Did you think they weren't going to notice the tension? I tried not to—"

"Look—stop trying, would you? Just stop."

He said no more.

CHAPTER FIVE

They avoided me the rest of the weekend. Christopher kept Jayne out of my sight with such apparent disdain that by Monday morning I was nearly convinced I was as toxic for my daughter as his twisted lip made me out to be.

I wanted to talk to her, but I couldn't even explain anything to myself yet. How could I make her understand?

Rich stayed home, but his marked escape from any room I entered shot fear through me. When I'd dogged him to the TV area, the mudroom, the kitchen, the garage, he finally holed up in the bedroom. From the sound of his stocky self heaving back and forth across the floor, I knew he wasn't sleeping any more than I was.

I went out once in the Jeep, to pick up a pound of his favorite French roast out of a thready hope that the aroma might lure him downstairs. When I pulled into the driveway on the return trip, I saw a movement in our bedroom window. Rich was backing away from the glass, caught in the act of watching for me. His broad shoulders looked shrunken in that instant, shriveled in loneliness. At least we shared that.

That kept me hanging on to the frail possibility that once the week started and our routine resumed, a piece of our life would fall back into place and I could begin to stitch it back together.

The only place I could start was with closure at Covenant and with Zach. I spent most of Sunday night composing my letter of resignation, and before eight o'clock Monday I was cleaning out my desk and bookshelves at the college.

I got into a saving rhythm that kept my thoughts from spinning out of control, until I came to the Faith and Doubt binders. Then I sank to the floor with a pile of my past in my lap.

Each pristine white notebook was labeled with titles Zach and I collaborated on with the students around a piled-high platter of fried calamari and fries at Tweeten's. I could see the kids working them over, their eyes narrowing and springing open in the gleam of neon fish signs. *Early Images of God*—No—*Infant Images.* Bursts of inspiration rose from prayer and shared purpose and unbridled laughter.

I ran my hand over the binder we'd finally labeled *Off His Lap and into the Trenches.*

"We were so close to God," I whispered.

The distance now left me hollow.

I stacked the binders as carefully as teacups on a chair by the door. The rest of my current teaching materials I dumped unceremoniously into a copy paper box. F&D had been the most meaningful thing to me at CCC that semester—since Kevin St. Clair had saddled me with teaching the ultra-dry "Religion in the Pacific Northwest" and two sections of Religion 102.

"What happened to Speaking in Parables?" I'd asked St. Clair when the preliminary schedules came out. "I thought we'd agreed I'd be teaching that."

"I'm still developing a sense of your take on the parables, Dr. Costanas," he said. The blowfish lips were fully operational. "I can't tell if you're a literalist or something else."

Beyond that, he'd refused to discuss it. That was the biggest obstacle in this relentless battle among the faculty. Zach, Ethan, and I—we all wanted to talk, to find out what common ground we had to work from. Kevin's camp always answered, "We have taught the Word as it was meant to be taught, and there is no reason to allow anyone to put a different slant on it." I would never forget the faculty meeting when Kevin himself had said, "The next thing you know someone will be declaring that the Prodigal Son was the victim of a wealthy workaholic father who never paid any attention to him." I guffawed right across the table.

The thing was, all Zach and Ethan and I, and a few others, wanted for our students was a chance to grapple with the possibilities, to pray together over interpretation.

A lump the size of my fist formed in my throat. I hadn't shed a tear over any of this, not even in the endless darkness of three AM. Now every one I'd been holding back threatened to break free, just as three girls, led by Brandon Stires, crowded into my office.

"So what's the deal, Dr. C.?" Brandon leaned a bony shoulder against the empty bookshelf. "The note on Dr. A.'s door says some new guy's taking over his classes."

Chelsea Farmer's eyes, perfectly framed in eyeliner, widened at the box I hoisted off the desk. "Are you leaving too?"

"Irreconcilable differences with the university," I said. "I was going to send out an e-mail, but—" I dusted off my hands. "Here you are."

I attempted a smile, which no one appeared to buy, and they all exchanged loaded looks.

"I've been asked not to discuss it, guys," I said. "I'm sorry."

Brandon elbowed his way past Chelsea, Marcy, and a new girl who'd transferred from Olympia in January. I thought her name was Audrey. Now I'd never know for sure.

"You can't even tell us what's gonna happen to F&D?" Brandon said.

Marcy's wide face flattened. "We talked about writing monologues we could perform. What about that?"

I tried to swallow. "I'll get together with Dr. Archer, and we'll set up a time to discuss it with you."

Brandon folded his arms. "What do we do in the meantime?"

"Keep meeting, interviewing people." For no reason that I could think of, I nodded vehemently at the dark-haired, diminutive Audrey. "You'll be okay, and I promise you, we won't abandon you. We'll get you a new advisor—"

"Like who?" Marcy said with a sniff. "Dr. St. Clair?"

"Dude—no! It'll go from the Faith and Doubt project to the Mandatory Faith Edict." Brandon jerked his head. "He'll want to rename it You Better Believe It."

I winced. "All right, so maybe we—maybe I could act as an outside consultant."

"That would work," Chelsea said. "What about Dr. A.?"

I'd come to the end of what I could pretend. "I can't speak for him," I said.

Marcy nodded. "You guys are a team."

I turned to an empty box and resisted the urge to stick my head in it.

"It'll be okay," I said again.

Nobody appeared to believe that. Least of all me.

When they were gone, everything was packed except two books that belonged to Zach—*Speaking in Parables* by Sally McFague and Paul Tillich's *Dynamics of Faith.* We'd talked about both of them, in those early days before we couldn't keep our hands off each other.

The theology department "secretary"—a round senior named Sebastian who never looked up from his NKJV when any of us made a request—let me use the master key to get into Zach's office to return them. I probably could have told him I wanted to rifle the place and he wouldn't have cared, or remembered two minutes later.

The aura of the tiny room overpowered me as I closed myself in—Zach's musky scent and herby-smelling tea stash and slicing wit still lingered in the air. Each word we'd spoken—beyond the yearning whispers to the real exchanges that led us to know that we thought and believed and doubted in identical ways—screamed now from the pages of the books he'd left behind.

Along with everything else. The electric kettle, the canvas bag he used to carry his overflow of papers, even the twenty-pound, leather-bound Oxford Annotated Bible were exactly where they'd always been.

I shoved my knuckles against my mouth. He wouldn't leave all this here.

So where was he?

When I got to Ethan Kaye's office, Gina took one look at me—told me I looked awful—and went directly into the inner sanctum. She was back before I could sink any further and ushered me in.

Ethan didn't have to tell me to sit down. I couldn't stand up. I barely made it to the Windsor chair before I broke down. Hard, from the pit of myself.

Ethan and I didn't have the kind of relationship where I poured out my personal soul. In fact, I didn't have that kind of relationship with anyone—except Zach. I choked myself back and buried my face in the handkerchief he tucked into my hand.

"It's finally hit you," he said.

"Rich knows. My kids know."

He let a short silence fall. "That's rough."

"I deserve it." I looked up. "I'm trying to tie up loose ends—I brought my letter."

"No hurry."

"I need to know—Ethan, where is Zach?"

His eyes narrowed.

"I don't want to see him for—that," I said. "But we need to get closure with the kids on the Faith and Doubt project."

"I have no idea where he is." Ethan's voice flattened. "And neither does anyone else. As of this morning, his e-mails are bouncing back. His cell phone service has been discontinued. To my knowledge he hasn't been seen since you left him on the boat Thursday night. I've talked to the police, the fire inspector—there's no trace of him in the—remains of the boat." He cleared his throat. "They've had divers in the inlet."

"What about whoever took the pictures? He would know." I choked back another threatening sob. "I should never have had a relationship with Zach, Ethan, but I can't just shrug off the fact that he's disappeared. Something has happened to him."

Ethan ran his hand across his mouth. "Or he simply left."

I stared at him. "Right or wrong, Zach loves me. He wouldn't abandon me to take the fall for both of us."

Ethan said something that I didn't hear, because I put my face into the handkerchief and wept until it hurt.

When the strange woman inside me finally shuddered out the last of it, Ethan handed me a glass of water.

"Drink this," he said. "And I want you to listen to me."

"I'm sorry. I didn't come here to do this. I'm fine."

"No, you're not fine, and you won't be until you get help with this. Hear me out."

I nodded and took a sip. He half-perched on his desk. The lines on his face drew long.

"I have a friend who's a therapist," Ethan said. "He's a well-known Christian psychologist—has a syndicated radio talk show, has written a couple of books. You may have heard of the Healing Choice Clinics."

I shook my head.

"Anyway, he's gifted. He doesn't see clients much anymore, but he would talk to you if I asked him to. We go way back."

"I can't go to—wherever—" My intellect seemed to have drained out with my tears.

"You wouldn't have to. He's on sabbatical up at Point No Point. That has to be a God-thing."

"I appreciate the offer, Ethan, but I can handle this."

His silence clearly said he didn't agree.

"All right, give me his name," I said. "If I feel like I need to, I'll call him."

"Dr. Sullivan Crisp. He was a student of mine twenty years ago, when I taught at Vanderbilt. I thought he was going to be a theologian. He turned traitor and became a psychologist."

I folded the handkerchief into a tight square in my lap and pushed it into my purse. "I'll wash this and get it back to you." I pulled out a white envelope. "Here's my letter."

I stood, and Ethan rose with me.

"Call me if you change your mind about Dr. Crisp."

"I will." It was a safe promise because I wouldn't reconsider. A new resolve was taking shape in the space I'd sobbed free.

I didn't go to the yacht club until the next day. Since my last night there, I'd discovered that the key must have dropped out of my jacket pocket. I was going to have to get someone to let me in, and there would be a better chance of that on a day when it wasn't freezing—outside my house or in it.

I still clung to the hope that my family would thaw, given a little time. But the passing of moments only drove Rich further into his cave and carved Christopher's disgust deeper into his face. Jayne couldn't seem to bring herself to look at me.

Rain or shine, I'd have to find Zach and put this behind me, before my entire life slipped away.

Both the sun and Ned Traynor were out when I hurried up to the yacht club gate the next morning. He was the one with the lovelorn Yorkshire terrier. His wife—a chatty lady who hung a wreath on the door of their slip for every occasion including Groundhog Day—wasn't with him, which was good. I didn't have time for a long conversation about the Yorkie's yearning to produce a litter.

"Hey, pretty lady!" Ned said. "I don't usually see you here this time of day."

"Which is probably why I walked off without my key," I said. "Would you mind?"

"So sorry to hear about Zach's boat." He shook his head as he gallantly swung the gate open for me. "We'll miss him around here."

I looked at him sharply, but he was busy shutting the gate with a flourish.

"Any idea where he's going to live now?" he asked.

"Not yet," I said.

Ned turned to me, hand jingling in his pocket. "You tell him he'd better swing by and at least say good-bye. You need me to jimmy the lock on the slip?"

I told him I did have that key. I didn't add that I planned to throw it into the inlet as soon as I was done.

Hurrying down Dock C in daylight was strange. Sunset was the closest I'd come in a while to seeing light shimmer on the narrow strips of Sinclair Inlet that showed on either side of the narrow walkway, and even that had been a risk. The few times I'd come before dark were at Zach's insistence that he wanted to see me with the "critters" again.

The sea critters, he called them. He said he'd never noticed the secret life that existed under the dock until the day last June when he took the whole Costanas family for a day-long fishing trip. Before he and I were us.

I'd confided in him that Rich had lost interest in everything, including me. Even the twenty-seven-foot Regal I'd bought him with my mother's inheritance money sat on its trailer in our backyard, forgotten like the rest of him. Zach offered to try to wake him up with an outing. Rich and Christopher had indeed both been entranced with the cabin cruiser, built in 1941 and restored by Zach.

Jayne, on the other hand, barely got two slips down Dock C before she was on her belly, pulling up a pregnant kelp crab. I plopped beside her, suddenly ten years old again, peering between the planks at the anemones waving like feather dusters and the sea stars groping with their suckered feet for something to hold onto.

Then Zach was there too, as enchanted as I, and Jayne lectured him on the ecosystem he was seeing for the first time. I propped my chin on my hands and basked in a contentment I thought I'd lost completely.

I never went out on the Sound with Zach after that day. The trysts that began in September took place right there at the dock, at night, pocketed in the cabin of *The Testament.* A few times, though, Zach convinced me to come when there was still light, so he could watch me flop on my tummy and bring up sea critters for him. He touched his first silken jellyfish with my hand holding his, saw his first shrimp swim, right across our side-by-side palms. To see me that way, he said, was worth the risk of someone spotting us.

I hurried over that hidden world now and let myself into Zach's slip. I wasn't prepared for what I saw.

The handsome vessel I knew was gone. In its place was a black skeleton, a lifeless tangle of ribs. The dock itself was remarkably uncharred—though not so surprising, considering Rich had been here to fight the flames. Every fire was a beast to him, he always said, a cruel, insatiable persona that had to be reckoned with. He fought never to let one take what didn't belong to it. Even the piece of white cloth hanging from a hook on the wall was unstained by smoke.

How, actually, could that be? It had to have been put there after the fire . . .

Hope quickening in my chest, I hurried to it. When I picked up my own cream silk blouse, the one I'd worn that night and obviously dropped, a sickening panic rose in my throat.

I don't know how long I stood there, clutching silk and trying to breathe. It was long enough to confront what Ethan Kaye had tried to make me see.

Zach had left. Deliberately.

Unless someone else has hung this here, my pathetic desperation said to me.

The fire inspector or the police would have taken it as evidence. This had been left for me—by a man who knew I'd come back for it—for him.

Then where was he? And why would he leave me to deal with all this on my own?

Estes and St. Clair had to be involved. Maybe because he was a man they'd cut him a break and given him the option to leave town rather than face Ethan.

Maybe they'd forced him to go—because he'd caught their photographer red-handed and knew they'd set us up.

That was patently ridiculous. No one knew we met on Zach's boat. No one knew we met at all.

Which led me back to the photographer—and the pictures in Wyatt Estes's file folder—and Zach leaving his burned home without a word. Not even to me.

I had the sudden urge to rip a life preserver off the wall and hurl it into Sinclair Inlet. I actually might have, if someone hadn't banged on the door to the slip.

"Mr. Archer?" a voice demanded. "Port Orchard Police. Open up, sir!"

CHAPTER SIX

I considered several options on the way to the slip's outer door—among them, hurling myself into Sinclair Inlet. In the end I opened up and said, "Can I help you, officer?"

Actually, there were two of them. One didn't look much older than Christopher and had less swagger than my son. The other one was tall and straight-backed, half-balding, and faintly familiar. I probably knew him from high school.

He flashed a badge from the inside of his nylon jacket and said, "We're looking for Zachary Archer."

"Me too!" I said. My voice sounded high and chipper and completely ridiculous.

"Mind if I ask why?"

"We teach together at the college," I said. "And he hasn't shown up for class so I thought I'd come—look for him."

I felt like I was committing perjury under oath—and he knew it. He squinted at me and nodded to the square-shaped kid, whose hand hadn't left his holster since I opened the door.

"Go check it out," the older one said.

Boy Cop nodded and hurried toward the boat carcass like an eager trick-or-treater. The other cop fixed his eyes on me.

"I'm Detective Updike," he said. "And you are?"

"Demitria Costanas—Demi," I said, only because I couldn't think of an alias. "The door was locked," he said. "How did you get in?"

My tongue thickened. "This door?" I said.

He glanced back at it and then at me, eyebrows raised.

I know, buddy, there isn't any other door. I patted my coat pocket.

"I have a key," I said. "Zach—Dr.—Mr. Archer gave me one—in case I ever—"

I let my voice trail off. Detective Updike lifted his brows again. "In case you ever what?"

"Needed to let myself in," I said.

You know, I wanted to cry out, *because it was so dark at my house, in my heart, that I had to get to his light before I lost myself.*

"So—you think something's happened to him?" I said.

"Do you?"

His eyes, small and iron blue, bored a hole through my forehead.

"I don't know," I said. "It isn't like him to leave without saying anything to—anyone."

"You know him well then," he said.

"Yeah, well, we work together."

He waited.

"We're friends."

He waited some more, but I pressed my lips together. Finally, he pulled a pad and pencil out of his pocket. "His employer has reported him missing," he said. "When was the last time you saw him?"

"Thursday night, a little after nine." I groaned inwardly. It sounded like I'd been rehearsing.

"And that was where?"

"Here."

He looked at me over the top of the pad.

"I came to talk to him," I said. "And then I—left."

"And you haven't seen or heard from him since?"

I shook my head.

"Did you expect to?"

I jerked. My purse slid down my arm, and the blouse dropped to the wet space between us. I took my time picking it up. There was no hurry; I could already feel Detective Updike eyeing it as Exhibit A.

"Did that come from here?" he said.

"It was on a hook over there. But it's mine. I left it Thursday night."

I was sure that the only reason the dock did not open and let me drop through was that I was being punished for unforgivable sin. The detective visibly came to all the correct conclusions.

"I'll need your address and phone number, Mrs. Costanas," he said. "We may want to ask you more questions."

There was no mistaking the emphasis on the *Mrs.* I gave him the information and ran like a vandal when he opened the door for me.

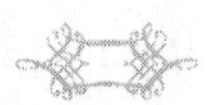

By the next morning, I was still running. I went through the house like a crazy woman that afternoon, cleaning things that had never been dirty—the screws on the door handles, the inside of the dryer. I'd torn through my Zach-fraught dreams all night, trying to find him, locating him in dumpsters and fishing nets and my own downstairs closet. When the kids had, literally, stomped off to school, I raced to Central Market for organic asparagus—all with the chased feeling that someone, something, was after me.

I couldn't come up with a plan. Tell Rich about the police, and risk the dropping of the other proverbial shoe? Don't tell him, and continue to live in nauseating terror that they were going to show up on the doorstep with an arrest warrant? Try to find Zach myself?

I always stopped there in the frenetic circle of thoughts. When I landed on Zach, on his suffering face that last night aboard *The Testament,* the pleading in his voice even as he said, "I love you because you're the kind of woman who will go back to her husband"—when I landed there, the fact that he had left me to face this madness alone distorted it into something I didn't recognize as Zach.

I didn't know where to go from there. It stabbed at me—that there was only one person who could ever help me sort, who could distill any craziness into its inevitable saneness. That was Rich.

It had been that way from the beginning, in New York, when I was an idealistic theology student at NYU and he was a firefighter with his boots planted firmly on the asphalt.

"What's with this?" he'd say to me when I hung up after an

angst-ridden phone call with my mother. "Your mother is your mother. All you owe her is your love and your respect. You don't owe her your way of life."

Why, I asked him, hadn't I come to that conclusion myself?

"Because you need me, Babe," he'd said.

Over and over again. Because it was true.

The road blurred like foggy glass in front of me as I drove home, a forlorn collection of vegetables in a bag beside me. The only thing that made sense was to go to Rich and lay it out: the scene with the police, the horror at myself that I'd let this happen. No matter what it cost, I needed Rich.

I always had.

I blinked back the fog and sat up in the seat. All right. I always did better with a Plan of Action, a POA, as Rich called it. Go back to the house, fix his lunch, make him listen as I told him about this latest knot. At the least he wouldn't want the trauma of my arrest for the kids. He'd know what to do.

But I felt the color drain from my face as I approached the house and let the engine slow to a whine.

A police cruiser was parked in front of our house.

There was a POA for this, the default every firefighter's wife fell into when a police official came within a hundred yards of her home. I peeled myself from the seat and somehow made my way through the garage. Rich had been burned. Christopher had wrapped his pickup around a tree. Jayne had tumbled from the stage. Once tragedy has entered a life, there is no end to the things that suddenly become possible.

I was nearly choking when I got to the great room and found Rich there. With Detective Updike and his sidekick.

The officer looked so incredibly smug, I wanted to hiss. I managed to dig up my professor voice and the determination not to humiliate my husband any further.

"Detective Updike," I said. I nodded at Boy Cop, who still had that ridiculous hand near his service revolver as if I were going to bolt for the kitchen knives.

They both nodded back. Rich wouldn't look at me.

"We were asking your husband some questions about Zachary Archer," Updike said. "But he ran out of answers."

"That's because this doesn't have anything to do with him," I said.

I crossed to stand beside Rich and felt his urge to step away. His face barely masked the confusion I knew was there.

"What do you want to know?" I said.

"After we talked to you at the yacht club yesterday—"

Rich stiffened.

"—we looked around—"

Updike nodded to the officer, who produced a bag. I watched as the cop reached in and pulled out what appeared to be two wet rags. A guttural sound gurgled in my throat.

"You recognize these, then?" the young officer said.

Everything in me recoiled as, with an obviously perverse kind of pleasure, he unrolled my bra and camisole.

"We fished these out of the inlet, under the gate at the yacht club." His eyes glittered. "I take it they belong to you."

"All right, you made your point." Rich jabbed his chin toward the cop. "You got something to say, say it—or get out."

Detective Updike put a hand up to the junior officer and looked at Rich. "We're almost done here. Mrs. Costanas—these are yours?"

I clamped my knees together. "Yes," I said.

"And how did they end up in the water?"

"I kicked them in."

"You want to explain that?"

I tried to harden. This man was a jerk, and I hated him. "No, I do not," I said. "But I will. They fell out of my hands when I was trying to get the gate open, so I shoved them off the dock with my foot. I was upset, and I wanted to get out of there."

"Upset because—"

Rich's arm twitched against me.

"Because while I was on board the boat with Mr. Archer, someone came out of the dark and snapped pictures of us. I gathered up my clothes and in the process I knocked over a candle, which set the boat on fire. Zach told me to go, so I ran. And that was the last time I saw him."

"So there was someone else on the boat with you two."

"Yes, but I don't know who it was."

"So there are photographs of the scene," the officer said.

"There were," Rich said. "I saw them."

I wanted to die for him.

"And where are they now?" the young cop asked.

"I burned them," I heard myself say.

Boy Cop looked disappointed, and I wanted to grab his throat.

"How did you get the pictures?" The detective looked from one of us to the other, like someone choosing between two half-rotten melons.

"They were delivered to me at the fire station," Rich said. "I don't know who and I don't know why. I brought them straight home and confronted my wife."

Boy Cop grunted.

Rich turned on him. "Would I be upset if something happened to the guy? No. Am I glad he's disappeared? Yeah. But do I think my wife did anything to the dude—you gotta be kiddin' me." Rich dragged his gaze to me. "She's in love with him, okay? If she knew where he was, she'd probably be with him. Now—you got anything else? 'Cause I gotta tell ya, I'm sick of you bein' in my house."

The detective stood up. "That's it for now. Mrs. Costanas, don't leave town."

I found my professor voice again. "I wasn't planning to."

"You either," he said to Rich.

He started for the door and I followed him, determined that he not spend an unnecessary minute in our home. He stopped, his face now so close to mine I could see the nicotine stains on his teeth.

"One more question. The secretary at your college—" He consulted his pad. "Sebastian Young. He said you borrowed his master key to get into Archer's office yesterday."

I closed my eyes.

"What were you looking for?"

"I wanted to return some books, which I did," I said.

"Did you find anything you'd left in *there*?" Boy Cop asked.

"Get out!"

I whipped my head toward Rich. He started across the floor, teeth set into a grind, eyes menacing.

"I don't need an escort," Updike said. He nodded Boy Cop out and followed him.

When they were gone, I leaned my forehead against the door. I didn't hear Rich make a move, not even as I turned to him and tried to see him through pained tears.

"Thank you," I said.

"Don't even start. I did that for our kids. I don't want them knowing anything about this." He sucked in a ragged breath. "Do you hear me this time? Don't tell them anything."

"I agree." The professor voice had been replaced by a thin plea. "I was going to tell *you* what happened at the yacht club yesterday—"

"You went back there—and to his office. You said it was over, and then you went looking for him."

"To make sure he *knows* it's over!"

"How many more clothes do you have to take off before he'll be convinced?"

He stormed up the steps.

CHAPTER SEVEN

At the moment, Dr. Sullivan Crisp felt almost nothing like a psychologist. And that, he told himself, was exactly what he wanted.

He'd picked the right place. The beach at Point No Point, the northernmost tip of the peninsula, stretched out before him like an endless playground strewn with oversized toys. It couldn't be further from the crowded too-adult world.

Here, the tossed-about driftwood of boys' forts, built long ago last summer, begged for reconstruction. Smooth rocks littered the sparkle-gray sand, silent to all but the youthfully savvy and sly, who heard their pleas to be skimmed or piled or collected in pockets.

Sully put his hands on his negligible hips and grinned. God had created a playland of scattered magical pieces for the putting together of puzzles. Here he could forget he was six-foot-two and forty-five years old and in self-imposed exile. He could be twelve, because in the world of twelve, possibilities were endless.

He jiggled the rocks in his pockets. Yeah. He could lounge in that log hollowed out into a weather-beaten chaise.

He did. And then he contemplated the pranks that screamed to be played on the plump woman who sat like a Buddha on her blanket a few yards away, reading her book in the cold.

Sully sagged against the ragged wood. He could do anything except forget why he was there instead of out fixing the world's psyche, one therapeutic method at a time.

"Maybe the psychologist needs a psychologist," he said out loud.

Buddha Lady glanced up from her book and then back, the way people did when they didn't want to be caught staring at the—unusual.

Sully adjusted the purple hat he'd picked up at Made in America, a funky shop down in Hoodsport, the day before. Had this woman never seen a middle-aged man in a tie-dyed ball cap? Maybe it was the scent of geoduck on him that got her attention. He'd just cleaned and marinated one, and she was downwind.

Or maybe it was merely the fact that he talked to himself. When you were used to bantering with people all day, it was hard to shut up.

Sully stirred in the log that cradled him like a frog in a hand. How many kites could you fly—how much geoduck could you dig—how much tie-dye could you buy before you were healed enough to go back to the depressed, the bipolar, and the narcissistic, and enjoy yourself again?

"Holy crow, I can't even get the Game Show Network up here," he said, for Buddha Lady's benefit.

She gathered up her blanket and her book and picked her way to a spot closer to the lighthouse. As Sully watched her, he saw Ethan Kaye appear at the edge of the bluff and shield his eyes with his hand. Sully could have kissed the man's L.L.Bean boots. He settled for untangling his long limbs from the chaise lounge log and loping up the sand to meet him.

It was only early March, but Dr. Kaye looked tanned. He always looked tanned. Probably the contrast of naturally olive skin with snowy white hair, which had been that color twenty-five years ago.

When Sully reached him, Ethan's round face smiled into creases Sully didn't remember, but the eyes were the same. Dark, direct, insightful as X-rays.

"Don't they feed you in Colorado?" Ethan said.

Sully grasped Ethan's solid hand. "You still look good, old man."

"And you're still the worst liar I ever met."

Sully squeezed his arm, clapped his shoulder, nodded repeatedly. What else did you do when you were looking at your mentor for the first time in five years, and seeing that he'd aged ten?

"How's Joan?" Sully said. "I forgot to ask you on the phone."

"Still an angel," Ethan said. "She's on a two-month European tour with her quilting club."

Sully grinned. "You didn't want to get in on that action?"

"I'd take up knitting if I thought it would help my situation any."

Sully tried not to visualize the venerable Ethan Kaye clacking needles.

"But I can't even get to Seattle, much less leave the country right now," Ethan said. "Kevin St. Clair would be behind my desk before I had my seat belt buckled."

The creases deepened. Watching Ethan's face had always been like reading a map of his soul. His was a transparency Sully could only aspire to.

"How's that going for you?" Sully said.

"The same. St. Clair already has three people—all of them men—lined up to interview for Dr. Costanas's position."

"What about the other professor—what was his name?"

"Archer. We can't officially replace him until we get his resignation."

"Hard to do when you can't find him."

Ethan scowled. "Oh, St. Clair will find him. He's already reported him as a missing person to the police, not that they weren't already looking for him when his boat burned up. They've been all over the campus."

Ethan shook his head. The wind set a shock of hair up at the crown. Though rooster-like, it didn't disturb his dignity.

"I have no doubt Archer just took off," Ethan said. "Left that poor woman to deal with this by herself."

Sully peered at him. "So you see her as a victim."

"I know it takes two." Ethan shifted his gaze uncomfortably, and Sully smothered a grin.

Ethan had always been the soul of propriety. He still referred to women's forays to the restroom as "going to powder their noses."

"So why is she 'that poor woman'?"

"Because I guarantee you she wouldn't have gone where she did without a lot of persuasion. And she's paying for it." Ethan moved his eyes from a passing tanker back to Sully. "I told you she needs help. And you admitted on the phone you were getting restless."

Sully took off the ball cap, shook it, put it on backwards. "I meant

I wanted to get started on my next book, revamp the talk show, open up a clinic in Nashville—not take on a client."

"I'm not trying to push you—"

"Sure you are."

"I thought while you were up here regrouping—"

"I'm regrouped." Sully rattled the stones in his pockets.

"I can see that," Ethan said dryly. He pressed his lips together, eyes searching Sully's face. "All right, this was a bad idea. You have enough to deal with."

"Holy crow—I supposedly still have four more weeks to 'deal,' and I'm dealt out."

Ethan's eyes didn't move. "You were in a pretty serious situation."

"Well, yeah—I mean, this is the first patient we've ever had commit suicide in the ten years the clinics have been open, but still, we have to look at it from the point of view that ultimately, it was his decision to take his own life. My people did everything they could."

"As I understand it, you were right in there with them."

"I took it all on at first, but at the end of the day, we have to let it go. Give it to God."

"So you're basically over it."

"If a patient gave me a 'yes' to that question, I'd say, 'Thanks for playing, but that is incorrect.'" Sully buzzed from the back of his throat.

Ethan gave a half laugh. "You still using that game show shtick on your clients?"

"If something works for me, I stick with it."

"I think it's job security," Ethan said. "If they aren't crazy when they come in, they are before you're finished with them."

"You done?"

"No. You haven't answered my question. You're over your patient shooting himself in his car outside one of your clinics?"

Sully squinted at the tanker, now a misty sliver. He admired Ethan Kaye's probity. He just didn't always like it.

"Like I said, I'm giving it a few more weeks. Making sure I don't show any symptoms of post traumatic stress. Meanwhile, I'm finding things to do. Speaking of which—you hungry?"

Ethan frowned. "Not if you're cooking."

"Ouch. Come on, I've got geoduck marinating."

"I hope you cook it better than you pronounce it. It's gooey duck, not gee-oh duck." Ethan's smile spread, crinkling his eyes. "Let me take you to supper. I don't need your miracle cure for appetite."

"That hurts, sir," Sully said. "That really hurts."

There were not one, not even two, but four vintage automobiles parked in front of the fish house Ethan pulled up to. Sully let out a long, slow whistle.

A 1967 silver Corvette Stingray. A cherry red '57 Ford Fairlane. A Camaro Supersport, 1966, blue. And a gold 1966 Pontiac GTO. Black vinyl top.

"I knew you'd like this place," Ethan said. "They all come here."

"They" were hard to pick out once Sully followed Ethan inside. The restaurant was dimly lit except for the candles in glass buoys, encased in fishnet, that reflected off the vinyl tablecloths. As far as Sully could tell, there was one of every kind of person drinking from plastic tumblers and licking their fingers as they ate fried onion rings, shiny with grease.

When they'd slid into a booth and Ethan had ordered a platter of what he referred to ruefully as "cholesterol on the half shell," Sully peered out the window at the Oldsmobile.

"Somebody's done a nice job with that," he said. "What do you want to bet it has the original tuck-and-roll upholstery?"

"Is that good?" Ethan said.

"Oh, yeah."

"You should know. You used to spend hours on your cars."

Sully nodded at the waitress, who set two mugs and a pot of coffee on their table.

"We're taking a trip down memory lane."

"Have fun with that," she said. She winked at Ethan.

When she left, Sully nudged Ethan's hand. "I see the women still flirt with you shamelessly."

"She knows who's leaving the tip. You work on cars anymore?"

Sully shook his head and poured the coffee. "No time. You take two sugars, right?"

"Black these days. Too bad."

"What is?" Sully said.

"I know of a '64 Chevy Impala going up for auction this next week. Estate sale. It would give you something to do while you're monitoring yourself for whatever—"

"PTSD." Sully sipped at the coffee and surveyed Ethan through the steam. Kaye's look was pointed.

"Anything to entice me into staying here so I can see this woman," Sully said. "Right?"

"All right, I admit it. From what I hear—and what I know of you personally—I really believe you could help her, Sully."

"You know this is ironic, don't you?"

"How?"

"You're the one who tried to talk me out of going into psychology. And 'talk' might be too mild a word."

Ethan cupped his hands around his mug, and Sully mentally kicked himself. Over the years he'd become proficient at steering Ethan away from this topic, and now he'd practically driven him there himself.

"I thought it was too soon after Lynn," Ethan said.

"Now *that* I'm over," Sully said.

"I want to believe that. Then you tell me you nearly had a breakdown because you lost a patient, and I have to wonder."

Sully set his mug firmly on the table. "I was already under a lot of pressure when that went down. I'd taken on too much, hadn't had a vacation in—well, ever. It was the proverbial last straw, and I had to delegate and get away."

Ethan took a drag from his coffee.

"This has nothing to do with anything except what it is," Sully said.

"You're the psychologist. You didn't get where you are without knowing your own mind. Which is why—"

"You want me to see your professor friend."

Ethan pinched the bridge of his nose. "It's haunting me. I had to let her resign—I told you."

"Right."

"And she has to take the consequences for her actions. I see that." The line between his eyebrows deepened. "But I feel responsible."

Sully twitched his lips. "Maybe you're the one who needs therapy."

"I might before all this is done." Ethan glanced across the room. "Let me just say this, and then I'll leave it alone."

Sully doubted that, but he nodded.

"This woman is a gifted teacher, and in my view she's only beginning to get into the depths of her spiritual journey. I've seen it over and over—the minute a person starts to get it, genuinely get it, something puts her to the test."

"So, what if she just didn't pass?"

"Then she needs another chance." Ethan looked startled at the vehemence in his own voice and cleared his throat. "I can't give it to her," he said. "But you of all people can. And not only because you're the best in your field. But also because you've been where she is."

Sully frowned into his coffee cup.

"She thinks she is the complete cause of the mess she's in," Ethan said. "She's taking total responsibility, even for the pieces that aren't her fault. I'm afraid of what that's going to do to her."

He put his hand up to stop the waitress, tray teetering, a few feet away. "I was afraid of that for you," he almost whispered. "You say you've gotten past it, and I trust that. Which is why there's nobody better than you to give this lady another chance at her life."

Ethan leaned back and gave the waitress a wan smile.

"Looks like that trip down memory lane got a little heavy," she said.

Sully looked at the heaped-high plates she slid onto the table. "Can you bring us a bucket to wring that shrimp out into?" he said.

"I can tell you're from the South," she said, making a less-than-successful attempt at an Alabama accent. "So don't be telling me you can't handle a little grease." She winked at him this time. "I'll get you some extra napkins."

Sully examined a tangled pile of fried-ness. "Is this calamari?"

Ethan didn't answer. Sully looked up.

"She has a thirteen-year-old daughter," Ethan said.

"Who, the waitress?"

"Dr. Costanas. For what it's worth."

Sully stabbed his fork into a gleaming breaded shrimp. "I'll think about it, all right?"

"That's all I wanted to hear."

CHAPTER EIGHT

I didn't go to church that Sunday. Rich hadn't been for over a year, but for me to miss would signal I was trapped under something heavy.

I knew people would question Christopher and Jayne and they'd have to hedge and lie, but those same folks were less likely to guess the truth from my absence than they would from my son sitting beside me in a pew, casting judgmental looks to rival the Reverend Jonathan Edwards. Christopher still made it no secret he considered me the ultimate sinner in the hands of an angry God.

So I opted to stay home when he left with Jayne, looking as she had for days—like she'd been shot but she didn't know how to fall down.

I wanted to help her, but she had a moat around her I could have swum in if she'd let me get close enough—but not with Christopher as her self-appointed bodyguard, shielding her from the evil mother. I wondered as I stood chopping onions that Sunday morning if he thought she might catch adultery from me.

When Zach was making me feel like I deserved the pleasure he gave me, I tried to find another name for it, but even the Bible wouldn't let me. One of the few times Jesus even talked about marriage was to mention that a spouse was justified in divorcing an unfaithful partner.

That had driven me to break it off. I didn't want to blatantly defy God. I didn't want a divorce. I didn't want to make Rich hurt.

That same fear and guilt and shame kept me making perfect hospital corners on the beds and ironing the boxer shorts and cooking three meals a day whether anyone ate them or not. It was my reason for peeling potatoes and wondering where I'd put the garlic press.

This meal might put Rachael Ray to shame, but I knew it would do nothing to assuage the guilt. I hoped that stew by pie by cheese-drenched casserole I could convince my family I loved them and was going to spend the rest of my life proving it.

The pot roast bubbled on the stove and an applesauce cake was taking golden shape in the oven when I heard Christopher's pickup roar into the driveway. The way he screeched to a stop was over the top, even for him.

I listened as he slammed every door between himself and me, until he stood before me, breathing like a locomotive. Jayne crept in silently and looked around as if she were searching for an escape hatch.

"Is this him?" Christopher said and slapped a newspaper onto the counter. When I saw the picture on the front page, I stopped breathing.

Zach's official faculty photo, his eyes bright in his intelligent face, totally unaware of the turmoil surrounding him. I felt an unfamiliar flicker of anger, which whipped into fear when I read the headline: MISSING PROF PROVOKES QUESTIONS.

"It doesn't mention you sleeping with him, if that's what you're worried about."

I looked at Christopher. Only two hot spots of red at the tops of his cheekbones colored his dead-white face.

"I'm only worried for you all," I said.

Christopher thumped Zach's picture with his fingers. "So this *is* the guy you cheated on Dad with."

I opened my mouth, and then I closed it, because I could feel Rich behind me prickling nettles up the back of my neck.

"Chris, throw that in the fire," he said.

He was between Jayne and any viable means of escape. She slipped up onto a counter stool and wrapped her long, loose skirt tight around her legs and the stool's. I wanted to pick her up and carry her out of there. I wanted us both out of there. I didn't have to look to know that Rich had finally reached his boiling point.

"That's a good idea," I said. "Let's burn it and get on with our life."

"What life?"

I did have to look then, to see whether that had come from my husband or my son. Rich's face was so hard it frightened me.

"Are they writing about our so-called life in the Sunday paper now?"

"There's nothing about us in there, Dad," Christopher said. "Not yet anyway."

"Stop this, Christopher," I said.

"What do you expect him to do?" Rich's voice descended to a dark place.

Jayne whimpered.

"I think you and I should take this upstairs," I said to Rich.

"Oh—so suddenly you want to protect the kids." He took a step toward me. "Let me tell you something, Demitria—if you gave a *flip* about Jayne and Chris, you would have paid attention to them, you would have been *here*, instead of giving those college kids everything that belonged to *our* children."

His finger was in my face, his breath hot on me. I thought wildly that he might hit me. It was the first time the idea had ever crossed my mind.

"Can you look me in the eye and honestly say that if you hadn't been so wrapped up in that college and your career and those kids, that this ever would have happened?"

I couldn't say that or anything else. My heart throbbed in my throat.

Rich hissed. "I don't know—maybe you would have."

He snatched up the paper and glared into Zach's face. The anger in his eyes glittered and hardened until it wasn't anger anymore, but cold hatred.

"Christopher," I said. "Would you and Jayne please go on upstairs?"

"You want us to, Dad?" Christopher said.

Rich wiped the newspaper from the counter with the side of his hand, narrowly missing Jayne, who sat still as a cocoon on her stool.

"You're not the woman I married." Rich snarled toward the face now mocking him from the floor. "I thought you were on my side."

Once again I looked at Christopher. "You and Jayne, upstairs."

"No need—we're through here," Rich said. "I'm going to go stay at the station."

"Why should *you* leave?" Christopher said.

Rich turned from the doorway, chest rising and falling like lava. Panic seized me.

"She's the one who screwed up." Christopher jabbed a thumb at me, and for an instant the son who looked like me was the image of his father. "I don't see how you can teach *Bible* classes and miss the whole part about adultery. It's like a major theme."

"I know, Christopher," I said. "Your father and I have already been through this."

"Yeah, but I still don't think you get it." He tossed his blonde hair back. "We can't pretend this never happened. It's like you want to say you're sorry and have us all say, 'That's okay, Mom,' and then— I don't know—" He wafted a hand toward the pot on the stove. "We sit down to Sunday dinner like the Brady Bunch."

"All right," I said. "I think that's enough."

Christopher made a sound with his breath, the kind that wiped out all conclusions but his own. "You gave up the right to decide what's enough for me when you stopped acting like a mother."

I yanked every tendon whipping my head toward Rich. He said nothing. He didn't even look up from the newspaper, now scattered across the kitchen floor like streamers from a party gone terribly awry.

"You know what, Dad?" Christopher said. "If you go, I go. I'm not staying here with her. Jayne shouldn't either."

Still nothing. No reaction from Rich as our life went through the shredder.

"Jayne and I are on your side."

Like a fingernail across a chalkboard, a line was scraped almost audibly between us, between me and my family. My husband was wrestling with his hatred and losing. My precious daughter sat staring at the countertop, face like an eggshell. One more angry word and she would crack into tiny pieces.

"Nobody's leaving," I said, "except me. It isn't fair for you to have to leave, Rich. And until we can all get a handle on our feelings we can't talk about this the way we need to."

I heard myself speak. I watched myself pack a suitcase. I felt Jayne's cold cheek against my lips when I kissed her good-bye. I saw Rich's silhouette in our bedroom window as I pulled out of the driveway, and I knew the stubborn set of his shoulders.

But it could not have been the real me who left her own home and drove to the Suquamish Clearwater Hotel in Poulsbo and checked herself in. The real me didn't have a family that would let her go.

All I could think of as I lay pulsing with fear on a hotel bed that night was that nobody had tried to stop me.

CHAPTER NINE

Dr. Ethan Kaye was at his best, Sully decided, when he managed a set-up without saying a word. The sign on the easel outside the tent read ESTATE AUCTION: PROPERTY OF EDITH ALLEN ESTES. Sully had to give his old friend credit.

He had already salivated over the '64 Chevrolet Impala on blocks that Ethan had sent him here to see. Holy crow—according to the sheet it didn't run and hadn't for ten years, but the body was perfect: no dents, no dings, no rust spots. A little buffing out, and she'd be a thing of beauty. He was so ready to get under that baby's hood he could already feel the wrench in his hand.

The fact that it was being sold by the Estes family—that was Ethan Kaye at work. Sully grinned and ducked into the tent. No doubt this was the same Estes Ethan was battling it out with at the college. He and that other character—what was his name, Saint Bernard?—the two of them were clearly out for Ethan's job. Jackals.

All right. He owed Ethan anyway. He could get the lay of the land for him.

Sully took a paddle from the young woman inside, who looked like she'd rather be elsewhere having a root canal.

"You know how to use this?" she said, face impassive. Only her string-of-beads earrings moved. Even the highlights in her hair stayed motionless as if they'd been ordered to.

"We're playing Ping Pong, right?"

"Funny." She appeared to be beyond eye rolling. "Will you be bidding?"

"Yes, ma'am," Sully said.

"Do you know how?"

"I do."

"Then sit anywhere," she said, and waited, clearly done with him.

Sully noticed after he sat down that all the women running the gig were the in-control type. Although he was sure there were a few hired hands mixed in, the core of them had to be of the same breed, possibly Estes. Every mane was some shade of yellow, though Sully was sure most of them hadn't seen a natural blonde strand in their dos in decades. They all moved fast, as if they didn't have time for any nonsense, but he was still struck by their eyes, large, blue, and sardonic.

He stretched himself up to full viewing height and checked out the crowd. Ethan said Wyatt Estes was a successful businessman, so Sully wouldn't expect him to be here overseeing the auctioning off of a relative's china. Still, he couldn't help scoping for a man who looked like he had big bucks and a college on a yo-yo string. He didn't see any guys like that—but the Estes women all fit that description. Including Paddle Girl, who appeared to be giving some poor man bidding instructions. Holy crow. If he didn't get it within the next seven seconds, she was going to slice him open with those eyes.

Interesting. She had a layer right beneath that smooth surface that might erupt occasionally—but Sully's guess was she never got it all the way out. He grunted. He could never resist a quick analysis.

Paddle Girl faded into the background when the bidding started for the Impala. There were a few lowballers who obviously only hoped for parts. Sully cringed at the thought of her being ripped up. A few of them made ridiculous bids but fell off, muttering to each other when two serious buyers jumped to attention. They apparently knew the potential of the lady and hung in as long as they could—until Sully grew tired of playing and jumped it to $5,000.

The crowd gasped as one, but Sully knew he'd basically stolen the thing. So did his rivals, who saluted with their paddles and gazed at him in undisguised envy.

He sat through the frenzied bidding on a few china cabinets and antique tables, just to observe the bizarre array of behaviors, but he got up to leave at the break and headed for Paddle Girl. A male version of the Estes women, minus the dyed-blonde, was talking to her, his own wavy gray hair grown thin with his seventies. The eyes and the unmoving expression were definitely from the same gene pool. He stood straight and solid, though gravity had been less kind to him. His conversation with the girl appeared to be intense, but Sully worked his way toward them anyway. He wasn't sure exactly how he was going to find out if this was Wyatt Estes, or what he'd say after that. That kind of thing usually worked itself out.

The discussion was clearly over for Paddle Girl by the time Sully got within two layers of people. The gentleman continued to speak near her face, but she directed her eyes elsewhere and didn't even pretend to be listening. Sully liked this girl.

As he elbowed past the line at the concession stand, she kept up her mindless scanning of the crowd until her eyes lit on him. He held up his paddle.

"You done?" she called to him. She said, "Excuse me" to the man and cut off three people to get away from him. The old guy watched her as dispassionately as she'd left him.

"Looks like you owe me," Sully said as he handed her his paddle.

"Where do you get that?"

Up close, Sully caught an aura of gold in her eyes. The attitude couldn't hide the fact that she was nearly beautiful.

"I got you away from the old codger."

"Yeah, well, that's not going to get you far."

"I don't want to go far," Sully said. "Can you show me who to talk to about picking up my car?"

"Follow me."

She led him along a row of now empty chairs and out a slit in the tent no one else seemed to be aware of. Sully suspected she knew all of life's shortcuts.

He waited until they were crossing the yard to say, "So, who was the old guy anyway? I think I've seen him before."

"You have if you live around here," she said.

"I don't."

"He owns something on every block in South Kitsap County." She looked unimpressed.

"Is he an Estes?" Sully said.

"Ya think? That's Wyatt. It's his aunt, by marriage, who died. He's here to make sure we women don't screw up her estate."

"Are you women likely to do that?"

"How hard is it to dump the money in a bag and hand it to him?"

The girl stopped in front of the Impala and eyed the tireless wheels. "You weren't thinking of driving this out of here, were you? Okay—see the blonde woman over there?"

Sully tried not to snicker. "They're all blonde."

"Cute. She's the one wearing the leather jacket—"

"Got it."

"She'll take your check or whatever."

"Thanks," Sully said. He smiled at her. She hadn't told him anything useful, not that he knew what he was looking for anyway.

He expected her to go back to her pile of paddles, but she folded her arms and looked at the Impala again.

"Seriously," she said, "what *are* you going to do with that thing? It's been sitting in Gramma's garage for, like, thirty years."

"I'm going to restore her to her former beauty. Do you think Gramma would approve?"

"Are you kidding? She spent like a hundred thousand dollars trying to do that to herself."

So he had heard right. Ellen Estes was her grandmother, which made Wyatt Estes her—

He was still trying to sort that out when the girl said, "So if you don't live here, what are you going to do, have it towed to wherever?"

"I'm going to see if I can find garage space to rent," he said.

"Good luck with that."

"Why?"

"You won't find anything like that in this neighborhood."

"Where would I look?"

She fiddled with her earring, the first behavior he'd seen in her that didn't seem conscious.

"I'd say Callow," she said. "Definitely Callow. They have a bunch of empty buildings there—I don't know if any of them are garages."

"Thanks for the tip."

"No problem. And can I just say—it is so refreshing to talk to a guy who isn't hitting on me."

Sully laughed out loud. "I'm twice your age."

"Doesn't matter. I've had seventy-year-olds ask me to lunch." She looked at him straight on. "I hate being hit on."

Sully was convinced.

Too bad he couldn't thank her, Sully thought the next day. She'd been right about Callow. Not only was there garage space for rent there, with no one else leasing the other two bays, but a camping trailer out back, which at first pass seemed livable, came with it. He was tired of motels, and this had—character. He'd be working on the Impala during the day anyway, when he wasn't doing legwork for Ethan Kaye.

There was no way he couldn't. Not after he told Ethan he'd bought the car and that he'd be staying in town for a while. Not after he heard the unspoken need in Ethan's voice, the need for someone to walk him through this, help him find out what he was dealing with.

"Come over and see her when she arrives," Sully said about the Impala. "And we can talk strategy."

"Strategy," Ethan said.

"For finding out what old man Estes and the Saint Bernard are up to, before they strike again. Uncle Wyatt is a control freak, I found out that much. He's not gon' let this die."

Ethan chuckled into the phone. Sully knew he'd get him with the Tennessee accent.

"When's she coming?" Ethan said.

"They're delivering her first thing tomorrow."

"You two bond for a while," Ethan said, voice dry. "I'll stop by after I leave the office."

"Pick up some sandwiches on your way over," Sully said.

"By all means. Please don't cook."

The Impala looked even better being lowered from the tow truck than she had amid the riffraff of Edith Allen Estes's golf carts and patio furniture. It was as if she knew she was about to be transformed back into the stunner she once was. Sully was sure he heard a long-suffering sigh when the driver set her down on the blocks Sully had carefully placed for her.

"We'll get you new shoes, babe," he told her. "Soon as you're well enough to stand up."

"This thing's in great shape for as old as it is," the tow truck guy said. He resituated the chew tucked in his cheek. "Some of the electrical still works."

"No way," Sully said.

"Dude, check this out. Go stand behind it."

Sully moved behind *her*—this person obviously had no understanding of what he was in the presence of—while the guy slid into the front seat. The Impala's trio of brake lights on each side shuddered to life, blinking beneath the film of dust on her red covers.

"Can you believe that?" the driver shouted back.

The lights flashed. Six red taillights. Again. Yet again.

Sully blinked, opened his mouth to tell him to stop. Couldn't.

They flashed again—in alarm—a panicked pounding of red through the dark.

"Stop! No—stop—something's wrong!"

The lights went out but the screaming went on and the darkness swallowed the rest of her up. Sully hurled himself forward.

"Okay—dude—I stopped."

Sully heard the last of his own shouts and stared down at his hands clenching the back bumper. He jerked his chin up. The tow truck driver stood at the Impala's hip, face whitening between scruffy tufts of beard. The taillights were out, the Impala was still, and Sully shook.

"Did that freak you out?" the guy said.

Sully forced his hands into his pockets. "Yeah, man, who knew she'd still have it in her?"

"Yeah. Seriously."

The driver eyed Sully and took a step backward. Sully attempted a grin he knew didn't cover the trembling in his lips.

"Hate to see what I'm going to do when I get her running," Sully said. "So—what do I owe you?"

The guy took the money and ran, though he did pause as he climbed into his truck and said, "I've seen guys get into these old cars before, but, dude, you take it to a whole new level."

Sully made himself go back to her tail. He fingered the lights, plowing through the greasy dust until the red glass shone clearer. She was *this* car, not that one. She was in *this* place, at *this* time, and that was where he was.

He'd told patients that—he'd written about it—he'd soothed the beast of the past in radio listeners who sobbed to him over the phone. He wondered now if they believed it any more than he did.

Sully grabbed a rag and went to work on the taillights again. He had to believe it, because it was true. The flashback was evidence that he wasn't ready to go back to Colorado, to work. Not a problem. He needed to focus on the now. On bringing an old passion back to life. On repaying a debt to a friend. Maybe even on bringing somebody else out of a dark place, like the one he'd been in. That was, after all, why he was in business.

Sully stood up, rag still in hand, and looked at the grungy office beyond the third bay. The landlord said he could use that too. Cleaned out, furnished with a couple yard sale chairs, it could make a decent place to meet with this Dr. Costanas.

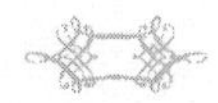

Ethan showed up around six with Reuben sandwiches. Sully found two metal folding chairs and set them on opposite sides of an upended box of the quarts of oil that were soon going to fill the Impala like a youth serum.

Ethan set the bag on the makeshift table and made the appropriate appreciative sounds over the car.

"As long as I have this place," Sully said as he unwrapped his sandwich, "you might as well bring your vehicle in for a tune-up."

"I'll be buying a new one before you get done with that—"

"Watch it now. She's sensitive."

Ethan smiled with his eyes as he chewed.

"So let's talk about the photographs," Sully said. "Did you bring them with?"

Ethan nodded, mouth in a grim line.

"How do you think Estes and the Saint Bernard got them?"

Ethan dug into the bag and produced a stack of napkins. "Estes said somebody gave them to him. He wouldn't say who, but I gather it was right after they were taken. He said whoever it was brought them late at night."

"I bet that put him in a good mood." Sully rescued a glob of sauerkraut before it dropped onto the table. "He looks like an old curmudgeon."

"He's still sharp. Goes to the office every day, still micromanages his conglomerate."

"He's playing this pretty shrewdly."

"We're not going to get any names out of him, if that's what you mean."

"What about the Saint—"

"St. Clair." Ethan's eyes crinkled as he wiped his mouth. "Kevin may be narrow-minded, but he's honest to a fault. If he says he doesn't know where the pictures came from, he doesn't."

"So Estes—and the photographer—are the only ones who know." Sully put his sandwich down on the wrapper and rubbed his hands together. "We had a patient—recently, in fact—whose wife paid a detective to follow him and take pictures of what he was doing."

"I thought that only happened on TV," Ethan said.

"This was for real."

"So what was the guy doing?"

"Blowing their life savings on sports bets. But the point is, what if that's what's going on here?"

Ethan grunted. "I would bet *my* life savings Rich Costanas did not hire a PI to follow his wife. In the first place, according to Demi, the photographer was already there when she got there, hiding on the boat."

"What if Estes hired him?"

"Why would he? Nobody knew what was going on between Archer and Demi."

"You sure about that?"

Ethan broke off a strand of cheese that stretched from the wrapper. "Look, Wyatt Estes has strong ideas about how things should be done, and he definitely uses his power to get his way. That makes him an opportunist, not a stalker. I firmly believe the pictures just fell into his lap, and he saw a perfect opportunity to take me down."

"So you think he was disappointed when your professor resigned instead of you?"

"Kevin St. Clair was. I think Wyatt Estes genuinely wants CCC to be an upstanding, morally pure educational institution, whatever that takes."

"That's what you want too," Sully said.

"We have different ideas about how that should be accomplished."

"And Kevin St. Clair?"

"He wants that—and more."

"Your job."

"Only because he thinks he can do it better." Ethan shook his head. "Their hearts are in the right place, which is why I don't think either one of them had anything to do with getting the pictures taken."

Sully nodded at the folder leaning against Ethan's chair. "Is that them?"

He cleared the box-table, and Ethan pulled out a thin pile of photographs and set them on it. Sully looked at the first one and felt his eyes widen.

"Pretty incriminating."

The man in the picture was largely hidden by the woman, his face buried in her bare neck. Sully could only see her naked shoulder and short blonde hair falling back as she welcomed him. She wasn't an Estes blonde. Hers was as real as everything else seemed to be.

Ethan slid the photo away, revealing a second. The woman now looked straight at Sully, as if he'd startled her. Her eyes were brown and soft and sad, even in the shock of the moment. Sully still couldn't see the man's face; she kept it hidden against her with her hands combed into his hair. He wouldn't have looked at him anyway. The woman held him with her pain.

"Do I need to look at any more?"

Ethan shook his head and slid them back into the folder.

Sully sat, hands folded on top of the box. "I don't think there was any force involved."

Ethan let out a long, slow sigh. "No, I never thought that."

"Looks like—I mean, what can you tell from a picture—but I'm betting all her struggling was on the inside." Sully shrugged. "Give her my number. Have her give me a call."

Ethan churned slightly in the chair. "I will, as soon as I can convince her she needs you."

Sully envisioned the picture again and leaned forward. "Don't let her wait too long, Ethan," he said. "She doesn't have that kind of time."

CHAPTER TEN

D*aylight basement apartment.*

I hadn't heard that term in ages. Of course, how long had it been since I'd apartment hunted?

The number of years was depressing. So was the hotel room. So was my savings account.

The one piece of advice I'd taken from my mother when I got married was to always have a little money of my own in a separate account. When she died from colon cancer in 1998, I put most of the money I inherited from the proceeds of her house and savings in there, in her honor. I felt good about that, since in life she made it so hard to honor her.

But "a little money" was an apt description now. I'd used the bulk of it to buy Rich's boat—my last big effort to bring him out of his funk—and in the preceding week I'd chiseled away a chunk of the rest of it, paying for the hotel room I couldn't sleep in, buying meals I didn't eat.

Rich hadn't called, on his own or in response to the messages I left him. I didn't leave any at the fire station. Knowing Rich, he hadn't told anyone there that we were separated, and in my current condition, my voice alone would give it away.

I went back to the classifieds, which I'd spread out on the bed. It would actually be cheaper in the long run for me to get a studio apartment. How long could the long run last, anyway? Most of the time I wasn't sure I could take it another minute. I was paralyzed at every knock on the door for fear it was a sheriff's deputy serving me with divorce papers. Rich's silence was excruciating, but it was better than a final decision. And as long as I had to hang in limbo, I might as well do it economically.

If my calculations were correct, I could go maybe two months before I had to get a job. I fought down panic. It wouldn't be two months—or even one—before Rich would take me back and we would work things out. No point thinking about work yet. If I did, I would surely go right over the edge I was teetering on.

DAYLIGHT BASEMENT APARTMENT. ONE BEDROOM. OVERLOOKING PUGET SOUND. $700 A MONTH, UTILITIES INCLUDED. PORT ORCHARD.

I circled the phone number, but I couldn't call yet. Maybe I should try Rich again, let him know what I planned. He wouldn't let me take this step. It was too permanent, too far from anything we'd ever thought of.

But then, so was my having an affair.

I sank down into the pillows and let the tears run out of the corners of my eyes.

"I've Got Tears In My Ears (From Lyin' On My Back In My Bed While I Cry Over You)."

Rich and I had howled over that song in reruns of *Hee-Haw*, watched when we were too poor to go to the movies and were so happy to stay home in front of a fuzzy fifteen-inch screen. When Rich tried to match the country twang in dauntless Brooklynese, I howled even louder.

We did laugh together back then. I hadn't laughed since two weeks ago when I'd met Zach's eyes in mirth at a faculty meeting and stowed it away for the precious time when we would be able to share it out loud—as out loud as our relationship could ever be.

How could I have loved that so much when I had to sneak and lie to have it? How could I be so sorry for it now—and yet miss it?

I sat up sharply. I didn't have answers. I could hardly stand the questions. I would call the number and ask about the apartment. I would put one foot in front of the other—

I reached for the classifieds, but they slid off the end of the bed, revealing the editorial page beneath them. A heading read: WHAT REALLY HAPPENED AT COVENANT CHRISTIAN?

Some people, it said, *have written that the recent faculty changes at*

CCC mean Vice President Kevin St. Clair is right about the way President Ethan Kaye is running the place.

I folded the whole section over, twice, and deposited it into the wastebasket beside the bed, on a cushion of my damp, wadded-up Kleenexes. I didn't need any more opinions of me.

I scooped the classifieds off the floor and dialed the number under *Daylight basement apartment.*

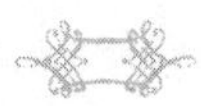

Sully turned the heat up in the garage office, again, and poured himself another cup of scalding coffee. The camping trailer was a bad idea. He didn't use the kerosene heater for fear of waking up—or not waking up—charbroiled, so he spent every night shivering under the two quilts he'd bought at Goodwill and half the next morning thawing out. He took a sip of coffee, winced, and opened the newspaper. He'd have to wait until his hands unfroze before he could work on Isabella.

That's what he called her. In the week he'd had her, he'd picked up a complete wiring assembly, new rotor and cap, points, plugs, thermostat, and carburetor rebuild kit. He'd barely started on the carb rebuild, but he could already hear the engine purring in his head.

He thumbed through the paper to the editorial section, which held all the action in Kitsap County. Aside from the occasional letter about the increasing absurdity of the television commercials for the Mattress Ranch & Futon Farm, everybody who took pen in hand had Covenant Christian College on their minds.

Things were heating up for Ethan, mostly because Kevin St. Clair and his faculty supporters were waving firebrands for a tightening of the rules. Sully skimmed one editorial. *Are we educating Christians or Revisionists?* the writer wanted to know.

Another one made a list of the issues Ethan Kaye allowed discussion on in open forums—divorce, capital punishment, the extension of grace to homosexuals, intelligent design. The piece was one long gasp at the dangers of debate over things the editorialist felt should simply be handed down as edicts to students so they could get on with spreading the Good News to all the world.

"Good news?" Sully said into his coffee. "I feel like I've just been spiritually mugged."

One last letter, tucked into a corner at the bottom of the page, chimed in with a different tune.

Some people have written that the recent faculty changes at CCC mean Vice President Kevin St. Clair is right about the way President Ethan Kaye is running the place. I don't think one has anything to do with the other.

Sully set his mug down on the upended oil case.

Sure, it looks a little suspicious. One teacher disappearing and the other one resigning. But couldn't it be a coincidence that at the same time Dr. St. Clair is pumping up his campaign against President Kaye, two profs leave? Nobody's talking about why they left. If there were a connection, wouldn't Kevin St. Clair be blabbing it for all the world to hear? I say we forget about the obviously messed up Drs. Costanas and Archer and focus on keeping a fine man like Ethan Kaye where he belongs—in the presidential office.

Holy crow. Who was this person?

Sully looked for a name, but it was signed only *"Fed-up Reader."* Unlike most newspapers where unsigned letters didn't go into print, the quirky *Port Orchard Independent*'s editorial page was one big debate in anonymity. Still, Sully thought, it would be nice to know who "Fed-up" was. He'd take him to lunch.

He reached for his cell phone to call Ethan, in case he hadn't seen he had a supporter, and the phone rang in his hand. He glanced at the ID.

"Good morning, Dr. Ghent."

A chuckle resonated in Sully's ear. Dr. Porphyria Ghent had a voice so deep, even her subtle laugh created the vibration of wisdom.

"It's almost noon here," she said. "The day is half over."

Sully closed his eyes and settled back against the rich tones. He'd always said if an anxious patient could spend one hour listening to Porphyria's voice, he wouldn't need an antidepressant.

"It's only ten here," Sully said.

"Ah."

She waited. Sully grinned. She was the only person in the world who cut him no slack. As honest as Ethan was, Sully could still charm him into letting things go. Porphyria was fooled by nothing.

"I'm up in Washington state," he said.

"So that's where you landed."

"You told me to get away and not come back until I could listen to a country music station for an hour without crying."

"And how's that going for you?"

"I haven't found a station yet."

He could almost hear her nodding, eyes closed. She'd be in her favorite Adirondack chair, wrapped in a blanket woven by a Seminole, watching the mist on the Smokies and simply nodding.

"Still bothers me some," Sully said. "But I'm coming to terms. We can't save everyone. That's abundantly clear to me."

"Is it now."

It wasn't a question, or even a statement. It was a rebuttal.

"So what are you doing up there in God's country?"

Sully got up and moved out into the garage. "You'll be happy to know that I'm rebuilding a 1964 Chevrolet Impala."

"That makes perfect sense. You have an anniversary coming up."

"Yeah," Sully said. "I know." He ran his hand down Isabella's chassis. "I think I'll spend it rebuilding her carburetor. Fitting, don't you think?"

"Mmm-hmm."

Only a black matriarch could make such a sound. Sully sagged before it.

"I don't know if I'll make my yearly trip to Mecca," he said. "This feels right. You remember Ethan Kaye?"

"Of course. Ah, that's who you're visiting."

"He's going through a tough time right now—a college mess."

"Is there any worse kind?" she said, chuckling again.

"I feel like I need to stand by him right now," Sully said. "His wife's in Europe, and his main supporters at the college are gone, which is a whole other story—"

"Sully to the rescue?" Porphyria asked.

"More like Sully walking alongside. I'm not giving him therapy, if that's what you mean."

"Mmm."

She let there be a velvet silence, which Sully didn't fill—until he felt her deep gaze penetrate through the wires.

"If it's all right with you," he said, "I'm going to play it by ear this year."

"Oh, it's all right with me," she said. "Long as you make sure it's all right with you."

"You know I will," Sully said.

"Mmm-hmm," she said. "Mmm-hmm."

CHAPTER ELEVEN

I moved into the daylight basement two days later.

Actually, "moved" is an overstatement. In thirty minutes I unpacked a pair of pajamas, the mini-toiletries I'd taken from my hotel room, and the same three outfits I'd been wearing for ten days. I kept telling myself I was only there for a short time. A very short time.

The apartment was furnished in Early Marriage—an eclectic collection that included a Wal-Mart dinette set, a mama's cast-off couch and love seat, and an old gate for a headboard, obviously an attempt to follow the instructions in one of those "Redecorate Your Home in a Weekend" magazines. The mismatched place fit me. The pieces of myself didn't go together much better.

Besides, the view of Puget Sound drew me straight to the built-in window seat. Even while sitting on cushions covered in mobile-home plaid, I could feel the Sound's charisma, and I soaked it in. It was its own shade of blue-green, unmatched anywhere I've ever been, and it rose in the wind in small peaks, like miniatures of the majestic Mt. Rainier, which towered faraway and magical as a knowing old sage.

For such an impressive body, Puget Sound maintained a calm and uncanny quiet. Supertankers were barred—one spill and an entire ecosystem would be extinguished. But the absence of something was not what provided the tranquility. It seemed to know something in its depth—because only a being of great wisdom could be so large and yet so at peace.

Puget Sound reminded me of God.

There on the window seat, I grew uncannily quiet myself. I'd emitted many outbursts toward heaven in the past two weeks—most of them along the lines of "God, forgive me!" "God, help me!" and

"God, why did I do this?" I knew, however, that those outbursts had little to do with God and everything to do with my self-loathing. I didn't expect my heavenly Father to answer.

Yet here was the sound, being still and knowing that God was God. Harboring His mysterious creatures—His Giant Pacific octopus and His black Dalls porpoise and His coveted silvery salmon. Mirroring His ever-changing sky, a seamless blue one moment, bowed with storm clouds the next. The sound simply did what God asked of it.

That came at me like an accusing finger. When someone knocked at the door, I nearly convulsed, then cried out, "Come in!"

"It's a safe neighborhood," said the voice that crossed the room, "but you really should see who's out there before you invite them in."

It was Mickey Gwynne, my new landlady, who lived upstairs with her husband Oscar, whom I'd yet to meet.

"It's actually Michelle," she'd told me the day she showed me the place. "But nobody calls me that except the IRS."

She was a little sprite of a thing, the kind who made me feel like Clifford the Big Red Dog beside her. She had an elfin face with a smile almost too big for it and a mushroom cap of fudge-brown hair. Clad in skinny jeans and an oversized green cable-knit sweater, she looked like a teenager. Only the weathering of sun and life on her skin gave her away as late thirty-something.

"Just so you know," she said now, "I don't make a habit of dropping in on tenants. I wanted to make sure you were settled, see if you needed anything."

"I'm good," I lied.

She nodded toward the nook of a kitchen outside the bedroom door. "Did you find the goodies in the refrigerator?"

"No!" I said. I started to get up, but she waved me back to the seat and dropped into a rocking chair that had at least a hundred thousand miles on it.

"No big deal," she said. "I know when people are relocating they don't have time to get to the market, so I left you some fruit—couple jars of my jam—an artichoke. They were on sale at Central Market."

"You didn't have to do that." My voice was thick.

"If you haven't even opened the refrigerator yet, it's probably a good thing I did." She looked around, probably at my lack of personal décor. "So," she said, "you like your view?"

"It's spectacular."

"On a clear day—which, in case you haven't noticed, hardly ever happens—you can see Seattle from here."

"I know," I said. "I live—well, I grew up here. Went to South Kitsap High—graduated in '83."

If Mickey thought I was rattling on like a moron, she covered it well.

"Did you go to college here too?" she said. "You look smart."

"No, I went to NYU—in New York City."

"No, you did not."

"I did—"

"The people we bought the restaurant from were from New York, which is why they called the place the New Yorker. They tried to do a fifties retro diner, but it didn't go over here." She gave a funny little grunt. "*They* didn't exactly fit here—obnoxious. But *you're* not that way—of course, you said you're originally from here."

I liked this woman. She didn't make me think of something to say, and I kind of loved that right now.

"So now we call the restaurant Daily Bread," she said.

She stopped to take a breath, and I felt I should contribute something.

"Is that the one on Main Street?" I hadn't been there, but it had a reputation for offering fanatically healthy food that didn't taste like grass.

"Best probiotic menu in town," Mickey said. "We prepare everything as close to natural as we can, the way God intended."

"Yum," I said stupidly.

"Come in and I'll make you one of my famous Synergy Smoothies, on the house." She gave me an unabashed critical review with her eyes. "With extra coconut milk. Don't you ever eat?"

Before I could answer, she put up her hand. Several rubber bracelets slid down her arm and disappeared into her sleeve. "You can tell me to mind my own business any time. I get the feeling this isn't the happiest time in your life."

I tried not to squirm. "It'll pass."

"So will you, if you don't get some omega-3s and protein in you." She put the hand up again. "Sorry. That's just me. Some women see your outfit, I see your vitamin deficiencies."

"Then you're in the right business."

Her open face invited me to say more, but I was suddenly exhausted. I felt like I actually had hauled armoires and steamer trunks full of knickknacks in on my back. The eyes I'd barely closed in a week chose that moment to become so heavy I could barely hold them open.

Mickey untwisted her pixie legs from the rungs of the rocker, stood up, and opened a cedar chest that served as a coffee table. "This is great for napping if you don't mind a few moth holes," she said as she pulled out an afghan in colors so loud I couldn't see how anyone could sleep under them.

She spread it on my lap and nodded like one of the older, wiser elves. "You should sleep well here."

When she was gone, I did.

Until I awoke with a start to a dark room. I thought fuzzily that the setting sun must have woken me up. Then I realized someone had tapped on the door. I stumbled across the room and felt for a light switch. Not finding one, I opened the door. In a pool of light from the outside lamp sat a grocery bag from Central Market.

I peered inside and found a pound of French roast, a container of what smelled like homemade chicken soup, and the *Port Orchard Independent.* A note at the bottom read, *Hope today is a better day. I promise I won't bug you.*

Back inside the apartment I squinted at the clock on the microwave. 6:00 AM.

I almost cried. I'd spent the last twelve hours not thinking about Rich and my kids and the house I'd been exiled from. For an entire half of a day, I'd escaped self-hatred. It was a gift.

Since I now had a reason for caffeine, I plugged in the one-cup coffeemaker and brewed the French roast as thick as espresso. I tossed the newspaper into the trash can, since it had done nothing but taunt me for days. But as the lid swung closed I caught the unobtrusive heading at the bottom of page one: NO FOUL PLAY SUSPECTED IN PROF'S DISAPPEARANCE.

I fished it out and started reading while the coffee dripped. Detective Updike said they'd found no evidence of a crime in the sudden disappearance of Dr. Zachary Archer. I detected a hint of disappointment in his quotes, but I was actually grateful to him and his baby-faced partner. That day in our living room, they'd at least provoked Rich into showing some life for seven seconds.

I wondered whether Rich had even taken down the new contact information I'd left him. So far neither he nor the kids had tried to get in touch with me. With a night's sleep behind me and some caffeine inside me, I couldn't stand the distance another minute.

I rummaged in the drawers and found a pencil and a notepad and set up at the wobbly dinette table. The first order of business—make a list.

FORGET ZACH

GET RICH BACK

FOCUS ON KIDS

GET NEW JOB

I skipped number one for the moment. The fact that it was even on the list produced more guilt than the other three put together. I went to number two and tried to break it down.

After several frustrating attempts, during which the rest of my coffee went cold, I could only come up with the profound thought that it would take time.

I looked at my bare surroundings. If I was going to be here for the time it took to turn Rich's heart, I was going to need some things to keep me from feeling like an alien to myself.

I went back to the house at two-thirty the next day, a time when I was sure Rich would be asleep and the kids would be in class. I was afraid if any of them saw me carrying out my pillow and my twenty-ounce coffee mug and the ratty sheepskin jacket I only wore for taking out the compost, they would conclude that I'd accepted my ousting from the house as final.

But Christopher was ensconced in Rich's chair in the TV area, scowling at the *Port Orchard Independent,* a publication I was really starting to hate. I felt principal's-office nauseated.

"I didn't see your car outside," I said.

"Did you see *this*?"

He snapped the *Independent* into a fold and thrust it against my leg.

With a profound sense of déjà vu I said, "What is it this time?"

Christopher squeezed out a derisive hiss that could have come from Rich himself and punched the footrest down with his calves. "Burn it when you're done so Dad doesn't see it."

I would have thrown the thing into the pellet stove right then if there'd been a fire going. As Christopher's footsteps faded into the second story, I sank to the arm of Rich's chair and forced myself to fumble the newspaper right side up in front of me.

St. Clair Makes No Denial of Cover-up at CCC, the headline said.

Zach gazed at me from his photo, seeming less real than he had the last time. I put my thumb over his face and read on.

Dr. Kevin St. Clair, Vice President of Covenant Christian College and Theology Department Chair, changed his no-comment position Wednesday night at a meeting of the Board of Trustees. When asked by board chairman Peter Lamb to give an official statement regarding the recent resignation of Dr. Demitria Costanas and the disappearance of Dr. Zachary Archer, both on the CCC faculty, St. Clair said, "Mrs. Costanas was not asked to resign but stepped down for personal reasons. No resignation request was made of Dr. Archer, and his whereabouts are unknown at this time."

In the wake of speculation over a possible link between the two events, the CCC pressed St. Clair for evidence of any unethical activity. His reply: "We can't rule that out."

I heard a rip and realized I was holding a torn piece of Section A between my thumb and index finger. So much for no publicity, St. Clair. Why didn't he just say it: "The two of them are rejects from Sodom and Gomorrah, and you haven't heard the last of it from me."

He was so careful not to lie, yet so deliberate in casting doubt. I fought the urge to shred the front page as if it were Kevin's liver lips. Above me something creaked, unmistakably Christopher's door, which had squeaked like a yawning puppy from the day we moved in. I riveted my eyes to the ceiling. He wasn't trying to sneak now as his feet fell with purpose down the hall in the direction of our bedroom. I strained to listen.

Was he waking Rich up with this? The urge to torture Mom must have overwhelmed the need to protect Dad.

I thought of fleeing. Behind that came a vision of me catapulting myself up the stairs and pulling Christopher out of our room, arms clasped around his ankles. But I could only stare at the newsprint.

There was more. Repelled by sickening anxiety and pulled by the need to do penance, I read on.

Ethan Kaye, embattled CCC president, was present at the meeting but still refused to comment directly on the sudden faculty vacancies. He told the board he was saddened by the effect the suspicions were having on the students and expressed a desire to "get back to the business of educating them."

Kevin St. Clair responded, "No—let us now begin *to educate them."*

My head shook.

Brandon Stires, theology major at CCC, told this reporter that rumors abound regarding the stability of Ethan Kaye's job.

"I don't know if [the rumors are] true," Stires said, "but if they boot him out, we lose the chance to understand what Christianity is about and move toward union with God. We're not going to get that from Dr. St. Clair."

Ethan's own words, quoted almost verbatim by Brandon, pressed down on my chest.

I had done this. I'd jeopardized a dream that wasn't mine to risk, and now its shards were trembling, waiting to fall from the crack I'd made. And they weren't going to crash on me alone.

Or had they already? My chest crushed me, so hard I could barely breathe. I gasped for air and felt my legs go numb.

Purse still on my arm, I shot from the chair, clawing at the newspaper to get it off me. The back pages paved the floor, and I slid across them as I careened to the front door. The pain was so suffocating I wheezed. My hands were almost too numb to find the knob.

Finally damp, cold air blasted in my face, and I all but collapsed on the porch. Dear God—was I having a heart attack? I shoved my head between my knees and tried to slow down my heart, or I was sure it would physically break. I didn't know how long I sat there, groping back from the edge of terror, when someone said, "Are you all right?"

I shook my forehead against my knees.

"Should I call 911?"

I didn't recognize the voice, and since my chest no longer threatened to rip open, I looked up. A stocky man stood before me on the front walk. Thirtyish, with a receding hairline that ended cleanly at a Chia-pet crop of perfectly rounded dark brown hair. The small blue eyes behind the rimless glasses showed real concern.

"How ya doin'?" he said.

"I don't need an ambulance."

He nodded so sagely, I expected him to pull out a paramedic's card and a stethoscope. "Heart condition?"

I smeared away the tears that pooled below my eyes. "Not that kind."

"You want me to help you inside?"

That was the last place I wanted to go.

"No," I said. "I need to leave."

"Like, drive?"

I nodded and stared at my Jeep. If it would only fling open its doors, pull me in, and take me away.

"You might want to sit here a minute before you do that," Chia Man said. "I'm not a doctor, but I think you might have had an anxiety attack. Try taking a couple of deep breaths."

I did, and felt a few nerves release their death grip on my shoulders.

"Take a few more. Concentrate on the exhale."

"You ought to be a doctor." My voice came back from far away.

"That would be a trip. How are you feeling now?"

"Better."

"Couple more breaths. Give your pulse a chance to slow down."

Slowly my heartbeat stopped pounding in my ears. I tried to smile at Chia Man, who watched me carefully.

"If you're not a doctor, what are you?" I rubbed my forehead. "That was probably rude—*who* are you? Are you a friend of Rich's?"

"Actually," he said, "I was looking for Demitria."

Even in my still-shaken state, I felt my eyes narrow. Nobody called me Demitria except Rich and people who were reading my name off a telemarketing list.

Or maybe someone trying to serve me with divorce papers. My pulse picked up.

"Would that be you?" he said.

"Who *are* you?"

"I'm Fletcher Basset. Reporter for the *Independent*—"

"Go away," I said.

I stood up and steadied myself, one tall pole of anger.

"So you are Demitria Costanas?"

"Get away from my house and leave my family alone. They are not part of this."

He peered at me calmly. "Part of what?"

I took the first step down, and he backed up, face still serene.

"Part of whatever it is you think you came here to find out. Now get off my property before I call the police."

"Hey—" He put up a hand. "It's cool. I'm gone."

He kept his eyes on me as he took a few more steps back and then turned to go. I watched him fumble in his jacket pocket and pull out something he muttered into as he made his way casually to his car.

I stayed until he was gone, though I could almost see a report of my near nervous breakdown on the front page of the *Port Orchard Independent.* Could it possibly get any worse?

Evidently it could, because the front door opened and Christopher stepped out.

"What are you doing?" He folded his arms, feet spread like a club bouncer.

"Leaving," I said. "But I want you to listen to me."

His shoulders jerked.

"There was a reporter here just now. His name is Fletcher Something—some dog name." Dear Lord, I sounded like an idiot. "Do not talk to him—and under no circumstances let him in the house or near Jayne or your father."

"Why, *Mom*?" Christopher said. "Are you afraid we'll tell him the truth?"

He might as well have hit me, right across the face.

"Don't worry," he said. "I'll make sure your mess doesn't drag the rest of us down."

He clicked my front door shut, and I stood there as outside as it was possible to feel. I balled my hands into fists, which is how I discovered that I still clung to the scrap I'd torn from the newspaper. I looked at it now.

My sweaty fingers had smeared the ink, but the image was clear—Zach's face, unchanged, unaffected. I peeled it off and wadded it into a tiny ball, but my hands were black with newsprint. As hard as I tried, I couldn't get it off me.

I found my cell phone and called Ethan for Dr. Sullivan Crisp's number.

CHAPTER TWELVE

I stood back and surveyed my decorating project: refurbishing the dining alcove. "Dining" was too rich a word to describe the kind of eating I would do at the rickety faux-maple table anyway, so I disbursed all the equally-as-unstable chairs but one, filled a Daily Bread coffee mug with pens and pencils, and set up my laptop facing Puget Sound. It was now my office.

I tapped the touch pad on the computer and brought my "work" to light: The List. It was all I had to do—and that fact sank onto me like the mist hanging stubbornly over the sound.

I jittered my fingers on the surfaces of the keys and missed the clacky sound my nails used to make. I'd gnawed them down to the tips of my fingers. I'd also taken to hauling on the same pair of sweatpants every day and skipping the eyebrow tweezing and the teeth whitening. In three weeks I had become someone I hardly recognized in the mirror. I woke up every day on the window seat, faced with nothing.

Except The List.

I drew myself up in the chair and took on my professorial posture and created a new page. GET RICH BACK went at the top. Under it, I typed

a. SEE DR. SULLIVAN CRISP

b. DO WHAT HE SAYS

I read the list again, and my eyes swam. Getting Rich back was the most important work I would ever do.

All right. Next page. I typed FOCUS ON KIDS.

CALL JAYNE

CALL CHRISTOPHER

Good grief. Here was a woman who wrote a doctoral dissertation on the role of story in spiritual growth, and yet the sight of those four words left me limp in the chair. All I had to do was pick up the phone. And all they had to do was—what? Hang up?

I reached for my cell phone, set in its charger, perfectly parallel to the laptop. I had to take this step, no matter what I might hear on the other end. At least it would be a voice I loved—even if it didn't love me back.

As the line rang I rehearsed. *Hey, Jay. It's still early—how 'bout I take you to school and we can get caught up—*

"Hello?"

For a shocked second I thought the voice belonged to Rich. It was quick and brusque and sounded as if it were in charge of the house. But it was Christopher.

"Hi!" I said.

Ugh. Too bright. Too rise-and-shine.

"Look, Demitria," he said, "I don't have anything to say to you."

Demitria? Had my son called me *Demitria*?

"What about Jayne?" I said.

"She doesn't want to talk to you either."

"No, I mean is she there?"

"She already left. Did you forget her schedule—or did you ever know it?"

My throat tightened. "I know her schedule, Christopher," I said. "She has dress rehearsal tonight, and I'd like to pick her up afterwards, so tell your dad—"

"I'm picking her up," he said. "It would be too weird for her anyway."

"Weird?" I said.

"Look, do you want to make her tell you to your face that she doesn't want you around?"

I squeezed the cell phone and charged across the apartment, the other hand clamped to the back of my neck.

"What are you talking about, Christopher? Come right out and say it."

"Okay. She doesn't want you coming to her play."

My neck muscles hardened beneath my fingers.

"After all this stuff that's been in the papers, she thinks everybody knows about your 'thing,' and she doesn't want a bunch of people gossiping about it when they see you there. Seriously—it would be weird for her to have to tell you to your face."

So you're more than happy to do it for her. I wanted to say that, and I would have, if my throat hadn't closed over the words.

"I need to go," Christopher said. "Anything else?"

Yes, I wanted to cry out when we hung up. *Everything* else.

Panic rose as I looked at the list again.

Focus on kids

How was I supposed to focus on my daughter when I couldn't even see her? When Christopher was sheilding her from me like a firewall? I realized I was still holding the phone—covered in my palm sweat.

I wanted to throw it across the room. It was an alien feeling, yet not as foreign as the one that came behind it: that if my son walked into the path of the flying phone, it wouldn't bother me a bit.

Yeah. It was time to get out of there. And there was really only one place to go.

Christopher worked part time at The Good Word, a Christian bookstore in Bremerton, one of the myriad small towns that fit together into the puzzle of Kitsap County. The store, shaped like a castle turret, beckoned largely female buyers looking for the latest in Christian romance or a nice plaque for the Sunday school teacher. Christopher's job, as I'd witnessed myself with mouth twitching, was to make them feel as if they were making such wise choices they might possibly want to expand their horizons even further.

He was in that very act when I pulled into a parking space at the gingerbread-trimmed window and watched through the drizzle on my windshield. He smiled over the top of the cash register at a middle-aged woman with a flattened perm who gazed at him as if her faith in the younger generation had been restored by his just-washed hair and the sincere nodding of his head.

My heart pounded again with the sickening urge to run from something I couldn't escape. I fumbled feverishly with the door handle, launched myself out of the Jeep, and tore unseeingly across the parking lot.

By the time I got onto the porch of the Victorian Teahouse, across from the bookstore, I could breathe again. In came the smells of strawberry-rhubarb pie and scent-saturated candles and the perfume of women who could sit calmly sipping tea and chatting about things that only a few weeks of my lifetime ago I had cared about too. Normal things.

I longed for a little bit of normal. So with a cup of chamomile and a finely chiseled slice of raspberry cheesecake, I sat at a table in a corner and fingered the lace on the tablecloth and watched. Watched until my son emerged from The Good Word, shrugging into his Northface jacket and slinging his backpack across slim shoulders that had not yet formed into manhood. He still had that walk—stalky and forward lurching, just as it had been at ten when he'd worked so hard not to be a little boy.

He stopped abruptly, and I realized as I followed his gaze that he'd spotted the Jeep. He lurched toward it and peered inside, hands on the hood, and then straightened to scan the parking lot.

Who was this bristling slice of man-child who searched for me as if I were invading his life?

I shrank from the window. I had no idea. And I didn't know when I'd stopped knowing who he was.

I didn't leave the apartment for the next two days. The List was still on the computer, though it went into hibernation just like I did. The only time I emerged was Sunday morning, when I went out to empty the trash that overflowed with Mickey's take-out containers from the refrigerator. Almost the minute I cracked the door open, she pounced as if she'd been staked out at the bottom of the steps leading up to her porch for hours. She was almost lost in a huge sweatshirt with a stand-up collar that reached her cheeks.

"I said I wasn't going to bug you—but that doesn't rule out checking to see if my tenant has died in her apartment."

Her eyes slid over me, and I surprised myself with a rusty laugh. "I guess you can't rule that out, can you?"

Mickey smiled like a wise elf, so that her eyes were sad. "Look, I don't know what you've got going on—and you don't have to tell me—"

She paused slightly, and I knew she hoped I would anyway. It made me laugh again. I sagged against the wall and folded my arms across the sweatshirt I hadn't taken off in three days.

She peered at me intently, between two strands of the mushroom cap that separated over her eyebrows. "I'm going to go ahead and get this out," she said. "Are you unemployed? Seriously, is that why you're holed up in the basement?"

Hers was not a face you lied to.

"Yes," I said.

Saying it was surprisingly like chipping off a piece of plaque from my brain. It left a breathing piece of freedom. So I added, "I had to resign."

"Meaning you would have been canned if you hadn't quit first," she said. "I hate that for you."

"I brought it on myself." Another chunk came loose. "I had to do the right thing."

"Which doesn't pay the bills or get you off the couch." She drew her neck up from the stand-up collar. "Here's the deal. Oscar and I have been talking, and we want to offer you a job at the restaurant."

What I did then gave new meaning to the phrase "burst into tears."

Her smile wavered. "Is that a yes?"

"I don't know what it is," I said.

"It's a step out that door. You can try it for a day or two, and if you hate it, no hard feelings. After I put you on a guilt trip, of course."

A mischievous laugh lurked in her throat, making me nod.

"Cool," she said, and picked up a handled bag from the step and offered it to me. "We'll see you at seven tomorrow morning. And, uh, charming as that outfit is, we'd rather you wore the uniform. This ought to be about your size."

She surveyed me in her open, hang-lipped, kid-staring-at-you-in-a-restaurant way. "Although I think you've gone down a size already since you've lived here. You're required to eat whatever lunch I fix you on the job. Otherwise you're fired."

"Yes, Boss," I said. Another chunk loosened itself from the hard place, and I actually felt myself smile. "This isn't a pair of micro-shorts, is it?"

"We don't do hooker wear," she said.

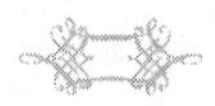

I'd passed the Daily Bread on Main Street in Port Orchard probably a hundred times, but I had only an inkling of what it was about. The fact that it still showed a certain degree of class in spite of the paint job on Main was a point in its favor.

In the nineties, during a downtown renovation project, the design-challenged city council hadn't been able to make up its mind how to redecorate Main Street. One night, after the petty infighting had gone on for months, a dentist and his son had painted all the balconies and storefronts the most hideous shade of bilious blue known to man.

Nothing could erase the graceful loveliness of the hill that streamed straight down to the water, but the juxtaposition of every-one-its-own-character buildings and the decorating-gone-wrong color scheme was jarring—if not a little bit embarrassing to the 8,650 of us who lived there.

But according to the city council, it was clean and done—and they were once again speaking to each other.

The Daily Bread rose above. The neat, simply penned signs that hung by hemp ropes from the main one proclaimed it to be *Beyond Probiotic* and *Foods Prepared As Our Maker Intended.* The only visions I had previously conjured up were ones of lava lamps and endlessly chanted tunes and too many wind chimes. So I wasn't prepared for the exquisitely real simplicity that waited inside.

The walls were a soft textured yellow, exuding health. The round tables, set in uncrowded fashion, each had its own Himalayan salt lamp, which, Mickey told me a few minutes after I walked in, provided negative ions that neutralized the harmful effects of electronics such as fluorescent lighting. The minute I breathed an air that breathed with me—an air of potted rosemary and drying basil and the zest of grated lemons—I believed her.

Mickey ordered my coat off and took me on a tour.

Only tea steeped in the pots on the uncluttered sideboard, each a different color for its matching brew.

"Coffee can totally tax the adrenal glands," Mickey told me. "We refuse to serve something that can injure the stomach and the esophagus with all that hydrochloric acid splashing up when the sphincter muscle between them relaxes too much."

I stared at her back as she led me into the beverage area. "This is Washington," I said. "How can you stay open without serving coffee?"

"Because people innately want to be healthy. And when they find out you don't have to eat what looks like the weeds somebody pulled out of their garden to do it, they go ahead and try." She turned to me in the doorway and smiled, eyes closed, so that she looked more marvelously gnome-like than ever. She opened her eyes and grinned at me. "Now, I'm starting you in beverages because I've already figured out you haven't waited tables before. I'm right, aren't I?"

I grinned back—and wondered what else she had figured out about me. My heart reached for her, yearned to tell her what was eating away at me. A woman who cared about the esophageal sphincter muscles of complete strangers might actually understand me. Even when I didn't. I ached to get it out—like the toxins she and Oscar were so eager to purge from their customers.

I didn't meet Oscar Gwynne until I'd made my first batch of carrot juice "cocktails," which people, amazingly, bought and, even more amazingly, drank. I stood at the sink—trying to scrub an impressionistic-style splatter off the organic cotton T-shirt that served as the top half of the Daily Bread uniform—when he emerged from the kitchen like a fuzzy bear. A pellet of frizzy grizzly-colored hair tumbled down his neck and seemed to continue into the quarter-inch beard that filled every crevice of his dimpled, clefted, chubby face. More hair peeked out of the neck of his T-shirt and rippled on the sizable arm that stretched out to me.

"You must be Demi," he said.

"And you're Oscar," I said, hand lost in his paw.

"Yes, and thank you for not adding 'the Grouch.'" He laughed soundlessly, shoulders shaking. "Mick always does."

"*Are* you?" I said.

"Absolutely not." He reached to an upper shelf, revealing yet another generous tuft of hair on his underarm. I wanted to scratch behind his ears.

"*Grouch* is Mick's MO," he said, bringing down a half-gallon bottle of olive oil in one hand.

"I heard that." Mickey appeared with a handful of paper slips and clipped them deftly to the revolving order holder. "Here's a demonstration—get back in the kitchen where you belong. I need two Synergy Smoothies and a Walla-Walla Omelet with a side of sauerkraut."

I felt my eyes widen. "Sauerkraut for breakfast?"

Mickey nodded. "Most of our regulars eat—"

"—lacto-fermented vegetables—"

"—with every meal."

"Great for the digestion," they said together.

A long, sparky look circuited back and forth between them. Mickey punched one of his furry arms. "So why don't you go in there and make it happen?" she said.

"Maybe I will." Oscar grinned hairily at me and lumbered toward the kitchen.

"Big lunk," Mickey said.

She disappeared back into the dining room, and I knew I had just watched a couple make love.

How did you do it? I wanted to cry after her. *How did you make it stay?*

One thing I was certain of: Mickey Gwynne had never been unfaithful to the big lunk. And she wouldn't be, no matter what he did.

Shoving my hair behind my ears, I went back to the juicer, turning it up high and loud so I wouldn't have to hear the thoughts that came next. My only hope was that this Dr. Sullivan Crisp could help me shout them down for good.

CHAPTER THIRTEEN

Sully always prayed before he saw a client—or counseled one of his therapists—or did anything that involved helping people make sense of themselves. In his view, if God wasn't in it, what sense was there to be made?

He sat that Monday afternoon in a sage green bowl of a chair he'd picked up at Great Prospects—the most extensive thrift store he'd ever frequented, and he considered himself to be a connoisseur. With finds from G.P. he'd transformed the grimy office into a session room, which, he admitted, would set the Healing Choice Clinics back fifteen years. But the two unmatched papasans, the lamp made from a parking meter, and the coat rack carved with a chain saw to look like reindeer antlers were an improvement over the orange plastic chairs he'd tossed out the back door along with the two-year-old Playboy calendar that had held a prominent greasy place on the wall. He'd completed the look with a great river rock he'd collected on the Hood Canal as a paperweight, and a Point No Point Lighthouse mug for holding pencils. Eclectic described it.

Sully pretzeled his long legs into a bow in the chair so that his knees shot up and provided props for his elbows. Resting his face in his hands, he cupped his image of God to his forehead.

Light. God was light for him, the only way to get his mind around the existence of life. And Christ—Christ, the Light from that Light, the only thing that made the path of life one he could continue on.

He watched the light behind his eyelids swirl, and he prayed into it. *God in Christ, the one Light, shine through me. Cast a ray from me onto her path—this child of Yours You've sent to me—*

And if Ethan was right, the woman he was about to see was trying to make her way through a tunnel that didn't allow her even a crack—

Dang. Sorry, God. Bunny trail.

Please—You are the Light—shine through me—shine through me—

A car pulled up, and Sully brought himself back. He couldn't resist the anticipation. You could tell so much about a client by the kind of automobile she drove.

High-pitched engine, probably a four-banger, light on its wheels. He'd guess some toylike vehicle, a car that had purpose, though clearly not cruising Main like Isabella. Practical, but with whimsy. Probably not a good idea to introduce himself to the driver with, "Hi. Let's start out with a good cry."

He untangled himself from the chair, tangoed between it and the pebble-colored one he'd bought for her, and stood in the doorway that opened into the garage. Through the big doors he could see a white Jeep Wrangler, and he grinned. Dead on.

A tallish woman climbed out and stood beneath a dark green umbrella, squinting at his building through the rain. She consulted the piece of paper in her hand, looked up again, and got a wry look on her face.

Sully chuckled. His digs were clearly not what she'd expected.

However, as she finally seemed to decide that this was the place and moved closer, Sully felt his brows lift. He'd consciously banished the boat photos to a far corner of his mind, but he brought into memory the faculty picture Ethan had shown him. This Dr. Demitria Costanas was far different from that.

That Demitria had seemed fully loaded with confidence. The wispy hair thing women of class seemed to do that made it at least *look* like they didn't have to spend hours in front of a mirror. Direct brown eyes, inviting opinion and promising hers would embrace yours. Level chin, straight shoulders announcing that they could haul a cord of wood and curve around a nursing baby, maybe even simultaneously.

Holy crow. Now her hair drooped, as did her posture, and her face was a mask, straining, he guessed, over an emotion beneath the surface. The hang of her head gave him a hint to what that was. "Skulkin' like a sheep-killin' dog," Porphyria would say.

Demitria Costanas—come on down. You're our next contestant on Your Life Is Right.

You just haven't found it out yet.

She kept the mask firmly in place as her sneakers squeaked their way to him across the garage. "I'm Demi Costanas," she said. "We talked on the phone?"

She extended her hand.

"Was that me?" Sully said as he shook it. "Or my secretary?"

Her eyes lifted in obvious surprise. A little light there—not much—but it flickered out. Her lips did twitch, though, as she looked around the garage and said, "I like what you've done with the place."

"You haven't seen the session room yet," Sully said.

He wafted a hand toward the office and followed her in. She barely looked around, obviously not there for the décor. What she *was* there for came out of her mouth before Sully even sat down.

"I don't want to be psychoanalyzed or therapized or whatever you do," she said.

We've prepared a little speech, Sully thought. He sounded his mental buzzer. Sorry, Mrs. Costanas, here on Jeopardy you must put that in the form of a question.

"All I want to do is get my family back. That's what I'm here for. Whatever I have to do to change myself so that can happen, that's what I want you to tell me. If you can do that, I'll talk to you."

Sully stifled a grin. She still had spunk.

"Goals are good." He didn't point out that the therapist and the client usually formulated those together—after they tried to get acquainted. He decided to go with the spunk, which appeared to be all that was holding her together.

"So," he said. "Do you have any idea what you think needs to be changed?"

"It's something heinous. You know my story—I'm sure Ethan has told you, and I really don't want to go into it."

Totally against contest regulations. I need to hear it from you.

But once again Sully skirted the rules and leaned back carefully in the papasan. "So the things that have happened to you have made you heinous?"

"No. The things I've done have happened because I *am* heinous." She kept her eyes directed at his knees. "There has to be something wrong in me to make me do what I've done to my family after all they've already been through—before."

They.

"They" brought the emotion pulsing behind the mask. We'll select a question from that category.

"You mean before you were unfaithful," Sully said.

The mask stiffened.

"What did happen—before?"

She sat further back in the chair, though her spine still didn't touch the back cushion. She kept her hands clenched around the purse in her lap, and Sully realized she was still wearing a navy P-coat, which she hadn't even unbuttoned.

"Can I take your jacket, by the way?" he said. There was, after all, that great coat rack.

She shook her head, but she still took it off and held it across her lap, under the purse. She was now two layers deep.

Sully was surprised to see her wearing what appeared to be a server's uniform. The words DAILY BREAD spread across the T-shirt, and in the baggy-legged drawstring pants, she looked as if she were wearing someone else's clothes.

"You want to tell me your story?" Sully said. "About that pre-affair time?"

The way she searched the floor before she began, Sully was sure she hadn't rehearsed this part.

"I don't know if Ethan has told you," she said, "but my husband—"

"Excuse me, Demi. What's your husband's name?"

"Rich. He was a fireman in New York City on September 11. He got there after the second tower fell."

She stopped, as if that were enough trauma for a man to have gone through in a lifetime. Sully had to agree. She was obviously controlling everything she said, but the hands she used to clench and unclench the purse also spoke.

"He lost a lot of friends, I'm sure," Sully said.

"He lost his twin brother. Eddie. Since then, he's never seemed the same."

"Because he isn't the same."

She finally pulled her eyes up to his. It was shame he was seeing, but it was murky now, as if something else were surfacing too, and muddying its color.

"It's not like he's a different person," Demi said. "It's like he's not a person at all."

Sully winced.

"The counselor who talked to all the wives told us it was survivor guilt." Her voice grew clearer, as if she were in territory she knew. "Almost three thousand people died, 343 of them firefighters, and the ones that made it couldn't help feeling it was their fault—why weren't they taken?" Her eyes flinched. "For some it helped that eighteen thousand people did survive, but that didn't do it for Rich. I mean, he lost his brother."

She glanced at Sully. He nodded her on.

"The thing is, Eddie only became a firefighter because Rich did, and because their father was one. It might have been in his blood, but it wasn't in his soul." Her voice thickened like a sauce. "That's what he used to say."

"Did Rich go to therapy?" Sully said.

She shook her head. "He wouldn't. I tried everything, short of threatening to leave him."

Sully heard her breath catch. Don't go there yet, he told himself.

"So what brought you to Washington?"

"There was nothing left for us in New York after Rich was suspended from the department. Before that he kept working, even though his captain advised him—practically begged him—to take a leave of absence and get help."

"He didn't."

"No, he didn't. He was the officer in charge at a call one night, and he made a tactical error—ventilated the wrong spot, and one of the other firefighters almost died."

For the first time, she sank against the back of the chair. "I know it was his fault, and it wasn't the first mistake he made after 9/11, but losing Eddie was so ripping for him, for all of us."

Ripping was exactly the word. Sully could almost hear the tear.

"He hit rock bottom, then?" Sully said.

"It was more like he was disappearing right there in front of us."

Sully watched her neck muscles go taut. He couldn't push her too much, or she'd have her purse and her P-coat and her pinched-in self out of there so fast, it would make the wheel of fortune spin. This would have to be about safety.

"So—how did that affect you?" he said.

"Me?" She shrugged. "I was desperate. I thought I was going to lose him, but I didn't even know to what. I talked him into coming out here, to start over. I'm from here originally, and it's so different from New York City. It was the only thing I could think of to do."

Sully propped up a foot on the papasan. He dug this part—hearing the story, starting to put together the puzzle. It was too soon to buy a vowel though.

"How did *you* feel about New York?" he said.

She blinked. "How did *I* feel?"

"Yeah."

"I loved New York," she said. "I went to NYU, and I met Rich in the city. We lived there all our married life, close to my in-laws, but with Eddie gone, and Rich's parents, there was nothing left for us there."

"When did they pass?" Sully said.

She furrowed her brow. This apparently wasn't on the script she'd prepared either. But she said, "Papa Costanas—my father-in-law—had a massive heart attack in 1997. Mama died before 9/11—Alzheimer's—she was in a nursing home. Then, of course, Eddie."

"That's a lot of loss," Sully said.

"Which is why Rich needed to get help—"

"No, I mean a lot of loss for you."

She squirmed, setting the chair at a tilt. She righted herself and said, "Rich suffered more than I did. I just wanted to help him."

Sully waited.

"Now I know I only made things worse."

"How so?"

Demi bugged her brown eyes at him. "I had an affair. I think that qualifies as worse."

This lady was determined to make everything her fault. Sully itched to take that road, but instead he said, "Let's stay with before the affair for a minute—can we do that?"

"Sure—I guess." She shook her hand in her hair as if she were stirring up anything that might be hiding there.

"Tell me about your relationship with Rich once you moved here, before the affair."

"At first I thought it was going to work out." She seemed to be taking out thoughts she'd stowed. "We bought the log home he used to dream about. I got the professorship at CCC, so he didn't have to worry as much about the pay cut he took coming out here." She stopped. "That might have started it. He never used to care that I had more education than he did, or that I made more money. But here it bothered him. A lot. And then I went and slept with a *professor,* for Pete's sake."

She put up a hand. Sully wasn't sure which of them she was stopping.

"You want me to go on?" she said finally.

"I'd like to hear more."

She fingered her purse. "At first everybody at the fire station—Orchard Heights—was great to him. He was a 9/11 hero."

No pressure, Sully thought.

"But that wore off—and then he didn't get promoted."

"How come?" Sully said.

"Something about his attitude. I don't know—that was about the time he started shutting down again."

"And where did that leave you?"

"This isn't about *me*!"

The sudden shrill seemed to surprise even her. She jerked in the chair and tried to steady herself with both hands, but the bowl tilted again.

"Look—" she said. "I want to know why I would hurt a man who's already been through hell and can't get out." She talked between her teeth. "I want to know what's wrong with me so I can fix it and get him back."

"So—" Sully picked his way. "If you fix yourself, that will automatically make things all right?"

The look she gave him almost made him laugh. The word *duh* was not far away.

"It makes sense to me," she said. "I'm the one who screwed up."

"Okay," Sully said. "So let me ask you this, then—just something to think about for a minute."

She jerked a nod.

"Can you think of anybody in your past—somebody important to you—who distanced himself or herself from you—so it hurt?"

Demi thrust her head forward so abruptly, Sully was sure there was a *Don't you* get *it?* in his near future.

"Why dig up my past?" she asked. She huffed out a breath. Frustration practically smoked from her ears. "I was a great kid growing up. I didn't lose it and mess up my entire life until six months ago."

Sully squeezed through the space he'd been prying open. "You say you want to know what's 'wrong' with you now. Well—your past is your present, and if we don't dig it up, it could also be your future."

She looked at him, and Sully could see the wavering that must be tormenting her every waking moment—and probably most of the sleeping ones too.

"I can't help you figure out why you've done what you've done unless I know more about you," he said. "That's all."

She didn't answer.

"And even then, you'll be the one figuring it out—"

"If I could do that, don't you think I would have by now?"

"No—because you need somebody to give you multiple choice selections. You game?"

She pushed two hunks of hair behind her ears and showed the first sign of letting go of the purse and its backup, the P-coat. That was good, since what he was going to try next could make her want to clobber him.

He leaned forward. "Are you ready to play Deal or No Deal?"

Her brow went awry. "Excuse me?"

"A little Game Show Theology." He tilted his head at her. "Look, Demi—I'm not trying to make light of what you're going through. But I have the feeling that you're worn out from working this thing—taking it apart and wringing it out and trying to fit it back together—and right now it's in pieces all around you. I'm not sure we can get them into a new picture unless we play with them some. That's what I'd like to do."

"Play?" she said.

"Just play," he said.

He was sure the corners of her mouth wanted to turn up, but there wasn't a smile left in her anywhere.

"Sit tight," he said. "I'll be right back."

He dashed into the garage and did a quick scan. Two tool cases and—what else? He snatched both of those up and tucked a metal bucket under one arm. When he set them next to his chair in the office, Demi eyed the collection incredulously.

Sully sank into his chair and picked up the empty toolbox.

"In case number one," he said, "is the possibility that you were born with a defective gene that makes you adultery material."

"Hello!" she said.

"I see we're not choosing case number one."

"How 'bout no!"

"In case number two—" He picked up a ratchet case. "The possibility that you don't believe any of the things in the Bible that you profess to believe. You've been a fraud all this time."

She blinked, hard. That was one she'd obviously considered. He was relieved when she discarded it.

"So much for case number two," Sully said, before she could reconsider. She was breaking his heart.

"Then how about case number three?" he said. "Which is, by the way, the only case left."

Demi looked at it, a wisp of wistfulness in her eyes. Good.

"In case number three"—Sully picked up the metal bucket—"lies the possibility that your husband distancing himself from you may have made it easier for you to justify your affair. Otherwise, you wouldn't have been able to do it."

She clenched the coat.

Ding-ding-ding-ding-ding, Sully said softy in his head. The right answer—because it was the one she resisted. Even now she was kneading the purse too. She would throw it at him without so much as a by-your-leave if he pushed even an inch further—although, in his opinion, the best work got done in therapy when projectiles were thrown.

When she reached over and picked up the river rock from the desk, he did prepare to duck.

"Please just throw this at me," she said.

Sully guffawed out an "Excuse me?"

"Let's get it over with. You know—like they used to do to adulteresses in the Bible." Her voice warbled with weak humor. It was the closest she was going to get to crying in this session.

"Maybe I don't want to know why I did it," she said. "Maybe I just need counseling for how to fix me." She looked ruefully at the rock. "Or maybe I need somebody to knock me in the head and tell me I'm an idiot for even trying."

"Which would help how?" Sully said.

"I don't know," she said. "I don't know anything."

Ding-ding-ding, Sully thought again. A place to start.

She was still looking at the rock, and Sully grinned.

"Just so you know," he said, "I haven't thrown that at anybody yet."

She gave a soft grunt. "Almost everybody else in my life has thrown one at me. Maybe you haven't met anybody as bad as me yet."

"How bad do you think you are?"

"Think about it. I'm a Christian. A professor at a Christian college.

A mother. A wife—I thought. And by the way"—she cocked her head. "Ethan told me you're a Christian counselor. I'm not exactly getting a sense of that here."

"Because I'm not quoting Scripture?"

"Well, yeah. We didn't even start with a prayer."

"Do you want to pray?"

"No," she said, before he even got out his last syllable. So—she was straight-arming God right now.

Sully recrossed his legs. "I can give you chapter and verse, and that's what some of my colleagues would do. But as you just mentioned, you're a professor at a Christian college. You have a doctorate in theology." He smiled at her. "You could probably tell me what verses to apply to this situation."

"We could start with the Ten Commandments," she said dryly. "Number eight, to be exact."

"Which you knew before you broke it. So me parading that in front of you would help how?"

"Exactly my point. If I'm this Christian, and I could commit a sin like this, maybe I'm basically a tramp."

"Do you really think you're a tramp?"

"No."

"Then you were right to begin with." He shrugged. "You did this for a reason, but it doesn't make sense to you now."

"Ya think?"

"At the time it did though, because it was based on a premise you believed then. You follow?"

"Go on."

"Maybe together we can find out what that premise was and how you got to it in the first place."

She lowered her voice in imitation. "And that helps how?"

"Because—when you had the affair, you were reacting accurately to what you believed. It was what you believed—the premise—that wasn't accurate."

"Give me an example."

Sully resituated himself in the chair. "If I believe it's every man for himself, I'm probably not going to show up at the soup kitchen to serve the homeless."

Her eyes took on the intelligent gleam he'd seen in the picture. "So if I didn't believe I was capable of being unfaithful to my husband, why did I act like I was? That's what we're looking for, right?"

"There you go. Now, I warn you, it might take time to figure out your premise. And then if you're still interested in change, we can help you develop one that's actually true. That's where God comes in and starts shaping."

"And that will help me get my family back?" she said.

He scooted to the edge of the chair.

"You're going to get *yourself* back. You didn't just cheat on your husband, Demi. You cheated on you."

She looked at him helplessly, as if she'd grown ten years younger since she walked in. Maybe a little of God's light was peeking through the cracks.

"Ever watch Family Feud?" Sully asked.

"What is with the game shows?" She finally let the corners of her mouth turn up. "Okay—yeah—years ago."

"On that show, within thirty minutes there's a winner and a loser, and everybody immediately starts to adjust to the new shift. You see what I'm saying?"

"Yeah . . ."

"You have your own family feud going on, as I see it—only it's going to take more than half an hour to determine who wins." He leaned so far toward her, his own chair almost tipped. "I hope everybody does, Demi."

And then he waited.

She pulled into herself as if she were gathering everything he'd dropped into her lap so she could take it away for examination.

"So I have to come back, then?" she said. Her tentative smile was bemused. "I'm not going away fixed today?"

"If you want to come back, I'll be here."

"How about tomorrow?"

"You might need a little more time to process what we've talked about."

"Process how?" She planted her fingers on the sides of her head. "Tell me what to do."

"Ding! Ding! Ding!"

"*What*?"

"That's what happens when you ask the right question."

"Do you have the right answer?"

"No—but you do. We'll take Childhood for $500. Will you find a picture of yourself as a little girl before age ten?"

She pulled in her chin. "That's it?"

"Put her where you can see her and talk to her often."

She didn't give him the incredulous *What?* this time. In fact, she seemed resigned to his inanity. "What do you want me to talk to her about?" she said.

Sully looked into the brown eyes he could imagine as dark pools of fudge on a child-face.

"Ask what she believes about herself," he said.

She straightened her shoulders and stood up, hand outstretched again. The college professor slid back into place.

"Thank you. I'll think about it."

"You want to come back a week from now? Tell me what you've thought?"

"Tentatively," she said. "I'll call you if I'm not coming."

Sully nodded. "Fair enough."

He walked her halfway through the garage, until she picked up the pace and went the rest of the way alone.

No little girl showed herself in the woman who drove away in the toy she came in. Sully leaned against Isabella. Little Demi had the answers. He hoped he'd have the chance to find out what they were.

CHAPTER FOURTEEN

H*i, Jay,*

I just had the most bizarre experience on the planet. As you yourself would say, it totally weirded me out.

I went to see a therapist. Counselor, shrink—I bet you'd have a funky word for it. That would have been strange enough—just going to someone I don't even know and telling him my deepest desire—to get you back, Jay. You and Dad and Christopher. That's all I want in this world—and that's why I went to him, because I hope he can help me.

But it was so *not-what-I-expected, and I'm not sure even you would have a word for it. Less like what you see on TV and in the movies, and way more like being on a game show—you know, Wheel of Fortune meets Who Wants to Be a Millionaire. There I was with Regis, Vanna, and Bob Barker all rolled into one.*

Are you getting a sense of how desperate I am to figure out what it was that made me betray you as I did—so we can be together again? Jay, please—

Mom

I put down the pen, folded the letter in half, and stuck it into my bag with the ten others I'd written to my daughter. Letters to Christopher had their own folder. So did the ones to Rich. I hadn't sent any of them. Every text message and e-mail I had sent to each of them—every day—had been ignored. If I didn't send the letters, I didn't run the risk of having them returned.

"Demi—meet my kid."

I straightened up from the bag and turned to greet the college daughter Mickey told me would be coming back in to help out at the

Daily Bread now that her spring break was over. I expected a younger elf from the gnome-like clan. I didn't expect a former student.

"Dr. Costanas!"

"Audrey?"

She was that little wisp of a thing who'd transferred in at the start of the semester. Of course she was Mickey's daughter, with a marvelous mouth that took up the entire bottom half of her face and fudge-colored hair that capped her head, probably no matter what else she tried to do with it.

"What are *you* doing here?" Her eyes were bigger and rounder than Mickey's, especially now.

Mickey squinted at us. "You two know each other?"

"This is Dr. C.!" Audrey dove at me and, to my surprise, put her arms around my neck. "I've missed you—everybody has missed you!"

"Okay—can I play?" Mickey said. She pulled a head of garlic from the bunch dangling near her head, but she kept her eyes on the two of us.

"This is Dr. Costanas, Mom," Audrey said. "She is—was—one of my teachers at CCC." Audrey stepped back from me, arms dangling as if she didn't know what to do with them now. "And the only one who was worth fifty cents for a box of Twinkies. I don't even know where they dug up the guy they replaced you with."

I must actually have looked as if I'd just had my nose hairs yanked out, because she prayed her hands at her lips and drooped. "I'm sorry—I guess you don't want to talk about that, huh?"

She had no idea how much I didn't want to talk about it. It was one thing to have Mickey now know where I was unemployed *from.* But if the why came out, there would be one more person I couldn't look in the eye. They were stacking up so high I could take a body count.

"But how cool is it that you ended up here?" Audrey said.

"Oh—pretty cool," I said.

"I mean, this is great for me. Like I said, we miss you. It just bites without you and Dr. Archer. But now we can, like, hang out—"

"Right now you're going to go ahead and hang out with the customers," Mickey said.

"We'll talk later," Audrey half whispered over her shoulder as Mickey ushered her toward the door.

That's what I was afraid of.

I reached for the celery and turned to the juicer. Mickey got herself in front of it, arms folded.

"Don't go getting that I'm-such-a-loser look on your face," she said. She nodded toward the dining area, where Audrey's voice lifted like the song it was. "You want me to get her off you? She can ask more questions than a civil litigator."

I didn't know what to say. I felt like my brain had gone through the juicer.

"Done," she said. "Do the apple-celery combination—and use the Granny Smiths."

As she started for the door, I leaned on the counter, looking down at the pile of stalks, struck with an aching loneliness. "I don't want her to not talk to me," I said. "I didn't get a chance to know her before I left."

"Feel free to get to know all you want," Mickey said, pushing the swinging door to the kitchen open with her back. "There're a few things I'd like to know myself. She just doesn't need to get to know *you* any better at this point. Am I right?"

"Thank you," I said to my celery.

"Don't mention it," Mickey said.

I didn't know what Mickey said to Audrey. Audrey and I worked side by side for the next few days, but she didn't ask me anything about why I left, what happened to Zach, or whether I was coming back.

She did talk though. While she grated lemons—over the washing of kale—between the words of the orders she called through the opening to Oscar, who, I figured out early on, was her stepfather.

"She can talk longer than you can listen to her," Mickey told me.

The first day I learned all about her roommate in the dorm, who listened to Kelly Clarkson and left her toenail clippings on the floor—and for Pete's sake, who needed to clip their toenails that much anyway?

I had to wait for the next day's lull to hear about Boy, the new guy Audrey was dating.

"Boy is *so* cute," she told me over the sink full of soapy muffin tins we were wallowing in. "I have never dated a guy so cute—no, he's hot. I mean it."

"Does Boy have a name?" I said.

"He does. But I'm not referring to him by it yet—you know, to my family, friends like you. I just call him Boy."

I stopped, hand suspended and full of soap. "And that would be because . . ."

"Because until I know a relationship is actually going somewhere, I like to keep it impersonal. If I say, 'It didn't work out with Boy,' people go, 'Oh, that's too bad. Next?'"

"But if you call him by name . . ."

"Then it says we have a relationship, and if it doesn't happen, it's a bigger deal to say, 'Percival and I broke up.'" She gave a sigh.

I took that to mean she'd had her share of Percivals. And what was she? Nineteen?

"So—tell me about Boy," I said. As if she needed an invitation.

I listened with deeper and deeper interest. There was something comfortingly familiar about that feminine, still-teenaged voice that tripped up and down its melodic ladder, making sounds and forming words that could only come from a girl-child trying to figure herself out.

We were well into an analysis of how Boy could be so, like, ridiculously intelligent and yet so—well, hot, at the same time, when I realized tears were backing up in my throat. She made me miss my daughter. Jayne was quieter, more serious, and less concerned with "hot," as far as I knew. She could have been Jayne nonetheless—but she wasn't. I was brewing jasmine tea with someone else's daughter, not mine.

"You okay, Dr. C.?" Audrey said.

"Does this jasmine scent affect your sinuses?"

"No—but—" She brought her voice down to conspiratorial level. "That nasty ginseng stuff makes me feel like I'm gonna throw up. Don't tell my mom, though."

"Your secret's safe with me."

"What are you two cooking up over there?" Mickey called from the table she was wiping down. "I don't think it's tea."

Audrey and I looked at each other and giggled. The moment I had a chance, I went into the bathroom and breathed hard until the tears were safely banished.

Audrey was off at two. I was too, actually, but since I had no place to go, I stayed and sat on a stool in the kitchen, grinding Himalayan salt while Mickey prepped the afternoon's goodies.

"So," Mickey said, "does my daughter have another new boyfriend?"

I looked up from the salt grinder, but she already had her hand up to stop me from answering. "Sorry—I'm gonna go ahead and take my foot out of my mouth now. Whatever she's told you, it was obviously in confidence. I wouldn't know what that feels like, mind you. Oh—late customer."

She hurried out to the dining room, pad in hand.

So—not so much with the mother/daughter relationship. That surprised me. I personally was almost ready to bare my soul to Mickey. I hadn't met anybody that non-judgmental and intuitive since Mama Costanas.

I stopped, hand full of salt crystals. What would my mother-in-law think of me now? Even the memory of her round, freckled, unwrinkled face cinched around me like a vise. I'd married a family as much as a man, led by a matriarch who would put her baggy arms around me, skin falling against me like panels of silk, and span the distance my own mother had enforced between herself and me.

My mind clicked back to the Daily Bread kitchen, where Mickey had returned to unroll a blanket of dough. Mama Costanas would have words for me now. I couldn't hear them. I could only hear myself cry.

"I've been wondering when you were finally going to do that," Mickey said.

"I'm sorry."

I reached for a paper towel. She stopped me with the sharp pause of her hands on the dough. "Touch that and you draw back a nub."

"You're paying me to work, not—"

"Right now I'm paying you to sit there and bawl your eyes out and hopefully tell me what's going on with you."

"I can't," I said. "You'll think . . . I can't."

"The way I see it, you can't *not*." She didn't take her eyes off the almond butter she smoothed across another flat of dough. She still didn't look at me as she rolled it into itself, a roll, a tuck, another gentle roll. "I'm going to go ahead and admit I know what's going on down in that apartment." Roll, tuck, smooth. "You've tried the pacing and the hand wringing and the forgetting to eat. Then came the hibernating. Now it's put a cheerful face on the agony that's ripping you up."

She used a tool like a triple pizza cutter to cut the roll into wraps, pecans peeking their faces out of the spirals. I cried on.

"You think I'm losing it," I said.

"No—I think you're doing everything you can to find it." She picked up each roll and placed it firmly in the pocket of a muffin tin. "That's the reason you ended up in our apartment and in our restaurant."

A sob bubbled from my nose.

"Now you're getting real." Mickey slid the muffin pan into the oven, closed the door, and folded her floury hands onto her arms. "You're here because this is part of you finding yourself." She nodded at the cinnamon sticks hanging in bunches over her head. "It's real here. You won't find anything fake. Including yourself."

I leaned forward on the stool, into a fold. She caught me in her dusty arms, soft as the dough that was so much a part of her. I felt her hand on the back of my head, kneading and smoothing.

"Talk to me, baby girl," she said. "Anything you say in this kitchen will flow right through me and disappear into the atmosphere." She held me closer until I melded to her touch, and I cried the loose, sweet, bubbling tears of a child.

By the time the pecan rolls were done, I'd told Mickey Gwynne everything. And when I was through, she simply said, "Oh, sweet baby girl, I'm so sorry."

"Not half as sorry as I am," I said.

"No—now you listen to me."

She took my face in both hands, and I knew by then I must be as smeared with flour and sweetness as she was. "You're a human being, and you made a mistake—"

"A big mistake—"

"And nobody wants to cut you a break. That's what I'm sorry about."

Her softness loosened my tears again.

"Good," she said. "You've got it going now—and I don't think you should stop."

"I can't feel sorry for myself," I said.

"Then let me. Let me be the one who gets that not one single person in your life is seeing you as a hurting woman who made a bad choice—like every other human being has." Mickey dug her thumb into her chest. The elfin face held firm, as if an edict were being handed down from a miniature throne of wisdom. "You said you're seeing a therapist?"

"Yeah."

"Go to him—her—whoever—when you need to drag yourself through your stuff. You pray, right?"

I closed my eyes. "I don't know."

"Are you saying, 'Please, God'?"

"That's about all."

"You're praying. Go to God when you don't know what to do with yourself. But, hey—" She touched my cheek. "When you just need to be a baby girl and pitch the fit you have coming to you because nobody will forgive you—come here—to me. I don't care if you spend all day crying while you're chopping nuts and doing dishes. I'll come through and tell you it's okay to keep crying. And—"

She put up a finger and turned to the muffin tin. She scooped up a wrap, happily spilling out its pecans and brown sugar from the smile of a fold, and cradled it in her hands before me. "And there will always, always be a cookie. Doesn't get any better than that."

I pressed it to my lips. At the moment, it truly didn't.

CHAPTER FIFTEEN

Sully couldn't get Demitria Costanas out of his mind.

Even four days after their session, when he was engrossed in finding out why Isabella's engine wouldn't turn over and had pulled the Impala's distributor, all he could think about was Demi, looking as mournful and slender as the thing in his hand with its connectors draping down in exile from where they belonged.

"What's up with you?" he said to them. "What's the disconnect?"

The hole he peered down into made him wonder about the places deep in her soul. When he took off the distributor cap and saw its crusted-down shape condition, he couldn't help wondering what lie she'd told herself that had brought her life to a freezing halt. When he saw her stuck in the gummed-up carburetor he disassembled on the table, he called it quits for the day.

Holy crow, you're obsessing, he told himself. *Get outta here and*—he grinned as he wiped his hands on a rag—*go obsess about something else.*

Ethan Kaye's situation provided the obvious next choice. They'd had lunch Wednesday, and Ethan ate what Sully considered to be a pathetic portion of the rack of ribs they shared at Metzel's, a clear signal he was brooding. That and the straight line that dug deeper than ever between his eyebrows.

"Jackals still after you?" Sully said.

Ethan nodded. "St. Clair hired an interim professor to replace Demi—the man looked qualified on paper, but he's completely obsessed with the Apocalypse. Granted, that'll lend itself to spiritual discussion, but he has the students making a timeline from the Book of Revelation."

Sully half grinned. "You're not serious."

"Oh, I'm serious as a heart attack."

"What about Wyatt Estes?" Sully said. "Heard any more from him?"

Ethan took to cleaning a miniscule speck of barbecue sauce from under his fingernail. "Are you sure this isn't crossing some kind of line for you—since you're seeing Demi as a client now?"

"I've thought about that." Sully sucked on a bare rib and set it on his plate. "A—I'm not planning to break any cardinal rules, but my situation with Demi isn't exactly conventional. The lines are a little blurred. And—B—my interest in Wyatt Estes is for you, Ethan, not Demi."

Ethan gave him a long look. "I'm going to leave the ethics to you, then. You know what you're doing."

"On a good day, yeah." Sully grinned. "So—what about Wyatt?"

"I still can't figure that one out. I know he wants the college turned legalistic, which is going to mean getting me out of there. But a man of his standing in the community—I can't imagine him being involved in that picture-taking thing."

"You mean with Demi and—what's his name—Archery Boy?"

Ethan's eyebrows knit together. "Archer." He gave Sully a closer look. "I guess my opinion of Dr. Archer has rubbed off on you."

That and the state Demi Costanas was in. Where *was* this guy who'd convinced that woman to risk tearing her life apart? But now that Demi was his client, he couldn't go there with Ethan.

"Anyway," Ethan said, "that still mystifies me. It seems like—"

"I know—we need to know where those pictures came from. I'd like to see what I can find out."

Ethan sat back. "You're really going to play detective, on top of rebuilding an old car and seeing Demi because I asked you to? I didn't mean for you to spend two-thirds of your time up here on my problems. You came to deal with your own."

Sully skirted that one. "I don't know how much good it'll do, but I'm going to start looking up photographers—see if I can't get a feel for who might have snapped the pictures. It would have to be a certain type." He licked his lips dryly. "Something from the sleazeball category."

"Whatever you can find out, I'll appreciate."

So on Thursday Sully closed up the garage and went in search of sleazeball photographers. Callow seemed like the appropriate place to start, seeing how the Laundromat across the street had been robbed twice since he'd moved in and the coffee shop around the corner was either a drug drop or merely a breeding ground for ptomaine.

It was obvious as he headed down the sidewalk on Callow Avenue, the main thoroughfare, that this had been a nice little American town at one point—the kind where people lived their whole lives getting their cuts of meat from the same butcher and being baptized, married, and buried in the same church.

There were no photographers, and he was about to turn down a side street when he found himself in front of a business that was obviously still a going concern.

McGavock's Bakery, the pink sign said. Since 1942.

Sully hadn't seen an establishment like that since he was a kid in Birmingham. Two large display windows were lined with paper doilies and still offered the remains of the day's baking. Letters painted across the glass read Home of the Famous Pink Champagne Cake.

The thought made Sully's teeth ache. Holy crow—it sounded like a recipe for diabetes. He was about to pass when something else caught his eye.

A girl behind the counter was dropping oversized cookies into a bag and remaining so otherwise motionless in the act that even the string-of-beads earrings that dangled nearly to her shoulders swayed only slightly. Sully peered shamelessly through the window. Ethan, he decided, had used the word *detective* too lightly.

The door opened, letting out a wizened old lady who was fairly pink herself and had, in Sully's mind, probably been buying her cookies there since the grand opening. He slipped inside and watched Counter Girl as she returned the tray of cookies to their case between a display of rum pudding cakes and several flats of plastic-looking petit fours. She looked up at him, and the eyes cinched it. Nobody else had those wide, blue, sardonic eyes with the gold flecks. This was the girl from the Estes auction.

"Can I help you?" she said, though Sully sensed that she wanted to suggest he either take a picture, which would last longer, or move on. But as she looked at him, recognition seemed to flicker. She didn't exactly smile—but she didn't look unhappy to see him.

"So," she said, "how's your car? Don't tell me you drove it over here?"

She looked out the window, a bemused look on her face. She obviously had no expectation of seeing the Impala out there at the curb, probably ever.

"She's not ready to be unveiled yet," Sully said. "So can I ask—"

"What I'm doing working here when I'm an Estes?"

Sully didn't try to hide his surprise.

"You know you want to know."

"Okay." Sully leaned on the counter. "What are you doing working here when you're an Estes?"

"Actually I'm not technically an Estes. I'm a Farris."

"Do you have a first name?" Sully said.

She straightened the pink apron she wore over the same-colored T-shirt. Sully was sure it wasn't a hue she'd chosen.

"Have we established you're not trying to pick me up?" she said.

"Oh, yeah—we got that straight at the auction."

"Then it's Tatum."

"What is?"

"My first name. And I'm here because I want nothing to do with being an Estes at this point in my life. You want to try the pink champagne cake or what?"

Sully had to grin. He was used to being the one who made everyone else's head spin. She had his in a mixing bowl and was going at it with an eggbeater.

"Sure, I'll try a piece." His stomach gave a warning gurgle.

She sliced into a pink concoction that sat up on a cake pedestal like a cotton candy castle dotted with icing puffs. As it fell onto the plate, Sully's worst fear was realized: pink inside too. It would match the Pepto-Bismol he was going to have to take later.

"So—do you want a cup of coffee, or are you going to try to gag it down dry?"

"Excuse me?"

She leveled those eyes at him. "You look like you're about to taste the hemlock. It's just cake."

"I can't wait."

The only thing making it worthwhile was the possibility of finding something out about Wyatt Estes.

Halfway into his second piece, he knew that Wyatt was Tatum's uncle, her mother's brother, and that he—more than anyone since his grandfather—had been responsible for building the sizable Estes financial empire in Kitsap County.

"So I take it your working here is part of a family feud," Sully said. He was having trouble resisting a plunge into Game Show Theology. That thing that simmered beneath her surface fascinated him.

"Sort of," she said.

Sully pretended to enjoy his next mouthful and waited.

"It has its benefits and drawbacks," she said. "Right now I'm the one doing the drawing back."

"Well put," Sully said.

"Oh yeah, I'm positively eloquent."

"Not to mention humble."

"Whatever." Tatum took the empty plate he pushed toward her. "You know," she said, "I'm not sure why I just told you all that."

"Because I'm new in town and I wanted to know who the movers and shakers are around here, and you were nice enough to tell me."

"Like you so care about movers and shakers," she said. "You live in Callow and own a thirty-year-old car."

"Don't let her hear you say that," Sully said. "She's sensitive about her age."

"Okay," Tatum said.

"Now I heard . . ." he said as he dug for his wallet to pay for the punishment that surged up his esophagus. "I heard that Wyatt

Estes gives a bunch of money to that college—what is it—Covenant Christian? Is he a major donor?"

She didn't miss a beat taking his money, poking numbers into the cash register, handing him his change. But when her blue eyes met his again, the gold in them had hardened.

"I wouldn't know about that," she said. "Look, I need to get back to work."

She didn't wait for Sully to leave before she disappeared into the back room.

CHAPTER SIXTEEN

I checked myself in the rearview mirror before I left the car in the driveway. My eyebrows were tweezed, but I hadn't used pencil. I went for groomed but not made up in the way Rich always said looked like a girl had been run through a floor polisher. I couldn't get the whole view of my face, but I could see that my bangs wisped over my forehead—deliberately careless—and my lips were smooth but not goopy. Rich would never kiss me when I was wearing lipstick.

"Like there's the remotest chance he's going to kiss me today," I said to them.

Or maybe ever. The thought tore a path right through my stomach, over and over. That was why I'd chosen to come to the house to get a picture of myself as a kid at a time when Rich would be getting up and, once again, the kids wouldn't be there. Although I was beginning to wonder if Christopher had somehow had a chip installed in me so he could track my every move and show up whenever I tried to finagle a moment with his father.

I climbed out of the Jeep and surveyed myself one final time in the side mirror. Between the dots of drizzle was the whole me, and to my own surprise, I didn't cut as pathetic a figure as I felt like inside. That was due in part to my kitchen crying sessions with Mickey.

I'd spent the last two afternoons, between lunch and the tea crowd, weeping shamelessly while she produced chocolate saveur. Make that weeping, wailing, and gnashing my teeth. She nodded and sifted and grated and passed me a cookie every now and then.

I let myself into the house and decided that the fact that Rich hadn't had the locks changed was a good sign. So was the fact that Christopher wasn't there.

But Rich wasn't home either, which surprised me. He should just be getting up, having a cup of coffee, turning on the TV, scratching his armpits like he always did for the first hour after he climbed out of bed. It ached in me that I knew him that well.

But the coffeepot was cold, and his bed hadn't been slept in. When I heard the Harley roar up the driveway, I found myself hurrying out of the bedroom—our bedroom—as if I didn't belong there.

Rich entered through the mudroom as I arrived in the kitchen. The infuriating guilt I felt was plastered all over me by then, I was sure. So naturally, I came out with a surefire way to get us back on track. I said, "Where have you been?"

His eyes narrowed down to slits, and his mouth hardened to a line. I had to take back what I'd thought earlier. I didn't know this man that well after all—because I'd never seen that kind of hardness on him. Ever.

Something in me caved. "I didn't mean it like that," I said. "I thought you'd just be getting up."

"I'm just going to bed," he said.

He got past me sideways. I stepped out of the way and tried not to think that if I hadn't, he would have pushed me.

"You're not going to work?"

"I just *came* from work." He was still moving, out of the kitchen, into the great room, toward the stairs. His arms sliced the air like scissor blades.

"You're working the *night* shift?" I said.

"I got demoted."

"That's not being demoted—"

We were both at the bottom of the steps now. He stopped, but a command for me to stay right where I was shot back at me. I froze, hand on the banister.

"You're a firefighter's wife, Demitria," he said. "You remember—they start you out putting you wherever they think you need to be—until you prove yourself—and then you choose where you know you need to be." He turned his head toward me over his shoulder, but he didn't meet my eyes. "When did I ever choose the night shift? For that matter, when did I ever pick evening shift?"

Never. And the reason why was something neither of us had to say. He always wanted to be there when his family was home.

He was halfway up the steps when I said, "What about Jayne?"

"What about her?"

"She's home alone at night?"

"We've got it handled, Demitria. I'm going to bed."

I probably would have cried—or torn up the steps and ripped the door off the hinges—if two things had been different in that conversation. I clung to them in the same way I latched myself to the stair rail.

You're a firefighter's wife, he'd said.

Not you *were.* You *are.*

It seemed like such a pitiful thing to hold me up, but I let it—as I stood there hearing the echoes of the other thing I fastened my hopes to.

Demitria. He still called me Demitria, the way no one else did.

And then the door slammed, and I was once again shut out. But it wasn't a place where I was willing to stay.

I peeled myself from the railing and looked at the cedar chest where I kept the old family photos. Coming to the house had almost nothing to do with finding a picture of myself at age ten. In fact, the more I thought about Sullivan Crisp and his bizarre Game Show Theology, the more I wondered if he was going to be any help to me at all. Finding the picture was just an excuse for coming over.

I stopped short of the chest. I needed an excuse to come to my own house and confront my husband? Didn't I have a right to fight for my family? Whether they wanted me to or not?

I lifted the lid. Was that stone coldness I'd seen on Rich what he wanted? Did Christopher like making me lick the dust? Did Jayne feel satisfaction in cutting me out of her life?

I couldn't say yes. And so I dug.

But anxiety gripped me as I got closer to the layer of what Jayne called "the antiquities." Looking into my innocent face was only going to more deeply embed the line I'd formed in my memory, the line that separated everything in my life into pre-affair and post—

"Stop," I said out loud.

The first few photos of a very young Demitria showed me in dress-up regalia entertaining the family with a one-girl show. Or me standing, grinning and gap-toothed, holding a certificate for excellence in one of about a dozen academic subjects or a trophy for some outdoorsy thing I'd reigned victorious in, or sitting at a piano leading the singing of an entire Vacation Bible School. Somehow none of those showed me anything I might have believed about myself—except that I could do anything and take first place. And make everyone love me at the same time.

I didn't know if that was what Sullivan Crisp was talking about, but I kept looking. The photo that made me hold it in my hand and gaze was the one I least expected.

It was a rather staged sitting of me, my mother, and my two brothers, all dressed up, as I recalled, to go to one of my father's speaking events. I actually smiled at it. Were we the poster family for 1970s doing-it-all-right or what? My mother with the wings in her layered hair and the polyester suit—with skirt, not pants. My older brother, Liam, with his too-big feet and too-short hair and wobbly smile that hadn't grown into the exact replica of my father's yet. My younger, dimpled brother, Nathan, with his chubby pink hands that later became the source of whispered concerns about his "sensitive" ways.

I sat cross-legged and ran my fingers down the sides of the photo. And then there was me. Was I not the lankiest, most vulnerably preadolescent child that ever was? My teeth, in the smile reserved for the photographer who took all of Daddy's publicity pictures, were big enough for two children, and I seemed to have more of them than most kids too. My hair was cut in a too-perfect pixie, and I remembered with a small pang that all the other girls had big loose curls they could flip around when they were feeling like they were, as Jayne would put it, "all that."

And the outfit. Oh, the outfit. Kneesocks. Pleated skirt that covered the tops of them. And could there have been more embroidery on that blouse? *Who dressed me?* I thought. Though I knew. I glared at my mother's face even now and might have actually read her the riot act on the spot for packaging me that way—if I hadn't noticed who was missing from the picture. Dr. Theodore Haven. My daddy. Where was his oh-so-real smile? His sandy-blonde hair that smelled like the Palmolive soap he always washed it with, much to my mother's chagrin? Even centered as we were in the photo, he was so obviously missing. There should have been a dotted outline where he was supposed to be.

I glanced at the date on the back. March 1975. That must have been right before the big Washington Association of Churches crusade for the ecumenical movement. It had to be the day when the photographer came to take a family photo for the newspaper, for a big opening event. I remembered now: Daddy was caught up in counseling someone with cancer or a wife abandoned by a cheating husband—although I wouldn't have been privy to that at the time. He said to go on without him—that we were the best-looking part of the family anyway.

I remembered feeling that day like I had no place to put my elbow when we were all posing. Even now, I could see how awkwardly I propped it on my own knee.

Now I untangled myself, picture still in hand, and stood up. This was the one. I didn't know why, but that little girl called to me to find out what she believed about herself that day. Right now, she was the only person related to me who reached for me at all.

Including the driver of the pickup that squealed into the driveway. I had to be right about that chip. I glanced at my watch. Did the kid never work or go to school anymore? As I listened to the progressive slamming of doors from Chris's vehicle to the kitchen, I suddenly felt like slamming something myself.

"So, Demitria," he said as he marched himself into the great room. He started to unfold his arms, curl his lip, spit out whatever he felt like.

Until I let the lid of the cedar chest drop. His face startled involuntarily.

"Christopher," I said, "no matter what you've decided to call me, I am still your mother—so stop right there with the attitude. If you can't treat me with some modicum of decency, don't talk to me at all."

I could barely believe the words were coming out of my mouth. He evidently couldn't either, because although he headed for the stairs, his motion held a slight hesitation, which made me say, "Come to think of it—you *are* going to talk to me. I'm taking you to dinner. Metzel's."

"I don't want to go anywhere with you," he said.

"Who said this was about what you want?"

He tried to harden—I could see it—and for a moment I wondered crazily if Rich had taught him to do that, or the other way around. But he couldn't quite pull it off.

"Look, I don't see how this is going to accomplish anything. You've disassociated yourself from anything that I—"

"Oh, Christopher, do shut up," I said. "Get in the Jeep—and I'm driving."

My bravado ran out once we got in the car, and we rode in silence to Metzel's, a favorite restaurant of ours in Poulsbo. I decided I wanted to be face to face with him across a table, with dozens of other people around that he might not make a scene in front of. Unfortunately the lack of conversation gave him time to refuel.

"I'm not going in there with you," he said when we pulled into the parking lot.

"Fine," I said. "No triple berry cobbler. We can talk here."

"I don't want to talk."

His teeth were so firmly clenched, he could barely get the words out. I didn't need to hear them anyway. I'd seen it before, this tightening against something he refused to let out. In fact, this could have been late September 2001, and Christopher could have been ten years old—crunched into a ball to shut out the hurt, the very curve of his spine crying out, *So what happens to me now? What happens to who I thought I was?* This could have been the night I tried to pull him onto my lap and said, "Please, son, if you're hurting, talk to me."

"I don't want to talk," he said again.

And just like then, there was nothing I could do to make him.

"All right, then," I said. "I'll talk. I want to say—"

"Did you know everything's gone down the tubes for Dad at work since you two split?"

"We haven't 'split,'" I said. "Your father obviously needs time to calm down—"

"Really," he said.

"Yes—really—and it's hard for him. You know what a tough time he has dealing with things—"

"No, I mean, you think you guys haven't split?"

"No, I wouldn't call it that."

"Oh," Christopher said.

A mean smile started across a mouth it didn't fit. I was starting to dislike my own son.

He turned to me, and I watched him deliberately form a triumphant sneer. "If you aren't breaking up," he said, "how come Dad hired a lawyer?"

CHAPTER SEVENTEEN

I brought my picture," Demi said.

Sully tried not to let his eyebrows rise. She walked in with barely a hello, took off her coat, sat herself down, and dug a photograph out of her purse—all with robotic precision.

"Hi, Demi," Sully said. "Nice to see you."

She looked at him, her hand suspended between them, holding the photo, and gave him a grim smile. "I'm not nice to be seen today. All I want to do is get to work."

"All right then," Sully said.

"And no games today, okay? I don't have time."

Sully caught the thickening in her throat.

She pushed the picture toward him. "My husband has hired a lawyer. Now can we get on with this, please?"

"I'm sorry, Demi."

He watched her fight the sag in her shoulders. No way she was giving in now.

"Looks like we better get to work then," he said.

She nodded and sat back an almost imperceptible inch. He could feel her eyes on him as he looked at the picture.

Holy crow—was this the Cleaver family? Minus a father?

"You were about half cute," Sully said.

"I was precious," Demi said dryly. "So what does it tell you?"

"I don't know yet." Sully wiggled his eyebrows at her. "Let's go in."

He got her to explain who the people were in the picture, leaving the obvious question unasked.

She finally said, "My dad was supposed to be there, but he got called away at the last minute."

"Busy man, your father."

Demi folded her arms, though she still sat close to the edge of the papasan, tilting it forward.

"Don't go into the corporate-executive-too-busy-for-his-family thing," she said. "My father was devoted to us."

"What did you call him?"

"Daddy," she said.

Sully felt a pang. Only a daddy's girl could say it like that.

"So—what called him away?" Sully put up a hand as she bristled. "None of this is a judgment, okay? I'm gathering information, not placing blame. We're here to learn about you. Deal?"

She looked around. "You don't have any of those cases in here today, do you?"

Sully grinned. "I'm prop free."

She gave the place one more glance. "Daddy was a major preacher. He had a huge church—Port Orchard Community—and he left it to enlarge his ministry to the Pacific Northwest when I was six."

Sully nodded. She was so fiercely proud of her father, it broke through her agony.

"He was only in his thirties then," she said. "But he spoke with this depth and wisdom—I've listened to his tapes as an adult. People flocked to his events, even in the early seventies when the traditional church was struggling." She finally sat back in the chair. "I wasn't aware of all of this at the time—but I do remember when I was about eight we had a big celebration because his first book sold well enough for my parents to remodel our whole house." She gave her nose a funny wrinkle.

"You weren't into remodeling?"

"I liked the house the way it was. Old—built in the early twentieth century—and it had all these nooks and crannies other kids' houses didn't have. And the backyard—now that was the best part. Old fruit trees that formed a canopy. My brothers and I climbed them, ate in them." She came close to a smile. "We even had names for them."

Sully nodded her on. He didn't want to interrupt the shimmer that was taking a chance on her face.

"The spring was the best. I made caps out of the blossoms and put them on my head and ran around like a wood sprite. Nathan—that's my younger brother—he followed me all around—I called him my sprite in training."

"What about your older brother?"

She smiled off someplace. "Liam—that was short for William—he was as enchanted by the whole thing as we were. He always hid it from Daddy that he liked playing with us in the yard. It was like he was afraid that if Daddy knew he made up stories and songs for Nathan and me, he'd be packed off to military school."

Sully felt his eyes widen.

"He wouldn't have, really," Demi said quickly. "I know Daddy was disappointed that Liam wasn't an athlete, but Liam believes to this day that Daddy wanted him to follow in his footsteps and be an evangelist, and he doesn't have the preacher presence."

"Do you think that's true? That your father was disappointed?"

She stared down an invisible line of thought. No wonder she was so successful at what she did. Sully didn't usually see that kind of focus in clients.

"I don't think Liam was meant to do the kind of work Daddy did, no, but that isn't a bad thing. He's a successful writer—he's had six books published—and he lives in New Mexico—has a darling wife—she's an artist. They have a daughter."

Sully got into his cross-legged, digging-it position. "So your dad's disappointment in him could have been real, or Liam could have formed it in his own mind. What do you think?"

"I don't know," she said. "I never got to know my father that way. I was only fourteen when he died."

Sully tried not to fall out of the chair. *Oh, by the way, one of the most important people in my life passed away when I was at a significant place in my adolescence. Didn't I mention that before as one of the losses I was enumerating in our last session?*

"Now, Nathan," she said. "He's an actor. He does well in regional theater in Seattle. He's celibate—I'm sure of that. And he's one of the loneliest people I know."

"You don't know, of course, if your dad ever picked up on—"

"I don't know if Nathan's gay, if that's what you mean," she said. "But he's not a man's man, and I know he felt Daddy was disappointed in him too."

"What about you?"

"I'm not disappointed in either of my brothers. I think they're both amazing."

Sully tugged at her line. "I mean, what do they say about your current situation?"

Her face took on that incredulous twist Sully was starting to like.

"You haven't told them?"

"Uh—how 'bout no! I'd like to keep them thinking *I'm* amazing, as well."

That was about as telling a thing as he could think of right now—but Sully returned to the track she'd been doing so well with.

"So, back to your daddy," he said. "What do you remember about him?"

She visibly focused again. "Even as a kid, I was aware that people respected him, that he was someone special." She sighed. "Like I said, as an adult I've watched films of his talks, and I understand why. He was handsome, charismatic—but the thing is, he was genuine."

"Define genuine," Sully said.

"He never used God-talk, you know what I mean? He wanted people to come to the saving grace of our Lord, but he never did that one long word thing, 'invite-Jesus-Christ-into-your-heart-and-make-Him-Lord-of-your-life.' He could unpack that and make it something people could embrace—and they did."

Sully saw a spark in her eyes. He nodded her on.

"He never judged or criticized non-Christians. He was a man ahead of his time." She stopped, probably at the shake in her voice. The poster child for self-control wasn't letting go easily.

"From what Ethan tells me," Sully said, "it sounds like your theology—your whole life's work, in fact—is like your father's. True?"

"Definitely."

He was sure she didn't realize she was now sitting up in the chair as if she were in the presence of something she could count on.

"He believed that God our Creator loves us, passionately, and that our hope in this world and the next is to have a deep relationship with Him—which goes beyond doing what God says in the Law. We're allowed to have doubts and fears and unbeliefs and take those to Him. Daddy always said the Old Testament was the story of God's relationship with His people—and that if we read it as our own individual thing with God—all the promising to stay close and the straying away and the coming back cowed but ready to be stronger—he said that was how the Bible should work for us."

"And that's what you believe."

"I do." She looked down for the first time since she'd arrived. "You wouldn't know it from the way I've behaved, but I do believe that."

Sully let her be for a moment. Then he said, "Where was Daddy on the New Testament?"

She took in a breath, as if she'd been forgetting to inhale. "He loved it. Loved Jesus connecting with people. Loved to talk about forgiveness."

Sully waited for her to make a connection. She didn't.

"Would you go to your father with this if he were still alive?" he asked.

She jerked to attention. "You mean, tell him about my affair?"

"Yeah."

She put a hand over her mouth. Sully watched panic shoot through her eyes.

"I can't even imagine it," she said through her fingers. "He would be so disappointed." She tightened her hand until her knuckles drained of color. "Why did you even ask me that? Now all I can think about is him out there in the everlasting, knowing all this hideous stuff about me."

"But not forgiving you?" Sully said.

Demi stopped. Her mouth worked, but no words came.

Ding-ding, Sully thought softly. Hold it in your mind, Demi. Let it speak to you.

Let it shed Light.

When she still didn't say anything, Sully ventured into his next tender step.

"That's a lot to think about right now," he said. "Especially when you can't know how he would respond adult to adult."

He saw her swallow hard.

"I don't know what to do with it," she said. "I don't know what to do with any of it."

"Let's sit with that for a minute," Sully said. "I want to ask you a few questions—these are easy ones."

She surprised him with an attempt at a smile. "The thousand dollar questions," she said, "as opposed to the million dollar ones."

Sully smiled with her and leaned on his knees. "What are you doing to take care of yourself?"

"What do you mean?"

"Are you eating, getting rest?"

She nodded and pointed to her shirt, the same Daily Bread top she'd worn to their previous session. "My new employers are feeding me—they're my landlords too. And they're my shoulders to cry on."

There was a relief. That accounted for her still putting one foot in front of the other.

"Anything else?" Sully said. "What do you do when you're not working and hanging out with them?"

"I'm trying to get my family back," she said, a little fiercely.

"By doing what?"

She bunched up her lips.

"You're going to think this is crazy," she said.

"Crazy is my business."

"I go to the Victorian Teahouse and I sit in the window and write letters to my family. Sometimes I write them at work when I have a break—but mostly I go to the tearoom."

"Do you get any response?"

She actually laughed. "No. This is the insane part—I don't actually send them. I just say what I wish I could say to them."

Sully could no longer hold himself back. "Ding—ding-ding-ding-ding!" he said.

"Why did I know you couldn't get through this whole thing without doing that?"

"I love it! Do you know psychologists go to school for years to learn to suggest letter writing to patients? Girl, you have instincts for healing."

"Then why aren't I getting any better?" she said, again, with fist-clenching fierceness. "Why isn't my situation changing?"

"Maybe you are getting better, but you don't feel it yet. That happens—or maybe you're writing to the wrong people."

She shook her head. "I don't get it."

"Maybe this is who you need to be writing to right now." He pointed to the pixie-haired child in the picture. "Write a letter to little Demi—tell her whatever you want to tell her."

"Why?"

"Because she's the only one who goes far enough back with you to help you see how you got here. By the way . . ." He tapped the picture playfully. "Have you asked her what she believed about herself?"

"No," Demi said. "I had a hard time justifying a conversation with a snapshot when my husband has just hired a lawyer."

"Priorities."

"Uh, yeah."

Sully steepled his fingers under his nose. "You have two things going on here. You have to deal with the current, concrete situation—and yet in order to do that, you have to also devote some time to figuring yourself out. Where are you with God right now?"

She looked at him as if he'd just brought in the Rockettes.

"Are you talking to God?" Sully said. "Hiding? Shaking your fist?"

"None of the above." Once again, the eyes went to the lap. "As much as I've taught and written about God loving us and wanting a relationship with us—I can't face Him right now. I know it's ridiculous—but I see Him standing there in line with everybody else, ready to throw a rock."

She looked straight at Sully, as if she were defying him to contradict her. Sully looked straight back.

"I can completely see why you'd feel that way," he said. "Just because you ask for God's forgiveness—or at least dump on Him—doesn't mean you're instantly going to feel better. Especially with everybody else gathering stones."

She tightened. Sully thought she went a bit pale.

"Rich is doing more than gathering stones," she said. "Or maybe a lawyer is one of them."

"A weapon to punish you."

Again the panic went through her eyes, and Sully felt a need to center her before she grabbed onto her own anxiety and let it haul her off.

"This work we're doing here," he said, "isn't theoretical stuff to explain you to yourself. Understanding is going to be so much a part of your dealing with the things you can't control." He softened his voice. "Like Rich consulting an attorney."

"If I could only do something." She jerked her chin toward the picture Sully still had in his lap. "Besides write a letter to someone I used to be."

"Then do this first." Sully disengaged from the chair and picked up the river rock from his desk. "Make a list of every person who seems to have one of these in his or her hand ready to throw it at you. Include people who aren't even around anymore."

"Like my father."

"Or your mother. We haven't even gotten to her yet."

"Uh, nor do we want to," Demi said.

Sully tried not to relish too much the thought of turning to the plastic lady in the photo.

"Try making the list," he said. "Even if it makes you cry, ticks you off, makes you want to ball the thing up and flush it down the toilet—do it."

"Okay, but tell me . . ." She pulled both hands straight back through her hair. "Give me a hint how this is going to help me."

"It's going to help you see exactly what you're dealing with," Sully said. "If you're going to win this—"

"Here we go."

"You have to know your opponents. This is going to help you focus. Trust me."

That *trust me* was an automatic addition, but he could see her reaching out to grab it and examine it.

"I can't even trust myself," she said. "How can I trust you?"

"Start with trusting God. Go through the motions if you have to. Tell Him you're making the list for Him—you're tattling about all the people who aren't doing what He said we should do."

"You are a bizarre individual, do you know that?" she said.

"I've been told that. But bizarre or not, I'm telling you the truth you have to be patient with yourself in this work."

"Do I have time to be patient?" she said.

He let a grin spread across his face, and he watched her roll her eyes.

"Okay," she said. "Go with the game show thing. You've been holding back this whole time, I can tell."

"Truth or Consequences," he said. "Remember that one? If you don't tell the truth, you get the consequences right away, right?"

"Right." She winced. "I got that part."

"But when you don't *know* the truth, you have to wait for the consequences—and those consequences aren't necessarily bad."

"I'm looking for the truth," she said.

"Yes."

"The truth I didn't have before."

Even before he said it she spun her hand in the air.

"Ding-ding-ding—"

"Ding-ding," she said.

CHAPTER EIGHTEEN

One for Rich Costanas," Sully said. "One for Christopher Costanas. One for Jayne. One for Kevin—"

Sully dropped the last stone into the burlap sack with the others and shook his head. Why couldn't he ever get that guy's name straight? St. Bernard was all he could ever think of—which at least made Ethan laugh, a rare thing these days.

And why should he laugh? St. Clair, that was his name, was making noises about asking the board for his resignation. Students were protesting in front of Huntington Hall—BACK TO THE BIBLE, their signs said. Where was it they thought Ethan Kaye had been—hell itself?

They were like predators, those people at the college—only their manipulations were so subtle, half the town was on their side and they didn't even know what line they'd crossed to get there. It was time to draw them out—Estes and St. Clair and the rest. Which, Sully thought as he reached into the bag of rocks and pulled out a small clam shovel, was why he'd chosen this spot. It didn't matter where he collected rocks for his next session with Demi, or that he was digging for geoduck when the tide wasn't at its lowest, as long as he was in front of the home of Kevin St. Sanctimonious.

Sully leaned on the shovel and looked down Hood Canal. He liked this part of Puget Sound, so much that it was a shame it was polluted with the likes of Ethan's nemesis. An inland fjord, the saltwater canal wound up the Olympic Peninsula like a playful necklace of funky little towns with names like Lilliwaup and Duckabush and Dosewallips. Houses teetered playfully on the edge of the shoreline, cozying up to the water at high tide, overlooking mucky flats at low.

The tide was almost low now, which meant a few people were out digging clams and picking the oysters they'd earlier "planted" in bales of oyster seeds and put in the water.

"Kevin didn't do his research when he bought that house," Ethan had told Sully. "He was so into the square footage and the granite countertops, I don't think he stopped to think about the fact that his view was going to be a mud flat half the time."

Personally, Sully loved the mud. It was April luscious, squishing noisily under his rubber boots. He loved the geoduck thing. Spotting a squirt arching over the sand—running to find it before it stopped to bury itself and you lost your place—peering down to see the ring of the neck playing hide-and-seek. It was play Sully couldn't resist. And with any luck, it would draw out the vulture.

Sully pretended to sight a telltale squirt, loped to it, and dug. He'd learned from the slow talking, practically barnacle-covered old guy at the Hana Hana Seafood Company that sometimes you had to dig a three-foot hole to get to the overgrown clamlike animal that lived half out of its shell.

Ethan had assured him that the longer and deeper he dug, right in front of Kevin's place, the more likely Kevin would come out with his hackles up. Especially on a Tuesday afternoon—St. Clair's day to work at home. Ethan predicted he'd be sitting in his turret at his computer, surveying his domain. And that he wouldn't be happy to see Sully digging holes in "his" beach.

Sully whistled and dug for the geoduck that wasn't, tossing shovelfuls of wet pebble-sand in chaotic fashion.

"I give it thirty minutes max before he's out there," Ethan had predicted.

He was over by fifteen.

Sully pretended not to be aware of the loose-limbed figure clad in khakis and a Mr. Rogers sweater until he was almost on top of him saying, "Excuse me."

Kevin scowled through baggy-lidded eyes. Sully had the vague thought that this man had lost all muscle tone, and yet he was only in his midforties.

"Gorgeous afternoon, isn't it?" Sully said. "Ya'll don't much get weather like this up here in April, do you?" He grinned sloppily, by design. "'Course it is only April first."

"You're aware that you're digging right in front of my home?" Kevin said.

"That your place?" Sully shaded his eyes unnecessarily with the shovel, dripping mud near the toes of Kevin's loafers. Who wore loafers to walk on a mud flat?

"It is." Kevin stepped back. "Now, this is not a private beach."

"Naw, I didn't think so. Pretty hard to own a beach, isn't it?" Sully waved the shovel toward the bundles of oyster seeds, once again sending the mud into flight. "I bet you'd like to, though. I imagine you could make yourself a nice load of cash selling oysters and clams. Not to mention these babies." Sully peered down into the empty hole. "I love me some geoduck, sautéed in olive oil with some of those—what do you call 'em?—croutons?"

"Look." Kevin ran his hand over his thinning hair without touching it, disturbing not a strand. "Like I say, this isn't a private beach, but I have a photographer coming over here this afternoon to take pictures of the place."

A photographer. No way it was going to be this easy. Sully had to scramble to keep from diving right at it.

"You're not selling?"

Kevin shook his head impatiently. "No, of course not. Local magazine wants to do a piece on it."

"Now isn't that great," Sully said. He tried not to exaggerate his grin, but this was too much fun.

"It *will* be great," Kevin said, "if it's not all dug up." His mouth seemed to grow larger with the scowl, which Sully watched with fascination. "I'm just asking you to move on down the beach—if you don't mind."

"Don't mind at all." Sully stuffed his shovel into the sack with the stones, making a point of jostling the bag so the rocks would create a clatter. "You sure got a nice place."

"Thank you," Kevin said coldly, and scowled at the bag, ear cocked to the sound.

He obviously wanted to know what else was in there. Sully almost chuckled.

"Can I ask what you do for a living to afford digs like that?" He waited for Kevin to tell him it was none of his business, but the man's chest rose beneath his crossed arms.

"I'm a Christian college administrator," he said.

Sully whistled. Though Kevin smirked at him, he went on.

"I'm a missionary, actually."

"I thought missionaries lived in hovels."

"I'm blessed. The kind of mission work I do pays well—though I try to give back."

"Oh, sure," Sully said. "Ten percent probably."

"Are you a Christian?" Kevin asked.

"Absolutely."

Kevin peered at him closely, drawing his eyes into a squint that strained the bags beneath them.

"Nice to meet a fellow believer. You are a believer, right? You're more than a 'cultural Christian'?"

Holy crow.

"Yes, sir," Sully forced himself to say. "So—what's your mission?"

"You know anything about Covenant Christian College?"

"I'm new here."

"You'll find out more if you read the papers." Kevin shook his head with studied rue. "It could be one of the finest faith-based institutions of learning in the country—and it will be if I have my way."

"What's stopping it?" Sully said.

"Liberals."

"Now, when you say liberals," Sully said, "you mean—"

"Liberals believe everything's okay, as long as it's right for you," Kevin said. "There are no absolute truths—they use the Bible to pick and choose what they want to believe, and they live by that, instead of by the one clear truth that Jesus Christ is the only Son of God, and that the only way to eternal life is through a steadfast, unwavering belief in Him."

"You have people at the college who think anything goes?" Sully said. He didn't have to work hard to sound incredulous.

To his surprise, Kevin edged toward him as if he were about to impart another absolute truth. Sully smelled fabric softener on his sweater.

"You would be surprised how they disguise it," he said. "They say they're all about letting the students explore their doubts." He grunted. "They would let them explore their way right into hell if it were left to them."

"*Them* meaning the current administration," Sully said.

Kevin nodded soberly and blinked his eyes against the wind that was picking up on the canal. It struck Sully that Kevin St. Clair clearly felt angst over this. He was hurting for his faith, for those who would water it down.

But there was fear in the man's eyes as well. Blinding fear.

"We'll get them, though." Kevin looked at Sully as if he were seeing him differently. "Sorry if I was abrupt with you earlier. I want these pictures to draw people into the article, because in my interview for it, I was able to express some of these same things. I want people to know what's happening. That's the way I've saved four other colleges."

Again Sully didn't have to pretend to be surprised.

"I hope that doesn't sound like I'm bragging," St. Clair said. "The glory goes to God."

Sully couldn't say anything.

And he couldn't get away fast enough.

I composed the list of stone throwers that Sullivan Crisp told me to make in my head about seventeen times before I actually put it on paper. The thought of writing it down produced too much anxiety at first, but I was seeing him that afternoon—and Demitria Costanas did not show up for class without her homework.

When I did huddle into a corner in the prep room at Daily Bread with a cup of jasmine tea, I flushed into a sweat from the neck up. Why was it so hard?

Because I was afraid there were going to be more names on it than I'd been willing to admit.

First I did what Sullivan said and silently told God I was doing it for Him. There was no answer, so I went on.

There were the usual contestants, as Sullivan would have called them.

RICH COSTANAS

CHRISTOPHER COSTANAS

JAYNE COSTANAS

I paused on that one. How could I know what my daughter thought? It had been weeks since I'd heard her halting adolescent voice or seen the subtle changes in her mood flit through her eyes like newly unfurled butterflies looking for a place to land. She was right in the middle of coming together as a whole Jayne—how could she possibly know how she felt about me from one flit to another?

My fist tightened around the pen. Maybe I shouldn't stop and have a conversation with myself over every name. No matter what Sullivan said, I didn't have that kind of time. I only had to hear the chime of someone entering the restaurant, and I was convinced it was the sheriff with divorce papers.

Okay, who else?

KEVIN ST. CLAIR

WYATT ESTES

I rolled the pen back and forth between my palms, which were now sparkling with sweat. It wasn't that long a list. It merely cut deep.

MY MOTHER

I could not go there—though there was part of me that believed she'd secretly applaud my unfaithfulness to Rich. She had disliked him that much.

MY BROTHERS

They would at least be disappointed. Actually, Nathan would say the church had done it to me. He blamed everything on the church—including our father's death. That was a stretch from a collision with a tractor-trailer rig on a slippery night, when Daddy was exhausted from a day of fighting for the church to take a more active role on the issue of domestic violence. Nathan had made that stretch like a yoga master, and never turned back.

Liam—I no longer knew him well enough to predict how he would react to anything I did. How had that happened?

I wiped my palms on my drawstring pants. I was stalling. Putting off writing down . . .

DADDY

A flood of pain came over me like a veritable tsunami. Not because I knew what he would think or what he would say or how he would look at me if I went to him with this. It was agony because I *didn't* know. I didn't know him at all.

I had come close—it was almost time for me to know him. Two weeks before he died, he'd told me he was taking me with him to an event in New York. All I could think about was having him to myself. I already had my suitcase packed except for my toothbrush. Six weeks after my father's death my mother discovered it and unpacked it. I wasn't sure I ever forgave her for that. I even had a list of topics I wanted to discuss with my father while we were flying across the country or eating genuine New York pizza or riding in the subway. I found that crumpled in my wastebasket the day my mother unpacked the suitcase. It was such a desecration of my father's memory, I secretly ironed the list and kept it in my King James Bible. It had moved to every translation I'd used since then.

"Hi—I'll be right with you," Audrey said.

I pulled myself back to the Daily Bread and looked up at the customer Audrey was greeting, a man with a Chia-pet crop of hair set on the back of a shiny head. Before I could duck behind the swinging doors, he caught my eyes with his needley ones.

"The person I was looking for," he said.

Audrey cocked her head at me like a puppy waiting for instructions.

"It's okay," I said, though my hackles stood up one by one. I folded the list and stuck it into my apron pocket as I moved toward him.

He stood, hands in his own pockets, surveying the restaurant. He seemed surprisingly interested.

"Great place," he said.

"You here for lunch?" I said. I could always hope.

"Sure—as long as I'm here I could eat." His eyes scanned the menu Audrey had painstakingly printed on the dry erase board. "What's good?"

"Everything," I said stiffly.

"Surprise me."

He moved to a table, still scoping out the décor, the display of teas, the case of baked goods. When he sat down, I marched toward him and took the chair across from him.

"All right," I said, "let's not pretend you came in here for the split pea soup." I leaned across the salt lamp and lowered my voice. "I've told you to leave me—and my family—alone. That includes my friends who own this restaurant. They don't need a scene in here."

He shook his head, hands spread like a jazz dancer's in front of him. "No scene intended. And I'm not here to pry."

"You're a reporter. Of course you're here to pry."

"Not about your personal life—please—that's not what I'm about."

My face must have shown that I thought he was as full of soup as he could possibly be, because he stopped smiling and looked at me soberly.

"Look, we got off on the wrong foot the other day."

"You mean when you tried to take advantage of me when I was in the middle of an emotional crisis?"

"I didn't mean for you to take it that way."

"Wasn't that the way it was?"

The Chia pet bowed its head. "Maybe partly."

"Thank you."

"But I'm on a different track now. I think I can help you."

I felt my eyes narrow. "Help me how?"

"Can we restart?" He offered me his hand. "I'm Fletcher Basset."

I took his palm halfheartedly. "You made that name up, right?"

"No, I think I just lived up to it."

"Sniffing around in people's business?"

We both pulled our chins in.

"I do that, too," he said. "But like I said, I may have information that could be helpful to you."

"What's our friend having for lunch?" Mickey said from the doorway. She wore her is-this-character-bothering-you look.

"Give me the split pea, please," Fletcher said. "It comes highly recommended."

Mickey looked at me, and I nodded. When she disappeared, with one last sweep of suspicion over the basset hound, I folded my arms on the table.

"Why would you want to help me?" I said.

"Because I want the truth." He looked straight at me with berry-blue eyes. "I'm trying to get to the truth of what's happening at the college."

"I don't know anything about it anymore," I said. "I've—retired."

He glanced at my shirt. "So I see."

I scraped the chair back, but he put his palm on the table. His eyes grew warm.

"Please," he said. "I think if you know the truth too, you'll be able to help both me and yourself."

"What kind of help do I need?"

"You need to be at that college," he said. "Every student I've talked to—except the ones out there protesting, who, it turns out, don't know you from Eve and have no idea why they're there—except one little jerk named—" He pulled a pad out of his jacket pocket and frowned at it. "Travis Chapman. You know him?"

I nodded. He wasn't one of my Faith and Doubt students, but he was in one of my sections of Religion 102. He spent most of his time regarding me as if I were an intrusion on his day, but I had no idea why. We'd never exchanged two words.

"The rest of them," Fletcher went on, "are saying you and Dr. Archer were the backbone of the program."

"Well, we're not anymore," I said. "Look—it's over. I have more important things to think about."

I got to my feet, his protesting hand notwithstanding. He slanted against the chair, but his eyes seemed to embrace the challenge. I wanted to slap him. I was experiencing that urge a lot lately.

"I don't believe anything is more important than what you were doing at that college," he said. "At least not according to your students. And I think you should know that your partner—"

"What partner?" My voice was shrill and I didn't care.

"Zachary Archer," he said. "He has no intention of picking up the pieces of the program—and if you don't, it dies. Now it seems to me that—"

I gripped the back of the chair. "How could you possibly know what his intentions are? He's disappeared. Nobody even knows where he is."

"That part's true. I don't know his location. But he hasn't disappeared. I interviewed him by phone."

The air went dead.

"I can't reveal how I got in touch with him." Fletcher looked at me closely. "You really didn't know he was around someplace, did you?"

"Nor did I care," I made myself say. "Why should I?"

"Wasn't he your closest colleague?"

I backed away from the table. "I'll make sure you get your lunch," I said. "And after this—stay away from me."

"Look, I didn't mean to upset you. I want to help—"

"Help me by getting completely out of my life."

I kept myself from shaking until I got into the prep room, doors swinging behind me. And even then I didn't get the chance. Audrey stood with her back to me, hunched over the chopping table, shoulders shaking.

"Audrey?" I said.

She straightened abruptly and turned to me, slapping at tears with her fingertips and working her face toward a smile she couldn't possibly pull off.

"What is it, honey?" I said.

"Don't you hate men sometimes?" she said.

"Often. Why do we hate men today?"

Her face crumpled. "Because they make you think they care about you and they make you open yourself up to them and then they stop calling and they stop returning your calls and they totally screw up your life."

Oscar came out of the walk-in freezer, took one look at us, and retreated into it again.

"Are we talking about Boy?" I said.

She nodded and put her arms around me, face in my T-shirt. "I don't know if he's ever going to get to name status. But he's C.J.—and I think I love him, Dr. C."

I tightened my arms around her. "I'm sorry you're hurting."

"I hate this. I didn't do anything wrong, but I feel like a loser."

She wept the way I had for hours on end the past few endless days. Her crying swept over me, and then got into me, and suddenly I was holding her out in front of me, both hands on her shoulders.

"Listen to me, Audrey," I said. "You are not a loser—that is the most ridiculous thing I have ever heard. You cannot let some guy who can't even make a commitment define who you are, do you hear me?"

Her eyes grew almost fearful, which may have been because my hands were squeezing her biceps.

"He has lied to you with his promises, and now you're the one who's taking all the foolishness and the self-put-downs. Don't do that." I pulled her back to me and held on. "Promise me that you won't do that."

Whether she did or not, I couldn't tell. She cried in my arms and made me miss my Jayne—and for the first time, hate Zachary Archer. From the broken pit of my soul.

CHAPTER NINETEEN

Sully put the last stone on the pyramid he had built on his desk when she knocked on the office door—so hard the whole thing teetered off balance and tumbled all over the desktop.

"Come in," Sully said, "but only if you're not armed."

Demitria shoved the door open and stood there, flushed and fiery-eyed.

Holy crow. The controlled Dr. Costanas on a tear.

"You wanted me to talk," she said. "I'm ready to talk."

She stuck herself into the papasan chair, rocking backward and recovering herself like a kid determined not to fall out of that swing. Sully slanted against the desk.

"You want to take a minute to breathe—maybe get centered?"

"No, I do not. I want to get this out before I explode." She pulled at her hair with both hands. "How could I have been so stupid? This is just getting worse."

"All right, then let's—"

"He's out there!" she said.

"He's out there."

"Yeah, sitting around, letting me take the flack for this whole thing by myself. He hasn't 'disappeared.' He's a complete psycho—and I thought I loved him! I threw away my whole life."

She stopped abruptly, chest expanding as she heaved in air. He could see her reeling herself in.

"Sorry," she said.

"For what? This is exactly what I think you need to be doing." He grinned. "If I didn't suspect you'd deck me I'd give you a series of dings."

She folded her knees up to her chest.

"I take it we're talking about Zach Archer," Sully said.

She shuddered. "A reporter told me he's been in touch with him—that he has no intention of coming back."

Sully eased himself into his own chair. "Do you want him to come back?"

"No!"

Sully waited.

"Yes—I want him to take his share of the responsibility."

Sully waited longer.

"Although I don't know why. What difference would it make?"

She shrugged, but Sully put up his hand. "Try not to do that, Demi," he said.

"Do what?"

"Slough off things because it doesn't make sense to be upset about them. If you're upset, you need to let yourself feel it. Then we can really look at it."

She gave him a look. "I'm upset."

Sully smiled. "And you do it so well. Nice job." He propped a foot up. "I was hoping you'd get angry at somebody besides yourself."

"Oh, I'm still ticked off at myself," Demi said. "How could I have been such an idiot? I'm like a little coed who fell for some guy's line—only I should know better. You know what really ticks me off?"

"Tell me."

"He got away without believing I meant we were done. Why does that bother me so much?"

"You really want to know?"

She gave him the look. "What else am I here for?"

He wasn't sure she was going to like it, but he had to go with it. He took the first step gingerly.

"As long as you still want something from Zach, you're still in the affair."

"No, I am not."

He stopped.

"Okay—okay—go on." She chewed at her lower lip.

"I get the sense that you'd like to have it all wrapped up with a bow."

"Right."

"But here's the thing—if you have a neat wrap-up, you leave with a final kiss and the feeling that you're abandoning something good." Sully leaned forward. "How does that leave it? Done—or still lovely in your memory?"

She watched him with that focus he could imagine her having in the classroom.

"Neat and tidy," she said finally. "But if it's rotten and lousy, like this has been, I won't wish I had it back."

"Ding-ding," Sully said.

"Yeah." Her voice gave. "We better get to that premise fast, or I'm going to have to believe I went completely nuts."

"You ready to get to work?"

She nodded. Sully waited until she got her face where she wanted it to be.

"You've noticed my collection of stones," he said.

"Yeah," she said, even before her eyes actually lit on them.

"There's one for every person on your list."

"Like the story of the adulteress." She twisted her mouth. "I'm not sure you have enough though. What do we do with them?"

"That's the point," Sully said. "You can't do anything about the people holding the rocks. Jesus didn't even order them to lay down their weapons."

Her eyes were now on the scattered pile.

"He said, 'If any one of you is without sin, let him be the first to throw a stone at her.'"

She saddened, as if the right string had just been pulled. "I wish He were here now."

"Who says He isn't?"

That thought seemed to make her squirm.

"You still having trouble going to Jesus with this?" Sully asked.

"Ya think?" She lowered her eyes from the pile to her lap.

"The woman in the story didn't exactly go to Him of her own free will," Sully said. "She was pretty much dragged."

He let that sink in. Demi finally looked at him.

"I know the feeling," she said.

"So as long as you're here—on the ground in front of Him, as it were—what does He say?"

She closed her eyes, as if the quote were written on her lids. "'Go now and leave your life of sin'—I think that's what it is in the NIV."

Sully stayed silent and watched impatience gather on her face.

"That's what I'm doing!" she said. "I'm not sinning anymore—I could cut my heart out for doing it in the first place!" She doubled her fists and banged them on her lap. "I'm never going to do that again—but what good does saying that do me now?"

Sully selected his next words carefully. "How do you know you won't do it again?"

She nearly convulsed from the chair.

"Wait, there's more," Sully said.

"There better be."

"You don't know you won't do it again unless you understand why you did it in the first place. I personally think that's why you haven't taken it to Jesus."

"Then why did I do it?" Her voice broke, and the words tumbled like the stones. "I have to know."

"I'm walking you through that, remember?"

"Do it." She shook her head. "I don't know if I can stand what I'm about to find out about myself."

"Demi," Sully said, "I'll risk it all on this: there is nothing you're going to discover that is plain evil, because that isn't you."

She gripped the sides of the chair and pressed her lips together. "Then let's do it," she said.

"You sure?"

"Yes."

"All right. Back to the post-9/11 days. You said Rich withdrew so far into himself you couldn't see him anymore. How did you put it—as if he were disappearing before your eyes."

"Yeah."

"You tried to pull him out of his depression—you even uprooted your whole life to bring him here, hoping it would help."

"Yes."

"But it didn't. Now—how were you feeling about yourself about then?"

"Like the most ineffectual, incompetent woman I could imagine."

Ah, she was racking up points.

"You weren't mad at Rich?"

"No." She chewed at her lip again. "Okay, yes—but then I'd feel guilty because he lost so much, why shouldn't he be depressed?"

"And hadn't you lost a lot too?"

"Well, yeah, but . . ."

"You were losing him."

She didn't even have to answer. The emotion drained from her face right into the sad cave of her chest.

"And when in the course of this did Mr. Wonderful come along?"

Her laugh was unexpected. "About nine months ago now—that's when we got to be close friends."

"Did you tell Zach what was going on with Rich?"

"Yes, like an idiot."

Sully buzzed.

She glared. "I won't call myself names if you won't make that obnoxious sound."

"No promises." He nodded her on.

"We were friends—good friends," she said. "It got to the point where my friendship with him was better than my relationship with Rich. I started confiding in him—what was I thinking?"

"Buzz!"

"Stop!"

Sully tilted his head at her. "I want you to see how often you beat yourself up. I know you realize what you did was wrong. But your guilt isn't necessarily going to get you to the answers you're looking for."

She sighed—a sigh so deep Sully felt it in his own chest.

"Okay," she said. "Let's just go on."

"What did Zach say to you when you confided in him—besides

the fact that he thought Rich was a complete moron for not taking everything you had to offer?"

She pulled her knees back up, feet propped on the edge of the chair, and hugged her thighs. "That Rich was cutting off his nose to spite his face. That I was the most nurturing woman he'd ever known. That I knew how to meet a man's needs."

"And when did he stop talking about Rich's needs and start talking about his own?"

Sully watched her struggle with that.

"I don't know," she said.

"Ding-ding. It's all so subtle when someone's giving you a chance to be who you so long to be."

Demi flattened her forehead against her knees. "But why did I let it go so far?"

"You're talking about sex," Sully said.

She didn't look up. "I'm starting to hate that word."

"Sex?"

"Ugh. I loathe myself when I think about being with Zach."

"Let me ask you this," Sully said, "and you do have the right not to play this round if you don't want to."

"What the heck. I've humiliated myself this much—I might as well go for it."

Sully watched the top of her head. "What was sex like with Rich before the affair?"

The head came up. "What does that have to do with it? If you're going to tell me that the reason I slept with Zach Archer is because I wasn't—getting enough—"

"I didn't say that, but if you want to go there . . ."

"Okay—no. It had been two years since Rich and I had—been intimate."

Sully forced himself not to let his mouth drop open.

"But that still doesn't excuse what I did. I'm a Christian! I know better!"

"Doesn't excuse it," Sully said, "but, Demi, it explains the temptation. It shows you why you were vulnerable." He held out a palm.

"It wasn't the temptation itself that was wrong. Zach and Rich both had a hand in that." He held out the other one. "It was giving it permission to become sin that got you in trouble."

"I should have resisted." Demi's face was falling hard and fast.

"No, you should have run—as long as we're talking shoulds. Any idea why you didn't hightail it in the other direction?"

"It just felt good—and I'm not talking about sex—totally." She looked down at her lap. "I liked who I was when I was with him. It was like I was the person I wanted to be."

"It's almost impossible to run from that," Sully said, "especially when you have to make the decision to run alone." He watched until she lifted her chin. "And Demi, you were completely alone."

"I don't know what you mean," she said.

"The right thing to do when you first felt attracted to Zach was to go to Rich, confess that to him, and ask him to help you. Give him a chance to step up to the plate."

Demi lowered her chin until she looked straight into his eyes. "You're kidding me, right?"

"No. I'm completely serious."

"I don't know what Rich would have done if I'd said that to him." The chin began to quiver.

"Under the circumstances, given his state of mind," Sully said, "what's your best guess?"

She nodded, as if they both already knew the answer. "I don't think he even would have heard me."

"Ding-ding-ding," Sully said softly. "I'm not giving you an out, Demi—this is the first step in your understanding yourself and forgiving yourself. And that takes us one step closer to that premise we're looking for."

There was no fight this time, no argument. "I'm tired," she said. "I don't know if I can think anymore."

"Good call," Sully said. "But I want you to sit for a few minutes, until you feel less raw."

"As if I could even move."

She closed her eyes, and Sully went to the desk and moved the stones back into their bag, leaving only one. It was the last big rock he'd collected after Kevin St. Clair left him on the beach to greet his photographer. This one Sully held until she looked up.

"You want an assignment?"

"I haven't totally done the first one. I don't talk to the picture." She sighed. "Will it move me out of where I am right now?"

"We won't know until you try."

She let out a long, resounding buzz. Sully couldn't hold back a laugh.

"Wrong answer, Sullivan," she said. "You were supposed to say, 'Absolutely. This will help you stop thinking of yourself as an incurable loser.'"

"It absolutely *might.*"

"That's the best you can do?"

"That's it."

She sat up and eyed the rock. Sully held it up in both long-fingered hands.

"I want you to take this stone with you," he said, "and find a use for it besides throwing it at yourself. Use it for a doorstop or polish your feet with it."

"Polish my feet?"

"Don't women do that—use stones to get the calluses off their feet?"

She put up her hand. Her eyes were returning to their wry state. "Stick to psychology, okay? Don't start giving out beauty tips."

"Noted," Sully said. "Whatever use you pick, do it when you get the urge to throw it at yourself. When you start calling yourself names or asking questions you can't answer except with more names—turn to this rock, even in your mind, and remember that you've made a mistake, but that mistake can lead to something besides stoning yourself. You can use it to figure yourself out."

"Tell me again how this is going to get me back to my family."

"You can only do what Jesus tells *you* to do: go and sin no more. Whether the rest of them put down their stones is up to them."

She put her forehead to her knees and slowly began to rock.

"I hate this, Sullivan," she said.

"Yeah, Demi," he said. "I hate it *for* ya."

As he watched her sway back and forth, he fought the urge that never went away, despite the years of training and the words of wisdom he himself had written. Don't become overly involved with your client. Let her feel what she needs to feel—don't try to take it away. The only way out is through.

But holy crow, it was hard not to lift the chin of this hurting woman and try to make it right.

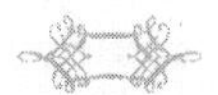

So hard, in fact, that he sent Isabella's heads out to be cleaned and the valves reseated. He had to let Demi work her way through the mire, but that approach didn't apply to Ethan Kaye. That situation he could speed along. Time to get hot on this photographer thing.

Kevin St. Clair, Sully now felt, had nothing to do with the procuring of the photographs. He was willing to use them, but he was way too eager for people to know about his mission to actually be able to pull off a clandestine plot. He'd have wanted to tell everybody who would listen exactly what he'd planned.

The answer had to lie with Wyatt Estes, and Sully's only link to him, tenuous at best, was Tatum Farris. Sully would rather down a bottle of pancake syrup than eat another piece of pink champagne cake, but he used it as an excuse to go back to the bakery. He'd be smoother this time.

He was staring into the case full of puffy castles, trying to work up an appetite for pink frosting, when Tatum appeared behind it, her chin barely rising above the glass top, feathered earrings swinging from her lobes. Sully wondered vaguely if anybody else even worked there.

"I'm surprised you came back," she said. "Your usual?"

Trying not to gag, Sully pointed to a small piece in the front. She slid out the thickest one in the case. Sully could see the rest of his bottle of Pepto-Bismol in his near future.

"Why wouldn't I come back?" he said.

"Because I was a complete snot to you last time you were here."

He pulled out his wallet, but she shook her head at him, face impassive—her default expression.

"This one's on me."

Sully shrugged. "I'll let you do that—this once."

He sat down and swallowed hard as she came out from behind the counter and put the cake in front of him. Maybe he could cut it up and shove it around on the plate the way he used to do with spinach so his mother would think he'd actually eaten some.

"Coffee with three sugars and two creams, right?" She lifted a brow. "I don't know why you even bother to put the coffee in there."

"Definitely coffee. And hold the sugars." As she headed for the pot, Sully said, "I actually came in here to apologize to you."

"For what?"

"For prying into your personal life."

"I don't actually have a personal life anymore, so you wouldn't have gotten far anyway."

Sully nodded and cut off a small, precise piece of cake with his fork, ready for a diabetic coma.

Tatum set his coffee on the table and folded her arms across her apron as she leaned against a case full of Easter cookies. "I'm the one who should be apologizing," she said, "although that's not my style."

"Really," Sully said.

"But since you're the first decent guy I've met in, like, years, I figure I at least owe you an explanation."

Sully shoveled a hunk into his mouth, making it impossible to do anything but frown and shake his head.

"I was having one of my I-hate-men days. Nothing personal. I just got out of a relationship that was going absolutely nowhere. Two of them, actually. Anyway, to answer your question about my uncle."

Pressing a napkin to his lips, Sully let out half the mouthful and squirreled the whole thing away in his lap. "Your uncle—oh, we were talking about Wyatt Estes."

"Daddy Warbucks." Tatum picked up his plate and headed for

the cake case again. Sully didn't protest, not with her taking him exactly where he wanted to go.

"Then he *is* generous with his money."

Tatum grunted. "Let's say he gives a ton to Covenant Christian."

"Ah."

"He also expects a ton in return, if you get me."

"I'm not sure I do."

She gave him a look as she approached with yet another mound of cake. "Yes, you do. As long as they run things the way he wants them to, he keeps opening his checkbook."

"And how does he want them run?"

She leveled her eyes at him. "For an auto mechanic you sure are interested in the academic world."

"I like to expand my horizons."

"Yeah, well, if you're counting on CCC, your horizons could shrivel up and disappear."

"No kidding." Sully fixed his therapist's poker face into place. "That bad, huh?"

"You don't even want to know. Uncle Wyatt may have closed his checkbook for good." A shadow passed through her eyes. "Wouldn't bother me. I have major issues with that place."

She planted her hands on the back of the chair opposite Sully's and pressed in, lips parted as if she were going to spew something across the table. But an engine firing on only three cylinders beat outside the front window, and they both looked. Tatum rocked the chair as she let go and stormed toward the door. Her shoes squealed to a halt halfway there. She thrust her arm toward Sully, finger pointed.

"Don't go away," she barked at him. "And don't let him leave either. Tell him I have something for him."

She tossed off the last part as she slapped open the swinging door into the kitchen and disappeared.

Sully rose halfway from the chair and watched a twentyish kid haul himself out of a scarred pickup truck. He seemed too tall for himself. In fact, as he lumbered toward the door, hands poked into his pockets, it appeared nothing about him had caught up to him, including his focus, which darted in six directions before he reached for the doorknob. He stepped in and blinked around the bakery.

Sully couldn't decide whether he was unfamiliar with the place or just had bad contact lenses. At any rate, this could not be the object of Tatum's rage.

"Tatum here?" he said, though he wasn't looking at Sully.

"She's in the back."

Sully was tempted to add, "Run for your life, kid," but he simply said, "She said not to leave. She has something for you."

"You better believe I do." Tatum made an entrance through the doors carrying a box almost bigger than she was. An assortment of items stuck out of the top, from a chartreuse teddy bear to a stale French baguette. Tatum marched up to the blinking kid and dropped the box without deliberation on his feet.

He yelped, but took a full ten seconds to even begin to pry his toes out.

Tatum remained in front of him, hands on hips, breathing audibly.

"What did you do that for?" he said.

"Don't even start with me, Van," Tatum said. "Because you do not *even* want to hear my list of reasons for wanting to break everything in here over your head. In fact, if you don't get out, I may."

Her chest visibly rose and fell, and the menace in her voice bordered on homicidal. Sully wouldn't have put it past her to go for the baguette. He cleared his throat, but neither of them looked at him.

"I still don't get why you're mad at *me,*" he said. "I'm not the one who—"

"Yes, do announce it to the entire bakery, would you, Van?" Tatum wafted a hand in Sully's direction, and Van shrank inside his flannel shirt.

Sully was having a hard time believing Tatum had ever been involved with this guy.

Van's chin quivered.

"Oh, please, don't make a spectacle of yourself," Tatum said. "Just go—and don't let the door hit you in the butt on the way out."

Sully felt a pang for the kid as he hunched over the box and turned toward the door. Naturally, half the contents spilled out, as inevitable as Tatum's eye-rolling exit to the kitchen.

"Let me give you a hand," Sully said.

Van scooped up two books and an over-sized valentine, dropping one of the volumes before he could get it into the box. Sully leaned over to pick up a square that floated his way—a picture of Tatum, obviously in happier times. She teased the camera with her smile, even then lighting up the corner of the bakery.

"You want this?" Sully said.

Van snatched it from him and after three tries managed to cram it into his back pocket. Somehow he got out the door.

Tatum emerged from the kitchen as the three cylinders banged the pickup down Callow Avenue.

"Now you see why I hate men," Tatum said. "No offense."

"None taken."

Sully watched her face smooth back into its mask.

"Thanks for staying."

"Didn't look like you needed any protection." Sully quickly scraped his chair back and stood up. "What do I owe you for the coffee?"

"There wasn't enough coffee in that cup for me to charge you." She almost smiled.

As Sully passed the cobwebbed hardware store, he forced his focus away from Tatum's veritable banquet of issues and back to Wyatt Estes.

Uncle Wyatt could be about to pull his funding. Did he smell another scandal? Was Kaye about to get blindsided again?

Sully wiped his mouth with the back of his hand and looked at the smear of pink on his skin. Ugh. He hadn't seen the last of champagne cake.

CHAPTER TWENTY

I tried to find a use for that stupid rock. I took it in the car with me to at least remind myself not to put myself down, though that didn't work well. On Wednesday I brought it into the prep room to observe while I rolled silverware. It seemed crazy at first—what wasn't?—until I discovered something strangely soothing about contemplating an inanimate object. At least it couldn't accuse me.

Maybe the rock gave me the insane burst of courage to call Rich. Or maybe my concern for Jayne just overrode anything he might say to me.

Almost.

He gave me monosyllabic answers at first, until I said I was concerned about her spending so much time alone.

"You had to rub it in, didn't you?"

I stopped.

"You're the reason I'm working nights, Demitria."

"This is not about you," I said. "I'm trying to talk to you about our daughter."

"She's fine. We're working it out. Anything else?"

I cramped my fingers around the phone. "Just because I was an unfaithful wife doesn't mean I'm not a good mother."

"Oh, you're a great mother." The serrated sarcasm sawed through me. "Only, great mothers don't lie to their kids so they can go off and sleep with somebody who isn't their father."

"Rich—for Pete's sake!" I said. And then I heard the click of me hanging up on him.

Sullivan torqued a head bolt down and thought it was too bad he couldn't do family therapy with the whole Costanas clan. He glanced at the manual he had propped on a cart. The head bolts had to be torqued down in order . . .

Rich would probably require years of extensive healing help. Sully had people who could do wonders with him.

And then there were the two children.

Sully torqued the wrench.

First get them out of that hole of a house with the despondent father—then shake the attitude out of that Christopher kid.

Dang, was the bolt stripped or what?

Typically kids that age turned against the offending parent, but these two didn't seem to have considered for a second what their mother had gone through with a depressed husband—especially since they themselves had obviously suffered in his silences too.

Sully wiped his hands and frowned at the manual. He was as stuck with those heads as he was with the ones on his car.

He tossed the rag and went into the office, where a cold frappuccino waited for him in the tiny refrigerator he'd picked up at a church yard sale. He'd offered one to Demi at their session yesterday, but she'd been too busy pacing—until he asked her the question that had catapulted her out of there like she was on the end of a large rubber band.

He was enumerating, with her help, all the things she'd lost in this crisis—including the ego boost she'd been getting from Zach. She gave Sully a death stare on that last one, but she didn't leave. Not then.

"You feel like you've lost everything," Sully said to her. "Including yourself."

"I have."

"So, then . . ."

He hesitated, but she stopped pacing and motioned him on.

"Then, if Rich divorces you—so what?"

He was sure the brown eyes would implode.

"Did you just ask me *so what*?"

"I know it matters, Demi. But you say you've lost everything already. Some of that you may not be able to get back. Some of it you can, with or without Rich." He held his breath.

She folded her arms across her chest, eyes swimming. "You're asking if I'm worth salvaging if I don't have my family back."

Sully ran his finger along his nose.

"I don't know," she said.

"That's better than no."

"Is it?"

"It's the only question you need to answer."

The slim shoulders strained. "Do you have a game show for this one?"

Sully nodded slowly. "I think it's *Survivor*, Demi."

"I hate that show."

"Uh-huh."

"I hate *this* show."

"I understand."

"I have to go."

There had been no desperation in her eyes, so he'd let her go to wrestle with herself.

He hoped she was winning.

He downed the rest of the frappuccino and headed back to the garage. When he leaned over to pick up the manual that had slid to the floor, he noticed the front door was slightly ajar. A paper bag printed with DAILY BREAD lay inside.

Bread? A stink bomb? A thanks-for-every-thing letter?

Actually, it was more than one letter Sully discovered as he emptied the contents onto the tool table. There were at least twenty, all folded neatly and each with a name printed in a different color ink. A single sheet floated on top of the pile.

Sullivan,

Who was that who left you in a huff? I don't even know who

I am anymore. Maybe that's what I need to find out. These letters are who I think I am. It's a start, huh?

Blessings,
Demi

Sully unfolded a few with the tips of his greased fingers. There were several to Rich. As many to Christopher. There was even one to Ethan Kaye. Most of them, though, were for Jayne—all in purple ink and written in curly cursive.

He turned to the Impala and gave her a grin. "Well, holy crow, Isabella," he said. "Holy crow."

CHAPTER TWENTY-ONE

A siren screamed me out of a coma-sleep early Friday morning. I came up on the window seat, straight into the covers-clutching, cardiac-arresting position of the fireman's wife, like I'd done for twenty-one years. The prayers cried out before I knew I was awake.

God—don't let it be Rich!

I squeezed everything so the fear wouldn't take me into places no one who loves a fireman should go: into suffocating smoke and flesh-eating flames and beams-turned-to-tinder crashing onto heads even helmets couldn't protect. Some wives didn't want to know anything about the fire-beasts their husbands fought, and most wouldn't have a scanner in the house. Others went to as many fires as their husbands did, cameras in hand. I always lay still and listened to the siren wail its agony and waited for the call.

Only tonight, there would be no reassuring ring from my husband. The thought that there might never be again drove me into the kitchen, where I flooded the room, and my spiraling psyche, with light.

Four AM. An acceptable hour to make coffee and start the day.

Another siren broke in, shrieked through our sleeping burg, faded to carry its fear to the crisis. A two-alarm.

I found myself cursing Sullivan Crisp with his, "If Rich divorces you, so what?"

This was "so what." I'd never know what was happening to him. I would be cut off from his breathing and his burping and the assurance of his still-existence at any given moment.

I snatched up the coffeepot. With or without him, I would keep breathing, keep making coffee.

So what if he divorced me? I would go on living. But who would I be?

I looked at the tangle of covers I'd dumped on the floor below the window seat. I was enmeshed in Rich even in my sleep. Whatever "premise" had claimed me and told me to risk that by giving a chunk of myself to Zach Archer—it was gone now.

So what if Rich divorced me? There would be an emptiness in my soul I could never fill. I put my head all the way down onto the cool counter tile and wept—because I might lose my husband.

It was a Mickey-cry I decided, when I was done and had all manner of gunk and tears to wipe off my face and the countertop. It was one of those cleansing cries that left me knowing something.

I loved. Wasn't that goodness in me, that I could love like this?

I wasn't the rotten excuse for a woman I'd named myself. I didn't know what to do with that. I only knew it.

Which was why I got dressed one more day and climbed into the car and drove through the morning mist toward the Daily Bread.

I realized halfway there I hadn't drunk that cup of coffee I'd poured. I flipped on the blinker and swerved into a parking lot, headed for the ubiquitous strip mall java shop.

As I pulled up in front I could see a line of people inside, waiting to order their lattes, so I leaned back to close my eyes—until the Jeep's plastic window rattled and I jerked up to a hooded figure, one brazen hand saluted over his forehead so he could peer in.

"*What?*" I said.

"Is this what you do all day?" a familiar voice said.

"Christopher?"

I fumbled to unzip the window.

"You just hang out at coffee shops?" he said when I got it open.

I looked around me. "No—what are you doing?"

He pushed his tailbone out so he could rest his lanky arms on the Jeep door.

"I saw you in traffic," he said.

"And you followed me?"

"I thought I'd see what you do all day."

I gripped the steering wheel. "I've told you in my e-mails that I'm working on Main. I even gave you my schedule—"

"I don't open your e-mails."

I gripped harder. "But you'll follow me into a parking lot to find out what I'm doing."

It was ludicrous, and I would have laughed, except that I saw his eyes dart away. It was the look he used to get as a little boy when he knew I was about to discover his ulterior motive for sharing a cookie with his sister or dashing off from the dinner table to do his homework without a cattle prod involved.

I sat up straighter. "You're checking up on me to make sure I'm not with someone."

"*Should* I be checking up on you?"

"You obviously think so."

"Why wouldn't I, Mom? With your record—if it looks like a tawdry clandestine meeting—and it smells like one—and it sounds like one—"

"Christopher," I said. "I want you to shut up—now."

He was startled enough to let go of the door. His next words were stiff. "I thought you should know what you've done to Jayne."

His words started through me like an ice pick, but I flung open the passenger door. "Get in."

"I don't—"

"I said get in."

He smacked my door frame with both hands, his version of having the last word. My mind raced as he crossed in front of the Jeep, shoulders hulking forward. How could I do anything to Jayne when I couldn't even talk to her?

Christopher folded half of himself inside the car. The other leg hung out in the drippy rain.

"What about Jayne?" I said.

"This is totally messing her up."

"Enough with the guilt trip. What's wrong?"

"She's grounded until, like, her sixteenth birthday. I told Dad to take her cell phone away, which he did."

"She's alone at night, and he's not letting her use her cell?" I scraped my nails through my hair. "What if something happens?"

"I'm there." His mouth went into a grim line.

"Why is she under all this punishment?" I said. "What could she possibly have done?"

"She's turning into you."

"What?"

He squinted one eye, as if I'd blown his eardrum. "We went to see her play."

I knew that. I'd spent that entire weekend looking at my watch, picturing her on stage writhing under the imagined grip of witchcraft, and swelling to her curtain calls. And I'd sobbed my gut out.

"She played this—well, basically, whore."

"She played Abigail Williams," I said. "She was a confused, messed-up teenage girl!" I shook myself. "It was a *character,* for Pete's sake."

"Yeah, well, Dad was ticked off at you for letting her take the role."

I chomped down on my lip. I wouldn't get into the fact that I'd tried to discuss everything Jayne did with Rich, and he'd grunted, "Whatever you think." I waved Christopher on.

"So afterwards, she comes up to us in the lobby and asks Dad if she can go to a cast party." Christopher gave the Rich-hiss. "She didn't notice he was already having a hernia. He said no, and she freaked."

"And he grounded her for that?"

"No, he grounded her for e-mailing her boyfriend about what a jerk Dad was."

"Her boyfriend?" I said.

"Oh, it gets worse," Christopher said.

He was nearly licking his chops, dispensing, at a maddening pace, information he obviously knew would shred my heart.

"What boyfriend?" I said evenly.

"The kid who played John Proctor. Josh somebody."

"Josh Elliston?" I said. "They've been friends since sixth grade."

"They're more than friends now. She told this kid everything about our current family 'issues' in an e-mail—so who knows who else has found out by now."

"Wait." I smeared my hand across my eyes. "How did your father find out what she wrote online? He can barely turn the computer on."

Christopher didn't have to answer.

"*You* told him," I said. "You got into her account—"

"Somebody's got to—"

"Not *you*!"

"Then who? Dad's barely functioning. He wouldn't eat if I didn't cook. He wouldn't shower if I didn't hose him off—"

"But you are not Jayne's father. She has another parent." I drove my thumb into my chest. "I am still her mother, Christopher. Now you tell me—" I got closer still, until I could feel his breath catch against my chin. "What have you told her about herself? Tell me you have not used the word *whore* with your sister."

"What do you think I am?"

"I don't know," I said. "At this point I do not know. Now you tell me."

He pulled back, far enough for me to see that some of the arrogance had seeped from his eyes. "I haven't said anything to her. She holes up in her room all the time."

"Are you feeding *her*?" I said. "Hosing *her* down?"

"It's not that bad."

"I can't see how it could not be."

I squeezed the steering wheel to keep from screaming. Christopher closed in on himself, the way Rich did.

"Listen to me," I said. "I am going to pick Jayne up from school today. Do not try to intercept me, and do not call the school and tell them not to let her go with me. You have no right to interfere with my seeing your sister. Am I clear?"

"Whatever."

"Christopher. Am. I. Clear?"

He gave his head another jerk, this time away from me. "Yeah," he said.

He wrenched himself out of the car and bent over to glare in at me. "I don't see where you get off being so self-righteous," he said. And then he walked away.

I didn't see it either. I only knew what I felt—what I heard—what I knew—because I loved.

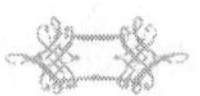

"It's on the house today," Tatum said to Sully when he ambled into the bakery that Friday afternoon.

That wasn't the bad news it might have been if he hadn't chewed a half dozen Tums on the way over. "What's the occasion?" he said.

"A thank-you for helping me with Van."

"The ex-boyfriend?"

"The freak show." She slid the knife cleanly into the quarter of a pink champagne she'd removed from under a glass dome. "With you here, he didn't get all dramatic. You want your usual sugar and milk with a shot of coffee?"

Sully grinned. He settled at a table and pulled one of Demi's letters out of his jacket pocket. Who said men couldn't multi-task? Tatum disappeared into the kitchen and emerged carrying a stack of cookie sheets dotted with Easter-egg shaped cookies. While she fanned them out on the display racks, Sully read.

Dear Christopher,

I don't know why—with everything that's going on, you'd think this would be the last thing on my mind—but I've been thinking a lot lately about you and me on 9/11. I've been wondering if you remember the way I do, like every detail is etched into the glass of my brain.

When I heard the first tower had been hit, I canceled classes and went to your school. You remember? I picked you and Jayne up, and we were on our way home when the second tower came down, and we'd hardly gone through the front door when the Pentagon was struck. A flawless, blue-sky day, and yet the world was coming to an end.

I will always have the picture of your face in my mind, son. You'd led a life full of love and safety and security, with your

Mama and Papa Costanas and your Uncle Eddie whom you loved almost as much as you did your dad. I'd never seen panic in you before. You went deathly white and your eyes were absolutely wild, and I couldn't hold you. Jayne crawled into my lap and rubbed my arm over and over, as if she were more afraid for me than for herself and her dad. But you—you kept saying, "Dad's in there. Uncle Eddie's in there. We have to do something!"

A phone call from the ombudsman confirmed that. Everybody had been called in. I could hardly keep you from running out the front door and all the way to the World Trade Center. The three of us huddled in front of the TV in that bright little living room in our row house in Queens. I tried to keep my voice low and level as I interpreted what was happening to the two of you. I thought it pointless to try to distract you. You were firefighter's children. You'd always known the dangers. You'd always known what the sirens could mean for us. Your bloodline told you to keep a vigil until everyone returned safely to the station.

Would you agree it was the longest day either of us could remember? Every siren call made me want to scream. My neck was strained from trying to catch a glimpse of your father on the TV screen. I gave up trying to keep you on the couch. You wanted to sit directly in front of the television, and every few minutes you'd touch it, as if you could feel your father's life there. You were only twelve, son. You were still such a boy, and yet your face started to take man-shape that day. The angles of fear cut away the softness, and I knew you would never be completely innocent again. That broke my heart as much as anything else.

When the phone rang, you got to it before I did. I could hear Captain Reardon's wife's voice, and I grabbed the phone from you. I know you remember this—you screamed at me, "I wanna know what's going on, Mom!" It was a voice I didn't even know. We had turned into versions of ourselves neither of us recognized.

Lydia Reardon didn't have any news, except that both your dad and Uncle Eddie were on the scene. She invited us to her house to watch with all the other wives, where there would be plenty of sleeping room for the kids. I wanted to go—we needed to be with the others who were suffering as we were. But I knew if I tried to move you from that house—where you had to be when your father came home—it wasn't going to happen.

From that moment, you sat apart from me and strained with every cell in your awkward adolescent body to take in what we were being told on CNN. If the phone rang, you answered it. If it was for me, you listened in. I held the receiver out for you, because that seemed the only way to hold you together.

You finally surrendered to sleep at two AM. You didn't wake up when the police officer came to the door. I remember stepping out onto the porch and fighting to keep the whole thing from blurring. That's what happened to me the day I opened the door at age fourteen to a policeman who told us my father had been killed in an accident. Everything smeared into the surreal, and cut off my grief. I couldn't let that happen this time. The poor officer was gray—both from the ashes and the shock he was obviously in. He knew your dad and Uncle Eddie, and his face worked against overwhelming pain.

"Tell me straight out," I said to him. "Is it Rich?"

"Rich is okay," he said. "It's his brother."

He told me Dad got out and Uncle Eddie didn't. He said he watched Rich fight everyone off and go back in and drag his brother's charred and broken body out of the rubble.

I wanted to go numb, Christopher. It was almost more than I could stand. But all I could think of was your father. I had a clear vision of that precious man holding onto his twin brother and feeling no life. Do you hear me, Christopher? All I could think of was getting to him, because no one can bear that kind of agony alone.

That's why I called Lydia Reardon back and asked for someone to come over and be with you kids. That's why I left with the police officer without waking you up to tell you. I wasn't trying to cut you out, son. I am your mother, but I am also your father's wife. I had to be with him, just him—and he needed me, just me.

I've never told you this, but they put me in an emergency vehicle so I could get to the workers' staging area. I cannot even describe the scene. It was every film clip of a third world country under attack I'd ever seen—superimposed on indomitable American soil. That bright, blue-sky day was a smothering gray night, and there were my beloved Yorkies, their faces blackened with ash and smoke, striped with rivulets of sweat and tears.

I found your dad sitting on a cot, a blanket around his shoulders, head in hands. He was so covered in ash I wouldn't have recognized him except for the shoulders. Several firefighters I didn't know were hanging out close by, but I could tell from the wary looks they were casting at him that they'd already figured out his was a solitary space. But I pushed into his circle of silence and I sat beside him and I put my arm across his back. It was like that with us, back then. I was never afraid to go to him and say, "What's the deal? What's going on?" Not the way I have been since.

At first his body was a knot. All he said was, "They won't let me go back in."

"You shouldn't," I said.

He looked at me and said, "Eddie's dead, Demitria."

And, then, Christopher, he cried. He sobbed—he wrenched himself to the very depths of his soul. I knew as I wept with him that when he pulled his identical twin brother out of what was left of the World Trade Center, it was like recovering his own body. How would he be able to live with that?

You never saw that kind of grief in him. Even I never saw it after that. Maybe that was the beginning of what has come to be for our family.

I stayed with him the rest of the night—got him to lie down on the cot while I sat on the floor. They let him return to the scene at daybreak, and I came home to you kids. Jayne was curled up on the couch in a fetal position. You'd just awakened, and I guess I don't have to remind you that you were livid because I hadn't taken you with me. I tried to get you to sit with me while I broke the news about Uncle Eddie, but you stood with your back against the fireplace while I gathered Jayne into my lap. When it was said, you went into the backyard and slammed your baseball against the fence, over and over and over. You were in so much pain, and I didn't know what to do except let you feel it all the way through. That was all I knew to do, Christopher. If I was wrong, son, I'm sorry.

I want you to know I believe I was drowning in that pain with you, and your father, and Sissy. With everyone, Christopher. All pain, all the time—that was all I knew for so long. If I made mistakes in that place, I am so sorry.

Mom

Sully folded the letter and tucked it into the folder. But its realness stayed in his hands and his gut. Was there no bottom to the pain this woman and her family had lived with the past six years? He choked and then let tears form.

"You okay?"

Sully looked up at a slightly misshapen version of Tatum.

"Actually, no," he said. "There is nothing okay about the tragedies of people's lives."

"You don't have to tell me that."

Sully tilted his head in surprise as she turned the chair across from him around and straddled it, forearms on the back.

"The difference between you and me," she said, "is you get emotional. I get bitter."

Sully slid the folder aside. "Bitter about—?"

"Men in general."

"And Van in particular."

She gave a faux shudder. "I don't know what I was thinking with him. Actually I do—he was a rebound boyfriend. That's always a mistake."

"He obviously hoped for something more." Sully leaned back ultra-casually. "I wonder what he's going to do with that beautiful picture of you."

She paused in mid earring-fiddle. Spider monkeys today.

"He dropped one," Sully said.

"I hope he burns the whole stack of them. He must have, like, hundreds. He thinks he's this photographer. It was like dating the paparazzi."

There was no way. No *way.*

"Does Van have a studio?" Sully said.

Tatum's face twisted. "Are you kidding? No—he's still in college—if you can call it a college. He's at CCC."

No way in *heaven.*

Tatum took Sully's plate and got up. "I don't know why I rattle on to you every time you come in here. Must be because you actually listen."

Sully scooped up the folder. "You're easy to listen to. Hey, thanks for the cake."

"Someday you have to tell me why you keep eating this stuff," she said.

"I'm hooked on it."

"Liar," she said, and disappeared behind the counter.

CHAPTER TWENTY-TWO

I called South Kitsap Middle School that morning to have the office get a message to Jayne, saying I would meet her out front after classes. Then I spent the entire day at the Daily Bread torturing myself with all the reasons that was a mistake.

What if she left school because she'd rather be suspended for truancy than have to face me?

What if Christopher told Rich, and Rich had the school ban me from seeing her?

What if Child Protective Services swept her away out a back door before I could get to her because Rich had reported I was an unfit mother?

"And what if monkeys fly out of my nostrils?" I said to the lentils I was pouring into a pot.

"That would be something to see." Oscar paused on his way to the gas range. "I hope you're winning that fight you've been having with yourself."

I looked into his whiskery-cherub face. Could there *be* any more compassion in this place?

"I'm going to try to see my daughter today," I told him. "And frankly, I'm freaking out."

He nodded his head of curls. "I get that. Mickey flopped around like a flounder all night worrying about Audrey."

I shifted—gratefully—to the dropping corners of his eyes. "She still having man trouble?"

"Who knows?" Oscar said. "She's in a funk, but she won't talk to either of us about it."

"I'm so sorry," I said. I covered the beans and headed for the door.

"The only person she'll talk to is you," he said.

I stopped in the doorway. "Is that a hint?"

"No." He didn't look up from a pot of steam. "It's a straight-out request. Mickey won't ask you, but I hate to see that kid suffering."

I was an expert on suffering, but that didn't make me an expert on fixing it. I was beginning to think there *were* no fixers. Only listeners.

But I went in search of Audrey and found her staring at a pot of oolong tea that had long since finished steeping. "Who does this go to?" I said.

She jumped.

"Pour a cup of chamomile for yourself," I said. "And meet me back here. I'll take this out."

Once I got the couple in the corner settled with their couscous and zucchini bread and their pot of oolong, I whispered to Mickey that Audrey needed a break.

She whispered back, "You are an angel from heaven."

By the time I got to Audrey and the chamomile, she was crying, big hunky sobs that shook her whole body. I folded her into me and rocked her back and forth. For a moment all I could think of was whether anybody was doing this for Jayne.

"It's official," she cried into my chest. "Boy dumped me."

"The cad."

"Oh, please don't, Dr. C." She shook her head against me. "I love him. He can't be a jerk if I love him."

Sure he could. My mouth tasted bitter, but I kept it shut.

"What did I do wrong?"

I held her tighter—as much to keep from going out and finding the Boy so I could smack him as to comfort her down to the bone marrow.

"I asked him," she said. "But he said it just wasn't working for him."

"Sometimes it isn't the right fit," I said through my teeth.

"But I tried everything! I was the perfect girlfriend!"

I pulled her out to arm's length and held her by the shoulders. "You shouldn't have to be perfect to please a guy, my friend. Either he loves you for who you are, or he doesn't."

She searched my face with her raw, streaming eyes, as if she were waiting for more.

"I know this hurts so bad you feel like you're going to split in two," I said.

"It so does."

I cupped her face in my hands before it could crumple again. "But when it stops, you are going to be so thankful to be rid of this person, Audrey."

She tried to shake her head, but I held on. "I know his kind. He probably thought he loved you, but he doesn't even know himself, so how can he possibly know you? He's a user."

"Then I'm an idiot!"

"No. He made you believe he was Mr. Wonderful. Nobody is savvy enough to see through that."

She nodded finally, and her face relaxed—but only for as long as it took for a new thought to crash in. She pulled away and buried her face in her hands.

"What?" I said.

"I can't tell you."

I watched her shoulders crunch together so that they almost met in front of her, and I knew what I was seeing. She was headed into a cave I had frequented myself, and I couldn't let her go there. I led her through the kitchen and out the back door. I once again held her face close to mine.

"You don't have to tell me this," I whispered to her. "But if you do, you have my word that I will not judge you."

"You would never do anything like this, Dr. C. How can you help thinking I'm a tramp?"

"Stop," I said. "I don't care what you did, you are not a tramp. Do you hear me?"

She nodded miserably. "I slept with him. I knew it was wrong, but I wanted to give him everything—and I wanted all of him." She crumbled, and I held onto her until she could catch herself again. "But now I feel so . . . dirty."

I let her sob. We stood there for a while—long enough for Oscar to poke his head out the back door, question me with *Okay?* fingers, and disappear back inside at my nod. Mickey, too, appeared and put praying hands up to her lips. This thing wasn't bigger than the love that surrounded Audrey.

When she was down to shudders, I looked into her face, blotchy with her inner mishmash.

"Let the shame go," I said to her. "You made a mistake, but it's done. Let it go."

"How do I do that?"

I bit my lip. Did I know? Enough to keep this child from losing herself in the pit I was only too well acquainted with? What *did* I know?

That I loved. Remember. I could love.

"Here's what you do," I said to her. "And it isn't going to be easy."

"Tell me." Her eyes welled again.

"Go straight to God," I said. "And dump it right at His feet. You go down with it if you have to." I squeezed her shoulders. "Then leave it there and go on and do what you know is right *now.* That other is done. It doesn't make you who you are. It just teaches you who to be."

She threw her arms around my neck, and the tears flowed again. If I weren't a veritable crying fountain myself in those days, I would have wondered where they all came from. But I knew.

"There's not a chance on earth Wyatt Estes would risk using a student for this," Ethan Kaye said. "I know Van Dillon. Estes would be out of his mind to trust that kid. Or any kid enrolled here, for that matter."

Sully turned halfway from the window in Ethan's office and tapped the glass. "Somebody's using students down there."

Ethan pulled himself from his desk chair with obvious effort and joined Sully at the full-length window. Below them a trickle of underclassmen stood, curved like question marks, propping up signs they seemed tired of carrying—as least as far as Sully could tell.

"What's on that one?" he said, pointing to a placard held by a coed with a cell phone in her other hand.

Ethan squinted. The crevices around his eyes deepened. "Feed your faith and your doubts will starve," Ethan read. He shrugged. "You can't argue with that."

"Who says you want your doubts to die?" Sully said. "The questions make you think, make you dig."

"You know that because you're not driven by fear."

"That's what this is about, isn't it?" Sully said. "Fear."

Ethan pushed his hands into his pockets. Sully watched his face—solid, sure, yet every line deepened with the gathering of thoughts. He'd seen it before in his mentor, but never with this kind of sorrow. Ethan Kaye had the look of a grieving man.

"I can't blame people for being afraid. We're living in chaos."

Sully glanced out the window. "Or on automatic pilot."

"They go into automatic pilot because they're afraid." Ethan sighed. "We were moving in the right direction before Kevin St. Clair came on board. I'm not blaming him entirely—he has supporters."

"Not the least of whom is Wyatt Estes."

"On the faculty too. But I was making progress there." He ran a tanned hand over his hair. "The students were speaking up about their concerns—over the war in Iraq, about environmental injustice, about the sickness of our economic standards. They were waking up to the fact that we can't cling to the myth of American innocence anymore, that we have to be self-critical and look at our systems—the assumptions that have shaped our values."

Sully grew still—reverent. This was the Ethan Kaye who had influenced him as a young man. This was the wisdom Sully had learned to live by in his early twenties—that he still embraced.

"We were getting the students to look at Jesus in the Gospels to answer their questions—grave, courageous questions."

"*We* being—"

"Several of the faculty, including Demi. And Zach Archer, I thought."

"He was a poser," Sully said.

Ethan chuckled. "You sound like the kids."

"Sometimes the kids can nail it."

"I think *you've* nailed it." Ethan's face darkened. "I should have fired Archer the first time I suspected him of an affair."

Sully felt his chin pull in. "He had an affair before Demi?"

"Probably. Last spring. St. Clair was all over it then, but I had no evidence. I should have gone with my instincts."

"And had a lawsuit on your hands." Sully tilted his head at Ethan. "You're thinking none of this would be happening to Demi if you'd gotten rid of him then."

"Yeah, that is what I'm thinking. But then, none of us is entirely responsible for anyone else's decisions, ultimately."

Ethan moved closer to the window and looked down. The thin sunlight slanted across his face, etching the lines of sadness more sharply. "I don't like the way this is panning out. But I have to believe God's in it—that there's a purpose."

He closed his eyes, and Sully let his own drift shut.

"We have to look at our own doctrine of sin in the church and be critical. There is nothing in the Gospels, coming from the mouth of Jesus, that says there are people who can't be forgiven." His voice dropped so low Sully had to strain to be included in the conversation Ethan was apparently having with God Himself. "I don't want my students to be blinded by a toxic faith that sees anyone as being outside God's concern—that justifies violence and sexism and racism and greed."

Sully opened his eyes to see Ethan pour his gaze over the scant line of students below.

"They can live authentic lives, but not by simply buying into doctrines they're not allowed to examine and experience."

He turned his eyes to Sully, though Sully was sure he was still seeing the fragility beneath his window. "Our striving with them is to be more like Jesus—who has grace for all."

Sully waited in the stillness that followed, but he couldn't rest. Not until he cleared the way for Ethan Kaye.

I wasn't in the line of moms-in-cars in front of Cedar Heights Junior High School for two minutes before Jayne emerged like a wisp of smoke from the press of students and moved toward me. I gasped when I saw her.

Jayne had always had a magical quality about her. Slender and supple, like all the tender, elusive things in nature. Blowing willows—tendrils of mist—puffs of lilac scent—she put them all to shame as she moved lightly, almost above the ground. She was not of this world, my daughter—as much as in her raw adolescence she tried to be.

The child moving toward me was not that Jayne. In four and a half weeks she had grown sunken and sallow, and her hair, darkened with pubescent oil, hung in languid strips on either side of a face I could hardly see because she kept it pointed toward the ground. I forced myself not to leap from the Jeep and scoop her into my arms and carry her to the nearest hospital.

She didn't look at me through the window. She simply climbed in and sat, eyes pointed toward her knees. She didn't even smell like my daughter.

I breathed in the odor of unwashed clothes and nervous breath, sucked back what was fast turning into shock, and tried to smile at the side of her head.

"Hey, Jay," I said.

"Hey."

"Thanks for not bolting."

She shrugged, as if she'd been practicing.

"Are you okay?"

Again with the shrug.

I struggled. "Please talk to me, Jay. Even a yes or a no."

"Can we just get out of here? Everybody's looking at us."

"I know the feeling. Where do you want to go?"

"I don't know! I'm tired of figuring things out!"

It burst out of her like pent-up exhaust—cloudy and foul smelling and unwanted. I put the Jeep in gear and wheeled us out of the school parking lot and took backstreets to get to the main drag. By then Jayne's face was ashen and she clutched the door handle.

"Do you have to throw up?" I said.

She nodded and plastered her hand over her mouth. I yanked the Jeep into a Dollar Store parking lot and reached over to fling open her door. She dove out and doubled over on the curb. I got to her just as she stopped retching. I didn't care what kind of response I got—I put my arms around her. I might have been hugging a broomstick.

"What have you eaten today?" I said.

"Nothing."

"How about yesterday?"

"I can't eat!"

No kidding. I ran my hand down her side, and even through the too-big sweater she hid in I could feel her ribs like rungs on a ladder.

"Come on, baby," I said.

I did try to scoop her up, but she stiffened, so I let her lean on me as I half carried her back to the Jeep. Inside, I lowered the seat back and covered her with my jacket.

"I feel stupid." Her voice was thin as a spiderweb.

You aren't the one who's stupid, I wanted to say. And for once I wasn't talking only about myself.

I got her to the Daily Bread as the afternoon crowd was filling the place and slipped her in through the back door. Mickey took one look at us and had Jayne in front of a bowl of chicken soup almost before I could hoist her onto the stool by the counter where I did my crying.

Oscar nodded Mickey away from us. She left with a reluctant, "You shout if you need anything." Then she couldn't leave without whispering to Jayne, "Your mother is a good woman."

Jayne's eyes were the size of nickels by then, and as pale. "Where are we?" she said.

"A safe place. Now—I want you to try to eat."

I spooned soup into her. After the first few tortured swallows, she opened her mouth like a baby bird and closed her eyes to taste. The dearness of it broke my heart.

So did the stiffness that returned after she'd downed a slice of

Mickey's zucchini bread and polished off half the smoothie Mickey set on the table as she "passed through." I could hear Oscar's warning voice from the kitchen.

Jayne pushed the half-empty glass away from her and folded her arms, so pitifully scrawny, across her concave chest.

"Better?" I said.

"I guess."

Should I wait her out? Try to force a conversation? Drop on my knees and beg her forgiveness? The fact that I didn't know how to talk to my own daughter was the most depressing thing I could think of at that moment. But if I didn't say something, she would pull back into her cocoon.

"I'm going to get to the point," I said. "Okay?"

She only tucked her feet up to the top rung of the stool and spread her long skirt over her knees like a tent.

"Jayne, I'm so sorry," I said. "I did something completely wrong. It is the most regrettable thing I have ever done in my life."

She fixed her eyes on the wall above my head.

"I would do anything to undo it, because I've hurt all of you, and I hate that. I hate it."

Still nothing. Except a learned hardening around her mouth.

"But I can't 'make it not be so.' Remember that from *West Side Story,* when Maria finds out Tony has killed Chino, and she goes to God and says, 'Make it not be so'?"

Jayne kept her eyes on the wall. "Bernardo."

I blinked. "Sorry?"

"He didn't kill Chino. He killed Bernardo. And he didn't mean to."

I held my breath.

"I don't want to talk about this," she said.

"Okay. Can we talk about what's going on with you?"

She finally looked at me. Something stirred in her eyes. "You don't want to know about me," she said.

"Of course I do. Jayne, I'm still your mom. No matter what I did, it doesn't mean I don't love you."

"Then why didn't you even come to my play?"

The air went dead—except for the echo of Christopher's voice in my head. She didn't want me there, he'd said. It would embarrass her.

"Christopher said you were probably too afraid to show your face," Jayne said. "Like, people would be talking about you, and you'd be embarrassed."

Ah. It was anger I saw in her eyes—only my Jayne didn't know how to feel anger, and the thought of it sucked her dry.

I, on the other hand, would give full vent to mine—later. For now, I put my face close to my daughter's.

"I got some bad information about that," I said. "And I'm sorry I listened to it. But, Jay, I would have shown up naked if that's what it took to be there."

"Christopher told you not to come, didn't he?" Her eyes flashed, and one almost transparent hand came up to slice the air. "I am so over him! He's trying to run my whole life!"

I nodded.

"I'm not supposed to tell you about anything that's going on at home. He says Dad doesn't want us to."

"But you haven't heard Dad actually say that."

"Dad doesn't say anything. At all."

I waited while she drew her knees in closer and hugged them into the curve of her chest. There was a decision going on.

"All right, look," I said. "Christopher is obviously trying to hold it together because your dad is having a hard time. But, Jay, he is not the boss of you. He's having as hard a time as anybody else."

She slowly shook her head. "I don't say that anymore."

"Say what?"

"He's not the boss of me. That's like so elementary school."

My voice shook with sudden hope. "What are we saying these days?"

"That Christopher is a total jerk and I can't even stand him and I go in my room and stay there because he's evil in his soul."

I put my hand up to my mouth. I couldn't laugh—not even in the flood of relief I felt.

"He's like taken over the house. He thinks he's this cook, which he is *so* not—I could make dinners better than the slop he's producing. But no, I have to do the laundry and clean the bathrooms. I'm like a slave!"

"What does your dad say about all this?"

"I don't know. I never see him." Her shoulders drooped again. "Christopher is gonna be so mad at me for telling you all this."

"What—are you going to run to him and confess?" I put a hand on her knee. She didn't pull back. "You don't have to answer to your brother."

"Then who do I answer to?"

The plaintive plea went through me, the cry of sheer loneliness.

"You can come to me, Jay," I said. "If you will."

"I didn't think you wanted to talk to me."

"Honey—I've called you every day. Sent you e-mails."

She stared, lips pressing until her skin went white. "I never got anything. I don't understand."

I did. I put my hand on my chest to make sure it didn't shatter into livid pieces.

"I'm here now," I said. "And so are you. I want us to—"

"Why did you have an affair, Mom?" she said. "That's all I want to know."

CHAPTER TWENTY-THREE

Sully looked at the official board of trustees photo of Wyatt Estes. The studio name, address, and phone number stamped on the back had seemed like a good lead. So had the photo credits on the Estes Enterprises Web site. But nothing had panned out. The corporate photographers were out of San Francisco and had as many awards as Ansel Adams. The local photographer was so old and deaf, Sully was hoarse from trying to communicate with him on the phone.

"We go from the sublime to the ridiculous, Isabella," Sully said to the Impala. He tucked his cell phone into his pocket and strolled around her.

If his first Impala were any indication, this one was going to purr like a lioness when he turned the key. She'd crouch over the pavement, energy gathering like a passion under the hood. They'd prowl the streets of Callow, engine growling . . .

"Yeah, baby," Sully said to the car. "Just like old times. Have I told you I used to be a bad boy?"

"You *are* a bad boy," Lynn had said to him the night he gave her the car.

He grinned at her, big and sloppy, the way he knew melted her. "Not since you tamed me."

"I don't want you tame—I want you *you.*"

He tucked her against him and rested his chin on the sandy hair that always smelled like clean itself. "You like your car?"

"I love my car—because you made her for me."

"You think she's you?"

She wriggled to face him and got her arms around his neck. Her brown eyes sparkled with the tears she was so easily moved to.

"What?" he said. "You're crying?"

"She's us, Sullivan," she said. "Like everything is us."

He smiled down into her face. "You won't drive her like a maniac?"

She'd wrinkled her nose at him. "At least not when you're looking."

Sully dabbed sweat from his upper lip. Memories are like any other thought that carries emotion, he'd told more than one client. Expect the feelings to flood in with them. The only way out of them is through.

"And I'm through," he told Isabella. "Good night, babe."

He wasn't tired though. It was only seven and unusually warm. He dragged the green papasan outside and sat back with a frappuccino and another one of Demi's letters.

Dear Jayne,

I miss you so much I can hardly stand it.

Sully rubbed a finger along his nose. Totally different approach from the one she took with her son, whom she crept around like an uncertain cat. This one had an almost puppylike candor.

But as long as I have to stand it—as long as it takes for you to forgive me, or at least hear me, it helps me to remember what we were—you and me together.

We were always easy, weren't we? Christopher and I were flinty with each other. Sometimes when you were small, and he and I were raising our voices higher and higher like we were chasing each other up a wall, you would cover your eyes with your little pink hands and squeeze your mouth all up in a knot. That's how you taught me not to yell at Christopher.

That's not all you taught me. You showed me how to be honest—to think through what I wanted to say and then say it. Outright. You were the one who finally said out loud, after one of our visits to Washington when you were five, "Why doesn't Grandma Haven like Daddy?" I couldn't tell you because I didn't know. I still don't. She took that sad feeling to her grave, I'm afraid. But you asked the right question—you made me admit that she didn't, you made me stop pretending that everything was wonderful. You never pretend that.

That's why you were the one who came home from Mama Costanas's that day and said to me, "Mama is acting funny." I don't know whether Christopher noticed or not. He's so male, isn't he? No, you were the one who said Mama forgot to feed you, so you had goldfish crackers for lunch, and she let you watch TV all day. No wonder Christopher didn't tell me!

But you wanted the old Mama, who told you stories "with her mouth," as you always said, not from a book, and let you help her fold the sheets like big girls did. Nobody else wanted to believe she was sick—and after she went to the nursing home—after Uncle Eddie found her in her nightgown in the backyard, looking for zucchini in the dead of January—you were the only one who still loved to go see her. You redecorated her room with your glitter pictures and balloon animals. Whenever they withered, you made more. You said she needed them.

That's how you taught me, Jay, to respect a life in every stage. You taught me about soul—that it's always there. You helped me live through the loss of my best friend. That's what Mama Costanas was to me, and I haven't had a friend like her since.

Sully rocked back in the chair and surveyed the wreath of mist forming around the light. That was a piece missing in Demi. As attractive and personable as she was—Porphyria would call hers a be-still-my-heart smile—she'd never mentioned female friends. She was probably the most alone client he'd ever had. And she wondered why she'd found unconditional comfort so irresistible.

"You've also taught me about yourself," I read.

I glanced up. Jayne was still on the stool, watching me, chin resting on her knees.

"You want me to keep reading?" I said.

"This is going to tell me why you had an affair, right?"

Her face was so hopeful, my heart once again tore right down the middle.

"I'm telling you what I know so far about why."

"'Kay. Then go on."

I closed my eyes momentarily. Dear God, I hoped this was right. It meant everything.

"We raised Christopher strictly by the book—whatever that is. He has always seemed to know what it contains because he's needed rules and consequences and consistent follow-through. He even knows how far to push at every phase—he never missed a stage 'the book' says a kid is supposed to go through."

Jayne grunted. We exchanged glances.

"But not you. Your dad and I realized when you were three years old that you needed to show us how to raise you. Threatening you, telling you what would happen if you did this or didn't do that—that seemed too harsh for a spirit born knowing good from evil and should from should not. All we had to do was explain—and then give you time to explore it in your own world. The only problem was finding out where that world was.

"Do you remember me searching the house in a panic after I told you Uncle Eddie had died, and finding you in the basement, sitting on a tuft of laundry with your eyes closed?"

I felt her nodding.

"You wouldn't leave your spot. I had to bring two cups of hot chocolate, and we sat there with the dirty clothes until we decided Uncle Eddie was with Mama and Papa, and that it was still okay for you to be sad for yourself and us.

"I guess that's how I knew not to panic that day when we'd been here in Washington for about two weeks, and you disappeared. Christopher freaked out and went off on his bike to check all the creeks. I made two cups of tea with honey and milk—you'd graduated from hot chocolate—and thought of hiding places where something might be normal for you. I found you in the storage shed, sitting on a stack of boxes we hadn't unpacked yet—your eyes closed—trying to understand why we left everything we knew and loved and came to this place where no one wanted to be your friend because you were an angel, not a regular girl."

"Mom," Jayne said.

"Okay, so that last part is my interpretation. Humor me."

"It was hard for you to sort all that out," I read on. *"Dad and I couldn't help that Uncle Eddie died—but* we *were the ones who chose to rip you and Christopher out of your home, away from the friends you'd grown up giggling and dancing with. You didn't know how to be angry. That's still hard for you, I know."*

I swallowed hard. No crying—not when she was listening and hearing me be the mom.

"That must be why you won't talk to me now, or answer my e-mails or text messages. You must be so angry with me—and that makes it hard for you to know how to be—at all. I'm angry enough with myself for both of us. That's all I know right now, Jay—that for a reason I'm still trying to figure out, I went against God and turned to somebody besides your dad for what I thought I needed. I didn't know how to be angry at all the things that had happened to us—I think I just wanted to feel better. I don't know—and I'm getting help to find out. But I promise you, it's okay for you to be angry with me. If you don't know how, I'll teach you—because I've had some practice. But I hope more that I can teach you how to love me again. It's my turn to teach you, the way you've taught me. Please, Jay, let me try."

"How do you explain an affair to a thirteen-year-old you've barely had 'the talk' with yet?"

Mickey tucked her feet under herself on my window seat. "I'm sure you were amazing."

"How can you say that? All you've ever seen me do is cry over the mess I've made of my life."

"Not true." She pushed the bowl of sunflower seeds down the seat toward me and scooped a handful into her cupped palm to pick from, like a little bird-woman. "I saw you with Audrey."

I fidgeted. Mickey held up a hand, two seeds poised between finger and thumb. "I'm not asking you to tell me what she said. As long as she has somebody like you to talk to, that's all I care about. By the way, she was like a different person after she cried on your shoulder."

I poked into the bowl of seeds. "Why is it I can have such perspective with your kid, but when it comes to my own, I don't even know how to be with her?"

"Looked to me like you were doing fine."

"It wasn't as bad as it could have been, I guess."

Mickey dumped what was left in her hand back into the bowl and brushed her palms together. "Okay, I'm going to go ahead and jump into territory that's none of my business. Stop me if you want."

I sank back against the cushions. "Go."

"When you brought her in there, I thought, *That child needs to be in the emergency room.* But ten minutes with you, and she came back from the dead." She twitched an eyebrow. "She probably did, if you know what I mean."

"She says it's bad at home."

"Bad? She's scary-skinny. She looked like she was afraid of herself, until you started reading to her. Here's the thing: that child needs to be with you."

I stared at my toes, now blurring before me. "It was so hard to take her home."

"Home for that girl is where you are. You can bring her here. She could have the bedroom—you never use it anyway. We'd cut you slack so you could take her to school on your way to work. Audrey could pick her up after class."

I shook my head.

"Why not? There's no legal document that says you can't have custody of your own daughter, is there?"

"There's no legal anything. Christopher said Rich hired a lawyer, but I haven't seen any paperwork yet."

Mickey bugged her eyes. "Why does Rich get to control everything? Why can't you get legal representation?"

Sudden anxiety shot me off the window seat.

"I'm sorry, Demi, but I don't get why you are so cowed by this man when it comes to your kids."

I stopped my march across the room and turned to her. "It's stupid, isn't it?"

"You have to stop it."

I dropped into one of the chairs, pushing aside the afghan. "You know what—I think it's more Christopher than it is Rich. He's actually lying to turn Jayne against me."

"Why are you letting him get away with that?"

"I just found out," I said. "And I'm not going to let him get away with it."

Mickey's eyes gleamed. "Now that's what I'm talking about. Do you have a plan?"

"I want to wring his neck."

"That's good for a start."

My cell phone rang. I picked it up and looked at the screen. *HOME.* I was almost too stunned to answer.

When I did, Rich said, "Demitria."

I grasped at his voice, deadwood as it sounded.

"Rich," I said.

"Look, did Jayne call you?"

"When?"

"Within the last hour?"

My mother antennae went up. "What's wrong?"

On the window seat, Mickey sat up straight and watched me openly.

"I don't know if there's anything *wrong.*" His irritation was forced. "She's not here, and I thought maybe she called you."

"I haven't seen or heard from her since I dropped her off at five."

He was silent. Anger lapped at me.

"Rich."

"I'll just keep looking for her, then," he said.

But I already had the phone halfway closed as I said, "I'm coming over." And I didn't wait for permission.

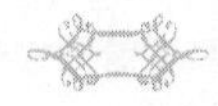

Someone different from the Demi I'd been living inside of barked half an explanation at Mickey and roared the Jeep all the way to the house. This Demi left her shriveling guilt back in the daylight basement and threw open the mudroom door as though she belonged there, confronting a husband who stood stiff at the kitchen counter.

"Are the police coming?" I said.

"No."

"Rich, we don't know where our daughter is." I snatched my cell phone out of my jacket pocket.

Rich reached across the counter and grabbed at it. I didn't even give myself time to gape at him.

"What is wrong with you! This isn't about your stupid pride, Rich—this is our child. Somebody could have abducted her."

"She left," Rich said. "We had an argument, and she ran off."

My thoughts rammed into each other like bumper cars—and somehow formed themselves into a line.

"I thought she might have gone back to you," he said. "She said she saw you today." He hissed. "You got her all upset."

"No, I did not."

I rounded the end of the counter and got close to him. He slanted away.

"We had a good talk," I said into his face. "Which we should have had long ago, except that Christopher has kept her from hearing from me." I shook my head. "What did she say to you?"

I could hear his teeth grinding. "I think I drove her out of here, Demitria."

"What did you say? Tell me—please."

He moved away, leaned against the stove, went restlessly to the refrigerator, where he supported himself with one hand over his head, his back to me. "I got up to get ready for work and she came into our—my bedroom. She told me I was being stupid and stubborn and that I ought to listen to you because this isn't all your fault." He gave me a look over his shoulder that didn't harden all the way to its edges. "That could only have come from you."

"No, because I didn't say any of that to her. All I said was that I am trying to figure out why I did what I did."

Rich kept his face away from me.

"I know you don't believe me," I said. "You don't believe a thing I say anymore."

"Why should I?"

"Because this is not about you and me—this is about Jayne. What happened after that?"

Rich shrugged. "I told her it was none of her concern—that it was between you and me. She said she didn't see how it could be since we weren't even talking to each other."

"And?"

"I told her not to take that tone with me," Rich said. "She said somebody had to." He stopped and set his jaw.

"Why did she run off?"

"Because—I told her to get out."

I put my hands to my temples.

"I meant get out of the room—but she left the house."

"How long ago?"

"About an hour."

"Did you not go after her?"

"No." He went for the stove again. "I figured she'd come back—where is she going to go?"

"Boys come back," I said. I headed for the mudroom door. "Girls wait to be found. But I guess you haven't figured that out." I nodded toward the stove that held him up. "Would you please put some water on for tea?"

Jayne was in the storage shed.

I peeked through a crack first and saw her narrow, diminished self almost fitting into it. She sat on a cooler between two pairs of cross-country skis, sorting out her mind. I knocked and heard a faint, "Go away, Dad."

"It's Mom," I said.

"Mom?"

"Can I come in?"

I didn't have to. She came to me—arms flailing to go around me, face searching for a neck to bury itself in. She cried until she went limp—that place where things can begin to make sense. I knew that place well.

"The tea water ought to be ready by now," I said. "Let's go inside."

"Is Dad there?"

"Uh-huh."

"Is he going to hit me?"

I pulled her away from me and stared into her face. "Hit you?"

"He was so mad I thought he was going to slap me. He didn't, like, raise his hand or anything. But it felt like he was going to. That's why I ran."

I crushed her against me, my hands tangled in her damp hair. She'd washed it since the afternoon.

"I'm with you," I said. "Come on—we have to go talk to him."

Talk wasn't something Rich was going to do. After the gush of relief when he saw us come in together, he turned his face from us and muttered, "I'm glad you found her."

It was the only cowardly thing I had ever seen my husband do. I wanted to claw the paneling.

"We have to talk about this," I said. "I'm going to pour some tea, and we can sit down and—"

"What is there to say?" Rich pointed at our daughter. "You don't need to worry about what's going on between your mother and me."

"Yes, I do," Jayne said, "because nobody's telling me anything! What am I supposed to do but worry, Dad?"

Rich turned his glare on me.

I glared back. I had never disagreed with him in front of the children about anything pertaining to them, and at the moment I resented him for putting me in this position.

He looked back at Jayne, though I wasn't sure he saw her. "I don't know what to tell you," he said finally.

She pawed at me until she found my hand at my side. "I'm scared," she said to him.

"Don't be," he said, tone short. "Everything is—"

"Going to be all right? It isn't all right! Mom's not living with us. Christopher has turned into Hitler. I don't even see you anymore."

Rich's eyes bore into me. He wanted me to make her stop—but I longed for the kind of release my daughter must be feeling.

"I can only do so much." Rich's voice was hard but thin, like a brittle bone. "What do you want me to do, Jayne?"

She squeezed my hand until I realized she needed me to squeeze back. When I did, she lifted her fragile chin and said, "I want you to let me go with Mom."

I stopped breathing. Rich's eyes went to me, accusing, and Jayne shook her head until the angel hair trembled.

"She didn't ask me, Daddy," she said. "This is my idea. This is what *I* want."

I watched Rich's Adam's apple rise and fall like an adolescent boy's.

"Jay," I heard myself say, "why don't you give us a minute?"

Her hand went limp in mine, and for a moment I thought she'd change her mind, hate me for not marching off with her in victory. But I heard a tiny sigh as she let go and hurried soundlessly to the steps. I didn't wait to hear her door close.

"I didn't put her up to this, Rich," I said.

He leaned, palms down between the burners on the stove. "I know that, Demitria. I hate this."

"So do I."

Rich lifted his face toward the ceiling. There was strain in every line—some of which I'd never seen before.

"I know you're sorry," he said. "But it's not enough."

"What more do you want?"

"I don't know!" His voice caught.

I pulled back. This had to be hope I was seeing, and I didn't want to breathe, lest I blow it away.

"I think Jayne should go with you." He jerked his head toward me, but he didn't meet my eyes. "She'll get more attention from you—it'll be better for her."

"And it *is* about her, Rich. Not about you winning or me winning."

He straightened and absently patted his back pocket. "Will you need money?"

"No. But, Rich, we're going to have to talk about money, and Jayne and Christopher—and us—soon."

"I'm not ready to talk to you without feeling like I want to tear the place apart, all right?"

It came out a barely controlled snarl, and involuntarily I startled back. While he stood there, staring down at the stove again, I went to the bottom of the stairs and called up, "Get some things together, Jay. You're coming with me."

I heard the Harley roar out of the garage.

CHAPTER TWENTY-FOUR

I was glad Jayne's first few days with me were over a weekend. She seemed far too jangled to deal with school or anything else.

I let her sleep as much as she wanted to and fed her a steady stream of nutrition pipelined from upstairs. Mickey insisted that I take Saturdays off from now on and stay home with her, for which I was thankful. I couldn't leave Jayne alone with herself again. As I watched her sleep, I was even more keenly aware of how pale her skin was, and how it stretched over her bony wrists and collarbone like cheesecloth, and how shadows passed over her face in her dreams. When she was awake she fell into long silences, as if she'd spoken all her words and only wanted to gaze out over the sound until she found more.

She did talk when she ate, which I coaxed her to do every few hours, and I managed to pull some fairly depressing information from her. Her grades, usually As with the occasional B, had fallen to Cs, with the threat of a D in pre-algebra. Teachers sent e-mails to Rich, at his request, rather than notifying me.

"Actually," Jayne said, "Christopher did that. I don't think Dad even knows."

I added that to my list of bones to pick with my son. There were already enough for an entire skeleton.

Jayne said she couldn't sleep at home at night because she was afraid, and she nodded off in class. Her teachers were threatening to call Rich at work.

"Has anybody asked you if there's trouble at home?" I said.

"I wouldn't tell them anything if they did."

"That's not the point," I said. "I want to know if anyone cares about the *why.*"

She shrugged and fell silent again.

In spite of Mickey's constant barrage of affirmations about what a blessing I was to the young female population, I groped for a way to draw Jayne out. "I love you," I said to her—every fifteen minutes.

"Love you," she sometimes mumbled. Other times she only nodded.

Maybe Rich was right. Maybe it wasn't enough to be sorry and keep loving. And maybe the Kevin St. Clairs were right. Maybe you didn't deserve grace when you'd screwed up this badly.

That finally got to me Sunday afternoon—the idea that the legalistic edicts of a blowfish could separate me from my child. I dried my hands from washing the teacups and went to her on the window seat where she sat with an open, unread literature book.

"What do you need, Jay?" I asked. "I don't know what to do—I need for you to tell me."

"This doesn't feel like home," she said.

I blinked.

"It always feels like home wherever you are, but there's no *you* here."

I grimaced as I looked around at Mickey's early attic décor. "I haven't done anything to it because I don't plan to be here that long," I said.

"But what if we are?" The look she gave me, full in the face, was imploring. "Dad is being stubborn. I told you, Christopher is evil in his soul."

I bit back a laugh again.

"It's true! Mom—I don't want us to go back there with them being all—stiff." She sent a gaze around the room. "If this has to be home, then can't we make it friendly? I'm sick of feeling like an alien."

I gathered her sweet, bony self into my arms. "Me too, Jay," I said. "Me too."

We didn't have much to work with, which meant a trip to the house. For once no one was there, and we crept around like thieves, gathering our own throws and pillows and pottery. Jayne made off with enough stuffed animals to start a small toy store, and I scored a set of wind chimes and a bird feeder, because she said she needed birds. I would have set up an aviary if I could.

It was almost eight before we were through home-izing, as Jayne called it. I had to admit we'd created a place where I didn't feel like a stranger to myself. I was positioning a book on Pacific Northwest sea life on the trunk coffee table when Jayne floated in from the bedroom and put something beside it.

It was the big rock Sullivan Crisp had told me to find a use for. My spirit sank.

"What's this?" she said.

I sighed. "It's a symbol of my anger at myself."

"Oh."

"I'm supposed to find something to do with it besides throw it at me."

"Yeah," she said matter-of-factly. "That would hurt." Her eyes took on their golden glow. "You already hurt, don't you?"

I could only nod.

She touched the rock. "Can I do something with it?"

"As long as you don't pitch it at me."

"I would never do that," she said. "You're my mom."

Then she carried off the rock that was nearly as heavy as she was.

Sully leaned back in the papasan chair and locked his hands behind his head. "You weren't expecting this, were you?" he said.

Demi shook her head. The bright spot at the top of each cheek made her sadness even more poignant.

"Sort of like winning a bonus round."

She rolled her brown eyes. She'd definitely been spending time with a teenage girl. "I'll call it whatever you want," she said. "I have my daughter with me—and that gives me hope for all of us being together."

Sully sighed inwardly. He hated this part—where responsible therapy called for bursting a bubble.

"You don't think so," she said.

"I didn't say that."

"You didn't have to. You've got that *sorry, wrong answer* look on your face. And thank you for not buzzing."

"It's not that it's the wrong answer," Sully said. "I'm still not sure you're asking the right question."

"My only question is 'How can I get my family back together?'"

Sully didn't nod.

"Okay—no—it's 'What made me do this stupid thing in the first place?' You keep saying if I figure that out, I'll be able to move on without being afraid this is going to happen again."

Sully rocked forward. "But you're still not sure that's the way to go."

"It's hard to work on the why thing when I'm afraid Rich is going to give up before I have a chance to figure myself out."

"Rich didn't call it quits when you took Jayne, right?"

"Right."

"He didn't say he *never* wanted to talk to you—just not yet."

"Not while he's still so angry." She focused sharply on Sully. "He actually scared me. And Jayne. She thought he was going to hit her—and that's not Rich."

"He's reacting—that's all I can say without seeing him."

Demi made a hissing noise that didn't fit her. "Like that's going to happen."

"We'd make a lot more progress. You could pray about asking him."

She jammed her hair behind her ears. "I'm still having a lot of trouble going to God. I told Audrey—I've told you about her—"

Sully nodded.

"I told her to throw herself at God's feet and ask for forgiveness." She looked wryly at Sully. "But can I do that?"

"What makes you any different from anybody else who's separated from God?"

Her face softened. "You *are* one of Ethan Kaye's, aren't you?"

"What gave it away?"

"He always refers to sin as separation from God."

"Yeah." Sully grinned. "Ethan used to say whenever one of those dyed-in-the-wool legalists started to talk about 'see-yun,' it was sure to be about policing genitalia."

Demi spattered out a laugh.

"He's cleaned up his act now that he's an administrator. Unfortunately, some people don't think he's cleaned it up enough."

"I haven't helped. Which brings us back to my 'separation from God.'" Demi tilted her head. "It does seem less final when you put it that way—like it's only a temporary separation and you can always go back. At least, I used to think that."

"Until?"

She looked at him.

"So—let me get this straight," Sully said. "Your Audrey can sleep with a guy, feel horrible about it, and go to God for forgiveness. Then she gets to go and leave her life of sin."

"Right."

"But you can't. Why is that?"

She closed her eyes. "I'm an adult. I should know better."

"You are, and you did."

"But I did it anyway."

"Uh-huh."

"And you think it's because Rich was ignoring me and I couldn't help him and we weren't having sex."

"What do you think?"

"I still think those are just excuses."

"Let's call them symptoms," Sully said, "of a marriage that was already in trouble. You tried to fix it."

"I did try."

"Running to another man wasn't your first response to being shut out."

"It was never my response! Zach found me—I didn't chase him." She curled her lip. "Does that sound like I'm blaming him? I do take responsibility."

"Responsibility? You're practically a martyr. Go ahead and put some of it on him."

Demi nodded absently. "I did try with Rich."

"Now bear with me when I ask you this," Sully said, "because I'm going to sound like a shrink."

"Ten bucks says you're going to sound like a game show host."

"When you tried and he didn't respond, how did you feel?"

Demi's mouth twitched. "You do sound like a shrink." She leaned her head back. "It made me feel like a failure as a wife—as a woman."

"And failure is never an option for you, is it?"

"I can't remember ever failing before this."

Sully saw her swallow.

"When I do it, I do it big-time."

"It's not like you've shot the pope."

"I can't minimize this."

"No, but you can keep it in perspective. You failed to meet Rich's needs—but you were able to meet somebody else's."

"Now you're going to ask me how *that* felt."

Sully nodded.

She put her hands to her temples and pulled at the corners of her eyes.

"It's okay to cry in here, Demi," he said.

"I feel stupid for crying over something that was wrong to begin with!"

"You felt good because someone needed you. Feelings themselves are not wrong."

"It's what you do with them."

"Which we've already established."

She was obviously determined to go down the guilt path to its inevitable dead end.

"All right," she said. "It felt good to have Zach need me and tell me I was good for him."

"Good?"

"Amazing." Her mouth crumpled. "It's sickening now, but that feeling of being wanted and needed after so long was irresistible."

Exactly the word Sully himself would have used. He held back a ding-ding-ding.

"So that was something *you* needed." Sully picked carefully through the possible phrasing. "And not only needed, but felt like you were entitled to, in order to be—"

"Be what?"

"You tell me."

"Give me a second." She cupped her face in her palms.

Sully had to hand it to her—she would do anything to put this back together.

"Okay—here's all I know," she said, bringing her head up. "If I'm not providing what somebody needs, what am I worth? Basically, I'm no good if I can't do that." She closed her eyes. "Please don't buzz me."

"I'm not going to buzz you," Sully said, "because I think that's the right answer."

Her eyes sprang open.

"To you, it was the right answer. To me—and to God—it's a false premise." Sully leaned forward, palms rubbing together. "And I think it's the one we've been looking for."

She stared at him. A light, the tiniest pinpoint, came into her eyes. "Then where's my ding-ding-ding?" she said.

"Ding-ding-ding-ding-ding!"

She sat up straight in the bowl-chair. "So—do you think Rich will get this? Understand why I did what I did?"

"I think *you* have to understand it first. We're going to work with it."

"But it's a start, right? I could go to him and try to explain."

"You could," Sully said slowly.

"You don't think I should."

"I think you have to consider that any reunion with Rich is going to have to be on more honest terms than your marriage was before. You going back to him is not necessarily going to pull him out of his depression over 9/11, for instance. How are you going to handle it if he continues to shut you out?"

She glared. "That hope was short-lived."

"Demi—this isn't a black-or-white thing. There *is* hope for you. You can work on this need to be all things to all people. And if Rich takes you back, that can help your marriage. But if you go back under the same circumstances, without dealing with your own premise, what's to say it's going to be any different?"

"It has to be," Demi said. "Because I'm not the same."

"And what about Rich?"

"I don't know." She turned her face away.

This was as far as he was going to pull her today. He could see her fighting back tears, and he couldn't let her leave that way. "You know what?" he said.

"Probably not."

"I think what you're doing with Jayne means God wants to use you." He waited until she looked at him. "No matter what."

"I have to go," she said.

He saw her shoulders shaking before she got to her Jeep.

The phone woke him up the next morning. He had to claw his way out of an entangling dream to get to it—something about Demitria driving Isabella and screaming *Where are the brakes? I can't find the brake pedal!*

He was going to have to get on those so he could get some sleep.

Meanwhile, the cell phone continued to chirp insistently while he rammed through the trailer, dumping over piles of clothes and peering under stacks of papers. By the time he located it between the cushions of the dinette booth, whoever it was had given up.

Who the Sam Hill was calling him in the middle of the night anyway?

He squinted at the phone screen. Eight AM. Those dreams really did have his timetable scrambled up.

Sully smeared his hand over his face and pushed a few buttons on the phone. Porphyria had called. What was it about *No, I'm not coming for the anniversary this year* that she didn't get?

He slid the phone across the table and tucked himself into the booth, feet hanging out to the flat excuse for a couch. He felt vacuum-packed into this place. Porphyria's calling him constantly to say he could still book a flight and be at her lodge in the Smokies on May 6 didn't help. She wasn't as subtle as she used to be, but she was just as insistent.

"You can run yourself ragged solving other people's problems," she'd told him, "but you cannot hide from your own."

Sully churned restlessly from the booth, stood up, banged his head on the tin can ceiling. Okay, no, he'd never get over Lynn. There had been a oneness with her, an *Everything is us.* You didn't get over love like that. You just learned to live without it.

When the phone rang again, Sully made sure it wasn't Porphyria before he picked it up.

"So you are alive," Ethan Kaye said.

"I'll take Famous Quotes for $200. Rumors of my death have been grossly exaggerated."

"Who was Mark Twain? Are you okay?"

"For somebody who hasn't had a cup of coffee yet, yeah, I'm good."

"I have information," Ethan said. "Nothing that really helps us—elimination maybe."

"Yeah?"

"I did a little snooping—actually, I talked to my secretary."

Sully pictured the plumpish platinum blonde in Ethan's office who all but pressed a glass to the door when he and Sully were conferencing.

"She says Wyatt Estes wasn't aware Tatum Farris was dating Van Dillon, because he wouldn't have met with family approval."

Sully snickered. "You want to tell me how your secretary knows that?"

"I have no idea, and I don't want to know—but you can take it to the bank. Gina has the 411 on everybody."

"I love it when you talk college," Sully said. He moved gingerly toward the coffeepot.

"I don't know where that leaves us. We've ruled out every possible photographer, and I'll tell you, Sully, I don't think it was a total amateur who took those pictures."

"So maybe we give up on finding the shutterbug and go at this from another angle."

"Do you have one?" Ethan's voice was suddenly weary.

"Not yet," Sully said. He abandoned the coffeepot. "But I think I know where I can find one."

Eight-thirty was too early for pink champagne cake. Anytime was too early for pink champagne cake. But a cup of coffee with three sugars and two creams would go good about now.

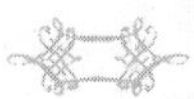

He'd never been to McGavock's Bakery before noon. It was a different place, with men in hammer-swinging jeans and flannel shirts crowding the counter, vying for donuts, and harried-looking women placing orders for baked goods.

"I need that Saturday—for Easter," one of them barked at Tatum.

She kept her unruffled expression in place and moved nothing but her pen, a myriad of pastries, and her earrings.

Sully took a seat at his table and watched her do a silent, intricate dance behind the counter with an older woman who also took orders and passed out free hot cross buns.

"Traditional Easter treat," she told each customer.

Sully hadn't even remembered Sunday was Easter. He wondered if Demi remembered. Holidays could be brutal in her situation.

"He actually emerges before noon."

He looked up to see Tatum standing beside him, steaming mug in hand. She put it on the table. It swam with cream.

"Y'all are busy in the mornings."

"That's how we stay in business." She let a smile pass briefly through her eyes. "You don't think your eating us out of pink champagne cake pays the bills, do you?"

Sully grinned.

"You want a piece right now?"

"How about a hot cross bun?" Sully said quickly.

"They're gross," she said. "But okay."

When she returned, she'd taken off her hairnet, and the highlights fell into their assigned rows. "You don't mind if I join you, do you? I've been here since four. I need a break."

"I gotta ask you something," he said.

"You want to know why a girl like me is working full-time in a has-been bakery."

"You're good."

"No—you're just obvious. You've basically been asking me that for weeks."

Sully gave her half a smile.

"I was in college," she said. "But I dropped out." She fiddled with a silver hoop earring she could have used for a bracelet. "It was so bad that I wanted nothing to do with the academic world. I didn't even want a job where I had to read or write." She looked around coldly. "This is perfect."

Sully chewed on a piece of bun. She was right, it was gross—but the longevity of its bulk in his mouth gave him an excuse to think through his next question.

"So that's why you didn't go into the family business," he said.

"I don't want to be identified with them in any way."

"That's pretty common for your age."

"My age has nothing to do with it. I want to be authentic, you know what I mean? Anything that smells like hypocrisy, get it away from me. Which is why I left CCC."

Sully slurped at his coffee. "There's no love lost between you and that place, is there?"

"Seriously. You expect a secular school to claim to be all about truth and wisdom and excellence and actually be all about money and prestige. Call me naïve, but I thought a Christian college would be different."

"And it isn't?"

"It's the biggest bunch of hypocrites I've ever seen. I could tell you stories."

Sully forced himself not to say, *Please do.*

"I won't, though, not with my uncle being a major donor. I do have some integrity."

Dang that integrity.

"But yeah, there's stuff going on over there that you would not believe. And I'm not just talking about the administration—although don't get me started on them."

He tried not to look like an eager hound dog, though he could feel himself practically drooling. "Students are a mess, are they?" he said.

"The students are only a mess because they're confused. I'm talking about the faculty." Tatum gave him a long look and then shook her head. "You are one of those people complete strangers talk to about their sex lives on airplanes, aren't you?"

Sully choked. "I can't say that I've ever had that happen."

"I bet I could tell you everything I know about CCC, and you'd never say a word to anybody—but I can't take that chance. Besides, it wouldn't do any good. I'll probably always be a little bitter." She gave him a sardonic smile as she scooped up his plate. "Did I not tell you those things were gross?"

CHAPTER TWENTY-FIVE

I knew Sullivan Crisp didn't want me to do it. And the startling thing was, I cared that he didn't want me to do it.

But not as much as I cared about getting Rich back. Which was why the day after our session, I let myself into the house with a letter in my pocket, made as much noise as possible clamoring up the stairs, and pushed open our bedroom door.

The room was a cave until I yanked the blinds up and let the light of a rare sunny day stream in. The sight it revealed was dismal, the odor worse. I'd smelled subways in New York that were sweeter than this.

I was working the window open when Rich stirred, his breathing still carrying the faint echo of a snore. The Rich I knew could come out of REM already shouting coherent orders to twenty firefighters and pulling on fifty pounds of equipment without missing a Velcro strip.

This Rich was red-eyed and disoriented, as if he'd been roused from the dead. I glanced at the bedside table and spotted a half-empty prescription bottle. Not that I hadn't thought of sleeping pills myself, but it jarred me. Rich wouldn't take so much as a Tylenol for a bruising headache.

I decided not to let his obvious stupor stop me. I sat on the edge of the bed—blocking his way out.

"What are you doing, Demitria?" he said. The words were fuzz.

"Saving our marriage."

He looked at me through swollen slits. "I told you I can't talk about this yet."

"You don't have to talk," I said. "I'm going to talk."

He half growled.

"I have something I want to say to you." I pulled the letter out of my pocket and unfolded it. "I want you to listen all the way through. You can say whatever you want to me when I'm done, but please hear me out."

He opened his mouth, but I plunged forward, reading as fast as I could.

"Dear Rich, I know it's hard for you to believe that I truly am sorry for what I've done to you and to the kids. If I were that sorry, why did I do it in the first place, right?"

He grunted.

"*I think I can answer that question now—the why—but I'm not sure you'll believe that either. I know what the pain is like, Rich, and I know how hard it is to keep your perspective in the face of it. So maybe it would help to look back—to before this happened—before 9/11—before there even was a 'why.'*"

Rich ripped the covers off and dumped his feet to the floor.

"Don't go—please," I said.

"I'm not going anywhere." His voice thickened, but the sleep had disappeared from it. He went to the window, his back to me.

I read on.

"What I'm remembering is the first months of us. When you told me even my toes were beautiful. When you were so proud that I was in college, even though you teased me about not having any mechanical sense. When you made me physically go through what I would do if my building caught on fire—the most endearing thing I could think of."

I glanced up at him. His head hung between his shoulders, and he rubbed the windowsill with his thumbs.

"I took cooking lessons from your mama, and I pumped your papa for your kid stories so I didn't have to feel left out of everything that had happened to you pre-me. I knew I wanted to be part of your family, part of you. That, and the fact that you were a gifted kisser."

"Demitria," Rich said.

I couldn't stop.

"You proposed to me two months after we met. It was so right, Rich. And it still is."

I grasped at the silence.

"It was a huge risk—as all the important things in life are, I'm learning. No, we didn't know each other well when we got married. I learned only after the ceremony that you snored. That you burped. That you wouldn't wear a tie ever again once that tuxedo came off and fell onto our hotel room floor. But none of that could overshadow your tenderness. Your appreciation of my jokes. Your calling out "Hey, Hon!" whenever you walked in the door at the end of your shift."

I paused, not for an answer, but for the courage to move into the next paragraph—the one that might bring him off the windowsill he leaned on.

"The only dark discovery I made was that when you were upset about something, you brooded. Whether it was work issues, a worry over Eddie, something I said to hurt your feelings, you closed yourself off and stewed, often for an entire day. Drove me crazy. I got the same feeling of dread that came over me in my childhood when my mother meted out the silent treatment. I took it from her because I had no choice, but I couldn't take it from you."

I drew in a rough breath.

"I cried. I pleaded. I slammed cabinet doors. All the things I never dared do with my mother. I don't think anyone had ever challenged your cavelike way of dealing with things, and over time, you began to at least tell me that you weren't upset with me and you just needed to think things through on your own. It wasn't my favorite compromise, but I learned to live with it. Until 9/11."

"Stop," Rich said.

"I'm almost through. Rich—please."

"I can't—"

"I didn't know how to help you. You wouldn't let me find a way, and that cut into the core of who I think I'm supposed to be."

I let the letter fall to the floor and took a step forward.

"Don't," he said.

"Just hear me then. I have this—this premise, they call it—that I live by. It tells me I'm supposed to be everything to everyone, and if I'm not, I'm a failure. Only you know me, Rich. You know I can't do failure—I have to find a way to make it right. And here's the screwy part." I was close to tears. "When someone told me I *was* right, I believed him—and that started my downfall."

Rich didn't move.

"I know I can't erase the past," I said. "But I'm learning from it, Rich. That has to count for something, doesn't it?"

He sank to the edge of the windowsill and parked his wrists on his knees as he stared down at his feet.

Did that sound too desperate? Dear Father in Heaven, I *was* desperate. This was my life—

"You think we could make it work?"

Rich's voice was small. So small I wasn't sure I'd heard it at all.

"What?" I said.

"You think we could make it work?"

Oh, dear God.

"Because, Demitria, I can never go through this again."

He looked up at me, eyes mapped with the pain I'd put there.

"You won't have to. It was the most horrible thing I have ever done in my life, and it will never, ever happen again." My voice begged, and I didn't care. He was saying yes.

"It can't be like before," he said.

"No—absolutely not."

"I don't know what we'll do about the house and the bills—but you can't go back to work—not if we're going to make it."

I blinked, hard and fast.

He fisted his hands, stretched his arms, gathered up control before my eyes. "I gotta believe that's what did it," he said. "You working all the time—you said it yourself—you wanted to feel needed, and that's where you did."

I studied his face. Tears had formed at the corners of his eyes, and the jaw muscles worked against them. I thought my chest would rip in half. He was asking me to give up a piece of my being. But I had said I'd do anything.

"If you stay home, we can do this. Maybe." His voice caught on a lurking sob. "I don't know, Demitria. This scares me to death."

I pressed both hands against my mouth as I sank gingerly to the sill, not touching him. "Me too, Rich," I said. "But we can do it. I know we can." And then I heard myself add, "If you want me to stay home, I'll stay home. We'll figure out the money."

Rich didn't take his gaze from me. "I want to believe you. Honest to God, I do."

We hunted for each other, eyes everywhere, my hands risking a reach for him. We almost found it—when I felt a presence in the doorway.

"There is no way," a voice said.

With my fingers still straining toward Rich, I whirled around. Christopher stood there, face white and angular, like a jagged piece that didn't fit what we were putting together. He inserted himself into the room, his eyes on Rich.

"You're not actually considering letting her come back," he said. "I thought you decided—"

Rich looked at me, face splotched, and said, "Your mother and I have been talking."

"So I see." Christopher lowered his eyes to me. "What lies did she tell you this time?"

Rich said nothing. Did nothing.

"Please send him away," I said between my teeth.

"Christopher, you're over the line, son," Rich said. "Go on—we'll talk later."

Christopher gave one long, disdainful hiss and left. I counted the steps until his bedroom door slammed.

Rich stood up and disappeared into the bathroom.

I sat, frozen.

He came back into the doorway in a T-shirt that smelled like exhaust.

"My career is not the only thing that's going to have to change if I come back," I said.

He stayed in the bathroom doorway, put his hand up on the frame.

I jutted my head forward. "Were you just going to sit there and let him talk to me like that?"

"I sent him away."

"After I asked you to. Rich, he doesn't run our lives. I don't know what we did with him that made him think he could take over, but that has to change."

Rich shook out the bedspread, smoothed it out, and sat on it. "I'll handle it my own way."

My face burned. "I need you to stand up for me with him, Rich," I said. "We both have to look at the way we handle him."

He snapped his head toward me. "I don't need you telling me how to deal with my son. It's been the two of us through this thing—"

"By your choice!"

"He's been a godsend," he said. "I couldn't do it without him."

"And now it's time you did it with *me.* And he can't be part of it—this is between us."

"Whoa, whoa, whoa." Rich put his hand up. "Let me get this straight, all right? You were the one who went out and slept with somebody else—now you're begging me to take you back, only you want to make the rules about how it's going to be."

I stared at him, hard.

"Christopher is not what's wrong with us. You—what you did—is what's wrong with us."

"Then when do I get to be right again? When are you going to forgive me, Rich—so we can be equals again?" My voice was shrill and shaken. "I want to come home more than anything in this world—but only if you forgive me, because you know what? I am not going to live in shame for the rest of my life. If you—and our son—are going to hold this over my head forever, then you can forget it."

I watched Rich recoil into himself, watched him plant his hands on his hips, heard him say, "Then I guess you can forget it."

I got hold of Mickey and asked her to check on Jayne, who was home alone. Then I got there too and made it to the window seat before I collapsed into myself.

But there were no tears. I couldn't cry. I couldn't claw at the cushions and call myself an idiot. I couldn't even wish I could take it all back.

Because I'd done the only thing there was to do. And now it was over.

I laid my cheek on my knees, head to the side so I could watch the last of the houses perched on the hill across the street blend in blackness into the sound. I'd expected to be devastated should this ever happen, but it didn't feel real. That "if" still lurked. I could go back—if I did it on Rich's terms. I'd thought I would do that no matter what they were. Sullivan Crisp had said I couldn't.

A curse on him and his game shows. He was right.

I looked at my reflection, now clear in the window. I looked like a woman who'd just had a bout with destiny and barely come out with her life. But she'd come out—hair in hunks, eyes sagging into carry-on luggage, lips chewed to a feathery red—but she'd come out, and here she was. With nothing left to do but figure herself out, or she was lost for sure.

I dug my face into my knees. I had to find my way—for Jayne—for what was left of my Christopher—for myself.

For God. Because if I let go of where I was going before—my direction, my call—where did that leave me with God? I grabbed my knees and held on and groped for my breath.

"Mom? Are you okay?"

I snapped my head up. Jayne stood halfway between me and the kitchen. She clicked on the lamp and flooded herself in strawberry blonde light.

"No," I said. "But I will be."

"Okay."

She padded toward me. She nestled onto the window seat facing me with something in her hands.

"Whatcha got?" I said.

"I made this for you."

She held it out to me, requiring two hands. It was the Sullivan Crisp rock—now shiny with a coat of pink paint and bright yellow stripes with blue dots.

"It was an ugly rock," she said. "So I turned it into an Easter egg."

I put my hand sideways over my mouth, and for the first time in days—weeks—maybe months—I laughed. It bubbled up from a spring I'd forgotten I even had, and it didn't stop.

She wrinkled her fragile brow. "Is it funny looking?"

"No—it's absolutely delightful."

"It's funny looking," she said. "But that's okay. You like it, right?"

"I love it. It is the most precious thing I have ever seen."

She set it down between us and surveyed it—dispassionately, I thought. Which made me giggle even harder.

"I might have an idea, actually," she said.

"Yes?"

"It's like transformation."

My laughter faded. "What do you mean, honey?"

"You said you were supposed to make it into something besides a weapon to use on yourself. Easter eggs are like new birth and all that. So it's transformed—and maybe we are too."

I looked at the girl who for an instant gave me a glimmer of a woman. Perhaps a woman wiser than I. And then she tilted her head at me.

"Do you think I could have an Easter outfit?" she said.

"Well—yeah—when's Easter?"

"Okay—you've been holed up in here too long, Mom. It's this Sunday. Hello!"

I laughed again.

"We'll go shopping," I said. "Only—I mean, you'll want to go to church."

"Not our church." She rolled her eyes. "Christopher's been making me go, and I feel like a beta fish."

"Excuse me?"

"In a bowl. All these people are looking at us like, *What's wrong with your family?* It feels weird because if somebody asks, I'm not allowed to tell them. So—no—can we find someplace else to go on Easter?"

"We will do whatever you want," I said.

She got up and put the Easter egg on our coffee table. "There," she said.

Now in full display, the rock showed itself lopsided and garish, with paint hardened into a drip on one side. If that symbolized my transformation, I had a long way to go.

But now I had a reason to go there.

CHAPTER TWENTY-SIX

You win."

Demi was barely inside the garage when she said it. Sully was still putting the intake manifold on, and he glanced at his watch.

"I know I'm early." She paused in her charge across the floor and drew her shoulders up to her ears. "Is that okay?"

"If you don't mind a little grease under my fingernails." Something seemed different about her today, something that sent his antennae up. He followed her into the office, where she was already pulling off her jacket. He couldn't name it yet, but a more vulnerable Demi sighed her body into the chair. He'd have to let this newness unfold. The prospect was delicious.

"So what do I win?" he said.

She looked at him blankly.

"You said I won." He sat lightly in his chair. "What's my prize?"

"Me saying you were right and I was wrong." She looked into her lap, and her face struggled against tears.

"I've told you, it's okay to cry here," he said.

"I can't. I'm all cried out."

"You want to tell me what's happening?"

"It's over." Even without tears, the pain streamed down her face. "I did what you said not to. I told Rich about my 'faulty premise.'" She made quotation marks with her fingers. "And I asked him to take me back." She let her head fall backward.

"It didn't go well?"

"You know it didn't. I mean, at first he said yes—if I'd agree to give up working."

Sully tried not to flinch. "And you said?"

"I said I would. It felt like we were so close to—" She pressed her fingertips into her forehead. "And then our son came in, and Rich backpedaled. He let Christopher just—take over. When I told him that had to change, he did an about-face, and I yelled at him. Yelled."

She closed her eyes, clearly seeing the scene for the thousandth time.

"I'm going to be the shrink for a second, okay?" Sully said.

She nodded.

"How did it feel to yell at him?"

She opened her eyes, and they flickered slightly. "When I was doing it? Kind of good. It's like he wants to hold this over my head forever—and I told him I can't live like that."

"Good."

"He told me if that was the case, I could forget about getting back together. I guess I got myself in a corner with no way out."

"You were right out in the open with him."

"Where you told me not to go."

"Only because Rich isn't ready." Sully pulled forward again and waited until she met his eyes. "But I'm not in charge here. I can guide you, but the choices are yours."

"I must have made the wrong one. It didn't work."

"It could have been a step."

"I want you to tell me what the next one is, Sullivan," she said. "I want you to."

The difference was there, in her voice.

Surrender.

Ding-ding-ding.

Sully kept his own voice soft. "I'm not going to tell you what to do. You know that."

"Yes, and I hate it."

"But I will take you to the next step, and if you want to make it—"

"I do." Demi straightened her shoulders.

"I warn you, it has more to do with you than with directly getting Rich back."

"I know."

"Do you swear to me that you know that?"

She put up a hand. "Give me a Bible."

"I trust you." He pulled a foot up under him. "Now—"

"What did you say?"

"When?"

"Just now—about trusting me?"

"I trust you," Sully said.

"Are you kidding—or do you really think you can count on my word?"

Her voice was the thickness of honey. Sully could taste the importance of the question, and he shaped his mouth carefully around his answer. "I'm seeing a different Demi today," he said. "This is the real Demi, I think. She's willing to look at the questions, the way she asks her students to do. And she's going to accept the answers. So, yes—I do trust you."

He watched that seep in, saw her face soften, witnessed the first tears in his office.

"Thank you," she said. "Dear God—thank you."

Sully wasn't sure which one of them she was grateful to. But he closed his eyes and said, "Amen."

"I can't believe I thought he was a goofball at first," I told Mickey the next morning.

"I still think he is." She gave her elfin smile over the shipment of supplies we were moving around. "But who cares? You're smiling."

"Am I?"

She stopped to regard me, a tub of coconut oil perched on her hip. "It's not an I-just-won-the-lottery smile, but it's hopeful. What did Bob Barker say to you?"

I did feel myself smile as I pushed the jars onto the shelf, labels out the way she liked them. "He said it's like starting a new game."

"Of course."

"All the mistakes you made in the last one are wiped clean. You get to start over, fresh and clear. I can't play Rich's game—or Christopher's—or anybody else's. I can't change them. I can only change me."

As I reached for a bottle of organic tamari, Mickey put her hand on my arm. "What if the rest of us don't want you to change? I'm kind of liking you the way you are."

I patted her hand. "It's the way I think about myself that needs to change. I think this is right. I don't totally get it yet, but I think I'm forgiven by God—my slate is clean—and now I have to live like a person who's been given a second chance."

"Is Dr. Barker telling you how to do this?" Mickey put up her hand. "I'm sure he knows what he's doing, but personally, I think you ought to get yourself a lawyer, drop-kick your son through a couple of goalposts—"

She stopped when I put my arms around her neck, tamari bottle in hand.

"You're such a trip," I said.

"Oh, baby girl, I'm a whole journey. I'm sorry. Oscar and I, and Audrey, we want you to be happy and come out of this with some dignity left. Enough with the shame already."

I stepped back. "I think the shame's going away. That's just—I think I have to fight to be allowed to hold my head up again."

"That I can get into. If he's going to help you do that, then fine." She turned back to a box of coconut flakes. "But I still think you ought to go ahead and bring that boy of yours in here so we can all go after him."

I'd actually been tempted. But Christopher must be operating under a faulty premise as well—one he'd probably never look at.

"Shouldn't Audrey be here by now?"

I looked up to see Oscar standing in the doorway with two plates up each arm, all steaming with fluffily-egged burritos.

"Not my day to watch her." Mickey's voice was like sandpaper. "Dock her pay when she gets here."

Oscar grunted. "Yeah, well, meanwhile, you've got four people out there waiting for breakfast."

"I can serve them," I said.

"You want to?" Mickey said. "I promised you wouldn't have to deal with the public."

"I think I'm past bawling into people's food." I nodded toward Oscar's heavily-laden arms. "But don't expect me to carry that many plates at once."

Mickey took two of them and, looking like the proud mother of a budding waitress, said, "Follow me."

Audrey didn't show up until two hours after her last class, which was unusual. In spite of Mickey's outward indifference, she watched the clock and looked furtively out the window, as neurotic a mother as any of us—though she was quick to switch to near-homicidal when Audrey's Nissan pulled up to the curb.

"You better get to her first and find out what her excuse is," she said to me. "Otherwise, she may lose several teeth, and I can't afford the dental bills." Mickey's mouth tightened. "Find out what's going on and get back to me, would you?"

The chimes on the door heralded Audrey's entrance, but by the time I got out front she was nowhere to be found. I must have looked quizzical, because the regular customer sipping a Chai tea by the window pointed wordlessly to the restroom.

"Audrey?" I whispered at the door. "You okay, honey?"

No answer. I was about to tap when she opened it just wide enough for me to slip through and pulled me in. We stood almost nose to nose between the toilet and the batik hanging, her eyes leaping at me as if she were about to fall over an edge only I could hold her back from.

"Honey, what is it?" I asked.

She put her hands to her lips and stared at me, wild-eyed.

"Audrey, breathe."

She gasped.

"No—nice big breath—let it out."

She did. I made her do it again, until she went limp, and then I pulled her into my arms.

"What happened?" I said. "Did you have an accident?"

"Big time."

I pulled her away to look at her. "Are you hurt?"

"No, Dr. C.," she said. "I'm pregnant."

"Come on, baby."

Isabella's motor churned. Tried.

"Come on, now, a little more." Sully pressed the gas pedal, and she tried again. The effort filled the air with gas fumes.

"Okay—I'm sorry, baby." He patted the dashboard. "You're not ready."

"Am I interrupting something?"

Sully jerked around, slamming his forehead against the top of the car door.

"Oh, my gosh!" Demi said. "I am so sorry—I didn't mean to scare you!"

Sully shook off stars and peered at her.

"Are you okay?" she said.

"I'm fine—are *you* okay?" He climbed out of the Impala, resisting the urge to check for a lump on his forehead, and kept his eyes on her.

"Is this all right, me stopping by?" she said. She drew her shoulders in and didn't seem to know where to put her hands.

He didn't have the heart to tell her that it wasn't. Their client-therapist arrangement wasn't the most conventional anyway. "What's up?" he said instead.

"I want to make sure. I'm in an awkward position, and I think I know what to do, only—I want to make sure I don't mess it up."

Sully leaned against the car and folded his arms. "Something with Rich?"

"No—Audrey. She's pregnant."

"Ouch. By Boy?"

"He says not—but Audrey says he's the only one she's been with, and I believe her."

"So—what's your awkward position?"

Demi shook her hand through her hair. "She doesn't want to tell

Oscar and Mickey. She says they'll disown her—which I absolutely cannot believe—but she's scared to death. I think if I hadn't gotten to her, she would have left town."

Sully nodded.

"I told her she's probably just letting fear get to her. She's in shock—finding out you're pregnant under the best of circumstances can throw you for a loop. But she refuses to talk to them unless I go with her."

"So—"

"How do I feel about that, right?"

Sully grinned. "You're learnin', girl."

"I feel like I should help. I have a great relationship with Mickey, so if there *is* any anger, I can probably mediate. She's always asking me to talk to Audrey, be there for her."

"So what's the down side?"

Demi opened her mouth, then closed it. He watched several ideas pass through her eyes until she looked at him with surprise.

"None, I guess. I was thinking maybe I'm not qualified, given my recent—activities."

"But now you're thinking—"

"Now I'm thinking, who knows better than I do what it's like to make a major mistake and have to put your life back together?"

"Ding, ding," Sully said.

Demi let one corner of her mouth go up, and then the other.

"Did I just figure that whole thing out myself, while you stood there and let me?"

"You sure did."

She smiled, all the way, and stepped right into him. Her arms were around his neck before he saw it coming. She squeezed, let go, stepped back.

"Thank you," she said. "You make me feel like—I don't know—whatever it is, thank you."

"You're welcome."

And then Sully said nothing.

The smile didn't fade from her lips, but it left her eyes. She looked around the garage as if her next words should be there, and when they weren't, she said, "Well, I guess I should go. Can I call you and tell you how it goes tonight?"

"We can schedule an extra session." Sully lined his words up carefully. "You want to come in tomorrow?"

The smile left her lips now too. "I'll call you," she said.

And then she escaped. There was no other way to describe the way she extricated herself from the scene and got away to face her own embarrassment. He wanted to call after her, to say it was his fault too, that he hadn't made the boundaries clear.

But he let her make the fast break, let her save face. Heaven knew, she needed that.

Dang.

He put both hands on the blanket he'd draped over the side of the car by the opened hood and let his head hang between his shoulders. Demi was just feeling the exhilaration of getting it, getting herself. He was the first person who'd trusted her in months. She was bound to feel like being spontaneous—like hugging.

He just couldn't let her.

You have to maintain a healthy distance from the client, he told his eager young therapists who wanted to do lunch with patients who'd made breakthroughs, who needed more of them than a session in an office allowed. *You aren't their friend—you're their therapist.*

"She is my friend," Lynn had said to him. "She understands me, and nobody else does."

Sully shook his head. No. No memories tonight. He had to think this Demi thing through, or he was going to lose her just when she was making progress.

He picked up a wrench and looked down into Isabella's waiting heart. "Come on, baby," he said. "You can do this. Get me through the night."

It was dawn when she finally turned over.

CHAPTER TWENTY-SEVEN

I couldn't believe I did that. Could not believe it.

I made it all the way back to the apartment driveway before I stopped the Jeep and banged my fists on the steering wheel.

You did *not* just hug that man.

I shoved my hair behind my ears. He hadn't taken the hug as a grateful client showing appreciation, either—I'd seen that in his eyes. Sullivan had drawn the same conclusion I had: that basically, Demitria Costanas was a sucker for any man who was nice to her, who showed any inkling of understanding her.

I felt wretched enough to run to my window seat and hide under a ratty afghan, except that Audrey's Nissan pulled up next to the Jeep. The curved-over waif behind the wheel looked worse than I felt.

Audrey opened her driver's door as if she were moving through a pillow. Picking up her purse, dropping her keys, retrieving them, all apparently took more effort than she could muster. She stood up, eyes large in her pale face. No doe in headlights ever looked so frightened, so sure that a terrible end was imminent. I'd seen that look before: every morning when I looked in the mirror and faced another day trying to make right what I'd done wrong.

"You're far more upset with yourself than they're going to be with you," I told her as I half carried her up the steps to her parents' house.

"I don't think they'll understand," she said.

"I do, and I'm not even your mom."

Audrey let her head fall against my shoulder. "Right now, I wish you were."

Mickey was crossing the kitchen with a basket of laundry when we came in. One look at us and she set it, teetering, on the counter.

"What's wrong?" she said. I gave Audrey's sweaty hand a squeeze, surprised it didn't wring out onto the floor.

"Come on, spill it." Mickey shoved the laundry basket from its precarious position and leaned a hand on the counter. Oscar was in the doorway, the remote control in one hand, the remains of an hors d'oeuvre in the other.

"Come on, Audrey." Mickey's voice was growing shrill. "You're freaking me out here."

"Maybe we should go sit down," I said. "Mick, do you have any tea made?"

Her eyes flicked in my direction, but basically she ignored me.

Oscar crossed to the trash can and tossed in his appetizer. "Aud?" he said.

"I can't say it!" Audrey said. "You're going to hate me!" She swiveled around and threw herself into my arms.

I looked helplessly over her head at Mickey.

"Oh, for heaven's sake, Audrey, we are not going to hate you." Mickey took Audrey's arm and pulled her from me. With her hand on the girl's chin she pulled her face close to hers. "Now what is going on?"

Audrey whimpered.

"Mick," Oscar said.

Mickey let go of Audrey, but her eyes kept her there. "What is it you're so afraid to tell us?"

"Promise me you won't think I'm horrible?"

"What—is—it?"

"I'm going to have a baby, Mom. I'm sorry—"

In all of the scenes I'd participated in over the past eight weeks, I'd seen and experienced more emotion, I was sure, than most people did in a lifetime. That didn't include the kind of grief I'd shared with my community after 9/11, which was almost unbearable. But I had never seen weeping quite like this. Audrey cried so hard, I was afraid she'd lose consciousness.

Mickey, on the other hand, watched her daughter sob from her soul without so much as a nibble at her lip.

Oscar stood with one hand over the lower half of his face, the other tucked into his armpit, swallowed in the girth of his arm. I could only see his eyes, which blinked hard, as if he were confused.

"Okay—you're going to make yourself sick, Audrey," Mickey said. "Come on—breathe." She folded her arms around her daughter as if she were dealing with some strange child on a playground. "Take a breath—come on—before you throw up."

Audrey gasped several times and nodded.

I was sure I was watching a scenario that had happened many times before. Audrey seemed strangely comforted.

"She's been terrified about telling you all day," I said. "She's been holding it in."

"She gets like this. Oscar, get her some water."

Oscar produced a glass, which Audrey drained while Mickey stood over her. The family dynamic was apparently restored. Time for me to leave.

"So what's the deal, Demi?" Mickey said.

"I'm sorry?" I said.

"Who is this guy?"

I looked from her to Audrey.

"You're going to make a lot more sense than she is, and you obviously know, so go ahead."

I couldn't tell what I was hearing in her voice—resentment, hurt feelings, out-and-out jealousy?

"He's the boy she's been dating," I said. "Um—C.J., is it, Audrey?"

She nodded.

"She thought she loved him—that he loved her."

"So she slept with him, without protection, and now she's pregnant." Mickey lifted Audrey's chin again. "Is that the story?"

"We did use protection!" she said.

"Oh—so it was an 'accident.'" Mickey lightly touched the end of Audrey's nose. "And a pretty stupid one, if you ask me."

I could feel my chin drop. She was kidding, right? But even if she was—at a time like this?

"I know, Mom," Audrey managed to say. "I'm so sorry."

Her knees gave. She seemed headed for the floor, and Oscar came in from behind and caught her under the arms. When he got her to her feet, her face was momentarily lost in his belly.

No one spoke for a few never-ending minutes. My instinct was to run downstairs and pull my long-legged Jayne onto my lap and rock her. And yet I had a hard time even moving toward the door.

Finally Mickey motioned Audrey into a chair at the kitchen table and sat down across from her. "So what does this C.J. say?"

"He says the baby isn't his." Audrey's voice was hoarse.

"Is it?" Mickey said.

"Mick!" Oscar said.

I could have hugged him.

"It couldn't be anybody else's," Audrey said. "I'm not some tramp, Mom."

"So that means he isn't going to give you any help," Mickey said.

Audrey nodded.

"Which is where we come in."

"I don't know," Audrey said.

"Well, don't be ridiculous. Whatever you decide to do, you're going to need us."

"I haven't thought about what to do."

"When were you going to go ahead and do that, Audrey?"

"She just found out twelve hours ago," someone said.

All eyes found me. Audrey's were pleading. Oscar's were still befuddled. Mickey's told me I'd said enough.

"Listen," I said, "I think this is a family thing. I should probably go."

I turned toward the door.

"Well, thanks, Demi," Mickey said. "I don't know when or if she ever would have told us if it weren't for you."

I turned to look at her, but her gaze was fixed on Audrey, eyes firm.

"Audrey?" I said. "Are you going to be okay?"

"She'll be fine," Mickey said.

And yet still I added as I opened the door, "Call me if you need me, Audrey."

A chill followed me out.

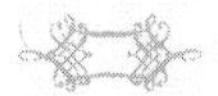

Jayne was curled up, wide-eyed, on the window seat when I got downstairs. I filled her in, and she nodded sagely.

"I guess her mom didn't talk to her about boys and getting pregnant," she said.

I didn't have an answer for that. I just didn't understand Mickey's reaction.

I was still trying to sort it out the next morning when, after a night of not-quite-sleep, I took a bag of garbage out to the compost heap, stepping carefully over Mickey's newly planted rows of peas and spinach and lettuce seedlings.

"I'm going to go ahead and say this."

I whipped around, dumping cucumber peelings short of the pile. Mickey was baggy-eyed and, if I weren't mistaken, a little sheepish.

"Hey, Mick," I said. "Are you hanging in there?"

"You do what you have to do, right?" She shoved her hands into the pockets of a pair of bedraggled cargo pants. "Look, I appreciate you being there for Audrey. The thing is, we can handle it from here."

I searched her face for a trace of the wise gnome who had virtually saved my life, but I could see only fatigue in the sun-ray lines at the corners of her eyes.

"How is Audrey?" I said.

"She'll live. After we finished with the drama, she finally got down to considering her options."

Even as I opened my mouth, I knew I was about to kick my own prop out from under me.

"What about her emotional state, Mickey?" I said. "She's only six weeks pregnant—she has time to look at what she wants to do. I'm more concerned about how she's going to handle it."

"That kind of concern isn't going to fix this problem." Mickey's hand came out of her pocket and chopped the air haphazardly. "Besides, she isn't the one handling it. That falls to Oscar and me." She looked hard at me. "You saw for yourself how she handles things."

"I don't get it," I said.

"That's because you didn't raise her."

"Audrey I get. It's you I don't understand."

In the pause, Mickey's mouth wanted to melt, and moisture lined up along her lower lids. But she pulled up whatever she selected to hold herself together and turned to plaster. "What's not to understand?" she said.

"You have shown me nothing but grace and acceptance ever since you met me," I said. "And as far as I'm concerned, what I've done is a whole lot worse than the mistake Audrey's made. I was just surprised you weren't more—loving, I guess."

"If I give her a hug and tell her it's okay, what does she learn?" Mickey shook her head. "I can cut you slack because I'm not responsible for how you turn out."

"How do you expect her to turn out if you treat her like she's committed a crime? She's already hard enough on herself."

"Not hard enough, obviously." Her consonants were hard. "Look—if you think treating Audrey like a victim is what she needs, then I wish you'd go ahead and stay away from her."

I stared at her. "You were the one who wanted me to be there for her in the first place!"

"I didn't know she was doing it with some guy she barely knew." Mickey stopped and looked as if she'd been poked. "Did you know about it? Did you know she was sleeping with him?"

I swallowed. "Whatever Audrey and I talked about was between us."

"I'll take that as a yes." She took a step back. "Like I said, we've got this handled. Thanks."

"Mickey, come on—you're upset."

"No, but you're about to see me upset."

"Mick!" Oscar stalked toward us with his palm up—as if that were going to quiet his wife, who was just warming up as far as I could tell.

Mickey's eyes were still on me. "I appreciate what you've done, but I think I know Audrey better than anybody. Just let us handle it." She planted both hands on her negligible hips. "Do you get me now?"

I got this woman, who bore no resemblance to the one who had put me back together. This woman was now in the business of taking her daughter apart, and then telling me to stand by and watch her do it.

And I couldn't.

"Where is Audrey now?" I said.

"Which part of this didn't you understand?"

"Is she here—or is she alone somewhere?"

"What is the *matter* with you?"

Mickey took a step toward me, but Oscar's big hand closed over her shoulder.

"Mick!" he said. "Back off."

She lowered her arm and closed her eyes. "I'm losing it," she said.

I had to agree.

"You're fine. Let's everybody go back to their corners and cool off." Oscar looked at me. "Why don't you take today off? You look pretty rough."

"She doesn't work on Saturdays." Mickey was already in a turn toward the house. "Maybe she doesn't work at all."

"What did I say about cooling off—before anybody says something they don't mean?"

She didn't answer him. He and I both stood examining the soil until she was gone.

"Did she just fire me?" I said.

"No. She just thinks she did." Oscar smeared his entire puffy face with his hand and let it rest on the sausage rolls at the back of his neck.

"I wasn't expecting that."

"It only happens when she's really stressed. She'll come back around." He grimaced. "I hope you don't take off on us in the meantime. Come to work Monday, and the air'll be cleared."

Did I not have enough yelling in my life right now? And enough lack of understanding? And enough unforgiving?

"Listen." Oscar's eyes were as soft as the folds around them. "I appreciate all you've done for Audrey. Who knows what she would've pulled when she found this out if you hadn't been there for her? Mick knows that too."

"Right."

"It wouldn't bother me any if you kept seeing her—and Mickey might even let you do that once she calms down. But for now, to keep the peace . . ." Oscar bobbed his head again. "Maybe you should give Audrey a wide margin. She's not here anyway. She went back to the dorm last night."

I felt my eyes widen. "You let her go be by herself after what she went through yesterday?"

"Mick felt like—"

"No, I can't let that poor girl go through this by herself. I just can't."

"She won't. Mickey will be there—she just needs time."

"Audrey doesn't have time." I stomped past him. "She's at the dorm, you said?"

"Dem, I'm really begging you here—"

"And I'm really telling you no."

I stopped behind him. He looked over his shoulder at me.

"You two can fire me, you can evict me, you can do whatever you want. But I refuse to abandon Audrey. Just so you know."

Mickey was standing midway up the steps when I passed under them to get back to my apartment. She was still the different Mickey. And that was fine. Because now, I was the different Demi.

CHAPTER TWENTY-EIGHT

Jayne was still asleep when I got back to the apartment, hair splayed across the pillow like filigreed gold, eyelashes kissing the tops of her cheeks. I crawled in beside her and listened to the soft, even breathing of a child safe and content. When she opened her eyes, she looked at me unsurprised, as if of course I would be lying there watching her sleep.

"Do you have a plan?" she said.

I propped up on one elbow. "A plan?"

"You look like you have a plan."

I pushed a curly tendril off her forehead with my finger. "I do. I'm just wondering if you want to do it with me."

"Is it about Easter clothes?" she said.

"It is—and it's about Audrey."

"Is she going shopping with us?"

"Do you want her to?"

"I like her," Jayne said.

"All right."

"What's the rest of the plan?"

"I wondered . . ."

I paused. This could be a mistake.

"Say it, Mom."

I sucked in air. "I wondered how you would feel about Audrey moving in with us."

"Are you going to treat her like another daughter?" Jayne said.

I studied her face. It was pensive, nothing more.

"I mean, I think you should." She came up on an elbow to face me, as if we were two girlfriends waking up from a sleepover. "She needs a better mom than the one she's got—the way Mrs. Gwynne was yelling at her last night."

"You heard that?"

She rolled her eyes. "Who didn't? I think she needs you."

My throat thickened. "You think that, Jay?"

"I *know* that. Mom, you understand. You don't expect a kid to be perfect."

I sat up and kissed her on the forehead. "What do you say we go find Audrey?"

We moved her in that night, complete with an Easter outfit and a basket full of that obnoxious plastic grass that you find under the rug and in the corners of drawers until Halloween. She'd opted for a high-waisted, large-print dress, leggings, and Jolly Rancher jelly beans.

"I hope people don't think this is dorky," she said as she held the dress up to herself in my kitchen. "I don't feel like being in a clingy sweater or something, you know?"

"Who cares what anybody else thinks?" I said. "They have no idea what you're dealing with."

"I'm gonna model mine," Jayne said.

She disappeared into the bedroom, and I enthroned Audrey on my window seat with cushions, afghan, and warm milk with nutmeg.

"It's been a big day," I said. "Time for you to let down a little."

"I feel like crying," she said. "I'm sorry. You're doing so much for me."

"Never be sorry for tears." It caught in my throat—where I'd learned that from. Her own mother should be saying this to her.

"I don't feel as stupid today." Audrey bunched the afghan up under her chin and let the tears trickle down into its holes. "You make me feel like the whole entire world isn't coming to an end."

"You're not, and it's not."

She looked deep into the afghan. "Is it okay that I miss C.J.? Even though he's treating me like crap?"

I closed my eyes. Zach Archer strutted past and didn't look back at me. "You can't help it," I said. "It's one of the things you'll deal with."

"If I can."

"When you can."

"Ta-da!"

Jayne made an entrance through the kitchen, spinning deftly around the chairs, the coffee table, and Audrey's duffle bag. Her three-tiered skirt swayed like a gypsy's.

"Okay, how fabulous is that?" Audrey said.

Jayne smiled pertly and looked at me. "You wanted me to pick the Jackie O. number."

"I know, I know."

The girls grinned at each other.

Tomorrow would probably bring an eviction notice, once Mickey found out what I was doing. But for now I sighed against the cushions and let them be girls, just girls, cooing over Jayne's beaded flip-flops.

I heard Mickey come downstairs early the next morning. I imagined her stopping to do a double take when she saw Audrey's car and steeled myself for a blowup.

There was, however, no knock at the door, nor any indication that I was being thrown out when I poked my head out. That was my first surprise of the day.

The second came when Jayne sat herself at the snack bar with her basket full of M&Ms and said, "I think we should go to the CCC chapel for Easter."

I stopped beating a bowl of eggs. Audrey stirred on the window seat.

"I love that," she said. "Dr. Kaye is preaching."

"Can we, Mom?" Jayne said.

"Let me think about it."

"The service starts at ten," Audrey said.

"It's eight-thirty now." Jayne hopped down from the stool. "I'll go take a shower first—that okay, Aud?"

"Wait," I said, eyes still on the spinning eggs. "Ladies, I don't know what other people are going to think of me going back there. I didn't leave under the best of circumstances."

"Hello!"

I turned to catch the end of a Jayne eye roll.

"Who cares what anybody else thinks?" she said, in a voice clearly reminiscent of my own. "They have no idea what you're dealing with."

I set the whisk on the counter.

"All right," I said. "Everybody get dressed."

Sully fidgeted with the tie all the way to the chapel. Neckwear had never been his thing, but he felt like he owed it to Ethan to get dressed up. He had to borrow the necktie from him, of course, and take a refresher tutorial in how to tie the thing. Right now it squeezed his Adam's apple.

He'd only been in the chapel once, to hear Ethan preach at a weekday service which, to his chagrin, only a handful of students attended. Today the place was packed, and the chapel itself was ready for all the people who went to church on Christmas and Easter and counted themselves good to go.

The sanctuary was a riot of uncultivated looking lilies and primroses, which separated only to form a path of oyster shells up to an empty rough-hewn cross.

"All right, Ethan," Sully whispered.

He squeezed into a back pew full of college guys in faded cotton polos and immediately took off his tie.

"Yeah, dude, lose that thing," said a long-armed, redheaded kid. "You were lookin' a little overdressed."

"Thanks," Sully said.

As a parade of swishing skirts and just-purchased pumps moved past, he saw familiar movement. A tall woman with a straight

Washingtonian walk took the aisle, flanked by two young women, and Sully sat up straight in the seat. It was Demi.

She apparently hadn't seen him, and, ushering the two girls into a pew in front, she wouldn't unless she turned around to gawk, which wasn't her style.

Sully decided he could slip out at the end of the service. It was going to be embarrassing enough for her when they did talk next—she didn't need to have that conversation here. Already, a row of coeds three pews up swiveled their heads toward each other as if on cue, eyes bulging like Ping Pong balls, mouths already shaping, "Are you serious?"

Sully looked at her as she sat in the pew between the two girls, looking down at the bulletin he was sure she wasn't reading. This was the last place he would have expected her, and another glance around told him he wasn't the only one. Less discreet than the coeds was the woman in top-to-toe pink who openly nudged the man next to her and nodded in Demi's direction.

Sully groaned. He'd have known Kevin St. Clair's baggy eyes anywhere.

A violin's sweet strain lifted above the din, sounding like sunrise itself and pulling Sully to his feet with the rest of the congregation. Ethan's voice joined the strings with the announcement, "He is risen! The Lord is risen indeed." The congregation responded with "Alleluia! Alleluia!"

Sully didn't know what had possessed Demi to come, but this was why he was here. His own Alleluia was belated, and the red-headed kid gave him a friendly smirk. It was Easter, and he was part of it.

"You ever heard him preach?" the redhead whispered when they settled in for the sermon.

"Oh, yeah," Sully said. "He's great."

The kid looked at Sully as if he'd grossly understated the issue. "He's *amazing.* I just hope this isn't the last time."

Ethan's voice hushed the sanctuary.

"Wouldn't it be great if someone came to you and said, 'I'll pay off all your debts. No matter whether they're foolish debts, notes you took out for less-than-savory reasons, accounts that have been in arrears for years—I'll pay them off. You'll be debt free.'"

The congregation nodded as one, with the exception of Kevin St. Clair, who, Sully noticed, sat self-righteously like a man who'd never used a credit card.

"And what if," Ethan continued, "this person said to you, 'I want you to be so grateful that you don't go out and incur more debt.'" Ethan smiled his I'm-right-in-there-with-you smile. "We'd all agree to that, wouldn't we?"

More head nodding. Sully grinned contentedly. He knew where Ethan was headed.

"Now imagine that same person saying, 'However, if you do get into more debt—and you will, simply because you're human and won't be able to resist the lure of ninety days with no interest—I will take care of that debt too.'"

Sully's gaze drifted to Demi, whose face tilted toward Ethan as if she were absorbing light. She slipped her arm around the dark-haired girl next to her and pulled her in, rocking the young woman's head until it fell onto her shoulder. She looked too old to be Demi's thirteen-year-old. Sully had the pixie-child on the other side pegged for that.

"You'd expect for there to be strings attached, wouldn't you?" Ethan said.

Demi rested her cheek on the dark head, which trembled beneath her. She had to be the pregnant girl.

Ethan said, "There are no strings."

Get this, Demi, Sully thought. *Get it for yourself, too.*

"'But I do have expectations,' your generous benefactor would say."

I knew every person there with a pulse felt like Ethan was talking directly to him or her. Ethan had a gift for sweeping each individual up with his eyes. Mine he held for longer than a fraction, and I couldn't tell if he wanted me to hang onto the words, or if he was merely as surprised to see me as everyone else obviously was. Kevin St. Clair had already delivered several looks, ranging from indignant to incensed, with flabbergasted in between.

"'I expect you to do things for others with the extra money you will now have,'" Ethan said. "'I want you to be generous.'"

By then Audrey was in my arms, crying silently as silk. On the other side, Jayne looped her arm around my elbow.

"You're doing that for Audrey," she whispered.

As I twisted to kiss her on the forehead, I felt as if a long-forgotten pocket inside me were being unbuttoned, containing a feeling I'd thought was no longer mine to feel. Warm and real and soft as a sigh, it whispered, *You are good.*

Ethan moved from his stance at the top of the shallow steps and down the aisle, so that he was even with our row. Unfortunately, if I were going to watch him, I was forced to have the St. Clairs in my line of sight.

I straightened myself up and focused on Ethan.

"Now imagine this fabulous person," he said, "instructing you to tell people who it was who got you out of debt and saved your life." Ethan's face seemed to deepen. "'Tell everyone you meet,' this person would say, 'and that I will do it for them, too.'"

Until then I could embrace every word Ethan said. But this part . . . these words . . .

Tell everyone you meet that I did this for you. That I forgave you. That I gave you a chance to make a difference in someone else's life in spite of what you've done.

As hard as I fixed my eyes on Ethan, Kevin St. Clair was still a palpable presence behind him, daring me to expose myself to the community that waited like a slavering wolf. How could I tell everyone Christ had forgiven me, when the very thing I'd been forgiven would humiliate what was left of my family and strip Ethan Kaye of his already shredded credibility?

How, in fact, could I ever share Christ's love publicly again?

Inside me, that pocket closed over itself and buttoned back up.

Ethan beamed at us. "Now, your debt-payer will warn you that this doesn't mean people won't try to take advantage of this new-found wealth, or even succeed sometimes. But he wouldn't want you to get all hung up on that and think you have to go into debt again in order to 'set things right.'"

Ethan's eyes settled on Sully.

You're talking about yourself, aren't you? Sully thought.

"He'd promise to help you through it, help you learn about yourself in the process."

Sully untangled his legs and refolded them.

"'Don't become bitter if thieves and swindlers get away with it.'" Ethan put an earnest fist to his chest. "'*I'll* take care of them. *I* will.'"

Sully felt as if his shoulders suddenly wouldn't hang on their own.

"There probably isn't a person here who wouldn't agree to all of that, if our debts could be wiped clean—and not only the ones we already have, but the ones we'll incur in the future, even though we swear we never will."

Ethan's voice softened. Whenever that happened in his sermons, we were at the place that I always clung to and carried out with me.

But today, this was the part where I closed my eyes and felt the pain in my chest and the thickness in my throat, the part where I grieved—for what I now could never do.

"Wouldn't it be fabulous? *Isn't* it fabulous?" Ethan held up both palms. "Substitute the words *separation from God*—what some might call sin—for the word *debt.* Replace the benefactor's voice with that of our Lord, Jesus Christ. See what happens."

The silence in the sanctuary was pure, the air perfect for rearranging the words in my head.

I'll pay off all your sin, Demi. You are sin-free.

I want you to be generous with your forgiveness.

I want you to tell everyone that I did this for you.

I want you to, Demi.

You have to.

"Mom?" Jayne whispered. "You okay?"

I looked down to see her hand rubbing my fist, clenched so tightly my veins stood out like strands of blue yarn.

You have to tell everyone I did this for you.

"People will try to take away your freedom from guilt, Jesus says." Ethan tilted his head kindly. "They'll try to shame you, pull you back into separation, tell you that you're stupid to believe He actually did this for you."

Almost of its own accord, my head turned and my eyes moved Kevin St. Clair into focus. He stared straight ahead, as if not looking at Ethan would cancel him out. If a word reached him, it bounced off like so much hail on tin.

But it reached me—wormed down into me—pulled open the pocket—curled inside. I didn't know what to do with it yet. I only knew it was there.

"That, people," Ethan said, "is what the Cross is about."

Heads tilted back, pulled by his words to the cross he stood before.

"The death we grieved once again last Friday, there on that cross, was the final payment on all your debts—your sins—whatever you want to call them. The shame and the guilt—" He raised an arm, dignified and strong. "Gone. Now hear—and hear me well—because this is the Easter message. In His eyes, no matter what you have done—at the foot of this cross, where we are today—"

He scanned the congregation, making sure, Sully knew, that every eye, ear, and mind was centered there. "It is as if it never happened," he said. "Never."

Ethan's eyes swept across the sanctuary and came to me.

"Never," he said again.

When he bowed his head, mine sank.

Now—I want you to be generous with your forgiveness, Demi. I want you to tell the world that I did this for you. You have to.

By the time the final hymn ended, the chapel was alive. Risen, I thought, was the word. The congregation burst into exchanges of the rush we'd all shared in. Through it, I heard someone call, "Dr. C.!"

A lumbering body topped with red hair came at me, trailed by what looked like every student I'd ever mentored. The Faith and Doubt group—my ultimate concern in a life so far away from me, it seemed like a mirage even as it surrounded me with khakis and polo shirts and teetery sandals—and idealism and love.

Brandon lifted me from my feet in a hug, and hands of all sizes and states of moisture rubbed my back and touched my arms.

"We thought you were in a coma or something!" Marcy said.

They coaxed a laugh out of me—which faded as I looked over Brandon's bony shoulder at Sullivan Crisp, turning away and elbowing his way toward the door like he was chased by a pack of dogs.

I patted Brandon to put me down. The kids closed me in, away from Sullivan's retreat.

"This is like a total God-thing that you're here," Chelsea said.

"You have to know Faith and Doubt is coming apart," Brandon said.

Marcy's wide face opened up to me. "Can't you please meet with us?"

"There's no way they can keep you from being a consultant."

"We'd meet totally off campus."

"You don't even know what's going on here."

"And you need to."

Marcy pressed against my arm. "This isn't just a project anymore, Dr. C. This is about keeping this place from turning into a convent—and I am not kidding you."

Brandon put his hand up. "Look, Dr. C.," he said, "I know we messed around a lot when you and Dr. Archer were working with us—but that was before we felt like we were living under the St. Clair regime. I mean, Faith and Doubt is about what Dr. Kaye was saying." He nodded, with a wisdom that belied the freckles and the frat-boy haircut. "But nothing like that is going on at this school. We can't let this keep happening."

I felt a warm hand creep into mine and looked down at Audrey. For the moment, there was no pregnancy in those eyes.

She made me say, "I'll see, you guys. I'll pray about it."

I hadn't said those words for weeks, but they tumbled from my lips as if they'd been poised for me to come back to them.

I want you to tell everyone.

As my students—still *my* students—filtered away, I felt a surge, small, but with a maybe in it. Maybe, in some way, I could.

My eyes went to the door. But I would have to do it without Sullivan Crisp.

CHAPTER TWENTY-NINE

Monday night I made a new list.

I'd abandoned the old one due to lack of results, but I read it over—wistfully—before I hit DELETE.

GET RICH BACK

A. SEE DR. SULLIVAN CRISP

B. DO WHAT HE SAYS

FOCUS ON KIDS

A. CALL JAYNE

B. CALL CHRISTOPHER

I looked up from the laptop.

Jayne was doing pre-algebra at the snack bar. Audrey studied on the window seat, between pained gazes out at the sound.

It was a far different scene from the vacuum I'd tried to escape from in my first list. Interesting, I thought, that my expectations had been so high—that I had thought by merely checking things off I could put my family back together. I felt a wave of anxiety. I wasn't much closer to any of them now than I was then.

Except for Jayne. And the whisper—*you have to—you have to—* that had followed me out of the chapel and everywhere since. Which was the reason for a new list.

That, and the terse conversation I'd had with Mickey the night before.

I was paying the pizza delivery boy—a large, original crust with pineapple and ham being our Easter fare—when she appeared on the steps. She barely waited for the kid to flee to his car under her bullet-eyed glare.

"I'm just going to go ahead and ask you," she said.

"Yes," I said. "Audrey is staying with us."

"I'm paying for a dorm room."

"Which she can't stand to be in by herself." I shifted the hot pizza box to my hip. "Listen, do you want to come in and talk about this? I know you don't eat pizza, but I owe you a meal."

"Look, I know I haven't been acting like Mother of the Year over this thing. I can't get my mind around it—I'm, like, disconnected from myself."

"I hear that."

She put up both hands, rotating her palms like she was erasing me. "Now Audrey doesn't want to be with me—and I get that—so you just do your thing and let me know if she needs anything from me."

Pain smeared her face—and broke my heart.

"I'm doing for her what you've done for me," I said.

"Don't try to go there with me again," she said. "I can't do it for her—I don't know why. And I have to tell you, it's killing me that you can. I feel like a piece of—"

"Do you want me to move out?"

She looked away.

I changed the pizza box to the other hip.

"If I put you out, that puts Audrey out too. I'm not Mommy Dearest."

"I never said—"

"Do you want to keep working at the Bread?"

I blinked. "Do you want me to?"

"You need the money."

"True—but I don't need the dirty looks."

"I won't bring it into the workplace. I don't want to hire anybody else." She blinked hard and turned and went up the stairs.

So I'd gone to work that morning, and, needless to say, I didn't sit on my customary stool and sob. Mickey and I avoided each other, and Oscar ran interference when our being in the same air space couldn't be avoided.

Mickey was civil and uncertain with Audrey when she arrived in the afternoon, but at that point I felt myself defrost. Audrey needed my hand on her arm when she passed by and my nod that she could make it through that order, that pile of dishes, that searing look at me from her mother.

The searing looks made me type now:

FIND A NEW APARTMENT

MOVE GIRLS IN

FIND A NEW JOB

And even

PRAY

There was one item from the old list I hadn't deleted. I shook my head at the popcorn Jayne offered me and pressed my fingers to my temples as I surveyed the screen.

GET RICH BACK

The pain and fear chugged in. No papers had been filed, no phone call came from a lawyer. Nothing. Even Christopher had been quiet.

I typed:

CONFRONT CHRISTOPHER

That had to happen soon. Putting his name on the screen trumped all fear and replaced it with the teeth-gritting, blood-pressure-rising ire I experienced every time I thought of the boy. The boy—who possessed less maturity than his still-a-child sister who at this moment held a crying Audrey in the kitchen.

"What's happening?" I said. I rounded the snack bar.

"I don't know," Jayne mouthed.

"It just comes over me sometimes," Audrey said.

"The baby?" I asked.

She shook her head. "I know I want to keep him, Dr. C. I decided that today."

"Are you sure?"

"This is my baby. It's the only thing I do know."

Behind her, Jayne was silently clapping her hands. I decided not to go into the ramifications of that decision. Who knew better than I did how making up your mind about something could keep you hanging on?

"I'm crying over stupid C.J." Audrey backed away and leaned

against the counter. "I called him again today—like a moron—because I thought after he had time to think about it, he might change his mind and help me. You know what he said?"

Let me guess.

"He said he made sure we used protection—so he didn't see how I could be pregnant by him."

"Hello!" Jayne said, a handful of popcorn halfway to her mouth. "Even I know there is no one hundred percent birth control! Well, except not-sex."

If I hadn't been so ready to flush the elusive C.J. down the toilet I would have had trouble hiding a smile. At least I'd done something right.

"And then he goes—" Audrey swallowed back a sob. "He goes, 'So if it looks like a tramp, and it acts like a tramp, it must be a tramp.'" She put her face in her hands. "I was never with another guy before him. I'm not like that. I'm not a tramp!"

"No, sweetheart, you're not," I said.

That was a feeling I knew, too, every time I let Zach Archer slither back into my thoughts. I wasn't a tramp who succumbed to a man's compassion when she was down.

When the girls went to bed, I reopened The List and typed:

Cancel therapy

I couldn't face Sullivan again. I wasn't sure I could face anything again. I was crashing.

Until the whisper.

You have to, Demi.

You have to.

The apartment I found Tuesday after another walking-on-porcupine-quills shift at the Daily Bread was in Gerst—a funky litttle village overlooking the scenic Puget Sound Naval Shipyard.

The complex, called Sherman Heights, consisted of a tumble of A-frames arranged on the side of a hill like Monopoly houses. Highway

3 roared below, but the place had a certain summer camp feel if you faced uphill. When I took Jayne and Audrey there that evening they were charmed by the creek that ran along the edge of the property, canopied by towering evergreens and willows that swept the foxglove-and-fern-covered ground.

They were less enamored of the cabin itself. While they thought the cedar tree, which grew right up out of the kitchen floor and up through the ceiling, was endlessly cool, their lips curled increasingly as they made the ten-second tour.

Tunnel of a kitchen with a curved eating bar.

A space barely large enough for two chairs and a love seat in the center.

A corner bathroom that opened into a closet with a random counter along one wall.

Narrow steps that led up to an alcove taken up with a double futon.

Period.

Jayne sat on the spiral stairs and hunched to look at me from under the metal banister. "It's kind of depressing, Mom. It's really dark in here."

I had to agree. The large window in the living—well, everything—room was shrouded in olive green drapes straight out of a 1970s mobile home.

"Here's your trouble right here," I said. "We're missing our view."

I yanked the cord that would, in theory, open them, but it snapped in my hand.

Audrey snorted.

"Okay, Plan B," I said.

I stood on one of the spindly wooden chairs and grabbed hold of the top of the curtains and hauled sideways. The rod gave up and came co-operatively out of the wall like a surrendering fugitive, and I felt myself falling backward—and then straight down, as the chair split and opened up so I could crumple to the floor, curtain rod, hideous drapes, and all.

"Mom!" Jayne said. "Are you okay?"

The mandatory daughterly concern was lost in that kind of laughter only an adolescent girl can produce. I looked up at Audrey, standing over me, keeping up in the eighteen-year-old version.

"That takes care of that issue," I said. "Now we have a view."

"Of the front of the Jeep!"

Jayne spewed spit and collapsed against Audrey. "I love it!" she said in a shriek.

"Good," I said. "We'll move in tomorrow."

The job situation was not as easily remedied. I was only half-hearted in my perusal of the want ads early Wednesday morning. Besides, I couldn't even hear myself read through the whispers.

I want you to tell everyone I did this for you.

There's no way they can keep you from being a consultant.

You have to, Demi. You have to.

God was not forthcoming about how I was going to make a living, however. I gritted my teeth and went back to the Daily Bread. One thing at a time.

We moved in that night, a process that took approximately two hours.

With my clothes hung up in my two feet of the closet, designated by color-coded markers Jayne cut out of cardboard, my laptop set up on the kitchen counter, and a throw tossed over the love seat to hide the bulging springs, I was in.

The anxiety pulsed. How much more readjusting could I do without letting go of hope? I needed to move forward with the list. I had to.

I sat gingerly on a backless stool at the curvy counter whose saving grace was its proximity to the indoor tree trunk. The smell of cedar was calming. So, in a sense, was the list when I brought it up on the screen.

FIND A NEW APARTMENT

Check.

MOVE GIRLS IN

Check.

FIND A NEW JOB

Maybe tomorrow.

PRAY ABOUT FAITH AND DOUBT

I'd done that, too. Since Sunday, every morning at 3:00 AM when I woke up, gave up on any more sleep for the night, and lay awake trying to stay inside my skin, God had shown up, almost viscerally pulling at me, and I had no choice but to go where He took me.

Once there, seeing the faces of my students who for those moments in the chapel passed into a place of gritty spirituality that went beyond grade-point averages, I couldn't get my mind around a clear plan. In spite of their voices touching me like eager hands—

a total God-thing

Faith and Doubt is coming apart

we'd meet totally off campus

it isn't just a project anymore, Dr. C.

We have to tell the world what it really means.

The question was—how?

"Dr. C.?"

I looked around the tree at Audrey, who stood in the doorway.

"I have to quit school," she said.

I was around the tree and on the love seat with her before the tears started.

"It's in the handbook."

"It says you have to drop out if you get pregnant?"

She nodded. "You can't be pregnant out of wedlock—you can't be cohabitating with a person of the opposite gender." She offered me said book, which I waved away.

"And as soon as I start to show, you *know* somebody like Dr. St. Clair is going to—"

"Stop right there—" I didn't add *before I throw up.* "You're, what, six, seven weeks along?"

"I think so."

I looked at her closely. "Have you actually seen a doctor?"

"No. I just did a pregnancy test. Two of them."

I made a note to add GET PRENATAL CARE FOR AUDREY to The List.

"There are only about five more weeks left in the semester," I said. "You aren't going to start to show until summer, Audrey."

"I counted, though. The baby's due in November. That means I can't come back next semester. And school is just starting to mean something, especially if you work with us on F&D again." She flopped against the back of the love seat.

I stroked the back of her hand and picked through my brain for an answer.

"The semester after that," I said finally, "you'll have a baby to take care of—if you're still planning to—"

"I saw a social worker at the clinic today."

I was startled.

"There are all kinds of programs I can get into, especially since I'm in school." She squeezed her hands together, as if she were putting a new self into place. "It's going to be hard, but this is my baby, and I want him."

"Or her," Jayne said from the loft.

I glanced up to see her belly-down on the futon.

"I want my baby to have a mother I know will understand her." Audrey put her arms around my neck. "I want to be a mom like you."

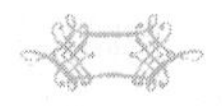

I was on the phone to Ethan Kaye at eight the next morning.

"Demi." His voice, though welcoming, was a thin version of Sunday's sermon baritone. "It's good to hear from you."

"It's good to be heard."

"How are you? Really."

"Hanging in," I said. "I actually called to talk about one of our—your students. I thought maybe you could help."

"Whatever I can do for you, Demi," he said. "You know that."

I stopped momentarily. There was something so eggshell vulnerable about him now.

You don't even know what's going on here, the F&D group had told me. *And you need to.*

I filled him in on Audrey's situation, complete with her fears of Kevin St. Clair barring her entrance in the fall. When I was finished, I expected the reassurance that all would be well in his hands.

It didn't come.

He did say, "There is no reason she can't stay here this semester. As long as she doesn't tell anyone." He paused. "You and I never had this conversation, did we?"

I was a little surprised, but I said no.

"As for next fall—I can't answer that right now."

"Because?" I said.

He drew in a breath I could hear through the phone. "Because I may not be here then."

We shared a stunned silence.

"You're not resigning?"

"No. They'll have to drive me out of here." He laughed without mirth. "And I can already hear the hoof beats over the hill."

"You've been hearing them for months," I said.

"They're closing in." His voice cinched. "That's all I can tell you, Demi. I'm sorry."

I switched my cell phone to my other hand and stalked along the walkway in front of the Daily Bread.

"You're not serious," I said. "Honestly, Ethan—is it that bad? Do they have something on you?"

"I can't say."

I moved into the alcoved doorway of the attorney's office that wasn't open yet. "You can say if it's about me."

He didn't answer.

"Ethan—is it?"

"Only indirectly, Demi. The board of directors knows nothing about your situation—and I intend to keep it that way. St. Clair and Estes kept their word on that—but they *have* used it as a reason to scrutinize any and everything. If I have even an inkling that they're going to bring you up, I promise to let you know, but I seriously doubt that they will. The circumstances of their knowing are still too shady."

The array of photographs slid through my mind, and my stomach clutched.

"You were in church Sunday. I was delighted to see you there."

"You were among the few. And you were preaching right to me, weren't you?"

I felt him smile.

"There wasn't a person in there I wasn't preaching to, including myself. You're free, Demi. Unfortunately, I don't think the likes of Kevin St. Clair are. If they succeed in running me out of here, it is not your fault and it is not your shame."

"Then let me help."

"You can't."

"From the outside. They don't have to know. The F&D group has asked me to work with them as a consultant, completely off campus."

"Demi—no."

I had never heard Ethan use that tone with anyone but the most recalcitrant of students—or Kevin St. Clair.

"I'm sorry," he said. "I have to ask you not to do that. It would only complicate things—and we don't need that."

I stood up straight, forced myself to answer. "I have to respect that, but, Ethan—this feels like God pulling me."

"I've said what I have to say. And I'll do what I can for Audrey Flowers."

When I hung up, I knew I had just participated in a conversation where the most important words were those left unsaid.

Sully made himself sit in the papasan chair, cell phone in his lap. He'd taken three trips to the door already, walked out onto the sidewalk twice. She wasn't showing up, that was obvious. The reason was too.

He picked up the phone. She couldn't turn her back on therapy now. Not when she was so close.

CHAPTER THIRTY

That evening, after my conversation with Ethan, I waited until the girls pulled away in Audrey's Nissan before I completely let down. They were on their way to get something—anything—to transform the bathroom from a painted phone booth into a space we could go into without needing Prozac.

"Thirty bucks and a trip to Tar-zháy should do it," I told them at the curb.

And then I went inside our hovel of a home and collapsed on the love seat. The back right leg gave way, and both the sofa and I sagged toward the floor. It was so fitting I didn't even get up to fix it.

This must be rock bottom. I don't know how long I would have lain there if my cell phone hadn't rung from deep in my purse across the room. I considered letting it ring—except that my daughter was out in a car with a girl who wasn't holding it together that much better than I.

I took the two necessary lunges and unearthed the phone from the depths of my handbag. But then I saw who was calling.

Sullivan Crisp. The last person I wanted to talk to right now.

Correction. I wanted to talk to him. That was the problem, why I couldn't answer and pretend I hadn't practically thrown myself at him.

I stood staring at the silent phone as it beeped with a message. I sank into the chair and listened to Sullivan's voice.

"Hey, Demi. Missed you this afternoon. Wonderin' if somethin' came up, whether you might want to reschedule."

I shook my head—as if he could see me.

"So why don't you give me a call? And listen—"

My breath pulled in on its own.

"Hey, we just need to talk. I'll have my phone with me the rest of the evening."

I pressed seven. "Message deleted," I was told politely.

This time I went face down on the love seat. I *liked* Sullivan Crisp's voice. It comforted and boosted me. That was all. I was just starting to trust him—but could I trust myself?

Sullivan was my therapist. He was a professional. I could call him. I should call him.

I sat up, ran my fingers over the keypad. But the look on Sullivan face when I stepped back from hugging him was all I could see.

There were probably other therapists.

I plunked the phone onto the coffee table, beside the Jayne-painted rock, and half expected a table leg to snap. All right—maybe *this* was rock bottom. Where would I go? The road to Rich was blocked. No career path was left—Ethan had made that clear. Mickey had put up a wall so high I would need climbing gear to get to her. The one light I'd seen with my F&D group was snuffed out. And now I couldn't even go to Sullivan and find out what was wrong with me.

I'm not sure how I ended up with the rock in my hand, but it shook there with my fingers locked around it, and the urge to hurl it was so strong I stood up and cocked it behind my head.

I had to get out.

Still clutching the rock, I dove for the door and tore it open. That rock was going, straight out into the dusk, right at the world I couldn't cope with anymore.

"Whoa!" a male voice said. "I'm not armed!"

I saw a silhouette of a bush of bristly hair. Sharp eyes gleamed at me. I let the rock fly—and then clapped my hands over my mouth in horror.

Fletcher Basset ducked. We both stared as the stone hit the ground.

"You don't mess around, do you?" he said.

"Oh, my gosh—are you okay?"

I rushed at him, prepared to do I-wasn't-sure-what. He backed up, but he was laughing.

"I've had worse than that done to me." He shook the Chia-pet head. The weak light from Sherman Heights's excuse for a streetlamp shone fuzzily on his baldness, but left his face in the shadows.

"I'm sorry," I said. "You caught me at a bad time."

I felt him smile.

"I seem to have a knack for that."

I leaned against the doorjamb. "No, I'm always having a bad time."

He nodded as if he knew exactly what I meant.

I straightened. "How did you find me here?"

Fletcher put up the jazz-spread hand I'd come to recognize as his all-purpose gesture. "I'm not stalking you. Your boss sent me."

My jaw came unhinged. "Mickey—at the restaurant?"

He nodded.

"Why would she do that?"

"I told her what I had to tell you, and I guess she figured it was important enough."

"What do you have to tell me?" I tightened my fists.

"I told you before that we could probably help each other get to the truth," he said. "I have news for you, and if you act on it, well—" He shrugged without nonchalance. "We both benefit."

"What news?"

"About Ethan Kaye," he said. "One of my sources tells me that there has been a threat."

My heart went right up my throat. "On his life?"

"I'm not sure. It was veiled. More than likely it's about his job."

"Veiled—what are you *talking* about?" My voice went shrill.

"I can't reveal any more than that."

"Then how am I supposed to believe you?"

"You don't really have any choice."

I squinted at him, hard. "And what would you know about my choices?"

Fletcher took a step forward so that finally the light hit his face. His left cheek was a garish shade of purple-blue and swollen to twice its cherubic size.

"What happened to you?" I said.

He attempted a grin, which only made it up on one side. "I told you—you're not the only one who has ever come after me with a rock—so to speak."

I shook my head. "You must have crossed the nosy-limit with him—or her."

"I wasn't even pushing that hard," Fletcher said. "This particular person isn't part of the mainstream—sort of fringy—but it's still indicative of the kind of influence wielded by the powers that be. " He grimaced. "They've attracted a fanatic."

"Do you need some ice or anything? That looks painful."

"I'm good. It kind of makes me look like a bad dude, don't you think?"

"Not at all."

His face sobered. "The point is, they're getting serious about putting Ethan Kaye out."

I sank to the stoop. "First of all, I have absolutely no idea how this helps me—or how I can help you find out anything."

"Then let me lay it out for you. Ethan Kaye has received a threat, which basically says he will be taken down from his position as president of CCC, no matter what it takes."

"I'm assuming this has something to do with—" I nodded toward his face.

"Maybe. And Ethan Kaye is losing support by the minute, which indicates to me that these people are trying to form an alliance. He needs you. There's a group of students over there struggling to be there for him, but they need leadership."

"Ethan has told me in no uncertain terms to stay away."

"So you do it unofficially."

"And possibly make it worse for him." I felt myself frown. "I still don't see how my getting involved is going to help you."

"I need somebody on the inside," he said.

It was so unabashed I had to look at him twice. He just blinked.

"You are unbelievable," I said.

"I try. So what do you say? You want to be a team?"

The kids had asked me. I was under no obligation to honor Ethan's request, not if it would help him.

Fletcher stirred at my side. "Look, it's not hard to see that your life is out of control right now. This is one thing you could do something about."

"You know what?" I stood up. "I can't give you an answer right now. I need to think about it."

He smeared his hand over his naked forehead. "I don't think we have a lot of time."

"Then it will be what it will be." My voice, even to me, sounded as if it were teetering on an edge.

After he was gone, I hurried back into the apartment, found the cell phone, and sat on the one unbroken chair, cradling it between praying palms.

"All right," I whispered. "I have to call Sullivan—I know I have to."

There was no pang—no shadow—no warning that I was headed into a dark place.

I swallowed.

Wasn't that how I got in trouble before?

No pang. Only the quiet.

I pressed the phone to my face. Tomorrow—first thing—I would call.

"Just don't let me fall this time," I whispered. "Please, God." I felt a tear trickle over my knuckles. "Please don't let me fall."

Sully draped one long leg over the other knee and leaned back in the Windsor chair in Ethan Kaye's office. He loved to watch the master at work.

"Gina," Ethan practically hummed into the phone, "tell Dr. St. Clair I am not available to see him right now. I'm with someone."

Sully didn't need the phone to hear Gina's reply. Her I'm-freaking-out voice oozed through the wall from the outer office.

"It is entirely none of his business who I'm with, Gina."

Sully grinned. Ethan really was good.

"You say, 'Dr. St. Clair, I am not at liberty to divulge that information.'"

Sully would have liked to have seen whether Gina could actually pull that off, but she evidently wasn't given a chance. The oak-paneled double doors to Ethan's office flew open, and Kevin St. Clair made an entrance that would have put Henry VIII to shame. He took the distance to Ethan's desk in two hard strides, leaving his angry footprints in the carpet. Both hands went to the desktop, and he jutted his head forward, lips first, until his nose nearly touched Ethan's.

Sully slid uneasily forward on his chair.

But Ethan sat back and said into the phone, "Thank you, Gina. That'll be all for now."

St. Clair breathed like a bull, and his thinning hair poked out in spikes at his collar, stiff with sweat. Sully shot Ethan a warning look, but by now Ethan stood so that his head rose above St. Clair's, still lunging across the desk. Before he could straighten, Ethan had him with the indomitable light of his eyes.

"Dr. St. Clair," he said, "this had better be a dire emergency. There could be nothing else that would make you think you could march in here when you were told that I was with someone."

St. Clair didn't bother to look behind him. He brought himself up to standing, wobbling off balance in the process.

"I see it as an emergency," he said. "This college is in a state of crisis."

His shoulders jerked as he reached into his jacket and pulled out a piece of paper. He was showing the restless, unfocused movements of a man on an emotional precipice.

Sully looked again at Ethan.

"All right," Ethan said. "I can see there's no getting you out of here until I let you have your say." He motioned to the chair across from Sully. "Why don't you sit down?"

"I can't sit. I can't eat. I can't sleep." St. Clair stuck up a random hand. "How can you stand by and let this school go down the liberal drain?"

"Spare me the metaphors," Ethan said, his voice still even. "What is it?"

"It"—Kevin said—"would be this." He planted the paper on the desk with a flourish. "A recent memo from you."

Sully resisted the urge to crane his neck.

"Am I misreading it—or does it state that you intend to change the ruling concerning unmarried pregnant students on campus?"

Ethan lowered his eyes to the paper. "Not only pregnant students," he said, "but students who have gone through drug or alcohol rehab successfully—anyone who's repentant, Kevin, and who is willing to live a new life." He looked up and lit his eyes across St. Clair's face. "Does this sound familiar, sir?"

"It doesn't sound like bleeding heart liberalism to you?"

It struck Sully that St. Clair never seemed to have answers—only questions.

Ethan shook his head and held up the paper, finger on the bottom paragraph.

"Sounds like Jesus to me. 'For if you forgive men when they sin, your heavenly Father will also forgive you. But if you do not forgive men their sins, your Father will not forgive your sins.'"

St. Clair was once again heaving breaths as he snatched up the memo and crushed it in his hand.

Sully inched, tensed, to the edge of the seat.

"You don't think I'll fight you on this, Kaye?" St. Clair said.

"I had no doubt of that when I wrote it." Ethan came out from behind the desk, grimness in his frame. "And, Kevin, if you and I had the kind of working relationship where we could sit down and discuss our differences, you would have been the first to know about this."

"What is there to discuss?"

"You tell me."

Before Sully saw it coming, St. Clair landed a fist on the desk. It came down on the edge, and Kevin moaned and pulled it back into his ribs.

Sully came to his feet, arms already out. But Ethan put up a hand and shook his head. Sully took a step back, but he couldn't sit.

St. Clair furtively cradled his hand. "Are you aware that this memo has gotten out among the students?"

Sully wanted to spit. Three guesses how.

"The solid ones are forming a protest out front," St. Clair said. "They're fed up with this liberal—"

"I find that interesting," Ethan said. "Usually it's the left-leaning students who do the protesting." He looked hard at St. Clair. "Now, I wonder who gave those kids out front the idea to start waving placards."

Sully's phone rang, and St. Clair whipped around, eyes startled. His lips pulled into an immediate accusation.

"Dr. St. Clair," Ethan said. "Dr. Sullivan Crisp."

St. Clair scowled, bringing his eyes into drawstring bags.

The phone rang again. It was Demi.

He left Ethan to make the explanation.

"Hey, there," Sully said.

He could feel Gina calculating his exit across the outer office.

A spidery pause filled the line, followed by a thin *hi.*

Sully let himself out into the hall and passed up the elevator in favor of the steps. He talked as he took them down two at a time.

"Thanks for returning my call," he said.

Once again a pause.

"So—we have an elephant in our living room, don't we?" Sully said.

"A what?"

"A big ol' animal that everybody wants to step around and pretend isn't there."

He could hear her sucking in a breath.

"You're talking about me hugging you."

"And feeling like you committed a major crime of therapy."

"Of therapy? Crime, period. Sullivan . . ." Her voice chipped off.

Sully stopped on a landing, one hip against a tattered sofa.

"It feels so good to have somebody listen to me," she said. "That's why I hugged you."

"I know that."

"Do you? I mean, really?"

"I do," he said. "Does that make you feel better?"

"No."

"Because—"

"I hate when you do this. Because I'm afraid that in my head it's going to turn into something else for me. This is how it started with Zach."

"Ding!" Sully's voice echoed in the stairwell.

A pimpled kid passing him on his way down the steps looked at him twice before continuing under a bulging backpack.

"I'm not Zach," Sully said when he was gone.

Demi gave him a soft grunt. "That doesn't help."

"But here's what will." He paused and planted his hand on the chipped plaster wall. "You, Demi, are not the same person you were when Zach came into your life."

"You're saying I could resist the temptation now?"

"I'm saying you would see it coming and run like you had a pack of rabid coyotes after you."

"Isn't that what I did when I skipped my appointment?"

Sully grinned and started down the next set of steps. "That's exactly what you did. But I want you to come back, and let's keep working."

He stopped again, hand on the door to the front hall.

"I have to come back," she said.

"You have to?"

"It's going to sound crazy, okay—but I think it's God."

Sully pressed his forehead against the door. "Ding-ding and amen, Dr. Costanas," he said. "What do you say we talk about you and God tomorrow—usual time?"

"Okay," she said. "Ding-ding."

Sully closed the phone with his chest. Yeah. He heard the hope. He pushed the door open into the hall, still grinning, and plowed into the kid with the hunchback knapsack.

"You don't want to head that way, man," he said to Sully. "Dude—somethin's goin' down."

Sully followed the jerk of the kid's head toward the front doors. A cacophony of shouts blasted through them—straight into the face of Ethan Kaye, who apparently had taken the elevator down and now stood in the doorway.

"They're about to riot," the kid said.

Sully jammed his phone into his pocket and tore down the hall, heart already pounding in his ears.

When Sully reached him, Ethan was facing the students with both palms and the full light of his gaze. The crowd was only about fifty strong, but they weren't taking orders from Dr. Kaye. Not one was older than nineteen, Sully guessed. Their mouths were wide, undulating, and spitting out anger.

"You're misinterpreting Matthew 6:14!"

"Jesus Christ wants sexual purity!"

"What's gonna be okay next, Dr. Kaye?"

The throng of young faces blurred together and twisted by rage was surreal, spewing words meant to be spoken in love. They were all distorted versions of Kevin St. Clair.

A ragged chant of "Resign, Dr. Kaye!" began on the fringe and gathered voices. Sully saw two passing students pause, shift their backpacks, filter in. Their lips were moving before they knew the words.

Sully curled his fingers around Ethan's shoulder. "Leave it alone," he shouted over them.

Ethan shook his head and stepped away, hands still up like futile flags over the rising drone.

"All right, folks, listen."

"No—you listen!"

"Resign, Dr. Kaye!"

"No resignation without conversation!"

A whistle blast tore through Sully, and he grabbed Ethan's arm. A bulky-shouldered student in the center of the chant held up one hand, his other one still poised at his lips post-whistle. The crowd settled into reluctant silence.

"You'll talk about resigning, then?" the kid said.

Sully focused on the face, pulled taut across the cheekbones, rigid with conviction.

Ethan lowered his hands and moved firmly forward.

"I'll talk about why you want me to resign," he said. "But not here, Travis. You know that."

Kaye calling him by name seemed to irritate the kid.

"What are you afraid of, Dr. Kaye?" Travis called out.

"I'm afraid of fear," Ethan said. "And that's what this is about."

A crack of silence went through the crowd.

Travis jerked his head, eyes darting. "We are not afraid to confess the truth of Christ crucified!" he shouted.

Only a few murmurs joined him.

"I'm not either," Ethan said. "But I am concerned about how that truth is lived out."

"As the Word says!"

Travis shot his arm up. A few Bibles rose in the air—though obviously not as many as he wanted.

"In the one true Word of God!" he shouted.

More arms raised, waving Bibles like picket signs.

"Then let's sit down and study the Word together."

Sully heard an edge in the sonorous tenor as he watched Ethan's back stiffen.

"I'm calling for an open forum."

"You have a forum right here!" Travis said.

"You say you want to confess the name of Christ—you want to live as He did."

A few of the Bibles paused.

"Did Jesus have shouting matches with His disciples?" Ethan said. "Even with the Pharisees?"

Travis took a step forward, face cemented. "Are you claiming to be Jesus now?"

Another crack went through the crowd. Sully watched a few of them shift where they stood.

"I'm claiming to try to live as our Lord did, Travis," Ethan said. "And what He did was to sit with those who had ears to hear."

"Yeah—well, we're tired of what you have to say."

Travis turned on the group, hardened eyes expectant.

"True enough," someone said.

A few others followed with halfhearted renditions of "Resign!" But most of them looked up at Ethan, and Sully watched faces emerge from the blur. An uncertain movement of eyes here. An irresolute sag in the cheeks there.

Travis alone remained hard, like a cardboard figure against the backdrop of reconsidered emotions. One perfect word from Ethan, Sully thought, and he'd topple forward and drift to the ground on his own air.

Ethan still stood with his arms at his sides, and Sully could almost see the energy moving up his backbone. The crowd watched him, faces now half open.

"You say you're tired of what I have to say." Ethan nodded. "Then perhaps I haven't fully responded to your current concerns."

"Like your lowering the moral standards!" Travis said, his voice like glass. He snatched a Bible from the hands of the shaken girl beside him and displayed it over his head with both hands. "Everything's here, Dr. Kaye. There's nothing to talk about."

"Except the fear behind your interpretation, Travis."

"This is not about me! It's about all of us!"

He looked around him. "All of us" kept their eyes on Ethan Kaye. This time the crack went through Travis. The thinned, hardened face shattered.

"You're the one who's afraid, Dr. Kaye!"

Before Sully could even register the movement, Travis charged the steps, Bible still exalted in upstretched arms, and hurled himself at Ethan. Amid the startled voices of the crowd, he planted the book against Ethan's forehead, knocking him backward. Ethan's shoulder blades thudded into Sully's chest.

"This is what you're afraid of, Dr. Kaye!" he screamed. *"This!"*

The crowd splintered, sending several bodies up the steps to pull Travis off. Sully wrapped both arms around Ethan's chest from behind and propelled him through the front doors.

"It's okay, Sully," Ethan said.

Sully let him go, and Ethan put his hand to his forehead, eyes closed.

"I cannot believe it's come to this," he said.

Sully planted his hands on the sides of Ethan's face and tilted his head back. An already fading red blotch wrinkled with his brow.

"I'm not hurt," Ethan said.

"Man, are you sure?"

He nodded and opened his eyes. In them, Sully saw he was lying. A deeper hurt shot through them.

CHAPTER THIRTY-ONE

Sully stayed in Ethan's office for the rest of the day. Through the interviews with security. The decision not to press charges or bring disciplinary action against Travis Michaels. The putting off of faculty members and administrative staff and curious community members who all wanted the story straight from his mouth.

As the day wore on without a glimpse of Kevin St. Clair, Sully's visions of wringing the man's neck grew more vivid. The lack of anger in Ethan was even more disturbing. For the most part his friend sat in a mulling silence that produced no visible signs of resolution—no straightened back, no determined shoulders. His face remained uncharacteristically cluttered, which created no small measure of uneasiness in Sully.

Darkness had crept in when Ethan declined Sully's offer to buy him dinner and suggested they both go home.

"You have to take care of yourself, my friend," Sully told him when they parted ways in the parking lot.

Ethan attempted a smile. "You think somebody else is going to come after me with a Bible?"

"I'm talking about in here." Sully rubbed his hand across his own chest. "I've watched this eat at you all day, and I'm not seeing you bite back."

Ethan swept his gaze across the darkening lawn that ran beside the Huntington Building and down the slope to the chapel.

"I don't know what God wants me to do." Ethan drew his brows together and stared long at the chapel. "For the first time in years, I don't know."

"In therapy we always advise," Sully said, "in situations where you don't know exactly what to do, don't do anything until you do know."

Ethan pulled his gaze from down the hill and let it rest in the middle of Sully's chest. "Thanks," he said. "I'll call you."

As Sully climbed into his car, he couldn't decide which hurt worse—seeing Ethan as a target, or not being able to help. The frustration burned in him.

He was still steaming when he turned down Callow Avenue. Eyes drilled to the windshield in yet another mental confrontation with Kevin St. Clair, he only peripherally caught movement in front of the bakery. When he turned toward it, the silhouette of two bodies pulled into a struggling knot, and Sully heard a scream.

He slammed into the curb, already wrenching the door open, and abandoned the car with the engine whining.

"Get your hands off me!" said an unmistakable female voice.

"Tatum!" Sully called to her.

Both bodies twisted toward him. The bigger, masculine one froze. Tatum raised her leg and landed a foot in his gut. The man moaned and curled over himself.

"I got him—I got him," Sully said. Although there wasn't much to it. Van Dillon was a sack of mush as Sully pinned his arms around him from behind and pulled him away from Tatum's poised foot.

"Let him go so he can get out of here," he heard Tatum say. "I can't stand to look at him."

As she watched Sully give Van a shove, her eyes dug into him with a fury that, Sully realized, mirrored his.

"What are you doin', dude?" Sully said. "You think this is the way to get the girl back?"

"In his dreams. I wouldn't have him."

"You had me when you needed me—to use me!"

Sully lunged for Van again, barely getting his fingers around a clump of the back of his shirt before Van could reach Tatum. Sully managed to get his arm pinned behind him and got him to the ground.

"Get in your car and go home, Tatum," Sully said.

"No way—I am so not letting him—"

"Slut!"

"Hey!" Sully tightened his grip on Van's arm.

"It's your fault too. You're the one who took—"

"Shut up!" Sully wrenched back on the kid's arm, and he let out a yell.

"Did you kill him?" Tatum said.

Van lifted his face.

"Go, Tatum," Sully said, "before this gets any worse. Call the police—do whatever you have to do, but get out of here."

Tatum's Volkswagen squealed from the curb, barely missing Sully's car, which still hung halfway in the street with the motor running. Van slumped again, and Sully let him go. The kid backed against the trellis pole that held up the bakery awning, his heaving bulk jarring against a backdrop of pink cakes.

Sully looked down at his fists and forced them open. "You have a lot of finesse, boy, you know that?"

Van grunted.

Sully nodded toward his belly. "You okay?"

"Fine." He lifted a face as blotchy as his voice. "Are you calling the police?"

"Me? No," Sully said.

"Then I'm going."

Van launched himself from the pole, but Sully held up his hand. "Only if you swear you'll stay away from Tatum."

The kid flipped his head back, sending a mop of hair off his eyes. "What's it to you? You her new lover?"

"Excuse me?" Sully said.

"Wouldn't surprise me." Van's lip curled. "Like I said, she's a sl—"

"All right—enough. Stay away from her, and I won't tell Wyatt Estes you tried to beat up on his niece."

Van blinked. "Who's Wyatt Estes?"

Sully looked at him closely. Even without a clear view of his eyes, the hanging lip proclaimed ignorance. He didn't know.

"Somebody you don't want to cross," Sully said. "Let me hear you say it."

"Say what?"

"That you'll stay away from Tatum. Say it."

"All right, all right—dude. I wouldn't go near her again anyway. She's not worth it."

"Good attitude," Sully said.

The kid started off, and then stopped. With one more fling of his head, he got the hair out of the way long enough to direct a knowing look at Sully.

"You should stay away from her too," he said. "She'll sleep with any guy, no matter how old he is."

Sully watched Van make his surly way down the sidewalk toward the battered pickup truck. *Lyin' sack of cow manure.*

He was suddenly exhausted. But one thought did get through before he drained completely: no way did that kid ever have anything to do with Wyatt Estes. But now, more than ever, Sully had to find out who did.

I realized as I got into the Jeep the next morning—after making sure Audrey was vertical and was actually going to drop Jayne at school—that I was thinking about the list, about Jayne, about getting myself strong enough to help Ethan Kaye. About other things besides how wretched I felt about myself. It was that kind of freedom you feel the first time you put on a pair of shorts when you've been clad in trousers all winter.

Washington spring was peeking out of the hideous blue window boxes, and Mickey was positioning a pair of chairs at a cozy table on the sidewalk in front of the Bread. Her head tilted as she surveyed them, cap of fudge-brown hair cupping her face, a satisfied elfin smile curving her cheeks. I considered going down the alley to the back door when she saw me. Though she dropped the smile, she didn't glare or, worse, fold those arms like a wall across her chest.

"Morning," I said.

She pushed a chair a quarter inch further into place.

"I hope I didn't mess you up yesterday," she said.

I blinked. "Yesterday?"

"That reporter was sniffing around here."

"He said you told him where I lived."

"I wasn't going to." She repositioned the chair unnecessarily again. "Well, at first I was. I thought you deserved having somebody digging into your business."

I couldn't conceal a complete gape.

"I never said I wasn't blunt," she said.

"No, I guess you didn't."

She put both hands on the back of the chair and leaned into her wrists. "But that's not why I sent him over to your new place—Audrey told me where she was living, of course."

"Of course."

"He said you needed to know what was going over at the school—said it would help you. Look, I'm not some witch."

"I know that, Mickey."

"And this doesn't mean I've gotten over your undermining my influence with Audrey."

I felt my eyes widen. "Is that what you think I'm doing? Like we're in competition?"

Her hand flew up. "I still want to see you get your life together." She shrugged as she turned from the chair. "I don't know why."

"Because you're a good person," I said.

She gave me a long look. "You are too. Too bad we're not good in the same ways, huh?"

The Jeep would whine up to the curb any minute, and Sully was still trying to pray—*trying* being the operative word.

The light was the problem. The sun had been spring-bright all day, drawing the denizens of Callow out of their dim bars and smeary-windowed Laundromats and onto the sidewalks, blinking in the glare.

Sunshine seeped into every crack of the garage and cast an

unaccustomed cheerfulness, giving Isabella her first chance to gleam under the buffing he was giving her. This was the kind of post-winter light that brought clients to the clinics in anxious bursts. People who'd been depressed all winter and blamed it on the wallpaper-paste skies now expected to feel better. When that didn't happen, they came in to find out why the promise of new life wasn't coming true for them.

Sully closed his eyes. Pray for Demi. This could be her cruelest spring ever. Who said that? Who said April was the cruelest month?

Dude, pray.

He breathed, long. Let the thoughts come . . . the prayer thoughts . . . Light of the World . . . blaze through the darkness . . . the darkness cannot put You out . . .

—Except the red lights—the flashes—swallowed by the night—by the inky blackness.

He cupped his hands to his face, pulled the Light to himself. Sometimes if he said it out loud . . . "You are the Life-Light. Be my Light to live by—shine through me to her."

—You can't help me, Sully—she says you can't help me—I have to listen to her.

"You are the Life-Light—bring me into the Light."

—Turn into the slide! Don't hit the brakes, baby.

—The red lights—flashes of alarm—spasms of panic.

Come on. "Every person who enters, You bring into the Light."

—or out—out and into the black—in long silence from the shrieking skid—lights gulped away—

"No—*into* the Light."

"Sullivan?"

Sully bolted out of the chair, across the office, into the fading light of the garage. Demi—how much had she heard?

How much had he said?

She was backlit in the big doorway, hand on the metal frame, peering in.

"I'm sorry," she said. "Were you on the phone?" She moved her thumb toward the Jeep. "I can wait, if you want."

"Absolutely not," he said. "You ready to go to work?"

With a nod she passed him and went straight to the office. In the doorway, she turned and surprised him by smiling. "You coming?" she said. "I have to get this done, Dr. Crisp."

Light shone in her eyes. The red ones lurking in the back of his thoughts winked out. By the time he got to his chair, Demi was pulling something from her purse.

"I brought this again," she said. "If this is going to happen, I have to do the homework."

Sully looked at the family photo she propped against the rock paperweight on his desk. The pixie-haired girl smiled obediently at him.

"Have you been talking to her?" Sully said.

Demi gave him the wry look. "No. I can't bring myself to do it"

"How come?"

"In the first place, I don't know when and where I'll have the chance. There are three of us living in a space big enough for one five-year-old. Jayne already knows I talk to myself in the bathroom mirror."

Sully grinned at her. "Doesn't everybody?"

"Do you?" she said, and then shrank behind a raised hand. "Sorry—I shouldn't ask you personal questions."

"Demi—relax. You're focused on your stuff now. You aren't going to do anything inappropriate."

She studiedly recrossed her legs.

"Demi."

She looked at him.

"Trust yourself."

No word could name the look that worked its way from her throat to her eyes. Sully watched in wonder what he always waited for in therapy, the moment of a genuine shift in feeling.

"It's hard," she said finally.

"It is for almost everyone. And most of the time it starts before you're even five years old." He nodded toward the picture. "By the time you were that age, you were probably already questioning yourself."

Demi grunted. "Are you kidding? I don't remember when I *wasn't*."

Sully turned his gaze on the posed woman in the center of the photo. "No help from Mom?"

Sully watched the tiny lines at the corners of her mouth harden into stiff threads.

"Do we have to talk about her?" she said.

Sully felt himself smile sadly. "Not today, but sooner or later you're going to have to deal with her if you want to get better." He leaned back. "I'm going to let you make the rules on this one. Tell me what you think is important about your mom helping you."

"She didn't 'help' me, Sullivan—she told me what to do in no uncertain terms—until the day she died."

Demi brushed her hand across her mouth, as if she were making sure the words had—finally—crossed her lips. Sully was still sorting out the last phrase, one that didn't really surprise him.

The mother died, too, and obviously left unresolved issues boiling inside her daughter. Another life trauma, and once again, Demi neglected to mention it.

Sully leaned toward her, arms on his thighs. "I don't think you realize how much you went through in your life before your affair."

She frowned. "I've known a lot of people who've lost their mothers to cancer."

"How old were you?"

"Thirty-five."

"And how were things between you when she passed?"

For the first time Demi stared at the picture. Her face worked hard.

"Demi," Sully said softly, "you've come too far to hold back."

"We had an uneasy truce," she said finally. "I brought the kids out here to see her every summer. Rich would've come, but I didn't ask him to. She was horrible to him."

"But you still came."

"She was my mother."

"And?"

"She would have made my life miserable otherwise."

"How so?"

"I wouldn't have been able to live with the guilt. She was alone—my brothers stayed away."

"It was all up to you then?" He scooted as close to the edge of the chair as he dared.

She squeezed herself in, opening and closing her hands against her knees. "I guess so."

"You guess?"

"No—I know! She said it—she said she'd suffered three heartbreaks already, and she couldn't take any from me. It was up to me. It was always up to me."

She whipped her face toward the picture, hands still clawing at her kneecaps.

"Right this minute," Sully said, "what do you want to do?"

"I can't."

"I think you can."

"I want to tear her right out of that picture and rip her into a thousand pieces like she did me—but I can't do that."

"Why?"

"Because it's wrong!"

"To be angry because someone put a burden on you as a child that no adult could possibly bear? That's wrong, Demi?"

She put her hand to her mouth.

"Let it go."

"I hate what she did to me! I hate it! I just—"

"Go ahead."

She snatched up the picture. "I hate what you did to me!" she said between her teeth. "No—I hate *you*! I was an innocent kid." The teeth parted, the voice teetered. "I was an innocent, and look what you did to me. You have no right!"

"What about that little girl?" Sully said. "Can you help her?"

Her eyes brimmed. "I don't know what you mean."

"What if she were Jayne and someone was telling her she was responsible for the happiness of an adult who didn't know how to deal with her own pain?"

"I would tell her—"

"Then tell her. Tell Little Demi."

Demi looked down at the picture, and Sully watched her gather. Slowly a finger came up to touch it.

"Don't listen to her, sweetie," she said. Her voice was tender as baby skin. "You're a child, and that's exactly what you need to be. She can go to other grown-ups. You just be a kid."

She cried, the loose, free kind of weeping that he savored in his office. These were the tears that healed.

"What does she want you to do now?" Sully said.

"Little me?" She looked back at the picture. "She wants me to let her sit and cry because her daddy isn't there for the picture. She misses him, and she's not allowed to miss him."

"Then let her miss him," Sully said. "It's okay."

He couldn't always predict how a person would respond to the first encouragement to parent herself, but Sully knew what Demi would do. He knew she would press the picture to her chest and cross her hands over it and rock forward in an act of purest maternity. He sank back and closed his eyes and let her cry.

Your Light has come, he prayed.

Light that will blink out in the darkness if you can't stop it. Red light—

"Oh—I'm sorry."

Sully jerked forward. A disco version of something vaguely familiar erupted from the floor next to Demi's chair.

She yanked her cell phone from her purse. "I have to take this—it's my daughter."

She slipped through the doorway, phone to her ear, talking in the same gentle tone she'd used for her own child-self.

Sully churned around the office. All this stirring up in Demi—that was triggering the flashbacks. Perfectly normal with the anniversary coming up, and too many late nights working on the car.

"Sullivan—I'm sorry."

Demi was in the doorway, face still tear-streaked, mascara dried in pools beneath her lower lashes.

"I have to go," she said. She picked up her purse and hung it on her shoulder without wasting a move. "Audrey's bleeding. I have to get her to the hospital."

"You okay?"

"I have to be." She went for the door, but she stopped there. "Can I . . . ?"

"Call me—yes," Sully said. "We need to follow up."

She gave him a firm nod and crossed the garage, shoulders resolute. The first shadows of dusk absorbed her.

After the Jeep whined away, Sully wandered, restless, over to Isabella, who looked buffed and expectant. Maybe the flashbacks meant it was time to take her out and get on with it.

Maybe, because he could think of nothing else to do.

CHAPTER THIRTY-TWO

An ambulance, lights still twirling, blocked the emergency entrance when we pulled into Harrison Medical Center, driving my anxiety up several more notches. A trauma ahead of us meant we'd have to wait forever for Audrey to be seen. Miscarriages weren't usually considered urgent—except by the women they were happening to. Audrey's quiet crying hadn't stopped since I'd picked the girls up at Sherman Heights.

"You take her in," I said to Jayne now. "I'll park and meet you."

Jayne climbed out, still with one hand on Audrey like a lifeline.

"You have your insurance card, Audrey?" I said.

Jayne poked her head back in. "Got it," she said. "Come on, Aud—lean on me."

I sat, white-knuckling the steering wheel, and watched my waif of a daughter support the wobbly figure as they made their way to the door.

Someone put a burden on you as a child that no adult should have to bear.

Was that happening to Jayne? I shoved the car into gear and wheeled around the ambulance.

Audrey was already in a curtained cubicle when I got inside, and Jayne was helping her into a too-often-washed gown that inevitably gaped open. Her vertebrae poked insistently at the skin of her narrow back.

"I've never been in a hospital before," she said. Her voice was frail.

"I had stitches one time," Jayne assured her. "It's not that bad. They give you Popsicles. Well, I was, like, ten . . ." She trailed off and licked her lips. "That was lame," she muttered.

"It was perfect," I whispered to her.

"Okay—looks like we have a few too many people in there." A

ponytailed nurse in a top printed in teddy bears breezed in. "You the mom?"

"She's like a mom to me," Audrey said and wrapped her fingers around my arm.

"Are you eighteen?" The nurse didn't look up from Audrey's chart.

"Yes."

"We're good to go then. You'll need to wait in the waiting area." She gave it a beat too long before she finally glanced at Jayne. "Where the chairs are."

Jayne begged me with her eyes.

"I'll come out in a minute," I said. "How about you get us some hot chocolate?"

She nodded, glared at the nurse's teddy-beared back, and hooked her arm around Audrey's neck.

"Love you," Audrey said.

"Love you more," Jayne said.

The nurse patted the examining table and nodded Audrey toward it. Now glaring at the teddy bears myself, I put an arm around Audrey's waist and boosted her up.

"After I examine you, she can come back in and give you support," the nurse said.

Audrey's frightened eyes went to me as she lay back on the table. "Support for what? Am I going to lose my baby?"

I stroked Audrey's forehead. "You know what? Whatever happens, we'll handle it, because we've got God."

"And you."

She closed her eyes and let the nurse slip her feet into the stirrups. Her fingers were still raking my arm.

Nurse Ponytail settled onto a stool and peered into Audrey.

"Ever had a pelvic exam before?" she said.

Audrey shook her head. Her face paled, leaving the dark eyes big and soulful as a puppy's.

"It's easier if you relax," I said.

"No need—done." The nurse tapped Audrey's knees. "You can scoot back now."

"Am I losing the baby?" Audrey said.

"Doesn't look like it." Nurse Ponytail peeled off a glove and dropped it deftly into a waste can. She had yet to make eye contact with either of us.

"You've spotted some, but you're not dilating—I don't see any fetal tissue." She pulled off the other glove and went for the sink. "The doctor will give you the final word," she said over running water. "He'll be here in—well, he'll be here."

"You can bring the other one in," she said over her shoulder as she sailed out.

Audrey devoured me with her eyes. "Does that mean I'm not having a miscarriage?"

"I think it means it's hopeful," I said.

She sighed, and I watched her settle her face. "Okay. I can hope."

Her fingers loosened on my arm, but I didn't move away.

"You know what's weird?"

"I know a lot of things that are weird," I said dryly. "What are you thinking of?"

"I was so scared when I found out I was pregnant—like, I didn't know what to do. But I'm even more scared about losing her."

"Her?" I said.

"I think she's a girl." Audrey reached across herself, plastic hospital bracelet dangling on her tiny arm, and put her hand against my cheek. "And I'm going to name her Demitria Jayne."

I pressed a kiss to her palm.

Jayne slipped in sideways through the part in the curtain. "The nurse said I could come in till the doctor comes." She rolled her eyes. "I bet she doesn't give anybody Popsicles."

"Will you two be okay?" I said. "I have to make a phone call."

"Don't leave me, Jay," Audrey said.

But I wasn't two steps outside the curtained cubicle when Jayne was on my heels. "Mom!" she whispered.

"Everything looks okay, Jay," I said.

"No—I wanted to tell you." She stopped me with a grab at my sleeve and looked furtively over my shoulder.

"What?"

"Dad is here."

I tried to keep the Demi-on-top-of-things face in place, but Demi-the-firefighter's-wife trampled her.

"What's wrong—is he okay?"

"Mom!"

I turned to look at Jayne, who trailed me toward the front desk, where I hadn't known I was going.

"It's not him, Mom," Jayne said. "One of the other firemen has something that's no big deal. Dad's just here with him. I saw him in the hall." She rubbed my arm. "Chill, okay?"

"Oh," I said. "Okay. Chilling."

I kissed the top of her head and let my heartbeat stop battering my eardrums. Of course. They didn't bring serious burn victims here—they were air-flighted to Harborview Medical Center in Seattle. Wives were called immediately.

"I thought you'd want to know he was here." Jayne lowered her voice to a whisper. "In case you didn't want to run into him."

That sliced through me.

Okay. Call Mickey, I told myself. I could trust *that* instinct.

"Go back to Audrey," I said. I headed outside to use my cell.

Oscar answered their house phone and immediately turned to mush on the other end of the line before I even finished explaining.

"We'll be there," he said. I could practically see his plump chin quivering.

"It isn't an emergency," I said, but he'd already hung up.

Only when I went back into the building, still folding my phone, did I second-guess myself. Did Audrey need Mickey here, telling her once again how much trouble she was causing? Maybe I should rehearse what I could say to them to stave off a full-out assault.

Or maybe I could just pray.

The thought came to me in a whisper, and I turned to it. I could pray. And I could love. I could trust that.

I slipped back to the waiting area and found the only chair not occupied by a taut body. The pain, the anxiety, the anticipation of sorrow hung over the place like an odor, and I sat down in the midst of it to pray over that part that belonged to me. When it refused to separate from the rest, I breathed it all in.

I hadn't prayed like that in months.

I wasn't sure how long I'd been there when I heard my name like no one else could say it. Before I even raised my head, I felt Rich above me.

"Hi," I said. "Who got hurt?"

"Baynes," he said.

A young rookie, if I remembered right.

"Is he okay?"

"It's minor."

His tone brushed me aside. Wrong again. How dare I even bother him . . .

"I was just asking out of concern, Rich." I stood, annoyance shooting up between my shoulder blades. "I need to get back."

"To that girl."

I paused and turned my head slowly back to him. "That girl," I said.

"Jayne told me she's pregnant and she's living with you." His eyes cut down to slits.

"Her name is Audrey." I lined myself up in front of him. "She needed help, and I'm helping her. Do you have a problem with that?"

He looked over his shoulder, and I saw the echo of my raised voice stir up a knot of people by the water fountain.

"Yeah, I do have a problem with it." Rich's *with* hardened into a Brooklyn *wid.* "What kind of influence is that on Jayne?"

"You're not serious."

"I don't like her hanging out with some girl who goes and gets herself pregnant."

I let out a dry snort that got another group shooting me a shut-up look.

"What's so funny?" Rich said.

"She got herself pregnant?"

"Everybody's responsible for what they do, Demitria." Rich squinted at me. "Or haven't you figured that out?"

I expected the anxiety and the guilt and the shame to smother me until I slunk away. It didn't. I only felt heat blossoming from my neck.

"What do you think I've been doing for the past two months?" I said. "I've *been* taking responsibility."

"For somebody else's problems—like you always do—instead of taking care of your own business."

"You are my business!" I said. "But you won't let me take care of you, so what am I supposed to do? What is it you want me to do? You tell me, and I'll do it!"

"We're done here," Rich said.

He stalked for the door, and I marched after him, all the way out to the red SUV with ORCHARD HEIGHTS DUTY CHIEF emblazoned on the side. I plastered myself against it.

"Move, Demitria." Rich hissed and closed his eyes, as he'd do if one of the kids had tried his patience.

"When you've told me what you want from me, Rich," I said. "What do you want?"

"I want you to feel the shame." He jabbed his thumb into his chest. "I want you to feel, in here, what it's been like for me."

"You don't think I do?"

"What I want is for you to make up for the pain you've put me through—and I don't think you can do that."

I stared and felt the full weight of what he asked fall on me.

"You want me to undo it," I said. "Do you know how many times I've wished I could? You're asking the impossible."

"I guess I am." Rich put his arm on top of the car and leaned, his back to me. Just as it had been for two long years. It had worked for him then, but it couldn't now.

"You're right." I let my arms drop to my sides. "I can't do the impossible. What else you got?"

He jerked his head sideways.

"What would you settle for if you couldn't have that?" I said. "What kind of wife?"

He stood with his arm still sprawled across the roof of the fire department car. "You really want to know?" he said.

"I do."

"I want a woman who loves me and respects me enough that she would never put herself in a position to be influenced against me by another man."

I held back the tears. Sullivan said not to hold back, but I couldn't cry now and drive him away.

"I know I wasn't that woman," I said. "But I am now. You can still have what you want."

He didn't answer—and the silence singed me.

"Rich, say something."

"I can't answer you."

Again, I expected the prickling of anxiety, the rush of shame, the paralyzing clutch of guilt. Instead, something visceral shifted inside me that I could almost measure. The anxiety and the shame and the guilt had played themselves out, leaving space for what in that moment shaped my thoughts and let them come.

"You don't have an answer?" I said. "Then I'll tell you what I want."

He turned on me. "What you want? I think you already tried to get what you want, and now you expect me to be your consolation prize."

"Excuse me?"

"I always knew it would only be me until somebody better came along. I knew it here." He knocked his flattened hand against the back of his head. "For a while I thought I was wrong—when you brought me out here—and then you—"

"Rich—what are you talking about?" I said. "I never—"

"You didn't know it, Demitria. *I* knew it."

The doors opened and two other firemen appeared, one with a bandage across his forehead and an eye swollen shut. I backed up, and Rich jerked open the car door and got behind the wheel.

"Mrs. Costanas," the uninjured fireman said to me, before he busied himself getting his buddy into the backseat.

For the first time, I believed anyone who called me that name might be wrong.

I forced myself to walk-not-run back to the emergency doors. Oscar nearly plowed me down as they sighed open. Mickey ran into him.

"How's Audrey?" Oscar said. His chin quivered, as well as every other part of him.

Mickey parked herself in front of him. "Where is she, Demi?"

"Follow me," I said.

All the dialogue I'd planned for warning them against slicing again into their daughter's heart was now stirred in with a shock I couldn't get my mind around. I might have thrown poor Audrey to the wolves if Jayne hadn't bolted from the cubicle when we were only yards away, her face glowing like Tinkerbell.

"The baby's okay!" she said. "Some women spot at first—or even their entire pregnancy—but that's all. And I got to see the sonogram." She threw her long adolescent arms around me and bubbled her laughter into my neck. "It was so cool, Mom—there's a real baby in there!"

I rocked her back and forth. On one pass, my eyes met Mickey's. I'd never seen such longing, such yearning, not even in my own mirror.

"You go on in," I said.

Oscar made a dive for the curtain, but Mickey grabbed his arm, barely getting her fingers across its girth. "I'm not sure she wants to see us," she said. She looked at me with eyes that ached to feel anything but what she felt. "Would you check it out first?"

Slowly I shook my head. "I'll go *with* you," I said.

I held back the curtain and heard Audrey chirp, a sound that faded when she saw her mother.

"I heard the good news," I said.

She tried to smile, but her eyes, on Mickey, were wary.

"Is it good news, Audrey?" I crossed to her. "For *you*, I mean?"

I saw her take a deep breath. "I love this baby, and I'm going to keep her and I want her to be okay."

Oscar jockeyed his huge self around Mickey and smothered Audrey in a hug that took *my* breath away.

Mickey didn't move from just inside the curtain. She folded her arms.

Folded arms. Turned backs. People operating on premises that were only walls of fear. That was all I was seeing tonight, and I was sick of them.

"Do you have any idea how she plans to pull off having a baby and having a life?" Mickey said. "When she can't even—"

"Why don't you ask her?" I said. "For once, why won't you trust her to use what you've taught her?"

The arms folded tighter. "So far, that hasn't been effective."

"Oh, get over it!" I shoved my hair behind my ears and went after her, until my face was nose-to-nose with hers. "She made a mistake and now she's taking responsibility for it—except that the people she loves don't want to let her. They want this one mistake to define her, for the rest of her life—and it doesn't. I *know.*"

I thrust an arm behind me to point in Audrey's direction. "What she does about it today, out of love and compassion and God, makes her who she is. Now, you can either embrace that and see her through, or you can define yourselves by your mistakes."

I pulled away in time for Nurse Ponytail to whip the curtain aside, tail in full swing.

"And if you break this young woman's heart any more," I said, "you are making the biggest mistake of your life."

I brushed past the nurse. "It's a little crowded in here," I told her.

Sully went back to close the garage door and stood there for a magic moment to listen to Isabella purr . . .

Hers was a grateful sound, he decided as he eased himself into the front seat. He took a second to appreciate the tuck and roll, then let her growl softly out onto Callow Avenue. These were the murmurings of a woman transformed in to her true self, the self she was meant to be.

Man, she handled nice. The new shocks, the new tires, all new grommets on the front end made her solid and tight. He could feel every pebble in the road. She was restored, not to what she used to be, but to what she could be.

Sully stepped on it, then slowed. The transmission dropped down, responding like she was part of him. Oh, yeah.

Halfway down Callow he thought of Demi. This was all he wanted for her, too—to move, free and whole. Everything was there—the intelligence, the love, the compassion, the blooming faith. Whether Rich Costanas dealt with his own issues and saw what he had in her or not, she would become authentic. He knew that potential when he saw it—even in the darkest hour. He could always see it—

Baby, this is only temporary. It happens to a lot of women—it isn't your fault.

It is my fault—it's my sin.

Lynn—stop this. It's clinical depression—you have to take the medication until your hormones—

Don't, Sully—don't get between me and God. I have to repent—I have to rebuild my faith.

A horn blew, and Sully mashed the brake, inches from rolling past the stop sign at Callow and Burwell Street.

He ran his finger across his upper lip and drew back sweat. Of course the car would bring back those kinds of memories. That, he told himself, was why he had to take her out tonight. Show himself he was reconciled to it. That was over, and this was a new time, a new car, a new life.

He sat back and gentled the accelerator, bringing Isabella to a purr again.

She swung to the right and Sully rotated the wheel into the slide. She righted herself onto Washington Avenue without so much as a sway.

Sully let a grin cut from earlobe to earlobe, let it split the time since he'd been this free, so he could drive straight through and into the future, the what-is-to-come—blocked only by the car that shot out of the side street to his left and across Washington.

Sully slammed on the brakes again, and Isabella pulled hard to the right. Man, he knew he should have checked those.

The other vehicle, something big and bulky and muscular, sped across the Manette Bridge to his right, taillights zigzagging in the inky blackness.

Don't hit the brakes, baby!

Sully jammed the gas pedal to the floor and squealed after the red lights that blinked like spasms of panic.

Turn into the slide—I told you—turn into the slide—

But the Impala screamed at him as the car went for the side in a path straight as a sword. The lights flashed one last alarm before they took flight out into the black, into the long awful silence.

Sully pumped his own brakes and lurched forward, slamming his chest against the steering wheel. His cry was lost in the deafening splash, gulped away with the lights as the Cumberland River swallowed them. Swallowed Lynn and Hannah—and his life.

From another place a horn blared, needlessly urgent in this place, where nothing was left to save.

"Hey, buddy—you all right?"

Sully heard the voice, but he couldn't turn to it, couldn't move—couldn't breathe.

"Somebody call an ambulance!" the voice yelled.

Sully managed to shake his head, but words couldn't find their way out of the chaos. His mind tilted sideways and slammed back and forth, back and forth as he struggled to stay real. A fear he couldn't run from seized every nerve and set it up on end. He was attacking himself with his own terror.

Groping through the panic, he found the steering wheel and held on.

You're here. This is now. Hang on.

Squeezing through pain, Sully found his voice and whispered what he told his clients: "The anxiety won't rip you off the edge—you aren't going mad—let it go—you can do this."

"Call 911," the voice said.

"No need," Sully said.

"You're shaking, buddy."

"Everybody okay?" A second voice, firm and sure.

Sully let himself open his eyes. A red light twirled, but it was real.

And so was the face close to his, talking in tight spurts between the teeth.

"Nobody went off the bridge, did they?" Sully said.

"You almost did," the first voice said.

"Okay—everybody back off—let the man breathe." The second man, close to him, took Sully's wrist. "Deep breaths, my friend."

He tried—tried from his gut—and spread his hands and wiped them on his thighs. His legs shook, all on their own, and he let them. "Panic attack," Sully said. "I need a reality check."

"You got it. What's your name?"

"Sullivan Crisp."

"You know where you are?"

"Manette Street Bridge?"

"Good so far. Keep breathing."

"It's May second."

"All day. How you feelin'?"

"A little ridiculous." Sully felt the tremors begin to fade. "Are we blocking the bridge?" He tried to move, but a firm hand gripped his shoulder.

"No, you got off the road on this end—see? You barely missed bouncing against the railing." The guy looked around, let his eyes glance at the dashboard. "Hate to see you mess up this ride. '64?"

"Yeah."

"Fix it up yourself?"

Sully nodded and sank against the seat. His heartbeat slowed. The guy let go of his wrist and rested his hands on the open window.

"There somebody you want us to call?"

"Who's us?" Sully said. He noticed for the first time that the guy wore a uniform.

"Kitsap Fire Department," he said. "We happened to be heading this way when we saw you go off the road."

"Well, thank God," Sully said. He leaned his head back, closed his eyes. Exhaustion seeped in.

"How 'bout that phone call?" the fireman said. "I'm not thinkin' you should drive right now."

Sully pawed at the tuck and roll and picked up his cell phone. "I got it," he said.

"Okay. I'll wait."

The man did what he himself would do if he found some poor dude on the side of the road, groping for the real out of an attack of sheer terror. Terror a person should only have to survive once.

"You want me to dial the number?"

"Got it." Sully stiffened his fingers to stop the shaking before he pulled up Porphyria Ghent. At the first ring, he put out his hand to the fireman. "Who am I thanking?" he said.

"Name's Rich." The man clasped his hand with Sully's, hard and tight. "Rich Costanas."

CHAPTER THIRTY-THREE

All weekend I was sure Mickey would call to tell me my services were no longer required at the Daily Bread or Christopher would phone to inform me his father was filing for divorce.

Sunday night, long after even Chris would be brazen enough to invade with a call, I lay on the love seat, plucking at the threads in a hole and trying to accept the inevitable. Once again, I'd brought it on myself—only this time, no matter how many times I replayed Friday evening's scenes in my head, I didn't see how I could have done anything differently and still bear being in my own skin. I finally melted inside myself and slept.

My blaring phone pulled me back into consciousness, and I simultaneously pawed for it and sat up to the realization that the sun pried between the slats of the blinds and both Audrey and Jayne were gone. Fletcher Basset's voice hauled me right off the love seat.

"Sorry to call you so early," he said, "but I thought you'd want to know first thing so maybe we can get on it."

"We?" I didn't even try to be pleasant.

"The board of trustees held a closed meeting last night. Word is it was about Ethan Kaye."

I staggered toward the cold coffeemaker, phone tucked into my neck. "How would you know that, if it was a closed meeting?"

"That's the scuttlebutt. I thought maybe you could find out more."

"Why?" I said, although I was already interested enough to stop with my hand on the box of filters.

Fletcher chuckled. "Don't try to tell me you don't want to know."

"I do. But why would I tell you if I did find anything out?"

"Because I can make it news, get it out there so people can make some noise about it before St. Clair and the rest of them sweep him out of there without anybody knowing."

"They don't have any grounds for firing Ethan," I said. But my stomach twisted itself into a knot.

"I can help," Fletcher said. "And so can you."

I shoved a hand through my couch-mashed hair. "Look, my last conversation with Ethan Kaye was not so good. I don't think he's going to confide in me."

"What about your friend Dr. Crisp?"

My fingers froze to my scalp. "Excuse me?"

"You and Dr. Kaye have a mutual friend."

I heard paper rustle.

"Sullivan Crisp—he was with Kaye when he was attacked by a student."

"He *what*? Wait." I shook my head as if I could make something, anything, fall into a slot it belonged in. "You could not possibly know that I know Sullivan Crisp unless you were stalking me!"

"Listen, Demi."

"No! Leave me alone, Bassett. Do you understand? Stay away from me, and do not call me again."

He was still sputtering when I slapped the phone shut. The thought of the Chia-pet following me to Callow, to Sullivan's garage, was nauseating. Only my concern for Ethan kept me from lunging to the bathroom unit for an embrace of the toilet.

A student had attacked him? Things must be completely out of control.

I shook my head again and dumped three scoops of coffee into the filter basket. If Fletcher Bassett could tail me all over Kitsap County, he certainly wasn't above lying to me to get me to do his dirty work. This "attack" could have been a few angry words tossed across the commons.

But I didn't actually think so.

I'd barely stepped out of the shower when the phone rang again. Sullivan this time. I'd already decided to ask what he knew about Ethan, but an un-Sullivan-like awkwardness in his voice stopped me.

"You okay?"

"No," he said. "But I will be."

I heard a labored breath.

"I have to go out of town, Demi. It isn't the best time, I know, but I have to take care of something."

That something was clearly himself. His voice sounded ready to break in half.

"I'll be back in a few days. You have my cell number."

"Sullivan." I put my hand to my forehead. How much could you ask the person whose job it was to do the asking? "Is there anything I can do?"

"You can pray," he said.

"You're scaring me."

"No. It's okay." The Sullivan voice I could count on crept in at the edges. "If you need anything, anything, I want you to call me. You okay?"

"Yes," I lied.

When we hung up, I did try to pray. But all I could think was, *You have to, Demi. You have to.*

Have to what? I was directionless in more ways than one. I didn't have any place to go this morning. No reason to get dressed. Nothing to do but finish a cup of bad coffee. Nothing to do except whatever it was I "had to" do.

Look at myself. That's what I'd been doing—and it was the only thing that had held me together this far.

Maybe that was the first thing I had to do.

The Victorian Teahouse didn't open until eleven, which gave me plenty of time to unearth the picture of me at ten with my mother and brothers and stop at Papyrus to pick out the right stationery for that pixie-haired girl who always wanted a ponytail. My cell phone rang when I was still two blocks from the tea house, and I didn't try to dig it out from the bottom of my purse while I maneuvered through traffic. I checked the missed calls list when I was settled at my usual table with a cranberry scone and an Earl Grey on the way.

I didn't recognize the number. Who did I know with a 650 area code?

At least it wasn't Rich or Mickey or Fletcher Bassett. I shook all of them off like a wet dog and turned to the scallop-edged stationery to complete the assignment I'd never done.

Dear Little Demi,

I've been looking at this picture of you—of us—well, you get the idea—and I think I owe you an apology. I was such a little rule follower, you know? I hated for Mom to give me that look with her eyes all slitted down into hyphens, because it meant her voice was going to get all tight and she was going to tell me I was being difficult. I was too much of a weenie to push her any further, into The Silence. I could NOT handle that. It was so cold and so dark in The Silence, and it scared me.

So—that's why I never even argued with her when she said it was time for a haircut, why I never told her I wanted a ponytail like every other girl in America. That's why, poor baby, if you weren't wearing a little skirt in this picture, it would be hard to tell you from Liam and Nathan. Now I know The Silence wouldn't have killed me—us—and now I know that maybe if I had "bothered" Daddy, like we weren't supposed to, and asked him about it, you might have gotten that ponytail, with a bow to match a dress with ruffles instead of a skirt with pleats . . .

But I didn't know. I was too scared to ask. And I'm sorry.

I stopped as I felt the server approaching with my scone, and I wished I'd ordered a chocolate chip muffin instead. With hot chocolate—and whipped cream.

"You know what?" I said, lifting my face.

"What, Prof?" he said, in a voice that put its velvet hands on me—and choked me.

For a fossilized moment I stared at Zach. The dark thicket of eyebrows tangled like brambles above the bridge of his nose. The liquid blue eyes swam in a network of thin red lines. His almost-gray hair shagged over the tips of his ears and the top of the collar of a wrinkled shirt.

He wrapped his long fingers around my arm, and I smelled his musk, melded with stale sweat. I broke out of emotional stone and looked down at his hand, but he didn't move it, and I couldn't peel it away. That would have required touching him back.

"Let go," I said. My own voice was hard.

The rayed lines at the corners of his eyes squeezed, but beyond that he looked unfazed. Nodding as if he'd expected me to say that, he took his time loosening his grip and let his fingers trail down my arm as he withdrew them. I forced myself not to shudder.

"I'm sorry, Prof," he said. "I know I've caught you off guard. I tried to call."

The voice was the only thing that was the same. Clear, bottomless, and, I heard now, practiced. Dear God, I found myself praying, was it always that way? Had he always been this dog-eared version of an image I'd dreamed up?

Zach slid himself into the chair across from me. I sat straight back in mine, my hands rigid in my lap. He smiled at me, head cocked—still "appreciating my assets."

The server arrived, scone in hand, and I waved her off. "I won't be eating," I said. "Bring me the check, please."

Zach looked up at her and shook his head. "Give me the check," he said. "I'm afraid I'm responsible for her loss of appetite."

"What do you think you're doing?" I said when she was gone. "You think you can just blow back in here and pick up where you left off?"

Zach's face went soft, making flaps on either side of his lips. The whole encounter became unreal.

"I should have waited until I could talk to you first before I showed up," he said. "But I couldn't. I had to see you."

Something cold and clammy crawled up my backbone. How had he found me? Had he followed me? Was everyone following me?

"You look wonderful," he said.

"I look heinous—because I have been through several circles of hell—thanks to you. Thanks to us."

He shook his head again, still smiling the appreciation smile, still trying to drown me in his Puget Sound eyes.

"I don't know where you've been all this time," I said, "and I don't care. But—"

"You care, Demi. The kind of thing we have doesn't die because we're apart."

"I cannot believe you said that to me."

I pushed back from the table and got to my feet. Zach grabbed my wrist, hard enough to stop me but not hard enough to shut me up.

"Let go, or so help me I will scream," I said through my teeth.

"Then promise me you'll sit down and hear me out. Please."

Nearby a woman gasped. Only in deference to her did I whisper, "You have five minutes. Now get your hand off of me."

Zach squeezed before he released my wrist. I thrust it into my lap as I sat down, and rubbed it the way a child tries to erase an unwanted kiss. "Say whatever it is you think you have to say to me, but don't touch me again."

"You can't leave until you hear me out—and when you do, you won't go."

I pulled my left arm from my lap and presented my watch. "Four and a half minutes," I said—though the four red finger marks on my wrist all but shot me from the chair. My skin throbbed.

"You have to understand why I left," he said. "If I'd stayed and confronted St. Clair and Estes with you, I wouldn't have been as strong as I knew you were. I would have confessed the whole thing—in detail."

He crumpled his mouth, into that look. I felt nauseated.

"I would have had to tell them that I felt absolutely no remorse for what we found together, in each other. Even Ethan wouldn't have understood that."

"And what about now?" I said. "You don't see it as wrong?"

"When is love like that wrong?" He leaned forward, fingers spread like fans on the tabletop. "They wouldn't understand that. They would only understand what I knew you would do—which was give them the legalistic response they wanted and free yourself. I knew you'd do that for us."

My jaw unhinged. "Are you serious? You think that's what I did?"

"I know you, Prof—which is why I waited until I was sure it was over with Rich. I knew you'd try to fix it." He pulled his palms together, for all the world as if he were praying. "I gave you space because you couldn't be certain as long as I was still here."

I couldn't even speak.

"I get why you're angry, Prof—but you see now, don't you?" He softened his face again. "You forgive me?"

Words found me, and I thrust them at him like javelins. "If you actually believe any of that, Zach Archer," I said, "you are sick."

His palms dropped from prayer to the tablecloth, which he squeezed up in his fingers until the saltshaker toppled over and the ice swayed in my water glass. The Puget-blue eyes narrowed and darkened as he jutted his head toward me like a promontory rock. His mouth broke into a jagged line.

I'd never witnessed an unveiling like that one.

"Don't ever call me sick," he said. "My ex-wife did that—don't you do it."

I tried fleetingly to connect with that. I never knew he'd been married.

"I did what I had to do—for you," he said. "Because I love you."

I shook my head.

"What?" he said. "What is that?"

"You did it for nothing. I don't love you, and I never did."

"Uh-uh—no—you can't say that." He smoothed out the tablecloth, righted the saltshaker, widened his eyes. "Nobody fakes that, okay?"

He tried to force the jagged line into a smile, but the transformation had been too complete. His lips teetered between desperation and barely concealed anger. I was frightened.

"I know I hurt you," Zach said. "You probably thought I abandoned you. But, Prof, don't let your pride come between us. We've come too far."

"Yeah. All the way to nowhere." I swept my unfinished letter into my purse and once again tried to get to my feet.

"Sit down," he said.

His voice was low, but his tone was menacing enough to freeze me there.

"Enough with the integrity act," he said. "None of this would have gone down if you'd gotten out of that marriage when I told you to. We could have left here and started over, but you forced my hand."

"To do what?" I sank back into the seat, a sickening sense of foreboding rising to my throat.

"To make Rich see it was over between you two. Come on, Demi—where did you think that photographer came from? You think I wouldn't know somebody was aboard my own boat?"

I shook my head.

"I got that kid—what the heck was his name—the shutterbug that took pictures for F&D."

"Van Dillon?"

"I paid him enough, you'd think he would have kept his mouth shut. Nobody was supposed to see those pictures except Rich."

"You?" I said. "You set me up?"

"What choice did I have? You were never going to leave him—sometimes you were as legalistic as Kevin St. Clair. And I swear to you, I never planned for Ethan or Estes to know. I don't know how they got the pictures. That wasn't my doing."

I scraped the chair back and snatched up my purse. "Your ex-wife is right," I said. "You *are* sick."

I marched, unseeing, to the front door. Zach was so hard on my heels I could feel his breath raising the hairs on the back of my neck until we both erupted onto the porch. He had me by the arm, pulled to the railing, before I could get to the steps.

"I told you not to touch me," I said.

"You never said that back then—not when you made me believe you loved me."

He had me by both arms now, and he shook me. My head lurched back and my teeth slammed together.

"I gave up everything for you," he said. "You think I wanted to lose my job—my boat—my reputation?" He shook me again. "Yeah, I did want to, because I thought it would get me you. Look at me."

I did, but I didn't recognize the twisted face that forced itself at mine.

"You think you don't love me now—I get that," he said. "But tell me you loved me then. Tell me I didn't sacrifice my whole life for nothing."

The unnatural gleam in those eyes told me I should give him what he wanted and walk away, safely. But the whisper in my head curled above the words being growled into my face.

You have to, Demi. You have to.

I wrenched myself away. "You gave it all up for nothing, Zach," I said. "And so did I. I never loved you—ever."

Before the slap of my words could register, before he could grab me again, I bolted from the porch and down the steps toward the parking lot. When I got to the Jeep, I turned around to see him at the bottom of the steps, his arms outstretched as he shouted at me.

"Only a whore would do what you did for me in bed if she didn't love me. A cheap—"

I blocked out the rest as I dove into my car and squealed from the parking lot, leaving a sick man to proclaim my guilt to the Victorian Teahouse and the Good Word Christian Bookstore.

CHAPTER THIRTY-FOUR

Sully could almost smell Porphyria's lodge as he nosed the rental car up the road that snaked around the Smokies to her door. Always lit fireplaces, paths of wet leaves, maples and oaks in new leaf. It all pulled him forward until he was suddenly, magically there, on the washed-out gravel driveway. The sun spattered his windshield and soaked his face, and he waited for the comfort of being steps away from her wisdom.

But his veins still raced with the fear that any minute he would once again see flashing taillights and follow them over the precipice of his sanity.

His cell phone rang. Demi's number.

"Hey, there," he said. "You okay?"

"I have no idea." Her voice was like wire.

"What's going on?"

"Zach. He found me, Sullivan—at the tearoom. I don't know how. It's like he was stalking me." She huffed. "Do I sound paranoid?"

"Tell me some more."

She did—a breathless story of Zach Archer hiring the photographer and setting her up to get her away from Rich. Sully struggled to keep up, especially when she mentioned Van Dillon. Setting that aside for later rumination, he followed her to the tearful conclusion, when Zach shouted obscenities at her in front of a place that had been her refuge.

"I'm so sorry, Demi," he said. "You're not thinking for a second he was right about that."

She paused an instant too long.

"Don't go there. Don't even drive by."

"How can I not? I did prostitute myself."

"Why?"

"Excuse me?"

Sully turned sideways in the seat. "Why did you have sex with Zach even though you didn't love him?"

"I thought I loved him—which doesn't make it right."

"We've established that. But what did you get in return? What was worth doing something you knew was wrong?"

She breathed, long and sadly. "The way it made me feel. Not just sexually, but—needed, wanted."

"Ding-ding," he said softly. "And you've already given all that to God, who has now wiped it away."

"As if it never happened." Demi's voice wavered. "I was starting to believe that."

"What's stopping you?"

"Hello! He dredged it up and screamed it at me across a parking lot for half of Bremerton to hear!"

"You believe some guy with a borderline personality disorder over Jesus Christ?"

"What kind of disorder?"

"I can't be sure without observing him myself, but this whole thing of arranging your life for you, and his outburst when you said he was sick—it smacks of borderline."

"It was creepy the way his whole face, his whole body, changed when I said that."

"Yeah—if you see him or talk to him again, I wouldn't use that word."

"I have no intention of talking to him again, ever. In fact, if he tries to get near me, I'm getting a restraining order. I'm going to have bruises on my arms from where he grabbed me."

Sully sat up and leaned against the steering wheel. "I want you to document that—have somebody take pictures. And do not, under any circumstances, open the door to him."

"He doesn't know where I live . . . I don't think." She seemed to trip over it.

"I'm not trying to scare you," Sully said. "Just don't take any chances. He's at the very least unstable."

"Was I a complete idiot to ever trust this man?"

"No. He's very good at what he does, which is, obviously, manipulating people. You're apparently not the only one he's fooled."

"He never mentioned an ex-wife. Way back when, he gave me this whole story about how he'd never found what he was looking for until me. And I bought that, like a moron."

"Buzzz!" Sully said.

"I have to admit I was gullible."

"Which gets you where? I think you ought to focus on how strong you were to walk away from him. You want to know how I see it?"

"Do I have a choice?" Wryness crept into her voice.

"I think you not only took away his future—this whole idea he had that the two of you were going to run away and live in bliss for the rest of your lives—you took away his past too. With you he thought he could actually love, unselfishly. But it was all about him, all the time, because that's the way with these people." Sully shrugged. "You snuffed out his illusion about himself, and he can't take that."

"He had to make it my fault."

"Ding."

After a heavy pause, she said, "Every door is closing, Sullivan. I haven't even told you about my last conversation with Rich—or what went down with Mickey." She hesitated again. "I'll fill you in on all that when you get back. You have things to take care of. Go do it. I'm okay now."

He curled his fingers around the phone. As soon as they hung up, he'd be treading emotional water again. There would be nothing to stall him from going inside and confronting himself with Porphyria. The thought enervated him to the tips of his toes.

Porphyria had been trying to tell him this for thirteen years. So had Ethan. So had God Himself. Now it ran through him like barbed wire. He couldn't ignore it anymore.

But there was still a trace of Demi in his mind as he made his way to the door.

So Van Dillon was the photographer after all. Either Zach Archer *was* a "moron," as Demi herself would say, or Van Dillon *wasn't.* Tatum had pegged him as one, although Sully had seen evidence of his general cluelessness the night he'd attacked her in front of the bakery.

That still didn't explain how Estes and St. Clair got the pictures. Maybe Van saw a way to make even more money than Zach had paid him, and sold the photos to them too. It was an ugly thought, but one he couldn't dismiss.

Nor could he bypass the possibility that Zach Archer was headed for a mental split. Manhandling Demi—exposing his dark side—verbally abusing her—those weren't signs that Demi was entirely safe.

Sully stopped at the top of the age-sagged steps. Maybe he should return to Washington and walk her through this. He'd made a commitment to her, and his own issues would still be here when he came back.

"I wondered when you were going to find the nerve to get out of your car."

He squinted at the silhouette in the screen door. Ebony. Tall within. Expectant in that way that offered only two choices: go to her with the courage it took to be healed, or run like a rabbit and live in fear of those taillights forever.

"Now if I can find the nerve to get from here to the door," Sully said.

"No need."

The door swung open, and she strode toward him in two magnificent steps, arms open. Sully fell against her and sobbed.

"The good Lord has enough nerve for both of us," she hummed in his ear. "He always has enough."

Sully thought he remembered every inch of Porphyria Ghent—until he was face to face with her again. Now he sat across from her on one of a pair of matching red-and-gold chintz love seats worn shiny by years of sit-downs with those brave enough for her wisdom. He knew, as he always did at these back-again times, that there was no way to recall all the details of her complexity unless he was in her presence. It kept him coming back.

She sat on the other love seat, coffee-colored hands folded in her lap. Every few moments she nodded her close-cropped head, iced in white like a cupcake. Now and then she let a still-black eyebrow rise and fall. Always her eyes stayed on him, in wonder, like a child's. A child with a soul as old as compassion itself. He'd forgotten the two tiny exquisite vertical lines on either side of her mouth, the only trace of wear on her face. He hadn't remembered the way her chin sloped back to her neck like that of a marvelous knowing turtle. How had it slipped his mind that her depthless java skin was all one seamless piece, like her self?

"Looks like you've been holding that back for some time, Dr. Crisp," she said finally.

Sully ran a hand under his nose and drew back mucus. He looked at her helplessly, fingers dripping.

"Kleenex is right there on the table," she said. And then her lips, full enough for thirty smiles, parted and lit her face, and the room, and Sully's heart. "You're still an incorrigible kid, Sully Crisp. I'm glad to see it. Now we can get some work done."

Sully blew his nose noisily and nodded toward his shoes. "You mind?"

"Take them off—and that ridiculous sport jacket. Did you think you were coming to a board meeting?"

"I thought I was a grown-up, Porphyria." He shrugged off the jacket and tossed it at the rocker next to the fireplace. It slid to the floor and lay like a puddle.

"There was your first mistake," Porphyria said. "It's the first one everybody makes."

Sully worked each shoe off with the toes of the opposite foot and folded his legs up under him on the love seat.

"Now grab a pillow."

Sully cocked his head at her.

"You'll end up hugging a pillow before you're through. You might as well go ahead and grab one."

Grinning, Sully selected a yellow-and-gold striped one from the comfortable tumble of pillows on the floor. As he pulled it to him, the tears threatened again.

"Let them come," she said. Her eyes were closed.

"You can feel them," Sully said. "You can feel my tears."

"And now so can you. Holding them back is the second mistake most people make." She opened her eyes and widened them at him. "Now suppose you tell me about the rest of them."

"The rest of the mistakes?"

"Starting with the last one you made—up there in Washington."

Sully let his head fall back and gazed around the room as he filed through what now seemed like an endless list of wrong turns.

Every nook and corner of the room burst with a drum or a zany carved giraffe or a cane carved and waiting for her to need its assistance, which hadn't happened yet, not even at eighty. On a dim square of wall, crowded between an illuminated copy of the Lord's Prayer and a photo of a tribal African woman and her slip of a baby, a diploma from the Graduate School of Psychology, Purdue University hung.

Porphyria Ghent, Doctor of Psychology, 1956. In its plain black frame, it didn't announce that she was the first African American woman to receive an advanced degree at that university. Nor did she. The education of this wise woman had taken place wherever she went, wherever she touched lives, wherever she found truth.

Sully looked now for another piece he'd forgotten, and it was still there. The prayer stand, in front of the dining room window that looked down over the mountainside, now frosted in lavender. That was her true classroom—the place where she went to her knees and wept and cried out and whispered. And listened.

"I made the same mistake I've been making for thirteen years," Sully said. He pulled his eyes back to Porphyria, who still watched. "I tried to help someone else find her answers, to keep myself from finding my own."

"I'm sure you did more than 'try to help.' I'm sure you immersed yourself into her issues like a fat lady in a hot tub."

"I did. You know I did."

"Well." She refolded her hands as if they were handkerchiefs she'd just ironed. "Why didn't it work this time?"

He shook his head. "I don't think it's ever worked completely. I look back now, Porphyria, and I realize that with every new project I took on—the clinics, the radio show, the books—I tried to bury it deeper, but a little bit managed to seep out." He gave her a wobbly grin. "I'm like a backed-up septic tank."

"Now there's a lovely image."

"I knew better. I would turn myself inside out not to let a patient do what I've done with my own stuff."

"You finished?"

"Finished what?"

"The self-flagellation. I don't want to interrupt you until you've got the job done."

Sully let his chin drop to his chest and watched his knees disappear in a blur. "That's why I'm here. If I don't stop, I won't be any good to anybody."

"Least of all yourself."

He looked up at her. She'd narrowed her eyes.

"You're saying I've had a death wish?"

"I'm saying you have had no regard for Sullivan Crisp, the man in pain." She fluttered a hand at him, like the ruffled feathers of a disgruntled dove. "Hear me, Sully. Hear me all the way down into the bottom of your hurting self where you can't forget it. Like everybody else, until you're dead—you're not done."

He wanted to laugh. He was afraid he'd cry. He did neither and simply sank back against the love seat.

"Now—are you ready to go to work?"

"Yes," he said.

"Then the Lord be with you."

"And also with you."

"Let us pray."

Sully's young wife, Lynn, had been so tranquil during her pregnancy. The anticipation of having a baby wrapped her in an almost-euphoria that at times glowed on her skin, at others sent her into reveries even he couldn't intrude on. Some evenings he watched her sleep, probably more deeply than the baby herself, and felt boyishly left out of her dreams.

He couldn't wait for Hannah Lynn Crisp to make her entrance—so that he, too, could be a part of her life. When she was born—peach-colored and fuzzy-headed and warm—he stood, first on one foot, then the other, while Lynn breast-fed her so he could hold her and croon her to sleep. He squeaked the floorboards as he paced endlessly to give Lynn a break from the colicky crying. As for diapers, he prided himself on being able to change even a poop-up-the-back in less than five minutes. It was all joy.

Lynn, however, didn't seem to share the pleasure. She wasn't sleeping. She wasn't eating. And the pregnant glow was replaced by a pallor that finally forced Sully to call her doctor when she refused to.

"This sounds like postpartum depression," the obstetrician told him, as briskly as if he were diagnosing tonsillitis. "Bring her in and we'll get her on medication until those hormones right themselves again."

He'd reassured Sully that her condition was common and easily treated. Maybe she'd benefit from some good therapy in case there were issues about being a new mother, but the medication would ease the symptoms so she could enjoy the baby and be able to look at things clearly. Sully collected himself in relief, packed Hannah into her car seat, and bundled Lynn into her coat. On the way to the doctor's office, he gave her an upbeat rendition of her condition and the ease with which it was going to disappear. She seemed less than convinced, but Sully knew she was just too tired to resist.

Sully had the prescription filled and bought the formula and fixed the first bottles, because on medication Lynn didn't want to breast-feed. He constantly reassured her that she was still a wonderful mother, and didn't mention it when he noticed little Hannah cried less and thrived on her new diet. Slowly, Lynn began to sleep and eat and even laugh. Hannah again became the light in her eyes. Three weeks after she started medication, Lynn told Sully she was ready to stop taking the pills.

"What does the doctor say?" he asked.

"I haven't told the doctor." Lynn directed her very-brown eyes to a tiny speck under Hannah's miniature fingernail. "Belinda says I don't need them."

Sully experienced a chill he later pinned down as a premonition.

"Who in the Sam Hill is Belinda?" he said.

Lynn's voice immediately rose in pitch, and her cheeks blotched the way they did anytime she and Sully headed into uncharted territory. "She's a Christian counselor I'm seeing. I met her at Bible study—she's licensed and everything." She pulled her hand through her hair and let it fall, defiantly, to her shoulders.

"You're seeing a counselor? Since when?"

"Since yesterday. The doctor said I could benefit from therapy."

"But you're doing fine on the medication."

"That's just it, Sully."

Hannah whimpered in her arms, and Lynn hurried to the swing to enthrone her there.

"That's just what?"

Lynn put her finger to her lips and shot him a look. He lowered his voice.

"What did this Belinda say about your medication?"

"Her name is Belinda Cox." Lynn's words were like a picket fence between them.

"You didn't even tell me about this."

"I wanted to meet with her before I told you."

"But I don't understand why you felt the need—"

"I'm feeling guilty, okay?" She put her hand over her mouth and breathed into it.

"Baby—guilty about what?"

"About not breast-feeding Hannah. Belinda said doctors give you medication to get you to stop calling them."

"What?"

"Sully—shhh!" She turned to Hannah, who dozed nicely to the rock of the swing.

"She says what I really need is a deeper faith in God, that He can guide me to be the kind of mother I want to be." Lynn's voice caught, and Sully watched in dismay as her face twisted against tears. "This is a lot harder than I thought it would be—being Hannah's mom. I don't want to mess it up."

"Oh, baby." Sully went for her, his arms already curved in the shape of her, but she backed against the wall.

"I think Belinda's right," she said. "I haven't gone to God with any of this, and that's why it all built up in me and I felt like I couldn't do it."

Sully dropped his arms to his sides. "Is this Belinda Cox a physician?"

"No—but she has the deepest faith of anyone I ever met. She knows truth, Sully."

"Lynn. Dr. West is a Christian. I'm a theology student—you don't think I have faith? Both of us know what this medication is doing for you—it doesn't mean you can't still go to God."

"As long as I'm depending on something other than God, He isn't going to help me."

The statement sounded so rehearsed, Sully had to look twice to make sure she wasn't reading it from a tract.

"Is that what *you* think?" he said. "Or is that what this Belinda person told you to think?"

He didn't mean for it to come out like a swipe at her ability to decide for herself. But the instant he said it he knew that was how she took it, and a door slammed in his mind—the sound of Lynn shutting him out.

They reached an uneasy compromise. She would ask the doctor how to come off the medication. The leaflet that came with the pills—the one he'd read the night they got them—warned the patient not to stop taking them abruptly. And if she showed signs of depression again, they agreed they would revisit the issue. He didn't offer to make the call himself, and he forced himself to trust her and not phone Dr. West on the sly. But he couldn't avoid watching her, scrutinizing every morsel of food she didn't eat, every sigh in the night.

The change was obvious within days. She woke up crying—fretted when Hannah wouldn't take the breast again—hurled herself on the bed when Hannah spit up. He begged her to at least call the doctor.

"This is just withdrawal," she told him tearfully. "I'm making progress with Belinda. God is here."

Sully prayed to God himself—and he had no sense of peace that any of this was right. The day he came home to find Lynn rocking a screaming Hannah, tears rolling down her own face, he broke his vow and called Dr. West from his study upstairs.

As soon as Sully told him what Lynn was doing, he said, "Do whatever you have to do to get those pills into her, Sullivan. And bring her in here first thing tomorrow morning."

Sully stopped. He realized there was now a plate of cold chicken and potato salad in front of him. Food always appeared as if by angel delivery at Porphyria's. He nibbled at a wing, poked his fork into the salad.

"Now I'm scrutinizing what you're not eating," Porphyria said. "Take a break and get that in you. You need sustenance for the rest of this."

Sully abandoned the wing to the plate and smeared his hands on his jeans. "The rest of this" stretched before him like a dark endless road, lit only by red taillights. He would rather swallow that chicken bone whole than go down it. But there was no road behind him to retreat on. He was stuck here, where he could only sink down—or he could move ahead into pain he wasn't sure he could endure.

He must be a sadist to be in the business of therapy. How many times had he coaxed clients to press on down similar paths, reassuring them the demons wouldn't get them, when those same demons had been threatening them for years? He could see Demi cringing in terror halfway down her road, Zach Archer snarling behind her, and no light before her. And he had left her there alone.

"Don't you do it," Porphyria said.

Sully snapped his face toward her. "Do what?"

"What you're doing—trying to find a bunny trail to go down so you don't have to face this."

"I think I can do the rest on my own," Sully said.

"Mmm-hmm."

"What does that mean?"

"I never took you for a coward, Sullivan Crisp."

"I've been a coward for the past thirteen years."

"And that brow-beating you're doing on yourself isn't working either. Come on, my friend. You know what you have to do. Rest. Eat. Then we'll go on."

He stared down at his hands, twitching in his lap. "I don't know if I can do it without going over the edge. I told you about the panic attack."

"Did you go over the edge then?"

"Nearly. You want to know what's ironic?"

"Mm?"

"The man that talked me down was the husband of the woman I'm working with—the man who won't take her back."

He let his voice fade as Porphyria shook her head.

"Bunny trail," Sully said.

"And you don't need it." She grew still. "It takes courage to go on with an experience like that behind you. You're always afraid your psyche will assault itself again."

Sully swallowed hard.

"You know the minute you emerge from that place of terror that you have to learn to live differently." She leaned in. "You have to learn to be your own friend and confidant and comforter. It takes courage to believe you can be." She sat back again. "Now—either eat your lunch or start moving through. You got no other choices. But I will tell you this."

He looked at her, and he knew his face begged her to tell him something that would take this cup from him.

"You cannot be the man you are, the man I know, and believe that God is going to let you drop off the ledge when you're facing the truth—His truth, Sully. Do you think for a minute that *I'm* going to let it happen?" She gave a marvelous grunt. "Who did you learn from, son?"

"The best," Sully said.

And so he stepped forward, back to May 6, 1995.

CHAPTER THIRTY-FIVE

Sully had made a point of coming home at breaks between classes to check on Lynn. Usually she was in the rocking chair holding Hannah. Dishes were piled, crusty, in the sink. Laundry erupted from the basket and spilled out onto the floor. The refrigerator refused to produce food when the last of it was gone. Sully was sure she sat in that chair with the baby all day. Whenever he came into the house he heard her whispering to their child—until she knew he was there, and then she shut herself down.

That evening in early May, Sully hurried home after a late class. A torrential spring rain had left lakes in the streets, and he fishtailed twice between Vanderbilt and their rental house in east Nashville. Whether the storm kept her from hearing him, Sully never knew, but he was able to slip into the kitchen and listen from the doorway. He could only catch a few words between Hannah's cries.

"Remember how . . . Mama loved you . . . if I can't, Hannah . . . always remember . . ."

Sully blew into the living room. Lynn clutched the baby to her neck as they both sobbed. His wife's eyes were so swollen, her voice so raw, he knew she'd been at it since he'd left that morning.

Sully went straight to her and pulled Hannah—hot, moist, and smelling of urine—from her startled arms. He picked up a half-empty bottle from the coffee table and put it in her mouth. Her sobs quieted as she gulped at it.

Lynn's did not. "Give her to me, Sully," she said.

"No. I want you to focus on me for a minute—please."

Sully propped Hannah up with pillows and the bottle on the couch and went to his knees in front of Lynn.

"You promised we would revisit this medication thing if I saw signs of depression," he said. He grabbed her hands so she couldn't use them to hoist herself out of the chair. "I'm seeing it, baby, and it's scaring me."

"I don't want to depend on pills."

"It's only temporary. This happens to a lot of women—it isn't your fault."

"It is—it's my sin."

She tried to wriggle past him. Sully pressed her back by the shoulders.

"Lynn—stop this. It's clinical depression. You have to take the medication until your hormones—"

"Don't, Sully—don't get between me and God." Her face was scarlet, her eyes stormy and unfocused. "I have to repent. I have to rebuild my faith."

Again she tried to break free, but Sully held on, with his hands, with his eyes.

"That's Belinda talking, Lynn, and she's wrong. I know you think she's your friend . . ."

"She *is* my friend! She loves me—she understands me—and nobody else does!"

Sully went cold. Hannah coughed and let out a scream, and Lynn squirmed away from him and snatched the baby into her arms.

"I can't listen to you when you talk like this, Sullivan!" she screamed at him. "Belinda says I can't let you change my mind."

"You don't think I understand you?" He had to shout to be heard over her hysteria, over the baby screaming. "I'm watching you disappear right before my eyes, Lynn."

"I won't disappear! She says I won't disappear. I just have to believe."

"Believe *me.* You have to take the medication—and we'll get you some real help."

"She's helping me."

"Let me help you."

"You can't help me, Sully. She says you can't help me, and I have to listen to her."

"No, you do not!"

"Stop!"

Hannah rose to a new level of screaming. Lynn pulled her tiny face into her chest and ran with her into the kitchen.

"Okay," Sully called after her. "Okay—calm down. Let's get the baby calmed down."

He dashed to the kitchen in time to see Lynn disappear through the back door, the baby in her arms, keys jangling in her hand.

"Lynn—do not get in that car!"

He shrieked now as he tore through the back door and down the steps, slipping on the bottom one and careening toward the mud. By the time he righted himself she was already halfway into the Impala, and in the overhead light Sully could see her wrestling to get Hannah into the car seat.

"Wait!" he shouted at her.

She twisted toward him, one leg still connected to the ground. Her swollen eyes widened, and in them he watched her slide into herself, to a place he couldn't reach. He had the one instant that she froze there to get to her, and he lunged forward.

"Lynn, stop, baby, please—"

If he had walked to her instead of throwing himself, would things have turned out differently? If he'd gone for her hand instead of the car door. If he'd done anything else—

But the sight of her once-shimmering face stiffening to a mask stayed forever behind his closed eyes. She wrenched herself into the car, yanking the door out of his hand with a force he couldn't control, and roared the Impala's engine into a rage. On the tuck and roll beside her, Hannah screamed—and slid down in the car seat she wasn't buckled into. Her tiny red face contorting in terror was the last image of her Sully had.

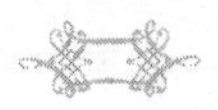

"I can't do this, Porphyria—"

"Looks to me like you're doing it, son."

A cool cloth pressed against his forehead. A cooler hand rested on his arm.

"You're brave, Sully," Porphyria said. "This takes courage, which you have."

Eyes still closed, he pawed for her hand. She turned her palm up and curled her fingers around his.

"Don't let go," he said. "If I go too far, pull me back."

"We have our hands on you."

"You and God?" He heard the fear in his voice—a boylike terror that made him cry.

"Father, Son, Holy Spirit—and me. You can't ask for more than that."

Sully nodded—nodded himself onto a dark road with only a pair of taillights in front of him.

"I have to go," Lynn said to him through the window.

"Let me go with you."

His cry was cut off by the spray of mud and gravel as she burned the tires into the driveway and shot backwards all the way to the street. The Impala swerved into it in a momentum arc that nearly landed it in the ditch. Sully wished in his tormented nights that it had. He could have saved her then.

He spent one crazed moment running after her on foot, until he watched the car sway through a sheet of water and surge on toward traffic-mad Gallatin Road. His keys were still in his pocket, and he fumbled for them on the way to the pickup.

Lynn was at a stoplight when he spotted her. He cut around a van and jammed his foot on the accelerator to catch up. He was within six yards when the Impala leapt forward on a still-red signal.

Sully shot after her, screaming for her to stop. A horn blared and Sully mashed the brake, stopping inches from another car. Eyes still straining for the Impala, he wheeled around the car and jerked in and out of the horn-blowing blur of vehicles. Ahead, through the drizzle, he saw her again. The taillights zigzagged as she took an abrupt turn onto a side street. Her shortcut to the Shelby Street Bridge.

The street was dark, cars parked along the sidewalks, owners tucked inside their houses, out of the rain. Veritable ponds flooded the roadway, and Sully had to slow down to keep from spinning out.

Lynn didn't. The Impala hurtled ahead, sending up a wake of frenzied water. Sully watched it swim sideways, the taillights flashing in alarm—a panicked pounding of red through the dark.

"Don't hit the brakes, baby!" he cried out to her. "Turn into the slide!"

The taillights blurred into a circle they shouldn't be in, and Sully knew she was going to hit one of the parked cars head-on. Horrified thoughts of Hannah clawed at him. Where was she now? On the floor? Sliding under the same feet that were shoving down the brakes?

The Impala spun in a three-sixty and hesitated only slightly before Lynn had her pouring through the puddles again. Sully followed the taillights, which still flashed on and off in spasms of panic. He screamed with every one—"Don't hit the brakes, baby!"

As heedless of his words as she'd been for the past two months, Lynn hurled herself on, making the last jog before she squealed left onto Shelby Street, into an inky blackness.

Power outage.

That was all Sully could put together before he heard the Impala scream. Her tires took an abrupt turn as she lunged for the bridge railing.

Turn into the slide, he would have screamed at her—if she were in another frenzied swerve. But the car went for the side in a path straight as a sword. The lights flashed one more alarm before they took flight out into the black, into a long and awful silence.

Sully pumped his brakes and lurched forward, slamming his chest against the steering wheel. His cry was lost in a deafening splash, gulped away with the taillights as the Cumberland River swallowed them. Swallowed Lynn and Hannah—and his life.

From somewhere else a horn blared, needlessly urgent in this place where there was nothing left to save. Only darkness remained, and the screaming that went on and on . . . silently in his head . . . through the plunge into psychology to save the world from the Belinda Coxes . . . through the adventures to peel his mind from a horror that haunted him. Straight through to now, when the screams cut through the gentleness of Porphyria's lodge and burned his throat, his heart, his soul, until he couldn't cry anymore.

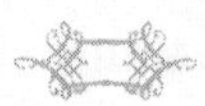

May on Puget Sound can look as if the world has been set free, and it did that year. God, I told the girls, was showing off—presenting us with splendid sunshine-drenched days, clear, soft air, and a profusion of blackberry blossoms that made our mouths water in anticipation.

People who appeared to have been hiding in the grave of winter climbed out, blinking, and felt their way to the shore and onto their boats and out to the farmers market to finger the organic cherries and gaze at the tomatoes and garlic and Walla Walla sweet onions, all bursting ripeness. Everyone and everything basked in the healing tonic of light.

I missed Mickey's daylight apartment, and just imagining myself on the window seat drinking in the sound didn't do it for me. I settled for the brook that ran through Sherman Heights, and the day I talked to Sully in Tennessee, I followed up our phone call with a late afternoon trip to a flat rock I'd discovered that was perfect for sitting and stewing.

I was halfway into a dragging up of scenes when I realized no hum of anxiety accompanied them. I went over the dialogue and reviewed the faces, but I didn't fall into a pit. I was actually trying to figure out what I could—and what I couldn't—do.

Sully would be proud of me.

I dug an oval rock out of the dirt beside me, a miniature of the one I perched on, and tossed it into the water amid the cheerful ripples. I breathed in my own courage. And I thought of Ethan.

Where was he in the mess Fletcher Basett said was going on at CCC? Who was left to bolster him?

"Hey, Mom."

I twisted to watch Jayne dance toward me, her creamy legs white as chick flesh gliding out of last year's shorts. We had to go shopping. As soon as I found a new job.

She floated down beside me and spread a newspaper before us.

"Did you know about this?" she said.

A pang of anxiety rippled through me. Every time I'd looked at a newspaper in the past two months, I'd seen an ugly piece of my own life displayed there for all to see. But the photo she pointed to was of the charred skeleton of a building.

"Metzel's burned down last night." She looked at me, sad-eyed. "Can you stand that we'll never eat triple berry cobbler again?"

I searched the picture for signs of a firefighter, the text for a mention of Rich's name. "Did you read it?" I said. "Was anybody hurt?"

"Nobody was even there—it happened in the middle of the night." She stopped and slid her pale hand over mine. "You're thinking about Dad, huh?"

"I probably always will."

"Does that mean you guys are getting a divorce?"

I looked up from the paper to see her eyes filling.

"I don't know, sweetie. It doesn't look good right now."

"Do you want me to call him? I could tell him he's being stupid again."

The laugh was out before I could stop it. "I don't think that would do it. But I did tell him what I needed to say. Now it's up to him."

She folded her arms and laid them across her propped-up knees. "I'm never getting involved with men."

"Not any time soon, anyway."

"I mean never. Dad and Christopher treat you like dirt, and you don't deserve it. Audrey's boyfriend is a total jerk—and she's like the best person ever." She shrugged the white shoulders sloping from the sleeveless blouse she'd unearthed. "I don't even want to go there."

I crooked my arm around her neck and pulled her to me. "They aren't all like that. Even your dad isn't like that. He's just hurting, and he doesn't know how to change."

I didn't know that until it passed through her eyes and left them in doubt. I couldn't let my daughter give up—on anything. And that meant I couldn't either.

"I'm going with Audrey to Wal-Mart, okay?" she said. The grave male dilemma was obviously over as she got to her feet and brushed her fanny with her hands.

"You two be careful—don't stay out past dark."

She pointed at the newspaper still spread across my lap. "I forgot—Audrey showed me another one of those letters, you know, about the college thing." Her face clouded. "I think it's about you."

I stared at the *Port Orchard Independent* long after Audrey's Nissan pulled out of Sherman Heights. Did I want to stir myself up again, reading somebody's opinion of what they thought was my life?

But the uncertain shadow I'd seen on Jayne's face made me turn to the editorial page. The letter was tucked down at the bottom. That was progress—it was no longer the main topic of editorial conversation.

Is anybody else tired of all this speculation about the resignations of those two faculty members from CCC?

I grunted.

I'd like to put it to rest, so hear me: their sudden exits had nothing—nothing—to do with the current problems plaguing CCC president Ethan Kaye. The controversy that is still bringing students and faculty alike into conflict is a separate matter, which, in my opinion, should be left for the college to sort out without the unwanted intrusion of public opinion. Whatever transpired between the two professors in question has no bearing on college issues.

I reached up a hand to flatten the prickles that rose on the back of my neck. Why didn't this person come right out and say my name and Zach's? And "whatever transpired between" us? Where did that come from?

I am not at liberty to divulge my source of this information, but I am asking the residents of South Kitsap County to trust me. Let's close the book on this thing and turn our attention to more important matters. Like—what can we do about that heinous shade of blue on our Main Street buildings?

I poked my index finger at the last line. *Heinous shade of blue.* The only person I knew who had ever described Main Street that way was Zachary Archer.

"You gravy-sucking pig," I said—out loud—my own voice as hard as the stone I picked up and hurled into the brook.

So now what? He had to make innuendoes about me in the newspaper, so there was no doubt in anyone's mind that we had "transpired"? And why the big separation from the CCC issues? Wasn't that too much of a protest—one he didn't even need to bother himself with?

I stopped, another stone in my hand. He'd told me he had no idea how Kevin St. Clair and Wyatt Estes got the pictures. How did he even know they *had*? Who would have told him? The only ones who knew besides Rich and me were Ethan and the two of them.

I let the stone fly. Zach had the pictures taken for Rich—but what was to stop him from taking money from St. Clair and Estes so they could use me to take Ethan down? Certainly not his integrity. I wanted to throw up in the blackberry hedge. I fished my cell phone out of my pocket and dialed Ethan's number.

Sully awoke in a bed on the second floor, between two yellow-curtained windows that drenched him in sunlight. A crow nagged him out of the four-poster onto his bare feet on the wood floor.

How he'd gotten down to boxers and T-shirt he didn't want to know. Not that it mattered. Porphyria was an angel before whom there was no need for male modesty.

Below he saw the angel in question waving to him, and he opened the window.

"I've got lunch coming!" she called up to him. "Your favorites. Out here on the veranda."

"I'm hungry," he said, "but I don't know if I can eat."

"You'll eat turnip greens and biscuits and redeye gravy."

Even from here he could see Porphyria's face draw the lines of a mother in charge, another layer of her complexity.

"No lamb tagine with spinach lentil something?" he said.

"Comfort food. Now get down here."

He found his clothes and reported to the veranda, where Porphyria waved him into a cushioned wicker chair. She picked up the conversation where they'd left off at the window.

"You've tormented yourself and you've blamed yourself and you've pushed yourself beyond the limits of helpfulness," she said. "And now you're going to eat."

And so they ate, Sully devouring Deep South cuisine until it did, indeed, settle his standing-on-end nerves. But he refused the cobbler, even soaked as it was in blackberry syrup, and felt the anxiety rising again.

"I still don't think I can handle this, Porphyria," he said.

She looked straight at him. "You can't. And that's the smartest thing I've ever heard you say."

He tried to grin. "That's depressing."

"Don't you start trying to hide under your humor again, Sully." She searched his face, eyes tear-shiny. "Whoever said anybody could handle watching his wife commit suicide and take his child with her?"

Sully met her eyes squarely. "You know that's what happened. They reported it as an accident, but you know . . ." He swallowed, retasting the turnip greens, now soured in his mouth.

"That isn't what's still in there eating at you."

"Isn't that enough?"

"It's enough, but it isn't all of it." Porphyria settled against the wicker chair. "What else, Sully? What else went through your mind when she took herself over the side of that bridge?"

He shook his head.

"Don't lie to yourself."

"Dear God—"

"And you sure can't lie to Him. Say it, Sully—and you can start to wake up from this nightmare."

He swallowed again, against the pain that strained at his throat.

"Say it, Sully—"

"I didn't save her. I could have saved her, and I didn't! I let my whole family die, and I couldn't save them!"

Sully put his face in his hands, but this time the sobs wouldn't come. His chest seized—his heart broke—but he couldn't cry.

"Let it go, son," Porphyria whispered.

"I should have made her take the pills. I should have gone to Belinda Cox myself and told her to leave my wife alone. I should have quit school and stayed with her until I knew she was better."

"That's a lot of shoulds. What about the coulds?"

Sully didn't look at her as he shook his head.

"*Could* you have made her take that medicine? Shoved it down her throat? *Could* you have stopped Belinda Cox from spewing her dangerous rendition of God? Gotten a restraining order?"

"I don't know."

"Maybe you could have. Maybe you even should have. But, Sully, you have spent the last thirteen years continuing to do what you didn't do back then, with Lynn." She reached over the remains of the lunch and put her hand under Sully's chin, lifting it like a child's.

"Now you've humbled yourself and admitted that you cannot handle this. What you can do is put God in charge, and let yourself be healed. Let yourself be forgiven for what you didn't do. Let yourself hurt while God soothes you and puts people in your life to comfort you. Let yourself open up to them instead of always being the one who fixes."

Sully felt his face melt into her hand. "I thought that *was* my healing."

She smiled sadly. "We doctors—we never take our own advice. Would you ever have let a patient get away with that kind of thinking?"

He was crying too hard to answer.

"You are an amazing doctor. You've saved thousands from living in desperation. That is God's work, but it can't heal *you.* What do we tell those souls who come to us wanting to be 'fixed'?"

Sully mouthed the words with her. "The only way out is through."

"You never went through until now. And here you are, still in one piece."

"Am I?"

Porphyria put her hands to the sides of his face and smiled into his eyes. Her warmth eased through his skin and into his veins. "You're beautiful, Sullivan Crisp. A little scarred, but beautiful. Are you humbly willing to work through this now—with God?"

He closed his eyes, pressed his forehead to hers. "Will you help me?"

"Ahhh. Those are the words I wanted to hear." She planted a kiss in his hair. "I have the rest of my life to help you, and it would be an honor."

Ethan sounded exhausted when he answered the phone, though he audibly tried to lift his voice when he heard mine.

"How are you, Demi?" he said.

"The question is, how are *you*?" I ran my hand across the folded newspaper, which I could no longer read in the shadows. "Have you seen the latest in the *Independent*?"

"I refuse to read that rag anymore."

The near-bitterness startled me.

"I hear that," I said. "But—this one got me thinking, and Ethan, there's something you should know."

I told him about Zach's sudden appearance, complete with his revelation about the photographs, and ended with my suspicions about his authoring the letter. The silence lingered on for a moment longer before he let a long breath fuzz through the phone.

"Thank you, Demi," he said. "That had to be hard for you to tell me."

"I want you to be able to avoid any more of their traps."

"We don't know for sure that you're right. I hate to think St. Clair and Estes would stoop that low, though I have no doubt that Archer would."

"Exactly."

He paused again, the quiet full of something more.

"I've hesitated in telling you this because I knew you felt bad enough."

"Is it about Zach?" I said.

"Yes—unfortunately."

His sigh curled around my insides like warning smoke.

"Before you—started seeing Zach . . ."

I silently blessed him for being so genteel.

"There was evidence that he had an affair with a student."

My chest swelled until I could hardly breathe.

"We couldn't prove it, although St. Clair tried, believe me. Zach of course denied it."

"You confronted him?"

"I had no choice, not with both Kevin and Wyatt Estes breathing down my neck. That's why I think you're probably wrong about any involvement between them and Zach." Ethan's voice softened. "I know this has to make you feel—"

"It makes me feel validated for walking completely away from that scumbag yesterday. Today I know he is out of my life forever and I'm forgiven for ever letting him in." I let the angry air out of my lungs. "And today is what I have right now. Today with God."

I could feel Ethan nodding his peppery head and creasing the lines on his face into a wise smile.

"You're okay, Demi. You're better than okay, aren't you?"

"I think maybe I am."

"Look, I'm sorry about that letter in the paper, but it sounds like this might be the end of that. I never wanted any publicity for you and Rich."

"You know what?" I said. "It is what it is. I'm actually kind of weary of Rich's paranoia about people knowing. It won't be long before everyone is going to know there's something up between us."

Ethan gave a soft grunt. "Does that mean you two are divorcing?"

"Looks that way."

"I wish I could do something."

"Just fight this thing that's happening at the college, Ethan," I said. "I heard there's going to be a hearing."

"A week from today." His voice went wooden again.

"Is there anything I can do?"

"Pray, Demi. Just pray."

"'Just' pray? Ethan, that's all there really is."

I hung up wondering where all this certainty came from. And then I closed my eyes, and I knew.

CHAPTER THIRTY-SIX

Audrey and Jayne pulled in just before the sun sizzled down over the horizon—not a moment before their curfew. I smothered a smile as I picked my way over the blackberry hedge and tried to do a firm mother-thing with my face, but they were giggling so hard, I gave it up and giggled with them.

"What are you guys up to?" I asked.

Audrey faced me, clutching a plastic Wal-Mart bag.

"I bought this cute maternity top, and Jayne says I look like Big Bird in it."

She yanked an impossibly yellow garment from the bag, and I shoved my fist over my mouth so I wouldn't guffaw.

"It's great," I said. "But, honey, what's with the feathers?"

Jayne absolutely squawked, and I would have, too, if we hadn't suddenly been blinded by a headlight beam. I shaded my eyes to see who was barreling up our pine-needle-paved road on a Harley.

"Who's that?" Audrey said.

Jayne's laughter died, and she backed toward the door. Her face took on an I-have-to-hide-now look that sent prickles up the back of my neck again.

"We better go in," Jayne said. "It's my dad."

Audrey nodded as if that were somehow clear and stuffed the Big Bird blouse back into the bag while she hustled behind Jayne. The screen door closed behind them as Rich killed the motor next to my Jeep.

I didn't want to look at him. I could feel the tension in his step as he marched toward me, and I didn't want to see it in his face.

"I have to talk to you, Demitria."

Those were the words I'd been wanting to hear for two months—but not the tone. "As your wife, or as one of your rookies?" I said.

He stopped at the edge of our stoop and stabbed a finger toward me. I put my own hand up before he could open his mouth.

"If you want to talk to me, I'll listen. If you're going to lecture me, I'm not interested."

He dropped his hand, but his eyes still glared in the feeble yellow porch light. "You interested in me knowing that you are still lying to me?"

I rolled my eyes. "About what?"

"How can you stand there and play innocent with me?" He jerked his head sideways, ran his hand down the back of it.

"*What?* What are you talking about, Rich?"

"You told me you were through with Archer—and then you meet him, right out in the open where anybody can see you with him—including your son!"

I froze. The bookstore—across from the teahouse.

"Listen to me," I said. "Christopher did not see what he thinks he saw."

A curse ripped from Rich's lips. "He saw you talking to him, Demitria—he heard him yell something about what you did for him in *bed*."

"He called me a—he yelled at me because I told him I never loved him and I never wanted to see him again."

"For how long this time, Demitria?" Rich's voice stretched beyond shaking, beyond anger. "You've been seeing him all this time, haven't you? All the time you've been telling me how much you want us to get back together, you've still been seeing him on the side."

"No. I—have—*not. Listen* to me, Rich."

"Don't try to tell me Christopher was lying."

"He only heard part of it."

"Wasn't that enough?"

"It was completely out of context."

Rich swore again, this time slamming his hand against the post that held up our overhang. "I hate that! Don't try to make this sound like it wasn't what it was, because I'm not buyin' it—not this time." He put his thumb and index finger close to each other. "After the other night at the hospital I was this close to believing that I oughta take you back." He hissed. "This is it, Demitria."

"This is what?"

"I'm done. I want a divorce. You'll hear from my lawyer."

I didn't say a word as I watched him stalk to the Harley and fire it up and fishtail through the pine needles to get away from me. When the taillight disappeared I sagged against the pole he'd slammed his hand into and felt the vibration of the anger he left behind. I slid down to the stoop. The doorstop rock dug into my back, but I left it there.

This was the moment I'd feared since the day Rich had turned to me with that brown envelope in his hand. I'd been so sure that I would die if it came to this—that my fear would turn on me and chew me up and leave me in pieces I could never put back together. But I was still here. I was still whole. I was so sad I couldn't even cry—but as the wash of nothing-left-to-do swept over me, I merely sat with it.

He'd been so close, Rich said. So close to believing he should take me back.

And then Zach.

Mission accomplished, Dr. Archer. You got Rich away from me for good, just like you wanted.

The rock in my back was suddenly unbearable, and I ripped it out and squeezed my hands around it.

"I hate you, Zach Archer!"

I brought the rock behind my head and tensed myself to throw it. But I couldn't let go.

You have to, Demi.

The whisper cleared a path in my head.

You have to tell everyone that you are forgiven.

Not by Rich. What good was—

You cannot be completely forgiven until you forgive.

I stared at the rock, wondering for a crazy moment if the thoughts were coming from it. In an equally crazy way, I supposed they were. The very rock I'd been throwing at myself I couldn't throw at anyone else.

Not even Zach Archer.

I put the stone back in its place and ran my fingers over the paint bumps. It was going to take time. It was going to take the Easter-Christ. *But Demi, no matter what it takes, you have to.*

I pulled myself up and opened the screen door. Jayne and Audrey were huddled together on the couch, faces halfway between guilty and frightened.

"You okay, Mom?" Jayne said.

"You heard."

"Enough."

"I'm okay, sweetie. We'll talk when I get back."

I grabbed my purse.

"Where are you going?" she asked.

"To find your brother," I said.

I hadn't been to Olympia College since freshman orientation back in August, and I barely remembered where the library was in the eclectic gathering of buildings that could be identified by decade. Christopher's truck was parked in the lot, next to a funky quadrangle that housed the designated smoking area. Even in my stiff-legged anger, I thought of the graceful slopes and sweet gardens of Covenant Christian College—and that made me homesick—and *that* made me angrier than ever.

The front door to the library suffered as I yanked it open. I climbed the steps to the mezzanine to survey the clumps of students below, and I found my son sprawled at a table in a corner, one lanky leg parked on the chair opposite him as he bent his head over a textbook. He needed a haircut.

I felt several students staring at me as I took the steps down two at a time and cut around the shelves to get to him. One of them darted out of the way so I wouldn't plow into him and mumbled something about me being a psycho.

"Christopher," I said. I made no attempt to speak at library volume.

He looked up and took several seconds to focus on me.

"What are you doing here?" he said.

"We're going to talk. Outside."

When he went into a snarl, I grabbed his sleeve and pulled him to his feet. The book slid across the table as he tried to grasp the edge to hold back.

"Now," I said. "Unless you want me to make a scene right here."

Judging from the whispers hissing from the stacks, that was already happening. Christopher heeded them and, with a killer glare at me, led the way to the door.

Once outside, he stood with his back to a bank of Plexiglas-covered announcement boards and put his hands on the hips of his wrinkled shorts. He tossed his head to flip the hair out of his face. "You talked to Dad."

"No, Christopher, he talked to me."

"What did you expect?"

I stepped in, my nose close to his. "I expected him to listen to me. But instead, he listened to you. And now you are going to listen to me."

He rolled his eyes.

"Stop right there, son." I took his chin in my hand and jerked it toward me. "Because you are still my son—and I have something to say to you."

He didn't move. I was sure that, like me, he'd never heard my voice sound like a pair of brass knuckles before.

"First of all, you are to stay out of the situation between your father and me."

"I don't think there is a 'situation' anymore."

"Shut up, Christopher." I stepped back so he could see me full face. "You told him what you thought you saw yesterday in the parking lot—or was it what you *wanted* to see? I think you have wanted us to split up from the moment this all came to light. Why, I don't know. And frankly, right now I don't want to know, because nothing you can say will excuse your behavior toward me in this."

"How was I supposed to behave? Walk around with my nose in your butt like Jayne does?"

"Ask me whatever possessed me to tear our family apart like this—that's what Jayne did. And I told her—and it wasn't an excuse, so don't even go there."

He pressed his lips together.

"She forgave me, Christopher, and that gave us a chance to rebuild our relationship. No thanks to you."

"What did I have to do with it?"

"You told Jayne I didn't want to come to her play. And then you told me she didn't want me there. Tell me—"

He turned his face away, and again I pulled it back.

"What else have you lied about? Besides telling your father I had a romantic tryst with Zach Archer."

"You did." He wrenched his chin from my hand. "I saw you."

"What you saw was me telling Zachary Archer to get out of my life because I never loved him and I regretted ever getting involved with him. He sought me out at the tearoom—I hadn't seen him since the night of his boat fire."

"What about what he yelled to you across the parking lot?"

"You mean when he called me a whore?"

He lowered his eyes and moved his lower jaw from side to side.

"Yeah—those were his parting words to me, weren't they? You heard them, but you chose not to share that part with your father."

"You can't blame me for you guys breaking up."

"You deliberately distorted what you saw and heard, and now there is no chance for us."

"Good!"

I felt the sting on my palm before I even knew I had slapped my son in the face.

He stared, his own hand on his cheek, eyes widened in an astonishment he couldn't hide. When he spoke, it was my turn to be astonished. His voice was thick.

"When I told Dad I saw you with Archer, he took off out of there to work like some crazed maniac escaping from a psych ward. That was the night of the fire at Metzel's—and he went off on a rookie when he dropped a hose."

I watched him swallow.

"Dad got suspended—because that was the second time he sent a fireman to the hospital."

My head spun. The second time. Had I seen his other victim the night I took Audrey there?

"So what do you think—Mom?" Christopher's eyes were red-rimmed and glassy, and his face worked. "I guess we both took him down. And if you're anything like me, you feel like a loser."

I let him go, back into the library, bony shoulders hunched forward like that little boy trying to be a man. My slapping hand stung at my side, burning away any satisfaction I felt two minutes before. I knew what it felt like to be him.

CHAPTER THIRTY-SEVEN

Sully was draping a cover over the Impala when he heard the toy-engine sound of the Jeep pulling up. Too bad he couldn't cover his pain the same way, just long enough to get Demitria through hers.

"I have to go back and finish this," he'd told Porphyria.

To his surprise, she'd nodded, the sun kissing her forehead, her nose, her chin as her head moved. "Sounds like she's almost there—and you have the final piece for her."

Sully knew she wouldn't put that into words for him. He'd had to mull it over on a walk through the woods, a slow stroll that brought him to his knees at a stump sprouting tender shoots. He folded his arms across it and rested his head.

At least he could close his eyes now without seeing red lights flashing in the darkness. He stumbled in darkness most of the time, even when he recited to himself what Porphyria had said. The shadows still fell across his soul. What would it take for the Light to flood in again, the way it did when he prayed for his patients?

It was there somewhere. Sully turned and leaned against his stump of an altar, face tilted toward the sun that mottled through the canopy of leaves above him. He felt so small here.

Dang. He *was* small. Like a kid just learning to live.

He'd felt a sad smile spread. *I'd like to solve the puzzle, he thought. Humble willingness.* He would have to give that one to Demi.

The Wheel of Fortune wheel was set up in the office, on top of the boxes of tools he'd packed to leave in Ethan's garage. It was a toy roulette wheel he'd picked up at Great Prospects and modified for today's session, and the puzzle board was ceramic tiles, letters penned in Sharpie. Only Vanna White was missing.

"You putting her to bed?"

Sully looked up at Demi, who nodded at Isabella.

"She's ready for a new owner," Sully said. "How are you, Demi?"

She seemed to appraise him, eyes drooping softly at the corners. "I've been better."

"Then let's talk." He wafted a hand to the office doorway, where she stopped and blurted out a laugh.

"Let me guess," she said. "Wheel of Fortune."

"Ding-ding."

She looked at him over her shoulder. "What—no evening gown for you?"

He had to grin.

"What do I do, buy a vowel?" She sank into the chair.

"Tell me what's going on first." He sat across from her.

"Christopher saw me in the parking lot of the teahouse with Zach screaming obscenities at me, and he gave Rich a slanted version." She took in a breath and held it before she went on. "And now Rich wants a divorce."

Sully closed his eyes for a second. "I'm so sorry."

"I took it out on my son—slapped him across the face. And then he told me that Rich took the news out on a rookie and sent him to the emergency room—casualty number two—and now Christopher feels as horrible as I do." She rubbed at the corner of one eye. "But he isn't speaking to me, and my husband has been suspended from the fire department, and things could probably be worse but I don't know how. You heard about the hearing coming up—for Ethan?"

Sully nodded.

"I told him about Zach so he won't be blindsided, but he doesn't think St. Clair and Estes were involved with him. Who knows what to believe? I hate the whole thing." Demi bent her forehead to her hand.

"So, which part of that can you do anything about?" Sully said.

She took a minute to bring her head up. "None of it."

"So who *can* you help? Besides Jayne and Audrey."

He got a blank look.

"I'll give you two consonants and two vowels. D-E-M—"

"Myself." She rubbed her hands on her thighs, clad in pink pants. She was crisp and put together—not the look of a hopeless woman.

"I learned something while I was gone," he said. "It's working for me, and I think it's the final piece of the puzzle for you too."

"You and I need the same thing?" She gave him an eyebrows-up look. "Go figure."

He turned to the puzzle board. "An attitude before God."

"They never give clues that good on Wheel of Fortune."

"This is the special Sullivan Crisp edition."

"For dense contestants, obviously." She pointed at the wheel. "Do I spin?"

"Go for it."

The wheel twirled and teetered and stopped with the ball between two pegs.

"What does that mean?" she said.

"It means you get to turn over a letter and start solving the puzzle."

"That's not how they play, is it?"

"I told you—it's a special edition."

She flipped over the first tile and displayed an H. "This could take all day, Sullivan," she said.

"Have at it, then."

"I'll be Vanna." Demi turned each tile over, smiling at an imaginary audience and framing the squares with her hands.

The attempt to cheer him up tugged at his insides.

"HUMBLE WILLINGNESS," she read. "An attitude before God." She traced the last tile with her finger. "I feel like I should kneel down and pray."

"That's how I felt when I discovered it. Well—when a friend of mine led me to it. My mentor, actually."

Her eyebrows lifted. "You need a mentor?"

"We all do."

Demi tapped the box the wheel sat on. "You're leaving for good, aren't you?"

He nodded.

"And who's going to be my mentor? I'm not done, you know."

"Demi, you know what?" He leaned on his knees. "Until we're dead, none of us is done."

"Lovely," she said. A quick smile faded. "How will I find someone as—I'm just going to say it—as amazing as you?" She wrinkled her brow. "And you know how I mean that."

"I do, and I'm honored." He grinned. "I'll help you find someone who at least comes close."

She brought her eyes up, shimmery and wet. "Whatever has happened to you, I get the feeling it was worse than a divorce and a rotten kid. If you're going to keep going, then so can I." She let the tears fall. "You've helped me so much, Sullivan. You've helped me start seeing who I am, and even if that didn't bring Rich back to me, it brought me back to me."

"Ding, ding, ding, Mrs. Costanas," he said.

They sat in the dewy-eyed silence for a minute.

"I want to do something for Ethan," she said finally. "I keep thinking that if the board knew about the pictures and had even a hint that they came by them dishonestly, they would give Ethan the benefit of the doubt."

Sully shook his head. "Ethan would never expose you to them. He promised you."

"I don't expect him to." She shoved a tear from her cheek with the side of her hand and lifted her chin. "But I can."

Sully slowly sat up straight. "You sure you want to do that?"

"If there was the slightest thing you could do for him, wouldn't you do it?"

He would, no question. He'd been trying for months—eating enough pink champagne cake to gag a maggot.

Somewhere in his head, a Light came on.

Maybe he could stand just one more piece.

The bakery was quiet when he jangled the bell on the door. Tatum appeared from the back, pulling off her hair net, and greeted him with a sheepish smile. "I thought you'd want to stay as far away from me as you could."

She leaned on the counter and let the smile vanish. "Okay—you didn't come in here for cake, did you?"

"You want to know something? I seriously hate that stuff."

"I knew that." Her hands went to her hips. "All right, what's going on? Did Van press charges against you?"

"No, but he did something—and I think you know what it is."

She stuck out her chin. "I'm trying to forget whatever I knew about him."

He watched her eyes. "Including the pictures Zach Archer hired him to take?"

Though she tried to form her usual thin layer of indifference on her face, the guilt was there in her eyes. "What's it to you?" she said.

"I'm a friend of Ethan Kaye's, and I want to help him."

"Yeah, well, I don't." She reached behind her and snatched up a rag, which she applied to the already spotless glass case. "I hate that college, I hate Zach Archer more, and I hate that woman even more than I do him."

"Dr. Costanas."

"Yes."

"Because . . ."

"Would you just give it up?"

"No, but it won't go past here." Sully pointed to his head. "I'm a therapist. I keep secrets."

She let the blue-gold eyes glint at him and tossed the rag behind her. "I thought therapists weren't supposed to lie."

"I didn't lie—I was here to rebuild a car."

"And pry into my psyche."

"Why do you hate Demitria Costanas?"

"Why should I tell you?"

"Because you could help a lot of people, Tatum. If not her, an entire segment of students at CCC."

"I have long since stopped caring about anybody at that college. In fact—" She gave him a plastic smile. "I wish it would burn to the ground or something. In my mind, they are all getting what they deserve—including Dr. Costanas, who, if you must know, took away the man I loved." She ripped off the smile. "Satisfied?"

"What about you, Tatum?" Sully said.

"What about me?"

"Don't you deserve to be able to face up to this so you can be healed, instead of turning into a bitter, cynical woman wasting her life in a bakery?"

Her eyes swam, and, he saw, she hated them for it.

"Is that the shrink talking?" she said.

"No—it's your friend talking."

She came out from behind the counter and marched to the door, and for a minute he thought she was showing him out. But she flipped the OPEN sign to CLOSED, and turned the deadbolt. With her hand still on it, she said, "Sit down. I'll give you ten minutes."

He sat dutifully and pushed out another chair with his foot. She turned it backwards and straddled it, leaving its back between them.

"Here's the deal." Her voice was cardboard. "I had a—call it an intimate affair—with Zachary Archer last spring. Technically it wasn't sexual, but it was enough for me to know he was the man I wanted to spend the rest of my life with. But just before classes started in the fall, he broke it off. He told me he'd had an attack of conscience about seeing a student. It was pretty romantic, actually."

Tatum licked her lips as if she were removing a bad taste. "He said it broke his heart, but he wanted to stop before we weakened and slept together. He respected me too much to do that to me. Can you believe I bought that?"

She pointed her finger at Sully. "Don't answer that."

"I do believe it. What woman in love wouldn't?"

"Anybody with half a brain. Anyway, I felt like he was protecting me, even when he said I should date somebody else, preferably a student. I took it to mean he wanted to avert suspicion. It was in the innuendo that we were going to end up together when I graduated."

Sully leaned across the table. "Tatum, from what I know about this guy, I'm sure that's exactly what he wanted you to believe. Don't beat yourself up."

She twisted her mouth. "Too late."

"So where did Van come in? Was he the diversionary boyfriend Zach told you to acquire?"

"Yeah. Zach even picked him out for me."

"So you two were still talking."

"He gave me just enough attention to keep me hanging on—I see that now. Which is why when he came to me in February and asked me if I would have Van do a 'discreet photography job' for him—" She pushed away from the chair back with her palms. "I was sick of Van by that time. He wanted a whole lot more from the relationship than I did, and I felt like a jerk leading him on. Zach said this job would get me out of it and set me free to go away with him."

Sully tried to keep the utter disgust out of his eyes.

"I was so ready to do that. Van was already accusing me of having a thing for Dr. Archer. I guess I wasn't hiding it all that well."

The impassive I-could-care-less face she was fond of putting on was a post-Zach development, Sully decided. She must have been a beauty to behold when she was in love.

"I did everything Zach told me to," she went on. "I gave Van a packet and told him to do whatever the instructions inside said. I have to say I was sort of weirded out by it—but I thought Zach wouldn't do anything that wasn't totally right, after he was so 'honorable' with me."

Sully nodded.

"So—the night he took the pictures—at the end of February, Van comes to my apartment, drags me out in the hall so my roommate won't hear, and says if I thought Zach Archer had any feelings for me, I was wrong. He shows me this huge wad of cash and says Zach paid him big bucks to take pictures of him and a woman, print them, and deliver them to the fire station with Rich Costanas's name on the envelope."

She tilted her head back and breathed in through her nose. "He shows me the pictures, and there's my Zach with Dr. Costanas—her half naked."

"I know," Sully said. "I've seen them."

Tatum blinked at him.

"Long story," Sully said. "Go on."

"It was like Tatum Farris ended right there—I either had to become somebody else or die." She put her head down, and her shoulders shook. "So now I'm a bitter little bakery girl—and I hate myself this way."

She cried like it hurt and stopped, Sully knew, long before she was ready. He handed her a napkin.

"Now," he said, "you want to tell me the rest?"

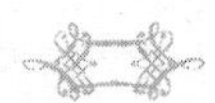

I had to admit it was manipulative, but I had to do it to get Rich to see me, and I had to talk to him before I went through with my plan. Jayne was more than happy to help, though I told her at least six times she was never to do anything like this herself.

"Whatever, Mom," she said. "You do what you have to do. He'll get over it."

It was so unlike my fairy princess of a daughter, I had to laugh out loud.

She called him and asked him sweetly to meet her at Java Joe's, that she needed to talk to him. That wasn't a complete lie. She did sit with him for ten minutes, telling him in no uncertain terms (she told me later) that he should listen to me for once instead of deciding to divorce me. From the ladies' room door I watched him rub the back of his head and try to look stern. He didn't quite pull it off.

When she reached up and pulled at her ponytail—our prearranged signal for me to enter the scene—I hurried to the table and slid into her chair as she slid out.

"I'll meet you out front," she said, and vanished among the tables.

Rich leaned back and simply sighed. The man looked exhausted.

"I'm sorry to hear about your suspension," I said. "I really am, Rich."

"Is that why you set me up—so you could tell me that?"

"No. I'm sorry about the setup, but you need to hear this."

"You used our daughter."

"She was a willing accomplice—and much more honest than our son, which is another story."

"What is it, Demitria?" he asked wearily.

I folded my hands on the tabletop and shook my head at the waitress who waved a coffeepot in my direction.

"What I've done has hurt a lot of people, and some of them won't let me make it up to them. But there's one person who I can help, and that's Ethan Kaye. I know you've always respected him."

Rich gave a jerky nod.

"There's a board meeting coming up to decide whether they're going to let Ethan go."

"That makes no sense. He's put that place on the map—he got you your position."

"I know that if I go to the board and tell them that Zach Archer set me up with those photos and somehow Wyatt Estes and Kevin St. Clair got them and tried to use them to force Ethan to resign—"

"Whoa, whoa, whoa. He did what?"

I blew out air. "Zach was the one who had the pictures taken and delivered to you. Somehow, the others got them too. I don't know for sure if he had anything to do with that—Ethan doesn't think so."

"This was the guy who supposedly loved you?"

"Don't start, Rich," I said, closing my eyes. "I know I was an idiot to ever trust him—and it isn't going to do me any good to tell you how deceptive he could be."

Rich swore under his breath. "The nice guy who took us all out on his boat. I bought it too." He cleared his throat. "Not that that's any excuse for you—"

"I said don't start. What's the point? You've already asked for a divorce."

"So why are you telling me this?"

This was the part I dreaded. "Because there's likely to be publicity, and I know you don't want that." I pressed into the table. "I have to do this, Rich. It's the right thing. I'm sorry if it embarrasses you, but people are going to know sooner or later. This way you can tell anybody you care about before they read it in the paper. Anybody else might even feel bad for you the victim."

He looked down. "There's nobody I care about anymore, except the kids. Do what you have to do." His eyes came up. "I'm surprised you want people to know what you did, though. You have friends here."

"They all know already—and besides, people can think what they want, but I know that one act of infidelity does not define me as a person. I can still do good things, and I can still love, and I can still serve God. That's who I am."

Something came into Rich's eyes and lingered there long enough for me to catch it and name it respect. He gazed back down at his hand.

"I hope all our conversations in the future can be as calm as this one," I said. "We're going to have to have some—about the kids and the property."

"Yeah." He shifted in his seat.

I scraped back my chair and swallowed down the emotional lump in my throat. "If anyone asks, I'll tell them you didn't deserve what I did to you."

Before he could answer, I wove among the tables and out to my daughter.

CHAPTER THIRTY-EIGHT

The air was misty the day of the board meeting, which seemed fitting. Sunshine wouldn't have worked for the uncertainty that shrouded the school as I made my way from the car up the hill toward the admin building.

I stopped at the top and looked down on the campus. The last of the day's protestors, lounging on the chapel steps in Northface, their signs dripping at their sides. People under a canopy of umbrellas moving into Huntington, shoulders nudged together in concerned conversation. I could see it all at once, and I knew what it meant: if I didn't go forward with the story I had spent all night receiving from the God-whisper, the struggle for truth through doubt would disappear.

And part of me would vanish with it.

Hanging the bag of rocks I'd collected from our brook over my shoulder, I picked my way down and went in through the back door. This might be the last time I climbed through that old stairwell with its battered couches and student clutter.

The board members were gathered at the front of the conference room, all looking decidedly Washingtonian at the front in their suits and polished hair. The place was swollen with people, and I stopped in the doorway to look for one with an unmistakable Chia-pet do.

Fletcher Basset waved covertly to me from the corner where he stood, a wireless earpiece in one ear and a pencil tucked behind the other. I nodded to him. Calling him to alert him to what I was going to do and to urge him to fill the place had been the source of much floor-pacing in the middle of the night, but I decided the light this might shine on the public debate was worth having to consort with a little weasel.

He looked less like a rodent than a concerned citizen at the moment, though. His eyes rested on Ethan Kaye, who sat still and distinguished on the front row next to Andy Callahan, right in front of the pompous St. Clair and Estes—and he covered my friend in unexpected compassion.

I marched myself up to Peter Lamb, the round, black-bearded chairman of the board of trustees, and put out my hand.

"Demitria Costanas," I said.

He seemed taken aback, which gave me a chance to hurry on. "I understand it's in the by-laws that anyone wanting to speak on behalf of a person who is up for dismissal is allowed to do so."

"So, I take it you'd like to speak," he said.

I'd never noticed the hint of a speech impediment, which made him sound less than chairmanlike. At the moment, I appreciated that.

"I do have something to say," I said. "As early in the agenda as possible."

"There is only one item on the agenda," Lamb said. "We'll call on you as soon as the position evaluation regarding Dr. Kaye is read."

I wanted to hand him a stone to throw while he was reading, but I just leaned against the far right wall, since there were no seats left. Fletcher had outdone himself. He'd filled the place, and there were still more neck-craners in the doorway, practically bulging the frame.

Peter Lamb mumbled the meeting to order, and people poked each other until all was quiet.

Lisping his way through, Lamb regaled us with "details" of Ethan's ministry to the college that made me want to chunk the whole bag of rocks over his head. The only thing holding me back was the uncomfortable scarlet his face turned as he went on about Ethan's creeping liberalism and the unrest it had caused among the students. How Ethan was not holding the line on traditional moral values, and how the consequences of that were becoming evident in the way students were expressing their disbelief in class. How the instances of pregnancy, drug use, and cheating were increasing as the truth was diluted.

I felt my eyes roll so far back in my head it would have made Jayne proud when he read that, due to the situations that had occurred under Ethan Kaye's watch, he must be held accountable for the failures in morality on campus and be dismissed from his position as president.

Half the room clapped when he finished. The other half joined in a low growl. The whole thing had so obviously been written by Kevin St. Clair. The only thing missing were the blowfish lips.

Peter Lamb held up a hand and bawled over the vocal chaos, "Excuse me—ladies and gentlemen. There is someone who would like to speak on Dr. Kaye's behalf. And then we will hear from others—" He looked anxiously at the second row. "On both sides of the issue."

As I elbowed my way through the standing rows of folks in front of me, the first real hush of the day fell over the crowd. If I hadn't known already that most people had put two and two together and come up with my affair, I was sure of it now. I thought of Rich, so worried about exposure that had long ago stripped our life naked before the world.

Peter nodded to me, his face still a bilious red above the beard, and muttered something about keeping it brief.

I leaned close to him. "It will take as long as it takes," I said in his ear. "So you might as well sit down."

By then the crowd was stirring. They hushed when I plunked the bag of rocks on the desk, opened it, and took them out to display them, one in front of each board member. The rest, all but the one I left in the bag, I piled at one corner. With the last one set on top, I turned to the now wide-eyed audience.

Only a few faces stuck out clearly from the mass. Wyatt Estes, jowls drooping on either side of his square mouth. Ethan, with the permanent vertical line between his eyebrows etched in deep, concerned surprise into his ruddy skin. Fletcher, nodding at me. And, of course, Kevin St. Clair. His baggy eyes grew smaller in proportion to the swell of his lips.

I drew in a breath. I was a teacher—and this was the most important lesson I would ever give.

"As this is a Christian college," I said, "I'm sure you're all familiar with the story of the woman caught in an act of adultery, as told in the Gospel of John." I pointed my eyes at Kevin St. Clair. "That's John 8, verses one through eleven, in case any of you brought your Bibles."

My eyes went to Ethan, who was shaking his head at me.

You have to do this, Demi.

"If you'll recall, John tells us that a group of teachers of the law and the Pharisees brought the woman in, having caught her red—well, handed. They reminded Jesus what the Law of Moses commanded was to happen to such women. She was to be stoned. They said to Jesus, 'Now, what do you say?'"

I turned to the stones on the board table and heard some uneasy shifting in seats.

"What we we often overlook in this passage is verse 6: 'They were using this question as a trap, in order to have a basis for accusing him.'" I swept my eyes over St. Clair and Estes. "On February 27 of this year, Dr. Ethan Kaye was presented with a similar dilemma. I was summoned before him—having been caught in the arms of a man who was not my husband, on the very night I had finally come to my senses and determined to end the affair."

Someone, a woman, gasped. The rest were silent.

"Wyatt Estes, who as you know gives a sizable sum of money annually to Covenant Christian College, and whose family's endowment provides a number of essential programs, placed before Dr. Kaye a series of photographs of me and my lover—former CCC professor Dr. Zachary Archer."

The group in the doorway tangled its voices together until Peter Lamb said, "Quiet, please."

"Dr. Kevin St. Clair was with Mr. Estes, and together they basically put the same question to Dr. Kaye that the Pharisees posed to Jesus. 'The laws of this college say that such behavior is contemptible and must be punished; now, what do you say, Dr. Kaye?'"

I strolled to the end of the table and rested my hand on the pile of stones. My heart pounded, urging me on. "Now, Ethan Kaye is not Jesus Christ, but as a true follower of our Lord and a man who tries to emulate the Savior, Dr. Kaye showed compassion to me, a sinner. I sinned, and I hurt not only my husband and my children to a degree that may never be fully healed, but this college as well. Yet Ethan Kaye forgave me."

My gaze went to Estes and St. Clair, stiff as a pair of iron bookends, holding up their self-righteousness.

"But Wyatt Estes and Dr. St. Clair, like the Pharisees in the story, were uncompromising in their treatment not only of me, a proven sinner, but of Dr. Kaye, whom they accused of establishing an atmosphere here on campus that condoned behavior like mine. They put as much of the blame for my sin on him as they did on me. In fact—"

I turned to the board. "They were ready to stone Dr. Kaye, metaphorically speaking. They asked for his resignation—which had nothing to do with my committing adultery any more than the Pharisees' threat to stone that woman had anything to do with her sin. It was Jesus the Pharisees were after, and in this case, Mr. Estes and Dr. St. Clair were hell-bent for Dr. Kaye. Yes, what I did was wrong, and I will pay for it for the rest of my life. But they merely used me as a wedge between Dr. Kaye's pledge to uphold the moral code of this school and his vow to show compassion. Sounds like what those teachers of the law were trying to do to Jesus. Doesn't it?"

In the back, Fletcher Basset nodded over the pad on which he scribbled. The bulging group in the doorway raised thumbs to me, and for the first time I realized they were students. Brandon Stires's red head rose above them all, pumping with nineteen-year-old earnestness. I felt a rush of energy.

"Somehow these upstanding men had obtained pictures of me in a compromising position. I don't know how, and I don't even venture to suggest that they procured them by less than ethical means. That isn't the point. More *to* the point, they used them to trap Ethan Kaye. To show that he would be soft on me and was therefore no good for the morals of this college."

I tilted my head at Ethan. He was still shaking his head, the direct eyes awash. "Unlike Jesus, Dr. Kaye had to sacrifice me to keep the college alive, and I was willing. I resigned rather than let him leave the office he has held with such honor. He had no other choice, as I see it—but in the wake of that decision, the stones have flown, and not only at me."

I stepped into the narrow aisle still left between the banks of chairs.

"People too cowardly to give their names sent letters to the editor of the *Port Orchard Independent*, rendering innuendos that cast doubt on Ethan Kaye. Protests were organized that involved students, most of whom had no idea what they were speaking out against, much less for. One unstable student got so caught up in the thing, he attacked a reporter and Ethan Kaye himself, and was not discouraged by the people intent on upholding moral values.

"The attempt to remove a man who has done nothing but try to do as Jesus did has been deliberate, manipulative, and as un-Christlike as anything I can imagine. No stone, to carry the metaphor further, has been left unturned . . . or unthrown."

I moved back to the front of the room. Wyatt Estes's jowls were quivering like bare nerve endings.

"In the midst of all this, in my own personal pain, I have had to ask the same question Jesus Himself asked. Where is the forgiveness that Jesus showed, not just for me, but for Ethan Kaye? Where is the chance to live a new life? To go on with the work we have been given to do by God our Father?" My shoulders went up in a shrug, unplanned, born of the indignation that rose in me.

"In the story, Jesus grew silent. He bent down and wrote on the ground with his finger. Here at CCC, here in Port Orchard, in all of South Kitsap County, His silence has also been deafening. What is written in the Word about things like compassion and forgiveness hasn't seemed to register with anyone here. Noses have been buried in the rules and mouths have spewed out rigid edicts and limitations that have nothing to do with seeking to know God, to having a relationship with Jesus Christ."

I bent down and pulled the last rock out of the bag. Its paint bumps felt familiar and reassuring against my palm. "Jesus said, 'If any one of you is without sin, let him be the first to throw a stone at her.'"

I plunked the big rock down, hard, on the table. "This is the rock I have been throwing at myself for two and a half months, and I am ready to set it down. If any of you has not sinned, in any way, be the first to hurl it at me, or at Dr. Ethan Kaye. Go ahead, dismiss him and deprive the students of this school of the kind of spiritual leadership that brings them into deep and authentic relationship with God."

No one moved. I pointed to the big rock that had taunted me for weeks, months, and swept a questioning gaze over the audience, half of whom could not look back at me.

"Do you remember what happened next in the Jesus story?" I licked my lips and tasted sweat. I was almost to the end. I could do this. "When Jesus made that challenge, people dropped their stones and left, one by one—the eldest first."

I looked directly at Wyatt Estes and Kevin St. Clair. "I suggest you do that. As Jesus told the adulteress, He doesn't condemn you. You can go now and leave this sin you're about to commit behind you. You can allow this college to continue to stand for what Jesus was and is."

I didn't expect St. Clair or Estes, or anyone else for that matter, to rise from his seat and go, head down, to the door. But someone did. Someone I didn't see until he threaded his way from a chair in the corner, along the wall, and through the student knot in the doorway. Rich never looked at me as he parted them and disappeared.

As I put my hand to my mouth, a voice, distinctly un-Southern and livid, rose from the second row. I turned to see Kevin St. Clair on his feet, his blowfish lips already in undulating motion.

"Is it not obvious that Dr. Costanas is merely trying to make herself out to be more than she is, which is a—"

"Watch yourself, St. Clair."

I stared at Ethan, who came halfway out of his chair.

St. Clair shoved the ubiquitous finger near his face. "How can you believe that those photographs were obtained illegally or unethically?" He shot the finger toward me. "But they—and the aspersions you have cast on my colleague and myself—guarantee that you will never work in the Christian academic community again if I have anything to do with it."

I felt my eyebrows go up. "Is that a threat, Dr. St. Clair?"

"It's a promise!"

I held my hands out, palms up, to the audience. Ethan turned not toward St. Clair but toward the door. The students jostled aside to let a short, blondish young woman squeeze into the room. Even in the midst of the turmoil St. Clair had managed to stoke, her face was expressionless—until she apparently found the face she was looking for.

Ethan held out one hand to her and motioned to Peter Lamb with the other. "Mr. Chairman," Ethan said, "there is someone else here who would like to speak."

"I protest," St. Clair called out. He placed one hand on a snakish hip for all the world, as if he were in full charge now. "It's time we heard from our side."

To my surprise, Peter Lamb said, "Sit down, Dr. St. Clair. You've had your say." He nodded to me. "You may have a seat, too, Dr. Costanas."

Andy Callahan, the school attorney, waved me to his chair and stood up in the aisle next to Ethan. I could feel the people behind us jockeying to see the diminutive young woman who came to the front as if she were on automatic pilot.

"Who's that?" I whispered to Ethan.

He didn't look at me. "Wyatt Estes's niece. I didn't think she was coming."

"Ladies and gentlemen, please." Peter Lamb produced a gavel and banged it on the table.

What was Wyatt Estes's niece doing here—speaking for Ethan? I wanted to glance back at Estes, but I didn't have to. I could hear him wheezing as he exchanged unintelligible hoarse whispers with Kevin St. Clair.

Peter Lamb pulled back from the girl, with whom he'd been having a whispered conversation of his own, and glared over the audience.

"Tatum Farris has the floor. Please, people, let's refrain from any more outbursts, shall we?"

"I only have a few things to say, and then I'm done—with all of you," Tatum Farris said.

I was stunned by the clear strength of her voice. Unfeeling as she might be, she was obviously a little powerhouse. I looked at Ethan, who leaned forward on his thighs, fingers to his lips.

"A student named Van Dillon took the pictures of Dr. Costanas and Dr. Archer," she said. "Dr. Archer paid him to do it, because . . ." Tatum stopped. "Well, that doesn't have anything to do with this. After he did what he was paid to do with the pictures, Van brought copies to me because . . . he thought I might be interested."

Why?

And then I knew. The pain that passed through her eyes in spite of her best efforts to appear stoic could only have come from one source. Zach had been involved with a student, Ethan told me. And here she was. My heart ached for her as if she were a sister.

"Let's just say I freaked out—and I took the pictures to my uncle, Wyatt Estes."

She looked in his direction. I heard him wheeze.

"It didn't have anything to do with morals, just so you know," she said. "I only wanted revenge on Zachary Archer and the woman he was with."

Her eyes flickered to me.

"I told my uncle I was sure he would want to know what was going on at the college he was giving money to." Her gaze went back to him. "I didn't tell him where they came from or why I had them—and he didn't ask."

Tatum looked at the ceiling, head tilted back so I could watch her swallow down what she didn't want to say. It was a thing I'd done many times.

"And then I called Zachary Archer and told him he was about to be in trouble and that as the most heinous man I had ever known, he deserved it. That, I assume, is when he disappeared—and that was exactly what I wanted." She brought her face down, mouth now struggling. "Dr. Costanas was let go, which was also what I wanted. What I did not want was the trouble this has caused Dr. Kaye, who is a fine man and good for the school. At first I didn't care what happened to this college—but after I sorted out that my real hatred was against Dr. Archer and Dr. Costanas, I felt bad for Dr. Kaye. I wrote an anonymous letter to the editor to try to shift the attention away from him."

I flipped back through my mind to find the one she was talking about.

"But it backfired. People started gossiping about the affair instead of defending Dr. Kaye." Her eyes shifted miserably. "So the other day, when Zachary Archer had the gall to come and see me, I threw him out, and I wrote another anonymous letter."

That one I could pinpoint. The one I thought Zach had written. I shook my head. Anybody tainted by Zach came away sounding exactly like him.

"Of course the paper printed my letters," she said, stumbling for the first time in the thickness of her voice. "After all, the Estes family does own it." She pressed her beautiful, hurting lips together and released them only to add, "That's all I have to say."

She darted for the door, shoving people aside. The doorway cleared, and as the buzz rose in the room and Peter Lamb pointlessly pounded his gavel, I blinked at what appeared to be steam wisping in through the top of the opening.

As if he were moving in slow motion, Brandon Stires covered his mouth and twisted his head to look up and then out the door. "Dude!" he shouted above the din. "There's a fire!"

CHAPTER THIRTY-NINE

The students bolted as one from the doorway, opening up the room to a haze of smoke that swelled the rest of the crowd into a frenzy. As bodies surged for the door, I heard my voice rise above the panic, kicking in with the response that had been hammered into my children and me.

"Stay calm!" I barked at them. "Get low!"

"Are you all right, Demi?" someone called to me.

Ethan, just a few feet from me, held back two flailing women.

"Tell them to stay low!" I called back to him.

He leaned over from the waist, shoved both women against him, and disappeared into the smoke. I looked around to be sure I was the last one out. The smoke was already making it hard to see.

Rich's voice was in my head. Move steady and quick. Don't run. It'll be the hardest thing in the world to do, but you have to.

I bent from the hips and forced myself to take a steady pace toward the door, but the smoke was thick in my face, coming down like a second ceiling. I dropped to my knees and crawled. Ahead of me in the hallway, people coughed and floundered in eddies.

"Get *low*!" I screamed at them.

I could hardly see my hands as I walked them out in front of me, one after the other. The floor was hot on my palms, which meant the fire was coming from below.

Plastering my hand over my nose and lips, I flattened to my stomach and got to the wall. Inch by inch I felt my way along, the shrieks and choking standing my nerves on end, Rich's voice in my ear holding me back from joining the terror.

Take the stairs. Then you can get help.

Ahead of me, the mob forced its way toward the main stairs. No one, apparently, had thought of the small staircase closer to the boardroom. They were lost in the fear of the pack.

I continued to inch, forcing myself not to cry so I wouldn't use up what little air was still left near the hot floor. My left hand slipped down. "The steps! Back here!"

My voice only croaked, and the now muddled thunder of frantic footsteps left me behind. I scooted forward until my whole arm was on the step, and I let myself roll to the next one, squinting to find the propped-open door to the hallway that I needed to close behind me. The heel of my hand protested in pain as I used it to dislodge the doorstop. The door labored stubbornly, letting in a downpour of smoke from the hall into the stairwell until I could get it closed. The stairwell ceiling filled, and I pushed my way down on my belly, head first.

The heat and smoke would rise and bank down the edges from the ceiling, Rich had told me. You want to get out before it pulls the oxygen out of the room.

I took in a gasp of air and held it. My eyes burned, and I squeezed them in and tried to remember what I was making my way into.

Plaster walls. What had Rich said about plaster? It held the heat more, didn't it, more than Sheetrock? I had to stay away from the wall.

Those ratty couches—synthetic and foam-filled. Once the heat hit them, they would erupt and chew everything around them.

I fought back rising horror and pressed my hands to the landing I'd now reached. The floor grew warmer—not yet hot enough to make me to pull away. But I could feel the heat on my back, and I didn't have to look to know the smoke was banking. If I could roll down to the second floor I could get out the window. That's what Rich said. Now . . . *get as low as you can and get out.*

Squinting through the stream from my eyes, I tried to see down and ahead to the turn in the stairs. Dark fog slid down the wall. *Don't breathe it in. Find the next steps and roll down.*

But as I pawed at the floor, my hands found no steps, and I had to take another gulp of acrid air to keep from hurling myself in every direction. The stairs were there, ahead of me. They had to be.

"Dear God," I said out loud. "Oh, dear God, please help."

My mouth filled with smoke, and I spit and coughed and pulled the neckline of my top up until it covered my nose. I tried to make my way down and slipped. As I went into a painful downward slide, black smoke fingered across the ceiling. I heard glass shatter. Dear Lord . . .

"Anybody up here—is anybody up here?"

God . . . had I heard a voice . . .

"Rich? *Rich*?"

"Demitria."

I got up on my elbows and made out a murky form emerging from below. His eyes were suddenly there, inches from mine, streaming at me from over a cloth that covered the lower half of his face like a bandit.

"Get down!" he shouted.

I flung myself to the step below. Sobs tore their way up my throat, and I choked them back.

"Lie down on your side and roll and keep going."

But I couldn't move. Above us the air split into titian flames that licked and groped for something to eat.

"Rich—the couch!" I screamed, and then gagged until I was doubled over.

I felt a shove, and I bumped shoulder over shoulder to the landing. Rich was on me before I could crab-crawl toward the door, which was wide open and billowing smoke.

"Put this on."

Something wet came around my face and I gasped into it. A thin stream of air reached my lungs.

"We have about thirty seconds—do what I say."

His voice went into me, and I nodded. This was Rich—this was the 9/11 hero.

"I'm going to get on top of you and crawl you down," he said into my hot ear.

I couldn't see anything but a black fog, so I closed my eyes and made myself move forward and down. Rich's body hovered over me and he put his hands over mine like paws and picked them up and put them down, steering me around another corner and down again. His chest heaved against my back, wet and hot right through to my skin. I kept my head tucked under and let him move me like a toy, and still my face above the bandana burned. I couldn't help buckling.

"Rich—are we on fire?" I tried to say.

His face came down next to mine and shook, searing my cheek. "It's just the heat. We're almost there."

His voice was unmuffled and raspy, and I knew he'd given me his own face cloth. And then there was air—cool and rich and on my head and in my face.

"Costanas—what are you doing?"

I felt myself being rolled over and picked up in jacket-bulky, unfamiliar arms.

"Give me a line," Rich said. "I can go back in."

"You need your gear."

"No, man, you need a medic—hey, over here! We've got a fireman down!"

I convulsed in the arms that held me. Rich lay at our feet, face to the ground. Even as I watched, his shirt melted away, and his skin hung like glue from his back. When his hair dissolved into ashes, I screamed, until someone put a mask on my face.

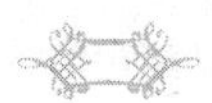

Sully stacked the last of the 10-W-40 on the shelf and glanced at the clock. The board meeting should be winding down by now—or exploding, depending on whether Tatum made the decision he hoped she'd made.

Wiping his palms on the back of his jeans, he went to the radio and snapped it on. Martina McBride filled the garage, and Sully let her take it on into news time. Maybe there would be a report—something to tell him whether dinner with Ethan would be a celebration or a wake.

Martina cut off so abruptly, Sully looked up to make sure the lights were still on.

"This is a KWOW Newsbreak."

Sully lunged for the radio, turned it up.

"A fire has been reported on the Covenant Christian College campus. Firefighters are currently on the scene, and it is reported that an estimated one hundred twenty people were in the school's administration building when it caught fire. Several engines have arrived, and we have Connye Lester live at Huntington Hall."

A roar came over the waves, with the static voice of a young woman yelling to be heard over it.

Sully snatched up his keys and left her behind.

He was halfway to Port Orchard, willing himself not to stitch frantically in and out of traffic, when the crackly radio voice lifted to the next level of rehearsed panic.

"Doug—we've just been told that the fire apparently started on both ends of the building simultaneously, which would suggest arson. Firefighters can't be sure of that yet, but all indications are . . ."

Sully jerked the wheel and screeched into a strip-mall parking lot, horns complaining behind him.

Arson. He closed his eyes, rapped his knuckles on his upper lip.

I wish it would just burn to the ground.

That was what she'd said.

In my mind, they are all getting what they deserve—including Dr. Costanas, who, if you must know, took away the man I loved.

There was no way—and yet Sully jerked the car into gear and crossed traffic to head back toward Callow. This time he did weave, leaning on his own horn as he tore for the bakery.

He saw her Volkswagen parked in front—at a rakish angle as if she'd been drunk when she pulled in. The CLOSED sign swung in the window, but the door was halfway open, and as he inserted himself inside he heard a voice from behind the counter, as if its owner were on the floor.

"Go away."

"Tatum—it's Sullivan."

He heard the sound of scrambling and the crinkling of paper and a cry that wrenched through his chest. Tatum's sob-swollen face appeared above the counter. Rivulets striped the dark smudges on her cheeks.

"Were you there, Tatum?" Sully asked. He picked his words gingerly. "At the fire?"

"I did it." She closed her eyes.

Sully took a quiet pace toward her. "You did what?"

"I went," Tatum said. "And I told them—and then the fire . . ."

"Okay, okay. Slow down."

He stepped closer, but she didn't move.

"Tatum," he said, "I'm going to help you sit down, okay?"

She was a post in his hands as she moved woodenly with him to the first table. He could feel the shock pulsing through her.

"Were you hurt in the fire?" he said.

"No. I ran out—I got away."

Sully swallowed. "You didn't inhale any smoke?"

"Did they all die?" She turned to him slowly, eyes shot with strain. "Did they all burn?"

"I don't think so, Tatum—the firemen are there." Sully put his hand carefully on top of hers. Only then did he realize she was clutching a paper that poked between her clenched fingers.

"It's my fault," she said. "If they die, it's my fault."

She opened her hand and looked down at a damp, crumpled ball. Sweat sparkled in the creases of her palm, and Sully drew in a long breath.

"Read it," she said. Her voice trembled at the edges. "You'll see—it's my fault."

Sully kept his eyes on her as he lifted the paper wad and spread it on the table. He looked down to see black calligraphy ink smeared at the edges of words that had been precisely penned.

"It was here when I got back," Tatum said. "Stuck in the door."

"Okay, it's okay. You want me to read it?"

"Not out loud."

Her hands went to her ears and she closed her eyes, as if Sully's silent reading would penetrate.

My dear Tatum,

You once told me that you wished all of Covenant Christian College would burn and smolder in ashes because of the pain it caused you. I've come to agree with you, and have decided to make that wish come true. I think I owe you that much.

This one's for you, Tatum.

It was signed with a flourish—*Zach.*

Sully turned it over and pushed it to the edge of the table, far from Tatum. When he put his hand on her arm, she startled and pulled her gaze painfully up to his.

"It's my fault," she said. "I went to the hearing and I told them everything, and I thought it would help. I thought I had finally done something right. But if they all die, it's my fault."

Sully caught her in his arms before she could fly out of the chair. Without a struggle she caved against him and sobbed.

"It's not your fault, Tatum," he said into hair that smelled of smoke and sugar. "He's a sick individual."

"I can't stand it!"

"Nobody can stand evil like that, sweet thing." He pressed her face into his chest. "Nobody."

And as she wept on, he wept with her.

By the time Sully arranged for her mother to come for her and explained to her what Tatum would need in the next twenty-four hours, in the next week, perhaps for a long time to come, he was afraid he'd be too late at the scene of the fire.

Too late for what, he wasn't sure. He banned scenarios of Ethan and Demi being carried out on stretchers, and pictured finding them calmly reporting their easy escapes to eager reporters.

Police barriers prevented him from parking anywhere on campus. He left the car on a side street, hoisted himself over a hedge, and scaled a low wall to cross from behind Freedom Chapel. He was in an instant night of smoke, although he couldn't see flames. When he emerged from its fog, there was only a great steaming skeleton of timber and stone that had once been Huntington Hall. The scenarios flashed, insistent, aggressive, as he pulled the neck of his T-shirt over his mouth and nose and loped the rest of the way.

At the top of the hill, a PBI-clad fireman in a shielded helmet stepped into his path, arms out.

"Sorry, pal—can't let you get any closer."

Sully peered at the name on his helmet. "Cauthen—I had friends in there. Were there any—"

"Cauthen—over here!"

The fireman moved away, one arm still stiff in Sully's direction. "Stay back. This thing is still live."

Sully waited until the man joined two other helmeted figures closer to the building before he made his way up the hill, breathing into his T-shirt. The toxic odors of gasoline and burned synthetics ate at the air as the mammoth thing steamed and dripped and heaved from a layer of smoldering coals. Tatum had indeed gotten her wish.

He got to another barrier and leaned against it, supporting himself with the heels of his hands. With his head hanging he gulped in air and fought back nausea.

"Found a body," a male voice called out. "Could be the perp's—it was handcuffed to a stair railing."

Another deep, smoke-raspy voice swore, attaching an obscenity to "psycho."

Sully strained to listen.

"One of those weird things—his briefcase was barely charred."

"Anything they can ID him with?"

"Initials on it. ZDA."

Sully let his arms go limp, head to the barrier. Something this grisly could not possibly be.

"Hey, you all right?"

Sully turned his head. The silhouette of an Afro took shape beside him in the smoke.

"I'm fine," Sully lied.

"I don't think anybody could be fine in this mess. You sure you don't need a little oxygen?"

Sully peered more closely at him. He wasn't wearing a uniform—nor did he have an Afro. His face was in fact pale around a pair of small intense eyes and extended far up his forehead into a Brillo pad of hair. It rang a faint chime in Sully's mind.

"I'm Fletcher Bassett with the *Port Orchard Independent.* Aren't you Sullivan Crisp?"

Sully straightened. "Was anybody hurt—besides that body they just found?"

Bassett nodded. "One old guy evidently had a heart attack in there—probably died before the smoke got him. Only one other injury that they know of—a fireman. Everybody else that was in the building has pretty much been accounted for, except for one girl they think ran out."

Sully nodded and scanned the scene, heart drumming.

"Too bad about the fireman too," Bassett said. "He was off duty—wasn't even wearing his equipment. He ran in there to save his wife."

Before Sullivan could register, Bassett put a hand on his shoulder. "Oh, man, I'm sorry. I think you know her."

Sully knocked his hand away and tore for the hill, half-running, half falling as he went.

"Richard Costanas!" he heard Fletcher shout after him. "They air-lifted him to Seattle."

CHAPTER FORTY

The hall in the Burn ICU at Harborview Medical Center was dim with an after-hours ghostly light as Sully hurried through it toward the two figures the nurse directed him to.

"Mrs. Costanas is down there," she told him at the nurses' station. "We don't usually let anyone in after visiting hours except the family, but since you're her doctor . . ."

As he strode closer, Sully saw that Demi's hair was uncharacteristically plastered to her head and she was wrapped in a man's tweed sport coat that hung off her shoulders and over her hands like a big brother's. It looked like one of Ethan's.

He slowed down when he took in the young man who faced her, his chin thrust at her, finger stabbing the air beside her ear. Everything about him lurched toward her in shapeless anger, and Sully's antennae went up.

He had almost reached them when he realized that the kid—who had to be Christopher Costanas—stood in the middle of a doorway that Demi clearly wanted to pass through.

"Get out of my way, Christopher," Sully heard her say.

"What part of this don't you get? You don't have any right to go in there."

Sully stopped and backed against the opposite wall. Demi could need him. From the sound of his voice, this kid stood on a thin place.

"He doesn't want to see you. He said that."

"He hasn't said anything to anybody, son. He isn't even conscious."

"I know him—you don't. He never wants to see you again." His voice teetered.

Sully saw Demi plant her hands on her son's shoulders and hold on in spite of his furious, adolescent attempt to twist himself free. Even from where he stood, Sully could tell from the startled look in the boy's eyes that her face, not her hands, held him there.

"I'm not going to leave you out this time, Christopher," she said. "You and I can walk your father through this together. You will know everything that's going on—you'll be a part of it."

The boy jerked his head back and glared down his nose at her, and Sully could hear him breathing—but he didn't pull away.

"You may think you know him," Demi said, "and maybe you do—but you don't know me. I take my share of the responsibility for that—but now is not the time for me to go into it."

Christopher jerked his head to the side this time, and a half-hearted hiss came out of his mouth.

"I love that man, and I am going to go in there as often as they will let me, and I am going to sit by his side until he himself tells me he doesn't want me there." Demi let her hands slide down to Christopher's elbows. "You can either come with me or not, that's up to you. Jayne will have the same choice when she gets here. Jayne will, not you for her. Am I clear?"

The boy's shaggy head made its final move, forward, as if he couldn't hold it up any longer. Demi pulled her hands away. He stepped aside and turned his back to her.

As Demi turned with him, her eyes met Sully's. "Sullivan," she said.

For the first time since he'd arrived, her voice broke. He went to her, hands extended to envelope hers. Her eyes were a mass of painfully red lines, and her face was gray with soot except for the space around her mouth and nose where an oxygen mask had obviously rested. But despite her rush to grab onto his hands, there was nothing fragile about Demitria Costanas at that moment.

"Thank you so much for coming," she said. "I didn't want to ask you—"

"You didn't have to. I came as a friend."

She nodded. "It's bad, Sullivan. They were afraid of internal burns to his lungs—there are none. But he has third degree burns on his back, his neck, the back of his head—40 percent of his body."

"I'm so sorry."

"He crawled me out with no protection on, no gear at all." She trailed a hand down the side of her face. "He covered me with his body so I wouldn't be burned."

"Demi," Sully said. "No guilt. He did what he had to do."

"You know something—I get that." She looked at her fingers and seemed to realize for the first time that she was wearing a mask of ashes. "He did it because that's who he is. And you know—being here with him—this isn't guilt, Sullivan. It's who I am."

"Mrs. Costanas?"

Sully motioned over Demi's shoulder at a towheaded male nurse in a gown and mask who poked his head out the door.

"I have to go," she said. "You want to come?"

Sully shook his head. "No—no, I think you're going to be fine."

Demi nodded and reached out to touch his arm. "Don't leave for good without saying good-bye."

And then she walked toward the nurse, with the stride of a wife who knew exactly what her husband needed.

Christopher finally dozed off in the recliner in the ICU family waiting room around 2:00 AM. I waited until he was breathing with little-boy evenness before I took the nurse up on his offer to let me sit with Rich for five minutes.

Dressed in full regalia—long paper gown, mask, gloves, and covers for my shoes—I sat back from the rocking bed that cradled Rich facedown and moved him constantly so fluid wouldn't collect anywhere. Rearranging him physically would be so excruciating it made *me* want to throw up at the mere thought of it.

We'd both known burned firefighters before, visited them in acute care wards and in rehab centers, listened to the stories of their agonizing recoveries . . . but to smell my own husband's scalded flesh . . .

He actually could have been anyone in that tangle of tubes and bags and wires and bandages. But I knew who he was, just as I always had. He was my hero—my burping, channel flipping, obstinate hero who had suffered so much and didn't have any more idea how to deal with that than I did. That was how he'd ended up here in a room where the inner workings of his heart were registered in stubborn beeps.

I stared at the screen and wished it could tell me how strong his pride was—whether it was going to forever keep us apart, even after I stayed with him and nursed him through the predicted months-long hospital stay and the myriad of corrective surgeries and the physical therapy I'd already been told he'd have to endure.

I was going to do that—feed him and bathe him and apply the pressure garments and listen to him curse through gritted teeth. I couldn't think beyond that—beyond Rich's pain. It wasn't only what he had to bear, it was what I had to suffer with him because I was the woman who loved him.

What I'd told Sullivan was true, though I hadn't known that until it crossed my lips. Ding-ding-ding, Dr. Costanas. It *was* me—the real me—who loved so deep and so hard that she would do all of that and more, with no hope that there would ever be anything else.

I bent my head, chin to my chest, and listened to the whisper.

You had to, Demi. Well done.

Sometime before dawn I fell into an exhausted sleep in the recliner next to Christopher's. When I woke to the sound of voices, I saw someone had covered me with a blanket.

"They said they were in here," somebody said in the hall.

My Jayne, voice fragile as lace. I scrambled out of the chair without lowering the footrest and stumbled across the room with the blanket trailing after me. She flung herself into my arms and clung to me.

"Mom, is he—"

"He's not going to die, sweetie," I said. "He's hurt really badly, but he's not going to die."

"Audrey—what are you doing here?"

Christopher's voice wrapped incongruently around a name he shouldn't have known. I pulled away from Jayne and looked at him. His face was bloodless down to his lips, which parted, shock-stiff, as if a gun were being held to his back.

"You know Audrey?" Jayne said.

I looked over my shoulder. Audrey stood in the doorway, in front of Mickey, whose brow was furrowed like a plowed field. Audrey's cheeks had no more color than Christopher's. I thought I had seen all the terror in that face the girl could possibly feel—until now.

Jayne looked from her brother to her "adopted sister" and back again. "I don't get it," she said.

I shifted back to Christopher, who looked like my son at twelve, ready to cave to a hidden misdeed.

And then from behind me I heard Audrey whisper, "C.J."

Five people attempted to restart their brains in silence.

Audrey's voice screamed in my head: *He goes, "So if it looks like a tramp and it acts like a tramp, it must be a tramp."*

Christopher was C.J.? He was Boy? The elusive, using, wretched Boy who had said that to Audrey was my son? The father of her baby?

"You?" Jayne said. "You're the jerk?"

I folded my arm around Jayne's neck and pulled her back before she could launch herself into Christopher's unnerved face.

"Who is this, Audrey?" Mickey said. I could hear her winding up. "Is this the kid that got you pregnant?"

Audrey gave a slow nod.

"This is apparently the kid," I said. I turned to Mickey. "I know I'm taking my life in my hands telling you this—but he's also my son."

All eyes went to Christopher, who shriveled like a raisin. I waited for the anger to rise in me. I was due, heaven knew. All the insults my son had hissed at me should have been more than ready to turn themselves around into the tirade the little hypocrite so richly deserved.

But then there was Mickey, watching me, expecting with her unblinking eyes what she herself had done to her child. What I had done to Zach, and to Christopher. What Rich had done to me.

When all any of us wanted was forgiveness.

I pushed my hands through my hair and shook it out with my fingers. Then I held out both arms, one to Christopher, one to Audrey.

"Well," I said, "it looks like there's some sorting out to be done."

"You think?" Mickey said.

I looked at Christopher. "And you will do it, son—you'll take responsibility for what you've done."

He blinked at me from beneath the shag of blonde hair that hung down over his eyebrows like shame-covering fingers.

"None of us can throw stones." I looked at Mickey. "None of us."

Jayne tapped me timidly on the arm. "Uh, you know what? I'm gonna go get a Coke or something." She started for the door, but she stopped when she got to Audrey. "Oh, my gosh," she whispered. "We really are like sisters."

With a hand clapped over the happiness only she was feeling at the moment, she scampered out, brushing past a still-stunned Mickey.

"What do you two need right now?" I glanced back and forth between the ashen-faced kids who had just collided with their future. "Alone time, or a couple of mediators?"

"Alone time," Audrey said quickly.

Christopher looked as if he would have leaped from the window if any of us had asked him to. Mickey followed me out into the hall, and I steeled myself for the verbal onslaught.

"I'm sure you haven't eaten since you've been here."

I turned and stared.

She held out an insulated bag. "I know how you get when you're stressed out. There's split pea soup in a thermos, sprouted bread—bunch of stuff. You need carbs and fat, and I know your electrolytes are a mess."

"Mick," I said. "I apologize for my son."

"Like we have any control over our kids." She lowered the bag and her eyes. "You handled it a whole lot better than I did—you handle everything better than I do."

"No. I don't."

"How's your—how is he?"

"I'm about to find out." I held out my arm. "Walk with me to the nurses' station. I could use the support."

She fell into step beside me, eyes still shifting from the floor to the side of my face. "Have you cried yet?" she said. "You know you're going to have to cry sooner or later."

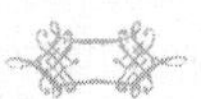

At noon Rich was still too groggy to talk. Twice they'd put him in a metallic bed with hoses that kept him wet while they scrubbed off the dead skin under water to stave off infection. This was among the most painful procedures a patient could go through, Ike, the towheaded nurse, told me, and they sedated him afterwards. When Ike began to describe to me that it was like being jabbed with hot needles, Mickey told him to "go ahead and take his poetry down the hall."

She was less hard on the reconstructive surgeon who explained that in a week they would embed Rich's left hand, where the most severe burns had occurred, beneath the skin of his lower abdomen to protect it and encourage skin healing around the fingers. There would, he told us, be approximately eight other surgeries after that, including the insertion of pins into his fingers so he would be able to use his hand again, and possible amputation of his pinkie.

"We have a 96 percent survival rate here," he assured me.

"Is that patients?" I said. "Or their wives?"

A social worker and a psychologist came to talk with us too.

"It's a whole team thing," Ike told me. "We have everything covered."

Still, I wished more than once that Sullivan were there, to assure me that the certainty I felt was real.

Several guys from the station came, gazed at Rich through the window to his room, and turned to me with eyes red-rimmed and wet. I finally told them I'd call when he was doing better.

I sat by Rich for five minutes every hour and let the kids have the other ten between them. After Christopher nearly passed out during his eleven o'clock stint, he gave his five to me.

It was a huge day for my son.

In true Mickey fashion, she practically spoon-fed me the thermos of soup and the herbal tea she commandeered. I was nibbling the edges of a hunk of flaxseed bread when she produced a copy of the Port Orchard newspaper.

"I didn't know if you'd want to see this or not," she said. "The fire made the front page."

I sat up and stared at it, waiting for it to take out another piece of my life. There was a half-page, full color photo of what was left of Huntington Hall—a black cadaver of a place, the smoke still curling up from the rubble piled shin-deep on the ground.

I felt nothing. Huntington Hall had never been the life of Covenant Christian College as far as I was concerned. My CCC was never about the ordeals Ethan Kaye suffered in his office with people like Kevin St. Clair, so nothing was lost for me in the lingering smoke and the oddly spared bits of office life scattered on the ground. I wondered vaguely if the Easter egg rock survived, or would be forever buried as it deserved.

I was about to fold the paper when I noticed something else in the picture—white and almost in flight behind the wreckage. I brought the paper close to my face and smiled.

"What?" Mickey said.

I lay it on my lap and smoothed it with my hand. "You can see the chapel now. With that big ugly thing out of the way, you can see Freedom Chapel."

I would have to share that with Ethan.

I was beginning to cave after my 3:00 PM vigil with Rich, and Mickey had run low on comfort food. She was out in search of a Central Market, Jayne in tow, and Audrey and Christopher sat in an awkward, painful silence on the other side of the waiting room. I was too frayed to do anything for them, which was the state Ethan Kaye found me in.

"You look like you're holding up," he said to me, hands covering mine as he sat next to me.

"Liar," I said.

"You never cease to amaze me with your strength, Demi. I missed it when you weren't there."

I filled Ethan in on Rich's condition. He told me about Wyatt Estes.

"Apparently he suffered a heart attack when he was trying to get out," Ethan said. "They've determined that he died before he was overcome by smoke."

"And what about you?" I said.

"I'm fine."

I squeezed his hand. "No, I mean the board's decision. I guess they haven't had time to reach one."

"They met this morning."

"And?"

He let out a long, slow breath from his noble nose. "I'm still president of CCC."

"It was unanimous, wasn't it?"

He nodded. "Thanks to you."

"And that little blonde thing. How on earth did you find her, Ethan?"

Ethan smiled, which I hadn't seen him do in a long time. "That was Sully's doing. Oh, I have something for you from him."

I watched him take a folded sheet of paper out of his jacket pocket.

"I still have your sport coat," I said. "I'll have it dry cleaned, but I'm not sure the smoke smell will ever come out."

Ethan waved me off and tucked the paper into my hand. "I don't think I would ever wear it again anyway. The fewer reminders I have of that time in my life, the better."

"I hear you." I curled my fingers around the paper.

"I'm going to leave you to read that." Ethan stood up, still holding on to one of my hands. "Demi—I'd love to have you back when you're ready. Kevin St. Clair has resigned, and I've called a faculty meeting to discuss where to go from here. I want you involved."

I closed my eyes and let that rise in my chest.

"Thank you," I said, "but Rich is my priority right now. Once he's recovered, then we'll see." I let go of his hand. "I know I can't ask you to wait that long—and it could be a while."

"As long as it takes, Demi," he said.

Sullivan's letter was short.

Demi,

You're on your way now, and I have to be on mine. If you and Rich want counseling, please call me and I'll set you up with someone to walk you through this next part of your journey together. I'm praying that happens, but Demi, if it doesn't, you know you have found you—God's you. It has been my honor and my joy to watch that happen.

Blessings,
Sullivan Crisp

I folded the letter in precise squares and held it between my palms. I was homesick for the *buzzzz* and the ding-ding-dings and the grins that couldn't be translated into words.

But as I pressed it, I felt something mournful and yearning ooze from it.

He had to do it, Demi.

Whatever it was, I didn't know. I only knew it would take more than Game Show Theology to get him through it. I hoped his mentor was someone who would shove him and coax him and be gentle with him. I hoped it was someone like him.

I was pushing couscous around on a paper plate when Ike the nurse came to the waiting room door with a new expression on his face.

"He's awake," he said to me. "You can have five minutes."

I looked at the kids. Christopher spoke the first words he'd said to me since Audrey walked in that morning: "You go, Mom."

I half ran down the hall, botching up the strings to the mask as I attempted to tie it on and letting Ike stick my arms into a paper gown and trying to listen to instructions on what topics to steer away from.

It turned out I didn't need those, because Rich had his face turned toward me, rasping at me before I even sat down.

"I can't talk much, Demitria," he said.

I started to cry. I wasn't going to, and yet there it was.

"You don't have to talk," I said.

"No—I've been quiet too long."

He breathed hard, and I glanced anxiously over the bed at Ike, whose back was to me as he busily turned knobs and dials.

"A little longer isn't going to hurt, then." Suddenly, I didn't want to hear what Rich had to say. The fear I'd been so victorious in battling all day shot through me, and with it every thought I'd shoved to the bottom.

He had lost his dignity, his career, and now almost his life because of me. No matter who I was now, he would never forget that, never get past it. It would be in every scar he lived with the rest of his life.

"I heard you talk," he said.

"Rich . . . shhh."

"At that meeting. I just want to say—I got no stones, Demitria."

I shook my head.

"I got no stones to throw, baby."

He dragged in another breath, and Ike squished toward us on his padded shoes. I leaned my face in close and caught the last wisp before Rich drifted off again.

"I was wrong too," he said. "I want—"

"I think that's enough for now," Ike said.

"You want what, Rich?"

"You can come back next hour. He should be more awake then."

I let Ike nudge me toward the door, but I couldn't take my eyes from the tiny piece of face that peered from a swath of white. Rich's eyes opened.

"You," I heard him whisper. "I want you."

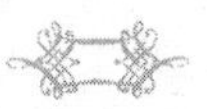

Sully had one last stop to make before he left Port Orchard. He'd said good-bye to Ethan, checked on Tatum, delivered Isabella to the auctioneer. The garage was cleared out, except for the Great Prospects furniture he left in the office for the next tenant to wonder about. As he headed out of town for the Seattle airport, there was one last thing to do.

He'd read about the funeral in the paper. There wouldn't be much to it—no visitation at the funeral home, only a graveside service. Ironically, Fletcher Bassett had reported that in lieu of flowers, donations should be sent to Covenant Christian College. Sully wondered who'd made those arrangements.

There were only a few cars parked at the cemetery, and so few people gathered in the rain that Sully had to ask which grave was Zachary Archer's. That didn't surprise him. After the news of the arson came out, who would have any respects to pay?

The body of Dr. Zachary Archer was found handcuffed to a stair railing on the north end of the building, Bassett had reported. *Investigators have named the fire an arson/suicide. College officials have no comment on any link between this and Archer's involvement in the scandal that was under scrutiny in the boardroom of Huntington Hall at the time of the fire, though Archer's name was mentioned at the hearing.*

Sully had been surprised by Bassett's final paragraph.

Reports from campus indicate that faculty and students are relieved at the board's decision to keep Dr. Ethan Kaye on as president. Students are equally as vocal about the possible return of Dr. Demitria Costanas.

She was going to be all right, Demi was, and so was Ethan. As he trudged through the drizzle toward the miserly-small knot of people at the gravesite, Sully wondered if that would be enough to make him believe he could ever get back to being of any use to anyone else.

The service was brief and dismal and couldn't have been more stereotypically hopeless. It had every element of a wasted life, from the dripping rain to the apathy of the four people who stood with their heads bowed and their minds obviously on shopping lists and afternoon traffic.

By the time the officiant muttered about ashes to ashes, Sully was sure he'd made a mistake. This was doing nothing but depressing him. When the black-coated man invited the "mourners" to pay their respects to the seated woman under the umbrella, who Sully assumed must be a relative who knew little about her kinsman, Sully moved out of the circle toward his car. Footsteps splashed after him.

"We meet again, Dr. Crisp."

Sully turned only briefly to see the Brillo pad of hair approaching. He stopped and put out his hand.

"Nice article in the paper," Sully said. "I appreciate what you did for Dr. Costanas."

Bassett shrugged. "She's a good woman."

"That she is."

"I don't know what your connection to her is," Fletcher said.

Sully gave him a half grin and continued toward the car. "Nor do you need to know."

"Okay—so throw me a bone here. Why were you at Zach Archer's funeral? I don't get that connection either."

You tell me, pal, Sully thought.

And then he knew. He knew as he'd known for Demi, and for Ethan.

"Off the record?" he said to Fletcher.

The Brillo pad nodded.

"I came because I needed to remember that even though this guy's through—I'm not."

"O-kay—"

"Because you know what, my friend? Until you're dead, you're not done."

And then Sully loped to his car, tears and rain dripping into his grin, because Dr. Sullivan Crisp was definitely not done.

ACKNOWLEDGMENTS

What a team we've had helping us create *Healing Stones.* Just in case you're one of those people who actually reads acknowledgments, we've tried to leave no stone unturned in naming them all. Pun intended.

Dr. Dale McElhinney, therapist/psychologist who kept us from setting the practice of psychotherapy back twenty years. His reading and re-reading of therapy scenes was priceless.

Ardi, Jayna, and Haven Fowler, and Barbara Dirks, who opened their home in Port Orchard, as well as their hearts, and made the town a character in itself.

Nick McCorkle, Joey Simms, and Bobby Cawthen, the Lebanon Tenessee firefighters who allowed Nancy to experience a fire first-hand, and Lt. Glen Pappuleas ("Pappy") of South Kitsap Fire and Rescue, who brought Rich Costanas to life. They have our utmost respect for the work they do.

Susie Cole, research cohort, photographer, and hand-holder whose cheerful support lightened the darkness of writing Demitria's journey.

Jim Rue, who though completely un-Rich-like, added valuable insights into the male world and gave the story a new dimension. His moral support was beyond measure.

Marijean Rue, who read, advised, made sure all college-speak was authentic, and kept the snacks coming. This book truly could not have been written without her.

The Writeen Crue, who field-tested and asked the hard questions we know our readers will put to us.

Lee Hough and Greg Johnson, our literary agents who paved the way for this opportunity and kept us afloat on a number of levels.

Our editors, Amanda Bostic, L. B. Norton and Jocelyn Bailey

who never ceased to amaze us with their insights, their tact and their ability to find every speck of literary clutter.

Our dear, dear friend Joey Paul, to whom this book is dedicated with love and respect. His championing of Sullivan Crisp and his belief in us is matchless.

READING GROUP GUIDE

1. *Healing Stones* was created first and foremost as literature, to be embraced and enjoyed. We hope you were able to immerse yourself in the story and know the characters as real people. Without destroying any of the sheer pleasure (as so often happened in your high school English classes, we are sure!), you might want to discuss some of these points.

   a. The story is written from two distinct points of view—Demitria's and Sully's. Which one did you relate to personally?
   b. Were there any secondary characters who captured you? Mickey? Jayne? Ethan? Porphyria? Rich? Chris? Tatum?
   c. Were there any characters who frustrated you? (i.e., made you want to shake, slap, or throw them out the window?)
   d. Which story line did you want to stay with most? Demitria and Rich's dilemma? The quest to discover who took the pictures? Sully's inner demons?
   e. Was there anything about the style of the novel that either delighted you or turned you off?
   f. Were you satisfied when you finished reading the last page?
   g. What do you think the next phase of Sully's journey will look like?

2. The theme of the book is, of course, forgiveness, on its many levels. It might be helpful to discuss how you define forgiveness—and how you've experienced it—before looking specifically at how it plays out in *Healing Stones.*

a. Were you able to forgive Demitria for her unfaithfulness to Rich, or did you think she pretty much got what she deserved?
b. Were you able to empathize with Rich in his inability to forgive her?
c. How did you feel about Christopher's reactions to his mother? Why do you think he responded so bitterly?
d. How, in your opinion, was Jayne able to forgive her mother when Christopher couldn't?
e. What was up with Mickey? She showed so much compassion for Demi, but when her own daughter needed some, she couldn't seem to produce it. What's that about?
f. Demitria needed forgiveness, surely, but what about the people she needed to forgive?
g. Do you agree with Demi's interpretation of the story of Jesus and the adulteress?
h. How about Ethan's explanation of how we are saved from our separation from God by the death and rebirth of Christ (as described in his Easter sermon)?
i. Kevin St. Clair and Wyatt Estes obviously had a very different view of grace than Ethan and Demi, but is there anything in the St. Clair/Wyatt take on forgiveness that you agree with?
j. Both Sully and Demitria had issues with forgiving themselves—and accepting God's forgiveness. How is that different from giving and receiving forgiveness with other people?
k. When Sully agonized over what he should and possibly could have done to save Lynn, Porphyria said, "Maybe you could have. Maybe you even should have." Did that surprise you? Discuss whether what Porphyria goes on to say about how to accept God's forgiveness and healing rings true for you.
l. Is it enough to simply be forgiven? What does the novel seem to say about what has to come after the acceptance of mercy and grace?

3. Do you have someone like Porphyria in your life? What does that person mean to you? Do you see yourself being a mentor to someone else?

4. In *Healing Stones*, we have tried to show people at their breaking points, where a decision must be made, and the decision will determine the direction of the rest of a person's life journey. Chat together about each of these characters' breaking points—where they occur in the book, what choice they make, and how they play out.

   a. Demitria Costanas
   b. Zach Archer
   c. Rich Costanas
   d. Jayne Costanas
   e. Christopher Costanas
   f. Ethan Kaye
   g. Sullivan Crisp
   h. Mickey Gwynne
   i. Audrey Flowers
   j. Tatum Farris
   k. You

5. Have you struggled with regret like Demetria did? Is there something in your past that you held inside, that you are only able to share with others now?

If you or your reading group has questions for us, please feel free to email either or both at: nnrue@hughes.net or sarterburn@newlife.com. Or if you would like to do a more in-depth study of *Healing Stones*, you can download the curriculum from www.nancyrue.com. We love to talk about what we're doing with the Sullivan Crisp novels, so do not hesitate to contact us. We are all on this journey together.